Proposing Mischief

Books by Regina Jennings

THE JOPLIN CHRONICLES

Courting Misfortune

Proposing Mischief

THE FORT RENO SERIES

Holding the Fort

The Lieutenant's Bargain

The Major's Daughter

OZARK MOUNTAIN ROMANCE SERIES

A Most Inconvenient Marriage

At Love's Bidding

For the Record

LADIES OF CALDWELL COUNTY

Sixty Acres and a Bride

Love in the Balance

Caught in the Middle

NOVELLAS

An Unforeseen Match (from the collection *A Match Made in Texas*)

Her Dearly Unintended (from the collection *With This Ring?*)

Bound and Determined (from the collection *Hearts Entwined*)

Intrigue a la Mode (from the collection *Serving Up Love*)

Broken Limbs, Mended Hearts (from the collection *The Kissing Tree*)

PROPOSING MISCHIEF

REGINA JENNINGS

a division of Baker Publishing Group
Minneapolis, Minnesota

Published by Bethany House Publishers
11400 Hampshire Avenue South
Bloomington, Minnesota 55438
www.bethanyhouse.com

Bethany House Publishers is a division of
Baker Publishing Group, Grand Rapids, Michigan

Printed in the United States of America

Library of Congress Cataloging-in-Publication Data
Names: Jennings, Regina (Regina Lea), author.
Title: Proposing mischief / Regina Jennings.
Description: Minneapolis, Minnesota : Bethany House Publishers, a division of
Baker Publishing Group, [2021] | Series: The Joplin Chronicles ; 2
Identifiers: LCCN 2021028779 | ISBN 9780764235351 (trade paper) |
ISBN 9780764239410 (casebound) | ISBN 9781493433865 (ebook)
Classification: LCC PS3610.E5614 P76 2021 | DDC 813/.6—dc23
LC record available at https://lccn.loc.gov/2021028779

Scripture quotations are from the King James Version of the Bible.

This is a work of historical reconstruction; the appearances of certain historical figures are therefore inevitable. All other characters, however, are products of the author's imagination, and any resemblance to actual persons, living or dead, is coincidental.

Cover design by Dan Thornberg, Design Source Creative Services

Baker Publishing Group publications use paper produced from sustainable forestry practices and post-consumer waste whenever possible.

21 22 23 24 25 26 27 7 6 5 4 3 2 1

To Shanna Lewis
For all the years of friendship,
but particularly for the day you
immediately said *yes* when I asked if you'd
drive me to the hospital to check on my husband—
eight hundred and seventy-four miles away.

The Kentworth Family

Albert & Laura Kentworth

Children

— Bill -m June

Finn Amos Maisie

— Oscar -m Myra

Willow Olive

— Pauline (Polly) -m Richard York

Corban Calista Evangelina

Calbert Kentworth -m Gretchen
(Grandpa Albert's Twin Brother)

Hannah Hilda Hank

CHAPTER 1

"When I told Pa I wanted to go to town, I didn't mean the feedstore." Maisie Kentworth reached over the side of the wagon bed and let the elm leaves swish against her hand as they passed. "That feedstore doesn't sell any phosphate drinks, and I aim to have me one of those today."

Her brother Amos pulled one rein tight, swerving to make the sharp turn into the feedstore's lot. "Welp, we gotta get feed, that's a fact, and ever since that Silas Marsh business, Pa wants to keep you on a short leash. So if you want to set foot off the ranch, it's church or the feedstore, or else you'll be tied to Granny's apron strings. Them's the only options."

Maisie grabbed the supple end of a branch and held it tight so that all the leaves were stripped away as it ran through her hand. Silas Marsh. She wished she'd never lit eyes on that man. She'd been staying in town with her cousin Calista when Silas entered her world. Charming, attentive, and romantic, the young miner seemed just what Maisie wanted in a man, but evidently she wasn't the only lady to feel that way.

Turning around on the bench and throwing her leg over the

seat back, she planted her sturdy boot in the middle of her cousin Hank's back and jostled him until he groaned and rolled over.

"Wake up. We're here." Maisie tidied her chestnut hair behind her ears and wiggled her freckled nose at the sweet scent of the feed.

Hank lifted his straw hat from his face and squinted at the sun. "What do you need me for? I thought we brought you to do the toting."

With a boot to his shoulder, Maisie shoved harder. "Get on your feet, Hank. It's time to work."

"Hank ain't afraid of hard work," Amos cheerfully put in. "He'll curl up right against it and sleep like a baby."

"What's your hurry?" Hank groaned. "I was out hunting all night. Give me a minute."

"If we have time to spare, we might could drive on into town to the soda fountain," Maisie said.

Hank bolted upright. "I do admire myself a phosphate cherry root drink." The flat, immovable planes of Hank's face gave his every pronouncement the weight of the granite tablets from Mount Sinai.

"There ain't no way." Amos set the wagon brake and wrapped the reins around the handle. "I have strict orders not to let Maisie anywhere near town." Even when Amos was serious, the sparks of merriment in his eyes didn't allow one to believe him.

"Now that it's settled," Maisie said, hopping out of the wagon, "how many bags of feed are we getting? I'll go sign for them, and you'uns start loading."

Despite their protests, Amos and Hank loaded the feed up with no lollygagging. By the time Maisie had the receipt tucked into her waistband, Amos and Hank were waiting in the wagon. From the anxious tapping of Amos's foot, it was clear that Hank had brought him around to Maisie's suggestion.

Maisie climbed into the back of the bed, and without another word, Amos slapped the reins and the team pulled them toward town instead of back to the ranch.

Maisie wasn't a troublemaker, but she needed adventure like a cornfield needed sunlight. Speaking of sunlight, she snagged the sunbonnet hanging by its ties around her neck and pulled it over her head. No use in making more of those freckles. When she was younger, running around in the sun, unconcerned about a smattering of freckles, she found ample adventure on her family ranch with her multitude of cousins. She'd grown up as independent and as free as her brothers or any of the boy cousins. But as she matured, she realized that adventure came in many forms, and a young lady could find better amusements than wrestling matches and throwing competitions.

Just outside her family's ranch was enough excitement to flip a corpse. Joplin had it all—society, music, and wealth. Unfortunately, it also contained a former beau of hers, and her family was determined that she not see him again.

Maisie wholeheartedly agreed.

"I ain't taking you all the way to the soda fountain," Amos said. "There's stretching the rules, and then there's pure stupidity."

"Then where are we headed?" Hank asked, then answered his own question. "We can go to Daniel's Drug and Miscellany. They've got shaved ice."

Amos grunted his approval, and Maisie propped her boot up on the side of the wagon bed to tighten a shoelace that had worked loose. She'd always thought Granny Laura was exaggerating when she talked about how Joplin could turn a girl's head plumb backward. Maisie had never believed her, but when her cousin Calista came from Kansas City, Maisie was sent to stay with her in town as a chaperone. Some chaperone she'd turned out to be. Before she'd gotten her bearings, she'd fallen as love-sick as a turtledove with measles and had decided that she'd be Silas's wife someday. If Calista hadn't overheard a young lady at the Children's Home, Maisie might never have known that Silas had sired children around the county.

She tugged on the shoelace, then whipped it into a tight bow.

Maisie had always thought of herself as tough and savvy, but it turned out she was neither. Silas's deception had shown her that her faith in him was misplaced, but so was her faith in her own discernment.

If only she could be like Calista—get herself an exciting job with the Pinkertons and travel the country hunting down crooks and no-accounts. 'Course, Calista had stopped that when she'd realized she was hunting with the wrong dogs, but Maisie still envied her adventures.

The mercantile appeared as they rounded the bend. The three Kentworths scanned the premises before rolling any closer, getting a feel for who they might encounter at the store. Not that they were worried about being tattled on—they were adults, after all—but sometimes life was easier if news of certain decisions they made didn't travel back to the Kentworth ranch.

"It's clear," Maisie said. "Prissy Jones is out of town, and I don't see sign of any of the Grosgrain family. No one else would bother to snitch."

"It's you that has to worry," said Amos. "Nothing wrong with Hank and me coming to town."

"Except you brought me," she said. "That makes you complicit."

"How do you figure?" Hank asked, his voice as level as his gaze.

"Because they've already determined that I have no sense. You're supposed to watch over me."

"If they're looking for someone responsible to keep an eye on you, they're barking up the wrong tree." Hank nodded toward Amos. "I say they get what they deserve."

Easy for Hank to say. Granny Laura was only his aunt and not likely to tan his hide.

Amid a debate over who should pony up for the ices, Hank and Amos got distracted by a weak bleating from behind the store.

"What do you reckon that's Wheeler's two-headed lamb?" Amos grinned so big that his dimples drilled into his cheeks. "I heard he was bringing it to town."

Even Hank seemed to light up. "Now that would be something to see," he allowed. "Let's go." He followed Amos around the outside of the drugstore.

"Hurry," Maisie called. "If we're gone too long, the folks are going to suspicion us."

She had seen enough carnival acts that she was hard to impress. The pity she felt for the animals wasn't worth the curiosity. Besides, she'd been hankering for a fancy treat ever since she'd gotten a pass to town. She'd contemplated how odd it was that a drink on the inside could feel as good as jumping into a spring did on the outside. She'd mulled over the merits of an ice drink versus a phosphate, but here she was, and nothing stood between her and this delight.

Except Silas Marsh.

As she entered the store, she saw him standing in front of a shelf filled with personal goods, no doubt buying more of that hair elixir that smelled like fresh lavender and potential.

"Is that you, Maisie Kentworth?" He sauntered across the drugstore while Maisie's stomach tried to push its contents back up her throat.

"What are you doing on this side of town?" Maisie growled. "You ain't supposed to come this way."

"I've made it a habit of mine. When I have a spare afternoon, I wander over here, hoping to see you. Looks like today my efforts were finally rewarded." He swept off his hat and ruffled his hair.

Maisie remembered ruffling that hair herself. That was before she knew.

"I've already said everything I have to say to you. If you're looking for soft words from me—"

"I'm not looking for anything from you besides reassurance. When we parted, you were displeased with me, and I understand why, but you were also discouraged and hurt. Knowing that I hurt you has weighed heavily on my conscience."

"As heavily as your illegitimate children?" Just saying the words made Maisie's gut twist. How could she have cared about him?

"I heard that your family blamed you—that they won't let you out of their sight—and that isn't fair. You're a smart woman, Maisie-girl. You shouldn't be treated like a child. You deserve freedom."

He was an uncommonly handsome man, full of confidence and charm. The fine creases around his mouth used to hold traces of black dust at the end of his workday. Maisie could never get him to stop smiling long enough to wipe them clean.

"I'm fine. Don't be troubled on my account." She cast a glance at the mercantile door, unsure what Amos and Hank would do if they saw Silas, but pretty sure it wouldn't benefit her.

"What troubles you, troubles me." He stepped closer. "I wish you'd let me explain to your family. Who are they to judge you? You're a good person."

Was she? She sure hadn't acted like it of late. All her sense had flown out the window when Silas came around. Thank the Lord she had a second chance. It was up to her never to get hornswoggled again.

"If you want to help me, then keep your distance." She stepped sideways, putting a barrel of brooms between them. "You're going to bring me nothing but trouble."

"I don't want to cause you trouble. I only want happiness for you—our happiness. There's nothing wrong with being happy, is there?"

"I'm not happy right now, Silas Marsh. Not one bit. Whatever this feeling is, it is not happiness."

His face crumpled into a sympathetic pout. "What can I do for you, darling? What will make you happy?"

"Cricket's wings! I told you: leave me alone." So adamant was she that she didn't notice the figures in the doorway until it was too late.

"What are you doing here?" Amos growled. "I thought we'd got rid of you."

"I'm having a conversation with your sister. It doesn't concern you." Silas spread his stance when he should've been cowering.

Maisie started for the door. "Let's go home."

But Amos was having none of it. That dangerous glint to his eyes was setting in. "Seeing how she's my sister, it sure as shootin' concerns me."

Poor Silas. He was keeping his eyes on Amos. He hadn't even noticed Hank working his way around the shop to get in his blind spot. Maisie shot Hank a silent warning. He waved her off and moved closer.

"I told you if you came within spitting distance of any of my kin, there'd be trouble," Amos said.

Mr. Daniel stepped out from behind the counter. "I don't want any trouble from you Kentworths." He marched between Amos and Silas and drew a pickax out of the barrel. "Whatever you've a mind to do, don't do it here in my store."

Amos reached into a bushel basket near the door and removed an orange. He squared up, blocking the door and any chance Silas had of escaping. "This coward can leave first." After tossing the orange and catching it, he perched it on his shoulder. "Just make sure you don't knock this off my shoulder."

For crying aloud, that orange was no better balanced than a tipsy field hand who'd just gotten off a barn swing.

Silas straightened, not one to back down from a fight. He turned to Maisie and, with a slight bow, dropped his hat on his head, then began whistling a tune as he tried to get past Amos.

Maisie held her breath. The orange rocked. Amos stared at Silas, waiting for the signal. Silas stepped around him and had nearly cleared the danger when a mighty crash sounded. It was Hank. With pot lids in both hands, he crashed them together like God's own thunder.

Amos flinched. The orange tottered. Silas paused and watched as it tumbled off Amos's shoulder.

"That's not fair, Amos," Maisie started, but it was too late.

Amos drew back and swung at Silas. Silas, quick as a flea, jumped to the side and swiped a tin labeled *Camphorated Dentifrice*. While Amos was readjusting his swing, Silas opened the tooth powder and flung it in Amos's face.

Amos roared from inside the white cloud of tooth powder, making Maisie think that the peppermint flavor wasn't as refreshing in the eyes as on the teeth.

"Get!" she yelled at Silas, but before he could skedaddle out the door, Hank caught him by the collar, jerking him back to crash into a stack of ebony-black coach paint cans.

Maisie covered her ears at the cacophony as Silas tried to squirm his way out of Hank's grasp.

"Get out of this store!" Mr. Daniel yelled. He brandished the pickax but didn't seem eager to join the fray. If he wasn't going to intervene, then Maisie would have to.

"Stop it!" she yelled. "Stop it, right now!" But they weren't paying her any mind. She spotted a painted panel propped against the door. With a grunt, she lifted it above her head and smashed the *Teeth Carefully Extracted* sign against Hank's back.

"You'd do that to your own kin?" Amos looked afright covered in white dental powder.

"When my kin are making fools of themselves."

"Traitor!" he yelled, then made a dive toward Silas.

Silas dodged and chucked a can of paint at Amos. It bounced off his shoulder before thudding against the floor.

"Woo-hoo!" Hank's mouth twitched. "Now we're in the thick of it." He swiped a ceramic jar off the countertop and hefted it to his shoulder.

"No!" Maisie and Mr. Daniel chorused, but it was too late. Hank chucked the crockery at Silas. Silas ducked, and the jar flew past him, toothbrushes slinging in its wake, and hit the wall of medicinal spirits opposite.

"I didn't do that. You can't blame me," Silas yelled, but Hank and Amos weren't dissuaded.

Amos dove for Silas again, but Mr. Daniel managed to slow him down by hooking the pickax through his suspender strap. He yanked Amos backward, knocking Hank off his feet as well.

Seeing his opportunity to escape, Silas jumped up on the countertop and ran the length of it, leaving white footprints with every step and bumping against the electric lamp bulbs with his head. He bounded off the countertop and grabbed Maisie by the shoulders.

"Don't forget, I never meant to hurt you," he said. One eye was blackened, and his lip was swollen, but it didn't keep him from stealing a kiss.

Maisie was furious. Reaching behind her, she grabbed the first thing that came to hand—a bottle of Phoenix Bitters Blood Purifiers—and smashed it against Silas's skull.

"Because of you, I'll never get to come to town again!" she yelled. She nearly crumpled trying to hold Silas's weight as he got his legs back under him.

"When you're ready to run away with me, that won't be a problem," he slurred. He looked again at her lips, then thought better of it and loped out the door.

Finally pulling free of Mr. Daniel, Amos trotted over the toothbrushes to watch Silas disappear down the road. He punched Maisie in the arm. "We showed him, huh?" he boasted.

"You've annihilated my store, destroyed my stock." Mr. Daniel clutched his head as he surveyed the damage. "You Kentworths are going to pay for this."

Glass crunched beneath Hank's boots as he turned to get a look at the carnage. He scratched the back of his neck as if he were seeing the mess for the first time. "Welp, if that cad Marsh wasn't here, this wouldn't have happened. You can't expect me to just stand back and let him insult my cousin."

"An insult?" Mr. Daniel could barely shake the words out of his mouth. Yanking a wide broom from against the wall, he swept up a pile of broken glass, dental powder, and toothbrushes. "You did this to my store over an insult?"

"Family looks out for its own." Amos stuck out his chest. "It was a good deed that was done today."

Maisie covered her eyes. She'd thought she could sneak away from the consequences of her actions for just half an hour, but consequences and bad decisions weren't finished with her yet. She'd have no end to the trouble this day had brought. The piper's price would be high, indeed.

"This looks like a fair offer on the mine, especially considering we hit water." Boone Bragg tapped his finger at each line of Darin Caine's proposal as he ran down it for the third time.

"I think I can get a little profit out of it before it's finished." Caine crossed one leg over the other and rested his hat on his knee. "Besides, if it's helping the son of my old friend Wallace . . ."

With Boone's father out of town, Mr. Caine had proven himself generous with his guidance and advice. Even before his father had left town, the payout in the Curious Bear Mine had been dwindling. In shaft after shaft, the ore had dried up, and when they'd gone deeper, they'd hit water. Boone had some experience with dewatering a mine. He knew to cut a sough in to let gravity do its work, making use of adits if the mine was in a hillside, but this was another matter. The opening shaft of the Curious Bear was low-lying. The mine had nowhere to drain the runoff. Pumps would be needed, and according to Caine, Boone couldn't afford the expense. It'd be better to purchase rights on a new prospect and keep his men employed.

"I don't think he's heard a word I've said. *Quel fromage*."

Boone lifted his head at Justina Caine's tight, high-pitched voice. Her eyes were slanted like a cat's, and when she was around, he felt like a mouse.

"I'm sorry. The numbers . . ." Boone pointed to the proposal in front of him as an excuse. What was Caine thinking, bringing his daughter to a business meeting? Yet there she was, perched on the edge of her seat with that indulgent look, as if she were forgiving him for an offense.

"Then you didn't hear me say that your mother was surprised you're treating me to brunch," she said.

"My mother is surprised . . . ?" Boone darted a look at her father, then back at her. "So am I. When was this decided?"

Mr. Caine laughed. "Your inattentiveness is going to get you in trouble, young man. But of course you're escorting Justina. She thinks you need a break from work, and I took your vague answer yesterday as approval."

Boone had had no intention of eating a brunch, much less escorting Justina and her boiler-whistle voice. Why couldn't the ladies leave him alone? Besides, it wasn't that he was inattentive. He paid attention to the things that mattered, and a brunch with Justina didn't.

But doing right by his miners mattered very much, and Darin Caine was a part of that solution.

Expecting their sons to learn to manage their finances, Mr. and Mrs. Wallace Bragg had given them their inheritance while they were still young. Boone's brother, Grady, had taken his funds and invested in the mines of Indian Territory. Boone had kept his investments local, but the Curious Bear's failure could threaten his other ventures. There'd be no more money coming from his parents, even if they could afford it. They'd promised what was left of their substantial estate to charity. This was the only help he'd get, and it was more than most people made in a lifetime. It'd be a shame if he lost it.

"When is this brunch?" he asked. If Justina had taken the time to telephone his mother in Florida, the damage was already done. Mother would rake him over the coals for getting trapped into this obligation.

"Tomorrow morning. Ten o'clock." Caine leaned back in his chair and cracked his knuckles. "Afterwards, I could go with you to Oronogo, if you'd like. I hear they have some promising samples coming up there. I know you've had your eye on those fields for months."

The money from Caine would give him the capital to keep his other mine, the Spook Light, going while starting afresh. Standing around looking at watery tunnels wouldn't solve anything. Boone had to get producing again, hauling out more of the ugly gray chat, as if Joplin didn't have enough piles of it already.

What would it be like to create beauty instead of dragging the unsightly guts out of the belly of the earth? Mining was dirty business. Like his father and older brother, Boone showed promise of being good at it, but he wished all that work produced something more pleasant than the zinc and lead ore that was shipped across the world. He wished he could discover something of beauty beyond the ladies who coveted the reward of his labor.

"I'm not ready to look at Oronogo yet," Boone said. "Give me time to go to the Curious Bear, gather our equipment, and get it cleaned out. If nothing changes, I'll have the paperwork ready, and you can take it over by the end of the month."

"Or there's another option. You could bring Bragg Mining into our collective. I'm firmly convinced that the future of Joplin rests on our abilities to consolidate. If we partnered together, we'd be able to bid our ore collectively. It'd decrease the competition and increase the profits."

"I've already told you, I'm not interested in consolidating," Boone said. "I'm just getting started. If the Curious Bear fails, I'd rather free up my capital to try another independent venture."

"So you've said, and I'm happy to help," said Mr. Caine. "It might be that you want to make an offer of your own someday soon."

Boone wrinkled his nose. "An offer on what? Are you selling rights on your mines? There's nothing else I'm interested . . ." His eyes flew to Justina before he realized that was the last place he should look.

Her eyelids fluttered, and her mouth stretched into an expansive smile. In his head, Boone heard the boiler whistle pitching higher and higher, warning of an impending explosion. Maybe it was time for his mother to come back. With her sharp eyes and sharper tongue, she'd protected him from the bloodthirsty machinations of the society mothers with single daughters. Now even the fathers were getting involved.

"Ten o'clock." Boone would mark the time like a condemned man going to the gallows. "I'll pick you up at a quarter till."

"Sounds good." Mr. Caine stood and held out his hand. "It's always a pleasure visiting with you, Boone. I know you'll do the right thing."

And according to Caine, the right thing for Boone to do was admit he couldn't manage water pumps himself and take Justina to brunch. Boone was worried that selling the Curious Bear might be a mistake, but taking Justina to brunch would be a disaster.

CHAPTER 2

It had only been a day, and already Maisie was going stir-crazy. She placed her hands between the barbs on the barbed wire and stretched it to the post. She had no more freedom than the cows she was penning in. No more choices, no more liberty. She might as well stand in the field and chew her cud with the same vacant stare as those looking past her now.

She wrapped the line of barbed wire around the post and held it tight while she bent the nail with a hammer. Tugging on the barbed wire with her gloved hand, she judged it secure. Taking the pliers, she cut the wire from the spool, then stood and arched her back to ease the muscles.

She'd been naïve in the matter of Silas Marsh. She'd felt so special when he wanted to hold her hand and squire her about town. She'd let him take liberties when they were riding in a mostly empty streetcar. She hadn't realized how bad his character was or what people would assume about her based on his previous behavior with women. Now her reputation was damaged before she'd even had a chance to build one. Not that it mattered. According to her pa, she wasn't to set foot off the farm without someone riding shotgun. Amos and Hank no longer qualified as protection.

"Sorry, girls," Maisie called to the cows still eyeing the fence. "We're all in the same boat."

But that wasn't exactly true, was it? Even at that moment, Maisie was on the outside of the fence. She looked down at her feet, and sure enough, they weren't on Kentworth property. There was nothing between her and freedom—nothing except her family's disapproval. Well, they couldn't disapprove of what they didn't know. That had been her mistake last time—taking off with Hank and Amos. She should've surmised that they would get her in trouble. But there was nowhere to go out here. The Kennedys' farm lay to the left, and the Curious Bear Mine was behind her.

Maisie cocked her head as she dropped her pliers and hammer into her pocket. Come to think of it, she hadn't seen much going on at the mine of late. Was it still operating? It bore looking into. Surely there was nothing wrong with investigating the goings-on within the proximity of their property.

As soon as she entered the clearing, it was obvious that the Curious Bear wasn't in production. No plume emerged from the smokestack on the ramshackle building. The three-story headframe looked abandoned. A pile of rocks remained from exploration, but in a mineral-rich area like Joplin, if ore wasn't discovered quickly, you might as well move on to the next prospect.

"Hello?" Maisie called as she looked around the corner of the office building. If you weren't from the tri-state area, you might think that the shoddy outbuildings were odd-shaped barns in the middle of the pasture. Besides the elevated track coming out of the headframe and the pile of rock dumped at the end of it, there was nothing to distinguish this plot from other farmland. She wiggled her toes inside her boots. Beneath her feet could be miles of dark, dramatic tunnels, but the topside was as dull as the june bugs that buzzed over it.

The door to the building was locked. Maisie had knocked before trying it, of course. The side door to the office, however, looked penetrable. Maybe it was unlocked, or maybe she jiggled the door just right. Either way, it opened.

With her senses on high alert, Maisie eased into the room. There was no use in calling out to see if anyone was there. Besides a forgotten hat, a pickax, a heavy chest, and some boards against the wall, there was no place to hide. Maisie dropped the metal hat on her head. A sunshine lamp, they called it, because of the lump of lard oil on the brim. All you had to do was light it on fire and you didn't need to carry a lantern. Maisie narrowed her eyes, imagining the darkness. What would it be like to work beneath the ground day after day? Did they feel as trapped as she did?

Something about the disorderly stack of lumber caught her eye. Those boards weren't propped against the wall, they were nailed down. Looking closer, she realized it was another entrance to the mine.

Of course they had another entrance. The miners usually rode the ore bucket in and out, but when the mine was newly started, they had to have a descent they could use. Now, with the closing of the mine, they had covered this entrance, but it turned out those planks weren't too secure.

With a strong tug, Maisie was able to pry off the main board, and that left a hole large enough for her to worm into. She stuck her head between the boards and felt the cool air on her face. She'd lived in the middle of mining territory her whole life but had never gone down into a mine. Was it different than a cave? She might as well find out.

She needed something to light her hat, and there was that heavy chest full of equipment. If it weren't for that lock . . .

Her hand fell on the pickax. It wouldn't take much to pop open that chest. She wobbled as she balanced the pickax over her head and aimed for the lock.

"Atta girl," Maisie said as the padlock popped open. Coming here had been the right thing to do. The lid was solid but not too heavy for her. It crashed backward, but no one was around to note it. She felt like a treasure hunter opening a pirate's chest. Her heart was racing, and she hadn't even gone into the mine yet.

Inside the chest was everything one would need to explore a mine. Matches to light her hat, a spool of twine, and more pick-axes. Maisie wiped her hands against her skirt. She wouldn't have dared go far, but the twine bolstered her confidence. With a line behind her, she could find her way to the exit even if her lamp went out. This could be just the adventure she'd been hankering after.

With the matches, she lit the lard oil on her hat, then carefully set the heavy thing on her head. Keeping as still as she could, she fastened the chin strap on tight, then picked up the twine. Leaving her pliers and hammer behind, she pocketed some matches, then heaved a pickax onto her shoulder. If she was pretending to be a miner, she might as well get rigged out.

Maisie headed toward the slanted opening in the wall. To make it inside with her gear and hat, she had to remove another board, but with the pickax helping this time, it took no effort.

The sunshine lamp worked so well that she almost forgot to anchor her twine. "Don't get overconfident," she scolded herself. "If this lamp goes out, you'll be in a world of hurt."

With the end of the twine tied to a board that was nailed across the opening, Maisie looped the rest around her arm and started forward, whistling a jaunty tune she'd heard at the Founder's Day parade last year.

She went down the concrete steps. Everything around her was concreted. She reckoned that kept the dirt from caving in and the snakes from crawling out. She shivered. She wasn't afraid of most critters, but snakes were her least favorite of them all.

The way was steep, the passage wide, and soon the concrete gave way to rock. The tunnel had deep pockmarks scratched out along both sides of the wide passageway. It looked like a giant had pressed its fingers into moist clay, only it wasn't clay—it was solid rock, but evidently just rock. If there'd been ore, those craters would've been cut out into full rooms.

The miners hadn't had any luck at this level, but that hadn't stopped them. Maisie followed the tunnel down a steep embankment, enjoying the feeling that she was completely alone. No one to disappoint. No one to disapprove.

The twine tangled around her wrist, forcing her to stop and straighten it before continuing. Slowing down gave her time to notice a crushing spot at the side of the tunnel. There was an anvil, and beneath it were shards and crumbles of stone. They must have brought samples here to test. She bent and rifled through the powdered rocks. Maisie didn't know a lot about mining, but when she'd spent time at Silas's claim, he'd shown her the shiny cubes of zinc that came so easily out of his ground. She'd recognize it, and she didn't see any here, but she regretted the memory.

She gave herself some slack in the twine and continued on. Those days had been the best of her life. They'd sat inside Silas's tiny house and talked about how easy it was to make a living on the rich claim. It was more than many of the wealthy of Joplin had started with. If Silas only had a reason to work, then he'd do it all day, every day, for Maisie. At that rate, it wouldn't take any time for them to build a proper house. Who knew? Maybe someday he would have a full-blown mining operation like the Bragg family.

Maybe she was being too hard on Silas. Maybe he had put his past behind him. Wasn't she supposed to be the forgiving sort? He was the only man who'd ever paid her court, and the way things were going, he was the only man who ever would. Unless God saw fit to drop a man from the sky and land him on the Kentworth ranch, Maisie wasn't going to have any luck at all.

Her thoughts troubled her sorely. If only getting Silas out of her head was as easy as swinging a pickax. If only she could muscle through the confusion and fix things right.

Tightening her grasp on the tool, Maisie bellowed a war cry, her voice echoing down the cavern as she drove it into the wall. Sparks flew. She straightened her hat, but it felt good. Again, she drove the pickax into the rock, turning her head to keep the chips from getting in her eyes. The sheer force of her strikes was satisfying.

Walking forward, she swung her pickax against the rock again. She would be a more restful person if she could do this a few hours a day. Every time Amos riled her up, *whack*! Every time she thought about how she missed the excitement of the city, *whack*! This could cure what ailed her.

But the next strike felt different, like the hardness of the rock had changed. Maisie craned her head forward, letting the light from her lamp reach the wall. Sure enough, where the crevice was deepest, the rock was a different color.

Wouldn't that be something if she found ore? Maisie straightened her back and lifted her chin. Maybe there was something worthwhile inside of her too. Maisie Kentworth, lady miner, finding treasure when all the men had given up. She lifted the pickax. There was nothing stopping her from hammering on all day—nothing until her family came searching for her.

She let the next swing fly with newly released power. Big chunks of rock crashed to the ground. Another inspection showed something very strange in the wall. The weak light from her hat caught on something white and reflected back at her.

Maisie ran her fingers over the bumpy rim of the dent. Were those diamonds? She whistled. Had she discovered diamonds? If so, she was going to fill her pockets and skedaddle . . .

But no, it wasn't her mine. Still, one would think she should get some kind of a reward, but finders keepers didn't apply to trespassers. No matter. The thrill of discovery was propelling her now. She had to see what was next.

With another swing, she hit the sparkling target, only to have it disintegrate before her eyes and her pickax get stuck in the hole she'd made.

"What in tarnation?" she grumbled. Those weren't diamonds. Even though she'd never owned one, Maisie knew diamonds were the hardest substance on earth. Whatever this was, it was breaking when she struck it. If it was just sparkling rock, then no one would mind if she took a piece home. She just needed the right piece.

As she worked, the hole grew bigger and bigger. There didn't seem to be anything on the other side of it. She expected to see another layer of rock eventually, but the darkness swallowed up her light. Even the sound was swallowed up and turned into a much-delayed echo.

"It's a cave?" Maisie dropped the pickax and unbuckled her hat. Holding it before her, she climbed over the debris she'd created to look into the hole. Leaning her hand on the jagged line of crystals, she pushed the hat through the opening and stretched it as far as she was able.

What she saw left her gasping for breath.

CHAPTER 3

Brunch? How many dinner breaks was a man to take in a day? But Darin Caine was a friend of the family and a prospective buyer for Boone's failing mine, so here Boone sat, the only man in a restaurant whose sole objective seemed to be making you wait so long on your food that you became hungry for lunch.

Justina was smiling at him over the edge of her teacup. Occasionally, when caught off guard, Boone had the disturbing realization that she was an attractive lady. Beneath the elaborate hair arrangement and the overly animated expressions, she could have been a beauty. Such a pity that her affectation had to get in the way.

"See, this isn't so bad." She lowered her teacup in triumph. "You could find much to admire about the situation here."

The chair was uncomfortable, the tea weak, and he had work to do. "It's a nice"—Boone looked above him—"building. I stopped by once while it was under construction but have never been inside." Now that he was thinking about it, he remembered the architect, Maxfield Scott, talking about the challenge of creating the large open dining room. It made sense how he utilized the columns around the room, much as Boone installed vertical support beams in the mines to prevent cave-ins.

Someone was coughing. It was Justina, but her ailment resolved with a smile as soon as Boone shifted his focus to her.

"Excuse me. The tea must have gone down the wrong way." She patted her mouth with her napkin and then, before Boone could get his wits, asked, "Why are you so resistant to socializing?"

Here was a subject he could elaborate on. He rested his forearm on the thick white tablecloth and leaned forward. "Do you really want to know?"

"Yes . . . I suppose." She gave an airy giggle. "I mean, there's nothing objectionable about—"

"The first objection," Boone said, "is that it interferes with my work. I should be at the Curious Bear right now, doing a final inspection. Instead, I'm here waiting for food I wouldn't normally eat, even if I was hungry."

The waiter slid two large plates each with a half serving of some sort of egg casserole in front of them. Boone caught the scent of dill, solidifying his opinion.

"The second objection is that being seen in public with you, or any other lady, raises the expectation that I should attend more social events. It will be assumed that I enjoy them, and then my reluctance to accept invitations is taken as an insult, which, as you can imagine, is quite tedious. Thirdly—"

"I know a solution that would make all those problems fly away." Justina fluttered her hand so that the lace on her sleeve shook like a drunken butterfly. "If you were always seen with the same lady, those expectations would dry up faster than a shaft with Cornish pumps. Everyone would know you were spoken for."

Cornish pumps. Another piece of business Boone should be attending to instead of this brunch. And yet Justina was making sense. Once a man was spoken for, he was no longer pursued. It was only eligible bachelors who were at risk. Just as he was falling into a deep contemplation of that new information, Justina interrupted again.

"Have you heard of the plans for the new Electric Light Park?"

she asked. "It's going to be the biggest tourist attraction in the region. Mr. Schifferdecker is bringing in a man named Peltz to oversee it. They say it will have gardens, rides, roller coasters, a skating rink, and a swimming pool. And it's all going to be illuminated by over forty thousand electric lights. Can you imagine? *C'est maléfique.*"

"Forty thousand lights?" Boone reached for his fork and knife. Perhaps if he ate this gelatinous mess, he could skip his midday meal and catch up on some work. "That's impossible."

"Well, I heard it will take $150,000 to build."

Boone nearly choked. "That's a fortune! It will take years for them to recoup that amount."

"Mr. Bragg?"

Boone caught the scent of lilac powder even before he turned. It was Mrs. Kleinkauf, who, along with her husband, owned the plot of land in Oronogo that he was considering purchasing.

"Are you enjoying your brunch?" she asked.

Boone cast a nervous glance at Justina, who was smiling proudly. "I haven't eaten a bite of it yet," he answered.

"I thought you never went to brunch," the matron said. "At least that's what you told Heidi and me when we invited you to join us last fall."

Had that happened? Boone had no recollection of it, but it sounded possible. "I don't usually," he said. "I never have time, but Miss Caine prevailed upon me to make an exception."

"I see." Mrs. Kleinkauf's cheeks were pink with embarrassment. "I'm sorry that our invitation was disagreeable to you."

"Not at all, it's just—"

"Have a nice meal, Mr. Bragg." She walked past them and out the door.

Boone's shoulders slumped. "I was hoping to buy their property," he said. "You don't suppose . . ."

"That Mr. Kleinkauf will refuse the deal with you because you slighted Heidi? More than likely. Matters of the heart should come first."

But they didn't for Boone, and he could see no benefit in pretending that they did.

Boone checked his map against his list of property owners again. He'd been correct. After escorting Justina back to the Caine home on Byers Avenue, he'd returned to his office to find a message from Mr. Kleinkauf. He'd decided to lease the property to Mr. Picher. Of course.

Another business casualty fallen to meddling women. That left only two speculative opportunities he was considering. He'd need to collect core samples to see what compensation would be necessary and then consult his board before making an offer. If all went well, they could break ground by the end of the month, and he could move on. No more standing in a dark tunnel, looking at a watery dead end.

He jotted down the addresses of the property owners and reached for his hat. He needed to take a last look at the Curious Bear, gather any remaining equipment, and then he'd make his calls. Most mine operators sent letters from their office, but Boone believed in the personal touch. Often it smoothed the way and avoided misunderstandings down the road.

As Boone left his office with his notes, he saw two parasols bouncing their way up his porch steps. He'd already suffered through a brunch. Hadn't he earned a reprieve?

Through the thick glass of the front door, he saw it wasn't Justina Caine, but it was nearly as bad. He couldn't remember her name exactly, but he placed her as the daughter of the lead-paint manufacturer. Her mother had once cornered him at a dinner and demanded that he share his proposed timeline for matrimony and fatherhood. Boone had been in the process of forcing himself to choke on hors d'oeuvres when his mother intervened.

No mother to intervene now. Boone headed toward his back door as Mrs. Karol, the housekeeper, passed him, alerted to the doorbell. Women, with all their frilly fragility, bored him senseless. He wasn't short-sighted enough to say he would never marry, but if there was some way to skip all the preliminaries that accompanied the ordeal, Boone would be grateful. He resented feeling like a prize in some contest, the rules of which he didn't understand.

He hurried past the kitchen to the servants' entrance, then out to his waiting buggy. The horse pawed expectantly, and Boone didn't hold him back when he burst into a run. He took the turn onto the street too fast and clipped his mother's rosebush with one wheel, garnering the attention of the ladies on the porch. Mrs. Karol must have told them that he was out, because they turned to stare at him with open irritation. Fine and dandy. If they didn't want to see him again, so much the better, but Boone feared they wouldn't be dissuaded. They'd come again and insist on pouting about how he'd avoided them the last time.

If only there were a way to get on with his life without the interference of all these women. They saw him as the heir of a wealthy man, but they had no idea that his fortune was in jeopardy. If his luck didn't change, Boone would be working for wages like the rest of the miners. He had to get his finances on solid footing.

His horse trotted quickly through the Murphysburg neighborhood, new mansions going up on every side. Dirt was piled high on the corner lot of South Sergeant Avenue in preparation for another sprawling foundation. All this money was from the dirty work he and the other miners did in the ground. He turned off the city street and followed the country road until he'd reached the special entrance at the Kennedys' farm for the Curious Bear Mine workers.

Too bad it hadn't worked out. Boone could've sworn that this spot would be productive. Perhaps it would've worked for him if he knew how to install and manage the large water pumps. He still wasn't convinced that he couldn't figure them out, but it was better to play it safe and hope for the best for Mr. Caine.

When he reached the headframe, Boone knew something was amiss. The side door to the office was ajar. He dismounted from the buggy and secured his horse. It wouldn't be the first time a worker stole supplies to trade for whiskey. Going inside, he saw that the equipment chest was open. Rummaging through the box, he figured that the value of the missing items wasn't worth bothering over. In fact, he couldn't figure out why they hadn't taken more. It wasn't worth breaking the lock on the chest, really. He looked at the boarded-up entrance shaft and saw that some boards had been pried off, but not enough for a man to fit through.

Then he saw the twine tied to the board, and his stomach twisted. It was a sure sign that someone had gone into the mine, and from the size of the gap in the boards, it was probably a child.

With a quick prayer for the safety of whomever he was going after, Boone removed his coat, stepped out of his Oxfords, and pulled on a pair of boots from the chest. Lighting a sunshine lamp and a handheld lantern, he trudged his way to the entrance. Another board had to be removed before he could fit through the gap, but now that he was through, it wouldn't take any time at all to follow the twine.

Boone ducked his head as he turned onto the narrower path that tilted downward. When was the last time someone had been here? Two days ago? Three? He was preparing himself for the worst—a child who'd fallen and hadn't been able to make their way out, maybe even a cave-in. For all he knew, whoever had trespassed might be long gone.

But then he heard footsteps running toward him.

Whoever they were, they weren't hurt. Not at that pace. And they obviously didn't see the light from his lamp, because they didn't slow down until they rushed right into him.

Swishing fabric, fast breathing, and then a grunt as Boone caught the trespasser with an outstretched arm. Holding the interloper at a safe distance, he tried to make sense of what he was seeing with the weak light from his lanterns. There was a skirt, so a girl? But then he got a better look at what the light revealed and what the shadows hid, and he recoiled.

A woman? In his mine? Would they never leave him in peace?

"You have to see what I found." Her voice was low—raspy—as if she'd just woken. "Follow me." She grabbed him by the wrist and tried to drag him deeper into the mine.

Was Boone losing his mind? This couldn't be real. "Who are you?" he asked. "Why are you in this mine?"

"I was fixing the fence just yonder and thought I'd hop over and take a look around. You'll be glad that I did. Come on."

"You thought you'd take a look around?" Boone dug in his heels. He hadn't hidden from half the society ladies in Joplin only to be snagged by a mine-dwelling trespasser. "You thought you'd break the lock to my supply chest and help yourself to equipment that you had no right to, then break through the barriers on the entrance. That's more than just stopping in for a visit."

Her eyes were shaded by the brim of her hat, but her mouth quirked. "You work here? Is that why you're riled?"

"I own the mine. For a few more days, anyway."

"Then you don't want to see what I've found, because then you'll have to wonder what kind of miners do all this digging and can't see what took me only minutes to uncover."

At last, here was a woman talking about something that interested him. Was there ore above the waterline? Had his men walked right past a blossom without seeing it? Not Gilbert. He was the best foreman in the district. And yet the quest for the unexpected, the thought that there might be treasure just behind the next blow of a pickax, was what kept the miners of Joplin digging, and Boone was not immune.

"Show me," he said.

She spun and raced away. As excited as he was, Boone couldn't run, not with the low ceiling liable to knock his hat off.

Women. Women everywhere. He'd snuck away from his own home to avoid them only to run into one deep in the bowels of his mine. Was there nowhere that he'd be free of them? But this woman didn't act like his presence meant anything further than another human she wanted to show something to. In other words, she wasn't acting like a woman.

She'd stopped running and tossed her pickax against the jagged wall of the passageway. The light from his lantern caught her brown leather work boots and her homespun skirt. Working on a fence, she'd said? She was dressed for heavy labor. And the hands waving him impatiently forward were probably used to labor as well. He felt his anxiety easing.

"Look." She stepped out of the way, exposing a hole in the rock.

"What? A cave?" He cleared his throat to hide his disappointment. Caves were as common as mules in this part of Missouri. But even as he approached, he saw the crystal lining the opening she'd made. Not just a crystal, but a crystal band that edged the whole area in glittering light.

Could it be a geode? A giant geode? A geode as big as a rain barrel?

She bounced on her toes as he leaned in farther, impatiently waiting for his response. Well, he'd respond once he figured out what he was dealing with.

Leaning against the broken wall, he extended the lantern into the darkness, going slowly so he didn't knock it from his hand when he hit the opposite side. But there was no opposite side. Boone frowned at the darkness and blinked to clear his eyes and pick out something definite about the space, but everything was shrouded.

"Hello," he called through the hole.

The girl clapped her hands together. "That's what I did too."

Because she was talking, he missed the return echo . . . but no. It came after she spoke. The hair on his arms rose with a delicious shiver.

"It's immense," he said, then called a greeting again, just to test his theory. The returning echo only confirmed it. "That's a big cave," he said, "but I don't know what good it'll do me unless it's filled with ore."

"Ore?" The lady shook her head, throwing light willy-nilly over him. "It's not ore you should be thinking about, but the room. Look at it again."

Boone wanted to look at her. What was she? Some kind of underground sprite? But he turned back to the opening. This time, instead of holding his lantern out, he held it against the nearest wall. The layer of crystal wasn't just around the rim of the hole. It covered every inch he could see. Even when the substance faded into darkness, twinkling hints of what was farther afield caught his eye.

"Do you think it's the whole room?" she asked.

That was an interesting question, and there was only one way to find out. Taking her offered pickax, Boone nudged her out of the way, and then, with a few hits, smashed through the wall. The sound of the falling debris told him that the decline wasn't sheer, but it was deep. He ducked his head and shoulders through the opening only to have her grab him by his belt and tug him backward.

"What was that for?" he asked.

She lifted her shoulders. "Sorry. I thought you were falling headfirst into the hole."

"I don't fall in mines." He raised his chin to get a better look at her face. Her eyes were wide-set and perfectly centered. He hoped she was trustworthy. With the exploration before him, he didn't need trouble. "I'm going forward. Should something disastrous happen, please send for help."

"You bet, mister. While I wouldn't cotton to telling my family where I've been, in a pinch, they're right handy."

With care, he stretched his leg through the opening. The long crystal prisms scratched against his trousers, and he could feel the sharp edges through his boots. Just as he'd thought, the wall of the cave was a steep decline. The crystals were not sharp enough to cut, but they were uneven. Grasping the edge with both hands, he eased his other leg over and hung a moment before trusting his footing enough to let go.

What he could see of the space that was lit by his headlamp told him he wasn't on the safe bottom part of the curve. Instead, all of his weight was being supported by a giant spear of crystal that had grown out of the wall. Below that was a lake, nearly fifteen feet down.

Precarious indeed.

As much as he wanted to explore, it wasn't safe. Not yet. With his heart thudding, Boone reached up for the edge of the opening, only to have his fingers pinched by an awful pressure.

"Ouch! What are you doing?" But then he was kicked in the head by a swinging foot. A skirt swished across his cheek. "Stop!" He grasped some limb, probably an ankle, and pushed it away. "There's not room!"

"I found this cave." She kicked to free her leg from his grasp. "I have every right to see it too!"

Oh, heavens. Boone had never seen the calculations for how much weight a crystal could bear, and he wasn't willing to experiment. Catching her by a more substantial area of her body, he shoved her upward. "This footing isn't safe. It can't hold both of us."

"I'm tired of being left out while you fellas get all the excitement. Let me down."

Boone was running out of ideas. Pushing a young lady through a hole in a mine while standing on a slick crystal spire was awkward. Especially when she and gravity and the darkness were fighting against him.

But then the darkness went away. In fact, it got very light, very quickly.

"My skirt," she bellowed. Now she began to kick in earnest.

The smell of burning fabric reeked, and as Boone looked up to see what could be the matter, she planted her boot on his face and jumped.

She toppled over the ledge as he wiped the pain from his nose, then hoisted himself up. Falling forward, he rolled into the passageway and safety.

Only it wasn't safe, because the woman was on fire.

Of all the nonsense. She was scooting backward along the passageway as she beat at her burning skirt. Of course, Boone would be expected to help. He sprang against her. Throwing his arms around her knees, he smothered the flames against his chest. The smoke stung his eyes, but his shirt squelched the burning. He turned his face away as the smoke dispersed from beneath him. She'd stopped fighting, and he could feel her long, deep breaths. In the semidarkness, the glowing embers were easy to see. He ran his gloved hands down her skirt until he'd sought out and suffocated the last of them.

She squirmed, and he realized that he was still lying against her. Lying against her and running his hands over more parts of her body than was proper for him to name. Having to clear the sudden fire in his throat, he coughed as he stood.

"I guess you owe me," she said as she scrambled to her feet.

Now that his headlamp had been extinguished, he had to lift his lantern to see. "How do I owe you? If I hadn't been here, you could've been severely burned."

"If you weren't here, your hat wouldn't have caught my skirt on fire in the first place." She lifted the edge of her tattered, burned skirt. She dropped it, but it barely reached the calves of her charred long drawers. "You got a gorgeous crystal cavern that I discovered, but all I got for my pains is a ruined skirt."

"If you found my pocket watch in my study, you wouldn't have any rights to it." He gathered the pickax and twine and motioned for her to go before him. "If you please, it's time to end your trespassing. I've got matters to attend to."

"Matters like exploring my cave?" she muttered, but she kept a steady pace until they reached the sunlight coming in the office window.

She shaded her eyes from the brightness, unused to the transition. Now that they were in the light, he realized how damaged her skirt was and how inappropriately short it had become. She saw him looking at her scorched woolen socks.

"Ain't no way in the world the folks are going to let this pass without an explanation," she said.

Boone's eyes slid closed. His mother had warned him in no uncertain terms what could happen if a conniving woman ever got him alone and claimed to be compromised. All his solitude, his independence—everything would be forfeited. Had he fallen into a trap?

He'd rather face it head on than wait for the outraged family to summon him. "What do you want me to do?" he asked. "Should I accompany you home to make an explanation?"

When she shoved him in the shoulder, he had to take a step back to reestablish his balance. "Go back with me? Yeah, that would be something! If Pa thought I was consorting with a fella, he'd come after you, and we don't want that. It's bad enough as it is." She unbuckled her hat, snuffed out the flame, then handed it to him. "I'll tell them the story, but I won't mention you. There's no need for that." She reached into her skirt pocket and emptied it of matches, which she dropped into the trunk, then gathered a pair of pliers and a hammer from the table.

"You'd do that for me?" She was unlike any lady he'd ever met. Not only had she found a wonder in the mine that he'd given up on, but now she was covering his tracks.

She wiped her nose with the back of her hand. "I ain't doing it for you, sir. I'm saving my own hide. Until next time, it was nice meeting you, Mister . . . ?"

Here was where the problem lay. She didn't know him. That

was why she was unconcerned. “Bragg,” he admitted. “Boone Bragg.”

But instead of acting the least bit impressed, she nodded. “It was a pleasure, Mr. Bragg. You and your mine gave me a few hours of reprieve. For that I’m obliged.”

And she left without further ado.

CHAPTER 4

Fixing the fence on the cow pasture hadn't gone as she'd expected, and for that she was grateful. It recollected her of her childhood summers when all her cousins came to the ranch. Adventures, discoveries, challenges, danger . . .

But she was an adult now. She had to put those things behind her. By the time she explained her ruined clothing and her wanderings, she'd be locked in her room, even if she left Mr. Bragg out of the retelling.

Maisie double-checked the fence she'd finished, then carefully placed the barbed wire spool over her shoulder, barely noticing as a few barbs poked through her blouse. It was nearing dinnertime. If she were lucky, everyone would already be inside, and she could sneak to the house without anyone noticing. If she could get out of these clothes and burn what was left of them, maybe she wouldn't have to tell at all.

Maisie reached the south pasture, which wasn't visible from the house, but she heard a whistled signal regardless. It was Hank, and when she saw where he was standing, she groaned. There was only one reason he would be waiting at the Secret Tree: there was trouble at home.

Maisie hurried across the pasture, the barbed wire getting more bothersome with every step. Whatever had brought Hank from across the river and his parents' ranch was a message of trouble. Of that she had no doubt.

Hank gawked at her burnt skirt. "What happened to you?"

"Nothing. Just found a cave and went exploring." She dropped the wire to the ground.

But Hank wasn't messing around. He grabbed her hand and pulled it to the trunk of the Secret Tree. "Tell me what happened. It's important."

It didn't matter that Hank was only a distant cousin. He still knew all the Kentworth lore. Even when they'd outgrown her brother Finn's warnings about the Secret Tree, they were still honor bound to tell the truth when beneath its branches and never to disclose the secrets revealed. To their thinking, it was as binding as swearing with a hand on the Bible.

"I got into Bragg's mine over on the Kennedys' land. They'd done a poor job boarding it up and left the equipment secured with a flimsy lock."

Hank snorted. "They were practically asking for you to explore it."

"I did explore it, and you won't believe what I found, Hank. It's a cave all covered in crystals. I've never even heard the like."

"Let's go." Hank tugged the waistband of his britches up higher. "I wanna see this."

Sometimes Maisie thought her family was crazy, but most of the time they were the most genuine people around. "I wish we could, but we can't. He caught me there."

"Who? The sheriff?"

Maisie wrinkled her nose. "No, Mr. Bragg. He owns the place. Chances are he won't let me come back."

"You made a discovery in his mine, and he won't let you come back? Where's his gratitude?" Then Hank's eyes narrowed. "He didn't catch you on fire, did he?"

"Actually, he did, but I forgot to account for his hat lamp when I was stepping on his face."

Hank considered this information. "Can't fault the man, then," he pronounced with the judgment of a sage.

"Don't intend to, but that doesn't mean I won't look for another chance to go in there. If I can change clothes without them catching me—"

"Hank, is that Maisie with you?"

Maisie and Hank turned to see her pa approaching on a horse. Him leaving off chores to fetch her did not bode well.

"Yes, sir," she said. "It's me."

"Get to the house. We've been looking everywhere for you."

"I was fixing to tell you," Hank whispered, "the sheriff came calling."

Maisie took another look at her skirt. If one could get locked up for general mischief, she was in danger of being arrested.

Picking up her gear, she walked out from the shade of the tree to meet her pa in the pasture. His horse flared its nostrils as she approached, probably spooked by her smoky scent. Maisie rubbed its nose to calm it even though her thoughts were running wild.

"What in heaven's name happened to you?" Bill Kentworth leaned forward, letting his wrists rest over the horn of the saddle.

"I ran into some trouble," Maisie said. "I'm on my way to clean up."

He looked doubtful. "The sheriff is at the house. What am I supposed to say when you look like you've been . . . What exactly have you been doing?"

"I was exploring a mine and caught my skirt on fire with a lantern."

It took her pa a moment to digest this information. "You were supposed to be repairing the fence," he said.

"I got distracted."

Maisie hoped she never felt as tired as her pa looked at that moment. "No matter. Sheriff Bigelow wants to see you, so you've got to face the music. And Hank too. Hank?" Pa raised his head and his voice to call for Hank, but Maisie was surprised to note that her cousin had vanished into thin air.

He couldn't have crossed the pasture without them seeing. Her first guess was that he'd found a depression in the ground and was hiding behind a clump of tall grass, but then she saw a dark spot in the tree and figured he'd climbed his way to a hidey-hole. Good for him. She lowered her eyes so Pa couldn't read them.

Pa extended his hand. "Drop the wire and hop on up here. Hank isn't my responsibility. You and Amos are."

On the way to their farmhouse, they passed in front of Granny Laura's home. As she rocked on the porch, Granny didn't acknowledge them but stared out at the horizon past them. Maisie wasn't sure she'd ever felt this level of displeasure before. Although Granny didn't look at her, she knew without a doubt that Granny had taken in every detail of her disastrous appearance.

When they reached her house, Maisie slid off the side of the horse, then stepped away as her pa dismounted.

With heavy feet, she walked up the steps and into the house. When her mother saw Maisie, she hopped off the sofa like she'd been goosed. She covered her mouth and plopped back down next to Amos.

"Pleased to have you join us." Sheriff Bigelow stood, the top of his bald head barely reaching Maisie's shoulder. "Have a seat."

"No," her mother said. "You're filthy. Don't touch any of the furniture."

"Fine," Maisie said.

"I hope I didn't catch you at an inconvenient time." Sheriff Bigelow drawled like he was smooching babies on the campaign trail.

"Actually, you did," Maisie said. "If you could return, maybe next year?"

"Maisie!" Her mother swatted at her with her hankie. "My apologies, Sheriff. She's always had a smart mouth, but here lately—"

"You mean since you confined me to the farm?" Maisie turned to the sheriff. "I have a grievance to report. These people have locked me up like a prisoner. I'm a full-grown adult, and they are treating me like an irresponsible child."

The parlor fell silent as they studied her disheveled state. The dog entered the room, sniffed at her charred skirt, then ran away with his tail tucked.

"If you want to leave, you can leave," Sheriff Bigelow said, "but if you live on your family's land, then you abide by their rules." He turned to her pa. "Is that the gist of it?"

"More or less." Pa didn't want her to leave and be on her own, but the time was coming. Maybe she could get hired on at the Pinkertons? How she wished she were more like Calista.

"Whatever you decide," the sheriff said, "you got to make two concessions. The first is that your family can never go back to Daniel's Drug and Miscellany."

"The whole family is banned?" Her mother's jaw dropped. "That's not friendly."

"The second is that you"—and here the sheriff pegged Amos—"don't harass Mr. Marsh any further. We can't have people accosting innocent citizens—"

"Innocent?" Amos tossed his head back. "Silas Marsh is guilty of offense against my sister."

Maisie stomped her foot, dropping cinders onto the braided rug. "The way you carry on, Amos. You know good and well I quit associating with him when he showed his colors."

"What do you have to say about the drugstore?" Sheriff Bigelow asked.

Maisie shot her brother a murderous look. No matter how badly she wanted to pin the blame on him and Hank, family had to stick together. "I told Silas I never wanted to see him again. He shouldn't have come."

"You shouldn't have been there." Pa looked ready to revive the flames of his indignation. "We told you to go to the feedstore, then come straight home."

Amos slapped his thigh. "Kentworths don't hide from their problems. If Maisie wants to go somewhere, she should be able to light out and go. It's on Silas's shoulders to make sure their paths don't cross."

"No," the sheriff said. "Legally, Mr. Marsh has as much right to go to Daniel's store as you do—more now that Mr. Daniel has banned you from setting foot on his property."

"Just as well," Amos groused. "He barely put any flavor on his shaved ice."

"Boy, you'd better watch your mouth." Pa glared at him. "You cost us the price of two calves with the damage you did to Mr. Daniel's store. I won't have you besmirching the quality of his products on top of that."

"The bottom line is this," said the sheriff, "if your boy here or your nephew Hank has any further conflict with Mr. Marsh, I'll be forced to restrain them." He turned to face Amos. "That means jail time, young man. You keep away from Marsh. This is your last warning."

"I'll be glad to stay away," Amos said, "as long as he doesn't come near my sister."

Maisie crossed her arms and tucked her hands beneath them. Would Silas stay away? Something in her gut told her that Silas would never shy away from her. As long as she was about, her brother and her cousin were in imminent danger. Either she stayed locked up, or they would be.

It was her freedom or theirs.

CHAPTER 5

The table in the boardroom of Bragg Mining was made of a solid slab of granite weighing a full ton plus change. Boone ran his hand over the cool surface and admired the swirls. The granite harvesters weren't the only ones who could discover beauty beneath the surface. He'd found something more than he'd ever expected.

When Boone had returned to the mine with his crew, he'd told himself not to be disappointed. There was no way the cave could live up to his memory of it. He'd allowed it to grow into something too fantastical. Too wondrous. But with a handful of his best men, electric lamps, ropes, and climbing harnesses, they'd made a complete exploration of the space. Two hundred and fifty feet long, fifty-five feet wide at the widest, and around fifteen feet tall above the water level. The cavern was immense, but what was more spectacular was that every inch of it was covered in dazzling crystals. He'd never seen anything like it. No one had.

And now he had to convince the Bragg Mining board that this was where their real opportunity lay. Once they were all seated, he began, delving quickly into the meat of the challenge.

"Despite the possibilities, this part of the mine has the same issues with water that the rest of it has. Three years ago, Father used Horace to install the water pumps at the Rosemary Mine, but since Horace moved away, we haven't installed any more systems. I know it'll take some work, but I'm capable of figuring it out. I think once you see the cave for yourselves, you'll understand how this could be profitable."

Or would they? The expressions of his board members were not promising.

"I can learn the pumps," he continued. "My company needs to advance in that area anyway. Once the pumps are going for the cave, we can take another look at the Curious Bear. Perhaps we'll find ore on lower levels. True, there might be easier ore for the taking, but we'll never have another chance at a miracle like this cave. That's why I'm canceling the negotiations with Caine and informing the crew that they'll be mining, but with a different objective. The highest spot of the cave is eighty feet down. It's southeast of the current headframe. We'll need closer access."

"Access?" Mark Gilbert, the foreman of the Curious Bear, stopped rocking in his chair. "What are we going to bring up out of there? There's no market for calcite crystals."

No wonder they weren't excited. They didn't understand.

"We're not bringing up anything," Boone said. "We're taking people down. We're leaving that place as pristine as we can—minus the water—and we're going to show God's hidden creation to the world. People will come from all over to see it."

It was as if Boone had just said something foolish and everyone was embarrassed for him. No one would meet his eyes. Was he making the right decision? It wasn't just a risk for himself, but for his employees and their security. What would they think about him rejecting a sure offer in order to turn a mine into a tourist attraction?

"Have any of you heard about the new Electric Light Park that Schifferdecker is planning? They estimate that it's going to take $150,000 to construct. Just imagine! And we have a sight more beautiful that's just waiting for us to show."

"It's not quite ready for show." As an adviser of Boone's father as well, Mr. Hunt had wisdom that couldn't be ignored. "It would still require a sizable investment to provide safe access. In my opinion, the sale of the mine should continue. Your solicitor has looked over Mr. Caine's offer and found it to be in order. There's no reason to disrupt it at this late hour."

Heads nodded all around the table. What would it take to convince them? Did he *have* to convince them? They were his advisers, but he had the authority to make or cancel a sale. Would he be able to finance the construction needed, or would he have to get a loan? Boone didn't cotton to the idea of investors. It'd be better to mortgage what was already his.

"Mr. Bragg? Are you attending?" Mr. Hunt's face came into focus. He flashed a worried look at the banker, then back at Boone.

Boone was doing it again—forgetting where he was and that there were people in the room. He tightened his mouth. It wasn't that he'd lost focus. He was perfectly focused on what was important to him. The men in suits didn't reach that level of interest, but they were trying to help him, and he'd listen to their concerns.

All he had to do was study natural wonders with the same intensity he'd studied mining, and he'd find his way from there. He always had before. The first thing was to make a plan. He reached for the map that he'd drafted after their excursion.

"Now, according to the survey, that high point comes out across the property line." He stood, rolled out the map, moved a coffee mug to one corner and a book to the opposite, and tapped the exact spot he was targeting. "We'll need access to construct ramps, stairs, and a catwalk for visitors. Electricity too. For people to understand the majesty of this place, it needs light. Something more than lanterns. We'll light up the whole place."

"Mr. Bragg, what about Mr. Caine?" Gilbert asked.

Caine? Boone adjusted his collar. He had suspected that the only reason Mr. Caine was bailing him out by offering to buy the mine was that he wanted Boone as a son-in-law, and after the miserable brunch the day before, Boone knew that could never happen. Keeping the mine would save him from an uncomfortable alliance.

"We haven't signed any contract. I'm keeping the mine."

Gilbert wrote something on his tablet, then passed it to Mr. Hunt. Did they think he couldn't see? But Boone wasn't a schoolmarm. They could pass notes if they wanted. Besides, he didn't need to confiscate it to know that it wasn't complimentary toward him and his decision. But this was an opportunity no one had thought to explore before, plus a chance to learn something that had held him back.

As the men gathered their papers and extinguished their cigars, Boone had his first real pang of doubt. Was he doing this because he thought it would be profitable, or was it for a less rational reason? Had he gotten his head turned by the novelty of the discovery?

Boone shook his head. Regardless of his motives, there had to be a way to make it profitable or at least self-sustaining. His parents had long admired his head for business, claiming he would grow to be even more successful than his father, but Boone had another side too. And he saw nothing wrong with indulging the dreamer as long as the business could be satisfied in the process.

The room had emptied of everyone except Mr. Hunt, who was politely looking over the map as he waited to be acknowledged by Boone.

"Right here, huh?" He tapped the spot on the map that denoted a low spot on the earth above the cave and the easiest access to the site. "This is outside your property lines. If I remember right, this outlet will open up on Kentworth land."

Boone lifted the mug of coffee off the map and took a drink. "I've heard of the Kentworths. Get ahold of Mr. Kentworth and arrange a meeting. I'll make sure he understands that this won't be a typical mining operation. There won't be piles of chat left everywhere or large areas of sod removed. We'll want a building of some sort erected. A visitor center, if you will, but its footprint will be minimal. Most important is that we'll need access to the road.

We'll probably have to widen the road to deal with the traffic. I'll tell Mr. Kentworth that it's bound to increase the property value of his ranch. He'll be the owner of prime real estate ere long."

The way Mr. Hunt's thick hair was parted and shellacked into two curves made it look like his head was in the grip of a sugar nipper. "It's not Mr. Kentworth. It's Mrs. Laura Kentworth. She's a widow lady who has run the ranch with the help of her family for years. Her son lives there, but no big decisions will be made without consulting her. And she's not likely to care about property values. The old gal doesn't need more money. She has everything in the world she wants."

"It takes a person with a weak imagination not to be able to think of anything else they want." Boone couldn't imagine not having a dozen dreams and plans rolling around at all times. "We'll just have to find something we want to give and convince her that's what she needs." He grinned. "That sweet old lady will be no match for us."

"You think so?" Mr. Hunt raised an eyebrow. "Well, good luck to you, Boone. You've bitten off a mouthful."

"Mr. Bragg?" His secretary, Mrs. Stein, stepped into the room. "Your mother is on the phone."

Boone smiled. If anyone would appreciate how horribly awkward his brunch with Justina was, it would be his mother. "I'll take it in here," he said and picked up the receiver as Mr. Hunt exited.

It was immediately apparent that Boone didn't need to tell his mother, because she already knew.

"What were you thinking, letting Justina drag you into that?" His mother's words came in short, strong bursts, like she was trying not to be overheard. "I've already heard from both Mrs. Yates and Mrs. Handel that you two are courting."

His plans for the crystal cave faded in light of this new threat. "We are not courting, Mother. I took her as a favor to Mr. Caine. Ask Father. I am considering a deal with him—"

"Whatever the deal is, you cannot allow her to hoodwink you

into any more social engagements. I cannot have Justina Caine as a daughter-in-law. That voice. Do you want to listen to that voice for the rest of your life?"

Boone dropped back into his chair. "Don't worry. Marrying Justina is the last thing in the world I want."

"Well, you'd best be careful. The way she and her mother are talking, you're practically engaged. If something isn't done to end these rumors, you'll end up with the reputation of a lothario."

Him, a lothario? No lothario ever made a name for himself with such scant skills as Boone possessed, but his naïveté made him an easy mark.

"Thank you for the warning," he said. "I'll set it all straight."

But his primary female concern involved a ranch-owning grandmother that he needed to visit.

Boone sat on a rough cowhide chair in the parlor and waited for Mrs. Laura Kentworth to return. He'd accepted her offer of lemonade mostly because he needed some time to compose himself. When he'd come to the elderly woman's ranch to talk to her about the cavern, he hadn't expected to find her astride a horse, wearing a bandanna over her face, leather chaps, and a Boss of the Plains hat. She told him that she'd been cutting the herd, sorting out which cattle were headed to their terminal destination in Kansas City aboard her grandson-in-law's trains.

Boone had heard that a railroad magnate had married into a local family, but he hadn't guessed it was this out-of-the-way clan that rarely came to town. No wonder Mr. Hunt laughed when Boone had talked about financial inducement. Boone would have to come up with something better.

"Here we go." Mrs. Kentworth entered with two Mason jars of lemonade. The glass felt cold in his hand even though there was no ice. With a grunt, Mrs. Kentworth plopped unceremoniously into her rocker and ran her fingers through her short-cropped white curls to dislodge the marks where her hat had crushed them. "It's kind of you to visit," she said. "I figured we'd be hearing from you sooner or later, but I'm honored that you came yourself instead of sending one of your people."

"I've heard a lot about you, Mrs. Kentworth, and thought you would be someone worth the trip, even if business wasn't involved."

"Hogwash." She eyed him sharply. "There's something up your sleeve besides mineral rights. I know how those negotiations are conducted, and they don't usually involve a visit from the owner."

"True. This case deserves special consideration because what I'm proposing doesn't involve a mine."

She lowered her drink. "You have my attention. Continue."

"Yes, ma'am." Boone set down his canning jar and moved to the edge of his chair. Talking about his plans was thrilling. "Earlier this week I was down in the Curious Bear and discovered something amazing. Now, I must ask you to keep this information private, but I think you'll understand why. I found a cave—a wondrous cave. One that people will come from miles around to see. It's a sight unlike anything you've ever considered."

Her eyes sparkled. "Tell me more."

"It's a huge, elongated room, and as far as we can tell, every inch is encrusted with calcite crystals. There's some barite too, but mostly calcite. Walking into it is like stepping into a geode. Most of the crystal is a pale gold, but some has a purple tint. The cavern still needs to be drained of water before we can see the whole area, but it's breathtaking with nothing more than a handheld lantern. Just imagine what it would look like when illuminated with electric lamps."

"Electricity? You're going to run electricity out here?" She looked at the hurricane lamp on the table next to her. "That would be something."

"There'll be a lot of benefits for you, Mrs. Kentworth. I'll improve the road to town so you won't have to contend with these washboard ruts anymore. If this venture is as successful as I imagine, your property will rise in value. There'll be shops, restaurants, maybe even hotels that want to locate out here."

"Hotels here at my ranch?" The lines around her eyes tightened. "Not sure that's something I'd cotton to."

"Maybe not hotels, but there would be people vying for the chance to see something special, something unique. Just think, God made this beautiful treasure and hid it for thousands of years. Isn't it exciting that it's being uncovered and explored in our lifetime?"

This seemed to please her. "'He revealeth the deep and secret things: he knoweth what is in the darkness, and the light dwelleth with him,'" she quoted. "Daniel, chapter two."

Boone beamed. He didn't feel like he'd convinced her, but he felt like he'd found a kindred spirit. "Yes, ma'am. Those are my thoughts exactly. Having been shown the handiwork of God, isn't it my duty to share it?"

She smiled fondly. "And what is it that you're asking of me?"

Boone pulled a folded map out of his pocket, a small copy of the rolled one he'd left in the conference room. "This is a sketch of the cavern. Here you'll see our current access point on the land we bought from the Kennedys, but you'll notice that it's quite a ways down the shafts until you reach the cavern. A more logical access is from this side . . . right here."

"Hmm . . . that looks like it'd be on my land," she said. "I sent one of my grandchildren out that way to repair the fence recently."

"You won't have to worry about the fence in that part ever again," he said. "We'll take care of it for you. We'd build a visitor center here, where visitors would purchase their tickets, and maybe a waiting room for the tours. Nothing too extravagant. There'd need to be access to the road and a place big enough for wagons to park while people are beneath the ground, but most of that can stay on the Kennedys' side. The space required from you would be minimal."

"And so would the offer you're making me?" she asked. When

Boone didn't answer, she crossed one leg over the other, letting the fringe on her chaps sway with her rocking chair. "No need to give me a dollar amount, dear. Not yet, because I have some requests that would be involved in the counterbid."

Boone braced himself. People often had unrealistic ideas of the worth of their land. It was up to him to help them see things more reasonably.

"From time to time, I have grandchildren who are looking for employment," she said. "Since this cavern is part of our ranch and you want to use our land to build your visitor center, I think it reasonable that a family member would be employed by this venture and have a say in what happens."

"A say? Define what you mean by *a say*."

"You'd be the boss, of course. Fifty-one percent of the decision-making power should come from you, but our family should have the next biggest piece of the pie."

"Mrs. Kentworth, I've had the rights to this mine for more than a year. I've invested in its development and am looking at considerable expense to start this new venture. I can't give away forty-nine percent of my interest."

"Not of the profit or ownership. Just that we have a representative that can give input on the decisions. That can speak their mind on what you're proposing. It'd only be fair that you pay a small stipend for the service, but not a piece of the ownership. I'm not an unreasonable person."

He breathed a little easier. "So, knowing that I'm still the primary decision-maker, you understand that your family's wishes could be overruled every single time? And you'd have no claim on the profits?"

"I understand. I think it's good for young people to learn something about business and not be stuck on this farm all the time. That's all I want for my grandchildren. That I can choose one who will learn from the process and keep us informed of your decisions, while informing you of our preferences." She reached for her lemonade. "If you agree to that, the financial compensation will be simple to arrange." Then she took a long drink, giving him time to think.

Hire one of her grandsons, let him sit in on the meetings, and even if he disagreed, there'd be no repercussions? What would it hurt? After all, everyone would know that the cave was found on Kentworth land. No one would think it odd that a Kentworth would be on the board.

On the board of the Crystal Cave. Boone smiled. He'd have to form a board, because this was an entirely new endeavor. One he couldn't stop thinking about. He'd need new insights and new advisers. He knew how to clear out a space underground, but he didn't know the first thing about hospitality, marketing, or tourism. Bringing new people on board made sense, and having a Kentworth involved wouldn't hurt a thing.

Mrs. Kentworth had done him a favor.

CHAPTER 6

"Welcome to the first meeting of the Crystal Cave Board." Boone rustled through a stack of estimates and sketches to find the list he was looking for. "If you will allow me to make introductions, first I have Mr. Hunt here on my right. Mr. Hunt has worked for Bragg Mining for twenty years, managing our employees and equipment, and has joined my company at my father's request. Any questions about our workforce go to him. Then there's the foreman of the Curious Bear, Mr. Gilbert. This will be something new for him as well, but with his experience underground, I know he'll learn quickly. Many of you know Mrs. Penney, who does publicity for many of our hotels and restaurants. She is bringing her experience in hospitality to share with us. My financial adviser . . ."

Heads turned as the door to the conference room swung open. Mrs. Stein stepped inside, her hands hidden behind her back. "I apologize, Mr. Bragg. You have a guest who's demanding admittance to the meeting. Mrs. Kentworth is here and brought her grandchild. . . ." She set her teeth as if merely saying the words was dreadful.

There was no telling how this country boy had decided to present himself. Boone didn't expect him to have a business wardrobe or city manners, but the family was respected. He'd make the best of the situation, because without access to the Kentworth land, the Crystal Cave might not open at all.

"Send him in."

"But, sir—"

"It's fine," Boone said. "This isn't our typical undertaking. We might as well bring in some fresh blood and opinions. Show him in, please."

There were some chuckles as the secretary retreated.

"Your staff is questioning your judgment." Mr. Hunt snapped his pocket watch closed and looked up at Boone. "She wouldn't have acted that way to your father."

Mr. Hunt was right, but Boone wasn't about to give Mrs. Stein any grief.

"We're in new territory," Boone said. "New for all of us. I'm inclined toward patience with each other."

Footsteps could be heard in the hallway. Boone's eyes lit on the empty chair next to Mrs. Penney. He'd get this fellow introduced, and then they could get started. Everyone turned toward the open door in expectation as a shadow preceded the Kentworth progeny.

Boone felt the air leave his lungs in a low-pitched rumble. It was the woman from the cave. This time her dress was clean, although poorly fitted, hanging off her broad shoulders with sleeves too short. Her hair was pulled tight, exposing her clean features, unpowdered freckles, and a widow's peak on that auburn head. She stood with her hands hanging artlessly at her sides and returned the stares of half a dozen curious professionals.

Boone leapt to his feet. Crossing the room with long strides, he stepped in front of her, shielding her from their view. "Can I help you?"

"There you are." She smiled as if his presence solved all her problems. "I'm here for the meeting."

"What meeting?"

"This meeting, I reckon." When she heard snickers, she looked over Boone's shoulder and smiled at the offender.

"There's been some mistake. This is a board meeting of a newly formed company. We aren't open—"

"Newly formed? You mean the treasure mine that I discovered?"

The laughter in the room died. "Mr. Bragg, does this corporation already have some shares spoken for?" his financial adviser asked.

"No, sir," Boone said. "This lady has no claim on the mine. She was trespassing. Miss . . . ?"

"Kentworth. Miss Kentworth," she supplied.

Boone's mouth popped closed. His eyes squinted. "Miss Kentworth, you say?" This was bad. This was really bad. "And your grandmother is . . ."

"Mrs. Laura Kentworth. She's out there sitting in the buggy, although I reckon she's sought a shade tree by now. I wanted to thank you for getting me off the ranch. If it wasn't for you, they would've kept me chained up like a lunatic uncle. I couldn't believe my luck when Granny told me you'd agreed to let me have a say in your business. What do I know about running a tourism spot? So that was mighty generous of you, especially after I kicked you in the face. 'Course, then you lit my skirts on fire, so maybe we're even in that respect. But I'm not one to walk away from something as incredible as that cavern."

Boone could feel the questions forming around the table. This was not what he'd signed on for, and it definitely wasn't what his investors had agreed to. But Miss Kentworth seemed oblivious to their shock.

She stepped around Boone to face the confused board members, her hands on her hips. "Well, if this is supposed to be a business, we'd best get after it. With all you fine people assembled, you'uns have got to have something better to do than gawk at me."

Spotting the empty chair, she strode to it and dropped into it without pretense. She was here to stay, and Boone was realizing that he could do nothing to prevent it. It felt like every step to his own chair at the head of the table was barefoot on broken glass.

He stared at his maps as he collected his thoughts. He had promised Mrs. Kentworth that she could send a grandchild, he just hadn't considered that it could be a granddaughter. He surely hadn't thought that the adventurous woman he'd met in the mine was a Kentworth. It all made sense now, but had he known, he would've been more circumspect with his promises.

Too late now.

"Gentlemen and Mrs. Penney, please welcome Miss Kentworth to the board. Not only is the access to this dig going to be through her family land, she is also the one who discovered the cave . . . while trespassing. I expect she'll bring a unique perspective to what we're trying to accomplish here."

With every venture, there were unexpected complications. He'd learned to make allowances for delays, expenses, and false starts. But no matter how much experience he had, he couldn't have foreseen the rouser from the cave coming to his boardroom.

Boone picked up his agenda and continued the meeting, and for once he wasn't distracted by thoughts more exciting than what was going on in the room with him.

Maisie tried to follow the discussion but found it awfully boring. Soughs, adits, water skips, Cornish force pumps—it was like she'd wandered into a foreign country and didn't speak the language. How could she contribute to a conversation on the oxygen content of air or the voltage of electricity needed to light the cave? Had they wanted to talk livestock or farming, then she might have some wisdom to impart, but not the logistics involved in this venture.

Maybe this had been a mistake. Having to sit still was as tough as a hickory knot. If they had cracked a window, Maisie might have been content, but without some air, she was getting antsy. She purred, thinking about the coolness down by the creek and how the air tickled over her skin after taking a dip. Mr. Hunt's cleared throat made her sit up straighter and stop daydreaming. Maisie planted both feet on the floor. She had to be here. It was her only shot at a life untethered from the farm.

"And while a decision is being made on the pumps, the promotional campaign will get started. We're going to run advertisements in all the local newspapers, of course, but also on the printed train schedules, so visitors from around the country will know we're here. The scientific community will be invited, but also your more common visitors—families, students, honeymooners."

"We could have parties down there." Maisie blinked at the sound of her own voice. Had she really said that aloud? But the idea had merit. "You could put a floor in when the water's gone. Build a stage. Have weddings, dances, parties. It'd be a gathering place like no other." Warming up to her subject, she leaned toward the group. "Otherwise people will come once to see it, and then they're done. But if you had a reason for people to come, a reason for people—"

"I like it," the woman sitting next to her said. "I'm Mrs. Penney, and as the marketing expert on this board, I think you have a genius idea. Daily tours will be essential in the beginning, but we could market this as a romantic getaway or the ideal place for a spectacular wedding."

"Hmmph." The grump across the table let the folds of his face crease even deeper. "Let's not muddy the waters. This is a scientific discovery, the largest geode ever discovered. I don't think a dark, wet hole in the ground is going to spark any romantic notions."

Maisie thought of how she'd looked after her foray into the cave. Her face covered in dirt, her skirt burned to ashes, the scrapes on her arms from pulling herself up out of the cave—not romantic at all. She tried to choke down a chuckle, but the marketer noticed.

"Wait a minute. You discovered the cave, didn't you? And then Mr. Bragg found you down there?" Mrs. Penney's eyes flashed from Maisie to Mr. Bragg. "That must have been a very interesting meeting."

Mr. Bragg's face had gone as white as milk. His eyes met Maisie's, and she read his warning. What had he told them? She didn't know.

"We did meet there," Mr. Bragg said at last. "She was coming out of the mine to tell me that she'd found something."

The mood of the room had changed. Grins were being exchanged, and there was a lot of rustling as the board members moved so they could keep both Mr. Bragg and Maisie in view.

"Of course you followed her into the mine to see what she discovered." Mr. Gilbert removed his cold cigar from his mouth so he didn't have to speak around the chewed end. "And I guess you discovered something too."

Well, that was enough of that. Maisie was in this mess because a man liked to run off at the mouth. She wasn't about to tolerate it from this fellow.

"You watch your stinking mouth. I don't like your insinuating." Rising to stand over him, Maisie cocked back her right arm, being how it was the one she favored. Mr. Gilbert threw up an arm and ducked his head at the same time. Then she heard the only familiar voice in the room.

"Miss Kentworth, don't threaten the board members, please." Mr. Bragg rubbed his hand tiredly down his face.

Maisie dropped into her chair. "Sorry," she murmured. "I'm easily riled."

No more rustling. Everyone sat stock-still, unsure what to do.

Mr. Gilbert must have been good-natured even at his own expense. "You don't brook any nonsense." With his off-kilter nose, he looked like possibly the only man in the room who had taken a punch. "If you hadn't had mercy on me, I'd be working on a fat eye right now. Serves me right. I didn't mean any offense."

"None taken," Maisie replied dutifully, although obviously she had taken offense. "I forgive you," she added, for that was closer to the truth. If she was going to be allowed to work with Mr. Bragg, their relationship had to be above reproach. She couldn't make the same mistake twice.

"Now that we have that behind us, let's look at the crew and who we think will be assigned to this project." Mr. Bragg flipped the page of a journal he was working on, and everyone bent over their papers to take notes. Everyone except Maisie, who had nothing to write on.

"We're going to talk later. I've got questions." Mrs. Penney's fair skin wrinkled around her eyes as she tossed a private smile at Maisie. If Maisie had known that Mr. Bragg was such an important man, maybe she wouldn't have kicked him in the face.

The rest of the meeting went slowly. Certain parts of it made sense, but other times Maisie allowed her imagination to roam over the elaborate room and intricate details of the furnishings. She owed Granny Laura for giving her this chance. Her parents had been one hundred percent against her leaving, but when Granny offered to chaperone in place of Amos and Hank, there was little they could object to. Maisie could just imagine herself strolling down the high-ceilinged hallways every day and chatting with these fancy people about the work they were doing to get the mine open. Maisie wrinkled her nose. With her luck, Mr. Bragg would put her down in the cave with a shovel and make her work with the miners. She was probably more suited to that.

The conversation in the room had halted. Maisie looked around to see what was the matter, and they were all looking at Mr. Bragg, who was staring at her.

"Did you hear me, sir?" the financier asked. "Those last numbers—do they have your approval?"

From the far-off look in his eyes, Mr. Bragg wasn't listening at all. His lips were twisted into a bemused smile, and he probably didn't even realize he was staring at Maisie.

When their eyes connected, he blinked. Then, aware of his surroundings, he cleared his throat and picked up whatever paper happened to be closest. "What was the question, again?"

The meeting continued, and he seemed determined not to look her direction again. City folk sure acted strange, or maybe it was just business meetings that made people act peculiar. Maisie wondered what Granny Laura was doing with all this time on her hands. Maybe she'd gone to visit her daughter-in-law Myra and Maisie's cousin Olive. Maisie wouldn't mind getting to visit with Uncle Oscar's family. Wait until they heard that she'd been to a bona fide board meeting.

Finally, the discussion wound down. Around the table they went, each verifying what they would work on before their next meeting. The man before Maisie said something about ordering more dynamite to blast the new access, and then it was her turn.

Maisie scratched her elbow as she tried to come up with something she could do. Then it hit her. "I'll reset those fence posts so you'uns can get to your new entry without setting our cattle loose. If my brother will help, we can get it done tomorrow, but if I have to dig the post holes myself, it could take an extra day."

She'd said something funny. The man next to her choked, then hid his face behind a piece of paper like there was something on it that he suddenly had to read. Mr. Bragg wasn't laughing at her like everyone else, but he was smiling like she amused him in a fond way.

The marketing lady patted Maisie's arm. "You take care of that fence, darling, but you and I are going to have a little talk. I want to hear all about you and Mr. Bragg meeting in the glass grotto."

Maisie shot Mr. Bragg a frightened look, but he had moved on to the next person, and soon everyone around the table had reported.

Mr. Bragg stood, which was the signal for the board to gather their things, although no one seemed to be in a hurry to leave. Instead, various members of the board made plans to meet and continue their work later. As far as Maisie knew, no one was going to come out and help her with the post holes, so there was no further discussion coming from her. She headed for the door.

"What's this I hear about you and Miss Caine?" Mr. Bragg's foreman asked him. "Does she know about this crystal cave yet?"

Instead of answering him, Mr. Bragg called Maisie's name.

"Miss Kentworth." The room silenced at his voice.

Maisie turned. "Yes, sir."

"A word please." But instead of coming toward her, Mr. Bragg walked to a door on the opposite side of the boardroom and held it open.

Was she in trouble? Probably. She didn't belong with these people. If only she could be professional like Mrs. Penney. The only skill she'd exhibited was the ability to break into a building and shimmy through some loose boards. It was no wonder she didn't fit in.

Not yet. But she wanted to someday.

CHAPTER 7

Having a lady like Miss Kentworth in the boardroom had been a mistake. How was Boone supposed to focus on business with her present? He might as well have turned a frolicking foal loose and let it kick up its heels. A foal would've been easier to ignore.

Boone held open the tall door that led to his private office and waited for Miss Kentworth to pass through it. She stopped within his span to survey the room. With its bookshelves littered with maps, rolls of ink-covered paper, and chunks of ore and rock with tags glued to them, he had to admit it was a mess. Except for his desk, which he kept spotless.

When she hesitated, Boone motioned her to a seat. He laid his hand on his leather-covered portfolio. A drafting pencil was arranged precisely parallel to it on the desk. No one could touch it without him noticing, and he noticed right then that it was moving. It bounced as the floor beneath his feet shuddered. Miss Kentworth had carried the heavy leather chair he'd offered her to the side of his desk and dropped it where there was no barrier between them.

Boone looked at the floor and calculated the exact distance from his desk to her chair. "Would you prefer my seat?" he said. "If you wanted to sit behind the desk, you could've asked."

"Well, we ain't eating supper, so I don't know what good a big table between us is. No reason to be yelling at each other from across the room, and it's one hundred percent proper. We aren't even within reach." Miss Kentworth stretched forth her arm and waved it, demonstrating that her fingertips didn't reach his chair. When he drew back, she asked, "Did I do something wrong?"

Boone lifted his chair and turned it to face her. "Just unexpected . . . and practical. Though now that I think about it, the practical is usually unexpected, isn't it?"

"Not in my world," Miss Kentworth replied. "Why would you do things that serve no purpose?"

Why indeed? Why did he have to attend entertainments that weren't entertaining? Why did he have to endure small talk when conversation could be boiled down to a few pertinent points? Why couldn't women escort themselves to brunch and leave him alone?

And why was he wasting his time talking to this woman? Maybe because for the first time, Boone didn't feel like it was a waste.

"Miss Kentworth, why are you here?" He'd do as she preferred and get to the point.

"I'm here because I'm on the board of the Crystal Cave." She crossed her arms over her chest, and he remembered the strength those arms must possess to break through a rock wall.

"But why you? Why did your grandmother choose you for this position?"

"If you knew my cousins, you might see that she's being sensible."

Boone was getting nowhere. He straightened his pencil in case it had moved since he'd straightened it last. "Miss Kentworth, we agree that we should be practical, so I'm asking what it is about this job that appeals to you. In plain words, tell me what you're hoping to accomplish by joining this project."

She lowered her eyes. Her brown lashes danced above her freckled cheeks. She gripped her knees, and the muscles in her arms tightened. "I want to be free," she said.

Boone was intrigued. The freedom to work, to think, without constant interruptions seemed an unattainable goal, but not one he expected to hear from a lady. "How will working here make you free?"

She looked him over, sizing him up, if he judged correctly. Then, with a slight nod, she began. "There's this man. He got it in his head that we should be hitched. At first, I entertained the idea, but when I decided agin it, he made a nuisance of himself. My family won't let me leave the farm now. Unless I have this job, or something similar, I might never—"

Before she could go any further, the door to his office swung open.

"Is the rumor true?" Mr. Caine skidded to a stop when he saw Miss Kentworth. Wherever he'd come from, he'd left in a hurry, because he wore no suit coat or hat, and the Caines were never seen in public undone.

Boone straightened. He hadn't realized how far he was leaning toward Miss Kentworth until he saw Caine's expression. But she'd been saying something interesting. He was already bored with Caine's conversation, and it hadn't even started.

"I'm not selling the mine," Boone said. "Not now. There's more exploration to do."

Caine's eyebrows rose. "More exploration? I thought you'd explored to your heart's content."

"I told you I was going back down there one last time before I signed the papers. That's what I did, and I made a fascinating discovery." Boone turned to Miss Kentworth. She smiled like a conspirator, and he felt like he'd found some freedom as well.

Mr. Caine was not a fan of freedom. "Above the water line? Are you sure? Remember, your parents aren't coming to your rescue if this mine fails. You need to make alliances that will be profitable to your future. I can help you."

Caine was talking about Justina. It had always been about Justina, and Boone was weary of it. Like Miss Kentworth had said, why couldn't things be straightforward? Why couldn't he discuss the purchase of a mine without bringing Justina into it? Why seed rumors around town about the two of them?

"I've got to see how this plays out," Boone said. "If I change my mind, I promise you'll be the first to know. No one else will get a bid on the land until it's been presented to you."

There. That should solve it. But if he thought Mr. Caine was going to accept his decision without comment, he was wrong.

"You are within your rights," Mr. Caine said at last, "but other people have rights too, and feelings." His nose twitched as he looked Miss Kentworth over. "I'll pass your regards on to my daughter," he said to Boone. "You might consider calling on her soon. I'd hate for your judgment to be lacking in this matter as well."

Before Boone could protest, Mr. Caine left, closing the door behind him.

Boone picked up his pencil only to slam it down again. The impertinence of the man. As if he were entitled to Boone's land, Boone's mine, and Boone's own soul as a gift for his daughter. Boone got to his feet and paced the office. These families were insufferable. They acted like he'd transgressed in some way if he didn't pay their daughters the required number of compliments. Didn't he have the right to remain single? His mother was right to be concerned.

Boone stopped at his credenza and picked up a piece of galena from the Spook Light Mine, shaft 8. This was because of Miss Kentworth. Seeing her in his office had caused Mr. Caine to think she had some bearing on Boone's decision not to sell the mine. He probably thought she had used some feminine wiles on Boone, which was far from the truth. Miss Kentworth didn't possess any feminine wiles. Although, according to the story she'd told him, she'd managed to entrap at least one unsuitable man.

Turning the shiny cube in his hand, Boone said, "Tell me more about this man who's harassing you."

She hesitated, probably not wanting to talk to his back, but Boone wanted to listen, and watching her caused him to miss words sometimes.

"His name is Silas Marsh, and he's a snake. I thought he was nice at first, but then I found out about his character. Unsavory to the core. I never wanted to see him again, but he took to following me around town. Everywhere I went, he'd pop up, trying to sway me. I'm never free."

Boone turned. Her story was his story. Perhaps the ladies in question had fine character, but he felt hunted just the same. "And your family? What do they think?"

"They won't let me leave the farm, not without a chaperone. When I did come to town with my brother and cousin, Silas made such a nuisance of himself that they lit into him. Now the sheriff is watching them. If Silas does anything more, they might get in trouble with the law. So here I am, stuck between a rock and a . . ." She nodded at the block of ore he held. "Either stay at the farm or risk getting Amos and Hank into trouble." She brushed the air, like there was a gnat pestering her, although Boone knew good and well that his office was gnat-less. "I reckon that's why Granny put me in this position. It'll keep me busy, and Silas wouldn't dare come on your property to harass me."

Boone looked at the young woman sitting in the light from the window. Was it sympathy for her or sympathy for himself that moved him? Was he imagining qualities in her because of their shared experience?

"Believe it or not," he said cautiously, "I find myself in much the same circumstance, but I'm being hunted by a bevy of ladies. It's gotten to where hearing any voice with a pitch higher than a foghorn makes me break out in hives."

Her brows lowered. "Why aren't women more reasonable about men? Why do they think men want a bird-brained nuisance? And to act like that with a man of your situation?" She shook her head in disbelief. "Obviously, with all the business you have going on, you'd need someone willing to roll up her sleeves and help you, not someone causing you trouble."

"Exactly." So many thoughts churned in his head that Boone had trouble catching them. What was it Justina had said? The only way to keep the women at bay was to settle on one? Then the rest would give up hope? It sounded drastic, that was for sure, but it might be something that a renegade like Miss Kentworth would consider.

"I don't mean to stand here and jaw your ear off." She got to her feet. "Granny will be anxious. So, if you have any instructions for me . . ."

"Sit." Boone pointed at her chair. "Give me a moment. I might have a solution to our problems."

He wiped his hands against his suit coat as he tried desperately to think of reasons this was a bad idea. But Boone had learned long ago that once he decided upon a course, it was next to impossible to see any other option. Besides, his initial judgment was usually sound, and his impression of Miss Kentworth seemed consistent with what he'd heard of her family.

She was looking up at him, her eyes large and curious.

"How old are you?" he asked.

"Nineteen."

"Christian?"

"Absolutely."

"You've never been married before?"

"Like I said, I escaped that fate."

Was he missing something? Was there some reason he couldn't do this? He tried to think of what his parents would say, but his mother had been adamant about him staying out of the clutches of the conniving women of Joplin. She'd always said that she'd rather him not marry than have him yoked to a show pony who couldn't pull her share.

Miss Kentworth was no show pony, that was for certain.

Maisie knew that look. She'd seen it on Amos's face once. It was when the well cover was being replaced, and Finn had bet him he couldn't jump over the hole. Amos had known that if he didn't jump, he would regret it forever, but at the same time, he feared taking the leap.

Whatever Mr. Bragg was getting ready to say had him scared that he was going to fall down the well.

Bit by bit, he'd scooted in his seat until he was nearly knee to knee with her. The dreamy look that had taken over him in the meeting was gone, and instead there was intense concentration. The excitement of a new venture, much like he'd exhibited in the cave, was reflected in his face, along with uncertainty. She could feel her pulse ticking up a notch.

"I've never made a deal like this before," he said.

"It doesn't hurt to ask," Maisie replied.

He looked at her hands, then leaned back in his chair and turned so that his legs were under his desk. Picking up the drafting pencil, he opened a drawer in his desk, pulled out a thick piece of stationery, and took off writing.

"What if I came up with a way to get you off the farm and free us both from being hounded by the opposite sex?"

"What ya got?" Maisie stretched tall in her seat but couldn't make out what he was writing. She felt important having the attention of such a fine man all to herself. Who would've thought she'd go straight from the cow pasture to reading over contracts with Mr. Bragg?

"I'll leave the starting date blank for now. The end date . . . well, there wouldn't be an end date. This contract would be permanent. Financial considerations . . . I suppose I could fix an allowance on you, but I'd expect you to share in the successes and, should they occur, the downturns of the venture, so it would be a risk on your part." His pencil paused. "What's your first name?"

"Maisie. I told you in the cave."

"Maisie Kentworth. I'm Boone, by the way. Boone Bragg, in case you forgot."

"This better not be an offer to buy me out," Maisie said. "If it weren't for me, that man would be getting your mine, and you wouldn't know about the cave until it was too late. Besides, no amount of money is going to solve my problems."

"But a protector might." He raised his eyes to hers. "Before I present this, let's think through the ramifications, shall we?" Scooting another piece of paper before her, he wrote *Pros* and *Cons* at the top, forming two columns. "We'll start with the pros," he said. "For you, one benefit will be that you can stay in town or visit your farm whenever you like. Also, you will be free from the harassment of this Mr. Marsh. If he still pesters you, it'll be my responsibility to address it." His pencil made straight strokes as he made notes. "As for me, I will forever be free from entitled girls and insulted fathers, and I will be free to conduct my business without wondering if there are ulterior motives behind offers." He drew his finger over his brow as he considered. "If I need a woman's input into my affairs, I'll have you, right?"

So far, everything Maisie was hearing sounded fantastic. She could hardly believe her luck. "Yes, you'll have me." That was why she was on the board, wasn't it?

"Now, before we get too carried away, we need to consider the disadvantages to this contract. Is there anything you'd like to address?" he asked.

Maisie cast about. A disadvantage to being able to leave the farm and work with Mr. Bragg? Not only was this the best thing that had happened to her, it was the only way out of her situation. She tapped her foot against the floor. Negotiations being what they were, she needed to come up with some way that she was inconvenienced. "I'd prefer not to spend all of my time in the boardroom," she said. "All day in there would be dull."

His eyes were so brown. "You're not a show pony, are you?"

Maisie snorted. "Cricket's wings. I'm worth my oats, but some work is more to my liking than others."

"I'll keep that in mind." He wrote *Too Much Boardroom* on the list and then added *Gossip*. "One con is going to be what people say. Will it bother you when they comment on our unusual partnership?"

Would it? Maisie agonized over the shame she'd brought her family because of her relationship with Silas. The Bible said that a good name was to be protected. There were things worse than being stuck at home.

"I won't disgrace my family," Maisie said. "If people got nothing better to do than ruminate over my business, then I don't guess I can stop them, but I won't do anything that deserves censure. Please don't expect me to."

Mr. Bragg moved to the pro column and wrote *Woman of Integrity*. "Back to the cons," he said. "Of course, neither of us would be able to pursue a romantic attachment. I can assure you that I've been given the opportunity to do so and have no interest in proceeding under the current atmosphere of the Joplin social scene. You might disagree."

What was he talking about? Romantic attachments? Hadn't Maisie just confessed that she'd been foolish in love? Was he worried that she'd misbehave while representing his company? She shook her head. "I don't have a beau anymore. There's no one—"

"Good. Then, I think this is the answer." He smiled as he removed the list and returned to the contract that he'd sketched earlier. "I'm used to business associates sitting on the other side of the desk, but this is a different kind of business."

Maisie shot him a sharp look, then turned the contract so she could read it. Certain letters jumped out at her.

Marriage.

She felt the impact of the word against her ribs. All that talk about gossip and romance—how had she missed his meaning?

Before she read any further, Maisie crushed the paper in her fist, wadding it into a ball. "What is this?" She threw it at Mr. Bragg, hitting him squarely between the eyes. "I told you I was hiding from a man, and what do you do? You ask me to marry you! What's wrong with you?"

"The best way to rid ourselves of unwanted attention from the opposite sex would be matrimony," he said.

"I came here for a job, not for a romantic entanglement." She'd seen Mr. Bragg's boardroom as a place of safety. She slapped her palm against her forehead. "Pa was right. I can't leave the property without men making donkeys of themselves. Who would've thought I'd shake out to be irresistible?"

His eyes flashed with triumph. "I don't find you irresistible. In fact, I'm perfectly capable of resisting."

"You don't find me attractive?" When it came to wooing, this man took a different tack.

"How about you?" He crossed his arms over his chest and jutted his chin up a smidge. "Do you think I'm attractive? Are you eager to join the chorus of ladies trying to lead me to the altar?"

"Evidently not! I'm running away like a bee-stung mare."

"And that's why this might work."

"You're out of your ever-loving mind, and I'm leaving." She turned toward the door, then paused. "But I'll be back for the next board meeting. You ain't getting rid of me that easily."

And with that, Maisie swung open the door and stomped away.

CHAPTER 8

Granny's black buggy was a thing of beauty. She'd bought it for herself a few years back to celebrate the ten thousandth head of cattle that she'd shipped up the railroad to the packinghouses. She only drove it for special occasions, so their trip to the Braggs' office had ranked high in her eyes.

Now, driving home, she wanted a full accounting of the meeting, but Maisie, who was hunched over in her seat, didn't feel up to snuff.

"If you don't tell me something," Granny Laura warned, "I'm liable to go back to that house and call young Mr. Bragg to account. Obviously, he trespassed against you."

Maisie kicked her foot against the dashboard. "What's wrong with men? Why can't a woman just go about her business without having to constantly mind them?"

Granny halted her horse. "We're going back."

"No." Maisie grabbed Granny's arm. "I can't go back. I'm so confused. How can a man who doesn't know you from siccum ask you to marry him?"

Even her unflappable Granny was flapped. "Mr. Bragg's son asked you to marry him? Was he in earnest?"

"As far as I could tell, but he's a hard fellow to read. I'm not quite sure what to make of him."

Granny grunted. "I've heard that about him. The family is well-respected, but the rumor is that he's difficult to know. Sharp, but singular."

"I can vouch for that." What to make of a man who told you that he didn't find you beautiful and he didn't want to get married, but then he proposed? All just minutes after being reminded of your first name?

Granny rattled the reins, and the horse started up. Her finely lined face was troubled. "What primed this offer? I can't imagine it was out of the blue."

Maisie watched a dragonfly land on her sleeve. God himself must have arranged for Granny to be her companion today. There was no one she'd rather chew this over with. "Mr. Bragg asked me why I wanted this job. I told him about the trouble we were having—how I was being hounded and couldn't get away from Silas. He said he had the same problem with some ladies he knows. Next thing I know, he was writing out a marriage contract and telling me how it would take care of everything."

"He presented it as a business deal?" Granny asked. "Nothing improper?"

"It was extremely proper." Maisie had always thought that a proposal should include a touch of indecorum.

"You never know what a day will bring." Granny chewed over her next words before presenting them. "From all accounts, he's a fine Christian man. That doesn't mean you need to marry up with him, but I don't think his offer was made with any harm intended. It was just a practical solution, in his eyes."

"You aren't waving his banner, are you, Granny? You don't even know him."

"If I thought he was of the same sort as that Marsh character, I couldn't let you go back and work with him. As it is, I think your reputation is safe from any rumors, especially as everyone knows he's been adamantly avoiding matrimony. No one would suspect—" She paused. "After your grandpappy died, I had my share of practical proposals. Had my share of the typical nonsense too, but there were men who presented themselves along with a list of benefits that would come from hitching up with them. I much preferred those who were honest to those who tried to cloud my thinking with romance just to get my ranch."

"But you rejected them all," Maisie said.

"The incentive was never enough. I'd already been married to one stalwart man. That was all I needed."

But Maisie would never meet anyone stalwart or otherwise unless God dropped him from the clouds onto her farm. And how would she know if He did? Maisie's judgment had failed her with Silas. She'd been fooled by a charming grin, persuasive words, and ardent kisses. If Calista hadn't heard the girl at the Children's Home name Silas as the father of her child, Maisie might have been married to him by now. As painful as it was, she thanked God every day that she'd been spared.

Mr. Bragg wasn't made of the same cloth. She could observe him with a clear mind and see that he wasn't perfect. Her emotions weren't swayed by flowery words or gazes filled with longing. By all accounts, Mr. Bragg was avoiding women as much as Silas was pursuing them. Even Granny vouched for him. And then there was the thought of living in that mansion in town and working with him on the Crystal Cave. When she stopped and thought about it, it was no wonder there were ladies of his set chasing him.

And she had thrown his contract in his face.

Granny stopped to let Maisie out at her house. Maisie kissed her grandmother's sun-bronzed cheek. Granny's practical assessment had settled her stormy thoughts. Maybe there was something admirable about a bare-bones proposal, but she doubted her grandmother had ever had such an awkward offer. Maisie slogged to the barnyard gate to check on the kittens hiding in the hayloft.

She'd be careful of her clothes. She'd already ruined one dress this week. Ma would be after her if she destroyed another.

From her view in the barnyard, Maisie could see the long drive that circled around to the back of their white farmhouse. A buggy was parked there. Someone had come to visit. It wasn't the sheriff. He would've ridden his horse. Who, then?

"Psst . . ."

Maisie spun around to see her cousin Calista standing in the darkened doorway of the barn. "How was your day with Mr. Bragg?" she whispered.

Maisie joined her in the cool shade of the barn. The musty smells of hay, horses, and leather unknotted the kinks that had been in her stomach since his awkward proposal. "You wouldn't believe it if I told you," she said. "Really. I don't believe the half of it myself."

Calista's sympathetic grin lightened some of Maisie's burden. "Sounds intriguing." And if there was anything Calista loved, it was intrigue. "You must tell me everything when we have time. Right now, Matthew is keeping the adults busy so I can talk to you alone."

Another twist of worry. If Calista had to bring her husband into the fray, then it was serious. "What is it?" Maisie planted her feet wide and braced herself for more ill tidings.

"Silas Marsh came looking for Matthew at the Lighthouse Center today. Silas told him you were in love with him and he wasn't going to let your family keep you apart. He thinks you're being mistreated. Matthew set him straight in no uncertain terms. He told him that you had made up your own mind. Silas should get his heart right with the Lord and leave the ladies alone."

Maisie's hands balled into fists. "How did Silas take that?"

Calista shoved her hand into her pocket, making Maisie wonder if she still carried that steel baton even though her detective days were over. "He took it like you'd expect. Denied that Matthew was telling the truth and promised to apply directly to you. He said he'd heard that you'd been spotted in Murphysburg and he was going to set up a watch there. That he knew you'd find a way to come to him, and the fact that you were in town meant you were looking for a rendezvous."

"I'll give him a rendezvous," Maisie growled. "I'll make his teeth rendezvous with the back of his throat."

But she couldn't. Not really. Silas was a miner and as good a fighter as she was. She'd probably need her brother to help her finish the job.

"You can't let my parents know." Maisie rolled an old corncob beneath her shoe. "If they get a whiff of this, they'll never let me go back to town, even to Boone's office."

"Boone?" Calista's eyes widened. "I didn't realize the two of you were so familiar."

"It was an eventful day."

"I'm not telling your parents—that's why I came out here—but I am worried for Amos's sake. It's not like Hank and Amos to back down once they've been challenged. If they catch wind of Silas's plans, they'll waylay him for sure."

Calista was right. It wasn't just Maisie's reputation at stake, but her brother's freedom. He would go to jail to avenge any dishonor against her. What was she willing to do to save him?

Maisie looked out the barn door at the farm spread before her. She could run away from home and disappear, but likely Amos and Hank would blame Silas, and they would still end up behind bars. Besides, imagine the damage to her family's reputation if their daughter took out like a thief in the night. She could give up any interest in the cave, not go back to town, and try to be content with her strawberry patch and the farm chores. That might keep trouble at bay, but at what price?

There was only one person who'd offered her a way out. One person who could give her a future while keeping her kin out of trouble.

"I have a message for you to deliver," she said to Calista.

Maisie would ask Boone for more information, plumb out his expectations, and ponder her options, but sometimes you had to stop dithering and get on with life.

He'd nearly missed her call.

When Boone heard the bell at the front desk of Bragg Mining, he'd called out to inform Mrs. Stein that he wasn't available for meetings. He needed to look over his figures and decide on the next steps. Tomorrow he would go to the bank and open a new account for the venture to keep the finances separate. By midmorning, Gilbert would have the crews down there, and they could start by moving the Kentworths' fence before they began digging. Then, once the cattle had been secured . . .

Boone heard a man's voice saying farewell. He moved to the window to watch as his visitor departed. The man looked familiar. Boone couldn't find a name for him, but he remembered thinking well of him. There was a lady with him, which was unusual for a business meeting. She stepped toward the door again, as if she were going to make another attempt to come inside, but her companion caught her by the arm. Whatever he told her, it was not to her liking. Normally Boone would let them continue on their way and check with the secretary as to the purpose of their visit, but some instinct told him that their mission was important.

He hopped to his feet and jogged out of his office, past Mrs. Stein, and through the front door. Hearing his approach, the couple turned. The man's eyes widened in pleasant surprise. Boone recognized him as the manager of the miner's center at the Fox-Berry Mine, but before he could greet him, the lady spoke.

"Glad you came out," she said. "I was looking for an open window."

Something about her mannerisms was familiar. She was dressed as fine as any lady about town, but as far as he knew, they hadn't considered climbing through his windows yet.

The man extended his hand. "I'm Matthew Cook. I'm the minister at the Lighthouse Center for Miners."

Boone shook it. "We make regular donations to your work. If you're looking for more, I'd have you call on my accountant."

"No, it's family business today. My wife has a cousin—she has a lot of cousins, actually—and we're here on her behalf."

Boone felt his spirits lift. Mrs. Cook bore a resemblance to Maisie in the relaxed way she held her arms and in her direct gaze. There was also that widow's peak in her hairline, although the hair he was looking at now was dark instead of the almost-red he'd seen this morning.

Her next words verified his suspicions. "According to Maisie, you are a particular friend of hers?"

"Is that what she said?" Boone asked. "Then I'm relieved, because I wasn't sure she'd claim me after our parting."

Unlike her husband's open smile, Mrs. Cook's stare could bore through galena without a pickax. "Perhaps this isn't a good idea." She took a step away. "Let me talk to her and make sure this is what she wants."

"It's too late," Matthew said. "We already told her we'd send him. Maisie has no problem speaking her mind."

"But sometimes she doesn't know her own mind. That's what's worrying me," Mrs. Cook answered.

"If Miss Kentworth needs me, it must be important." After his awkward proposal, Boone thought he'd be the last person she'd apply to for help.

"She asked if you would meet her at the Secret Tree in the southeast pasture," Matthew said. "Going from the Kennedys' farm, you turn in . . ."

Boone formed a mental map of the meeting place, noticing that it was between his mine and the Kentworth homes.

"It's the only oak out in that field. Stands alone. You can't miss it." Matthew looked at his wife, then spoke even though Boone could tell she wasn't pleased with his words. "And she said to bring the contract. I guess it has something to do with the mine? That's all she said."

The contract? Boone ran his hand through his hair. Was she going to go through with it? His heart pounded. Was he sure that he wanted to? Ever since her refusal earlier that morning, he'd tried to convince himself that he was fortunate to have gotten out of the offer. He'd told himself that his hasty decision could've ruined his life. But despite all his sensible self-lectures, he couldn't shake the feeling that his instincts had been true. There were more pros than cons on his list.

"I'll head out there right away."

"If you have a minute," Mrs. Cook said, "I'd like to look that contract over. What exactly does it entail?"

But Boone didn't let people poke around in business matters that didn't involve them. "You may ask your cousin about it. If she's agreeable, I'm sure she'll tell you everything. Now, if you'll excuse me."

Boone closed the door on her protests and went to his office to pull the contract out of the trash. He smoothed it flat, but it was still terribly wrinkled. For a moment he considered copying it anew, but time was of the essence. He couldn't leave Miss Kentworth standing beneath some tree in a field; not when she'd dispatched her family to him with such urgency. He folded the contract and slid it into his breast pocket. Getting this settled would free his mind up for more important issues concerning the Crystal Cave. First matrimony, then water pumps. A wedding couldn't be allowed to completely derail his plans.

Riding past the entrance on the Kennedys' land to the next pasture, Boone saw the tree in question. Tying his horse to the fence, he bent, pushed the barbed wires apart, and ducked between them, knocking his hat off and snagging his pant leg in the process. No matter. Mrs. Karol took care of such niceties.

He picked up his hat and settled it back on his head. Only then did he see Miss Kentworth striding from the woods that lined the pasture.

He took a moment to observe her. She was still dressed in the serviceable gown she'd worn to his office that morning. She covered the ground with a healthy stride, unconcerned with appearance or grace but still managing to lay claim to both. To his surprise, she looked no less angry than she had at his first offer. The thought struck him that perhaps she'd come to berate him further.

Instead of coming straight to him, she headed toward the tree and waited for him there. Boone made his way to her, watching for cow pies along the way. The tree shaded his face, making it easier to see her in the shadows. Upon further inspection, it wasn't anger firming her chin, but determination. Good. He'd rather avoid messy emotions.

"I came as soon as I could," he said. "Immediately. I left your cousins standing by their buggy as I rode away."

"Put your hand on the tree," Miss Kentworth said.

"What?" Boone looked over his shoulder to see if he was being baited for the amusement of some unseen audience.

"This is the Secret Tree. If you tell a lie while touching it—even a sin of omission—it will pull up roots and come to you at night. Its prickly fingers will reach into your window and snatch you out of bed, then crush you like a bug and feed your body to the birds that live in its branches." She shrugged. "At least that's what my brother Finn always told us."

Boone turned his head to look at her askance. "You can't expect me to believe this tale."

"You might not believe it, but I had to warn you just the same. I would hate to have your blood on my hands."

"I don't lie," Boone said. "It's not in my nature."

"That's what a liar would say. Put your hand on the tree."

She was agitated, and she wasn't hiding it. Her hair had

pulled out of her braid and was sticking out in all directions like a daisy's petals. He remembered her refined cousin's threat to climb through his window and thought that no matter how you dressed this family up, there was still a wild streak running in their veins.

He leaned his hand against the trunk of the tree. "Am I doing it right?"

"Do you have any children—acknowledged or unacknowledged?"

He dropped his hand. "No! Why would you ask that?"

Her eyes flashed. "Put your hand on the tree and answer again."

This was the most hostile and personal contract discussion he'd ever been a party to. "I have no children."

"Could it be possible that you have some that you are unaware of?"

Boone couldn't help his incredulous smile as the gist of her question became clear. "Are you asking me if I've ever—"

"Just answer the question. Hand on the tree, thank you!" Her cheeks were flushed, but she persevered. "Is it possible—"

"It is not." He'd thought that having a straightforward woman like Maisie Kentworth around would be less difficult. He was mistaken.

"Would you be pressuring your wife for . . . favors?" She crossed her arms as a barrier between them.

Boone paused. "That would be unconscionable for a contract that was purely business. On the other hand, given the unique nature of our agreement . . ."

"I'm a stranger," she sputtered. "How could you even think—"

"I have no interest in seducing a stranger."

"And when we're no longer strangers?"

Boone leaned against the tree. This required some thought. "I understand your outrage, Miss Kentworth. Discussing the possibility of romance seems indecent at this time, but you have to project what our feelings might be in the future. Marriage is forever.

Do you really want to forgo the possibility of anything personal between us?"

She dropped her gaze. "I thought I'd found a man I could trust once before. Call me gun-shy."

Boone had to admit that he found her candor surprising. He hadn't thought she'd be so blunt. Perhaps it was on account of her former beau. Under further consideration, it made sense. She'd been harassed before. "I'm a man of principle. I have no intention of misusing you."

Her eyes followed the tree trunk up its height. "Let's walk."

"No. It's my turn. Put your palm on the tree, please." Funny how she balked when he expected her to follow suit. "What happened in the last hour that caused you to send your cousin after me?"

Her index finger traced the pattern of the bark. She didn't bother hiding her annoyance, but she answered as requested. "They heard that Silas was going to follow me to your house and press his suit again. If he did and Amos and Hank got word of it, there'd be trouble, and my kin would wind up in jail. I started thinking about what you said, and I saw the sense in it. The only way that Amos will feel he doesn't have to protect my honor is if I have a husband to do it."

"Do you expect me to go to jail for you?"

"If Silas comes around, I can protect myself. I'm not afraid of him. The important thing is that Amos won't feel that it's his duty to shush him." Then, looking at her hand on the tree trunk, she added, "Besides, if Granny learns of Silas's plans, she won't want me to go to town, even with her riding shotgun. Before too long, I'll be stuck at home and won't be able to work with you."

"You want to work with me?"

Her eyes softened, and she chuckled. "That's why we're doing this, isn't it? Of course I want to work with you."

He looked at the tree. Yes, her hand was still on it. She meant it.

Boone reached into his pocket and retrieved the contract. It was good, thick paper and was still readable despite her rough treatment. He held the folded page out to her. "This gives you equal ownership of the Crystal Cave. We'll be partners on that, and you'll have a say in the decisions made on that venture."

"I thought a wife shared everything of her husband's," Miss Kentworth said. "When my grandpa died, Granny got the ranch."

"You might want to share an opinion on the running of the cavern before I'm dead, right?"

She nodded. "Good idea."

Boone prided himself on being forward-thinking. He was good at spotting potential problems and safeguarding against them.

"What's this about social engagements?" She pointed to the contract. "What am I agreeing to?"

"You agree to appear with me at three social events per financial quarter. I don't relish these appearances, but many times business relationships are strengthened at them."

"What kind of social events? Like barn raisings and hoedowns?"

Boone's mouth twitched. Miss Kentworth was going to hit the Joplin social scene like a wildcat in a henhouse. "There'll be music and dancing, so it'll be similar."

She shrugged. "I enjoy a musical diversion as much as the next person. I can clog up a storm when called for."

"I can't wait."

"And what about your rights as a husband?" Maisie asked. "There's nothing on here about that."

Was he a hypocrite? He claimed he wanted nothing to do with courting and romance, yet he couldn't quite agree to never enjoy the charms of his wife.

"Children," he said. "Someday we'd want children, wouldn't we?"

"The Children's Home had a baby raffle earlier this year." Her eyebrow rose as her mouth twisted into a smug smile.

Boone pulled out his pen. "We will table the discussion on children until after the cave is a success. I'll write that in. *No marital benefits until the cave is successfully opened.*"

"No *discussion* on marital benefits until the cave is successfully opened," Maisie amended.

After a pause, he scratched in the words, then handed the contract to her.

"If I sign this, we aren't hitched yet, right?" she asked. "We still have to stand before a preacher."

"I want to do everything right. I'll talk to your father, then—"

"No." Miss Kentworth flattened the contract against her chest. "You can't do that. He'll say no, sure as shooting."

Boone's face tightened. He'd been so used to running from matrimony that he hadn't considered there'd be people who *weren't* trying to marry their daughters to him.

"If your parents don't approve, then what are we going to do?"

"I'm a woman grown. It'll be rough going at first, but when they think it over, they'll come around. Besides, I already floated the idea past Granny."

"What did she say?"

"She didn't commit for or agin. Said it was an interesting proposal, though."

"Your cousin's husband, Pastor Cook—will he marry us?"

She shook her head. "I don't imagine so, and once we ask, he'd be obliged to tell my folks. Better keep it to strangers."

Boone looked out over the field. Getting this settled was already taking more time than he'd allotted for the day. What would be the most expedient?

"I hate the thought of not saying our vows of holy matrimony in a church, but under the circumstances, I can bring a preacher here. I have a connection at the courthouse who will be able to get the license ironed out." He felt the relief of watching a plan come together. "He can conveniently forget to run the notice in the paper. If I can get it by tomorrow . . ."

"I'd be your wife that soon? Are we crazy . . . Boone?" Miss

Kentworth caught and held his gaze. She was putting her trust in him.

"What other people think doesn't matter. We can make this work."

He wouldn't let her down.

CHAPTER 9

"I'm going to pull up those potatoes this morning," Maisie told her pa. She lifted a bushel basket out of the stack that rested in the hay. According to the plans she and Mr. Bragg had made, she would be wed by noon. Her family had no idea.

"Sounds good, honey." Pa held the new ax handle against the sander as he pedaled the machine. "We know you'd rather be in town like Calista and Olive, but you've been a good hand out here. You've shown a lot of maturity by not bucking against our rules. Maybe in another few months, if that Marsh man has moved on, you could get some freedom back."

Another few months? Perhaps she was making a mistake. Maisie loved her farm. She enjoyed the work, the space, the family. She could be happy here for another few months.

But what would happen then? Eventually she'd run into another man who'd sweet-talk her. He'd tell her how beautiful she was, how she was the only gal for him . . . and like a fool, she'd trust him. Then, sooner or later, she would learn that he wasn't who he said he was. Maybe he'd leave her and break her heart, or maybe he'd stalk her and she'd never be free from him.

Either way, Boone represented safety to her. He didn't care

about her looks—he'd barely looked at her so far. She didn't love him, so she couldn't get her heart broken. And everyone who knew him knew his reputation when it came to women—above reproach.

Without his protection, either her family would forbid her to keep working on the cave, or Silas would make such a nuisance of himself that her kin would get in trouble defending her honor. It was the only logical thing to do.

Yet she knew her family wouldn't understand.

Going to her pa with the bushel basket on her hip and a rake in her hand, she bent and pressed a kiss to the top of his straw hat. "Thanks for watching out for me. I detest being a bother. As soon as I can get this mess settled, I will."

"Don't you worry," he said. "We're here to hold the reins until you get control. That's what family is for."

Pa was going to be furious when he found out what she'd done.

Because she didn't want to tell a fib, Maisie went to dig the potatoes. Thudding the rake into the soft, worked soil, she caught a stolon and pulled the potatoes to the surface, shaking the excess dirt off them. Here it was, her wedding day, and she was digging potatoes. She hiked her skirt up to her knees and squatted, yanking the potatoes off the stolons and placing them inside the basket. She might as well be doing something useful. There was no reason to get all pretty for the ceremony. She stifled a chuckle at the thought of Boone's face if she showed up all dolled up and painted. He'd turn tail and run. That was what she liked about him. She could look as rough as a cob, and he paid no mind. It was kind of nice.

The bushel was soon filled. Maisie rested the rake against the garden fence and checked the sun. It was about time. Would she get a chance to take the potatoes home after the ceremony? She didn't know what Boone had in mind, so she couldn't be sure. If not, her family would eventually find the potatoes when they came looking for her.

Dusting her hands off on her skirt, Maisie trotted toward the edge of the ranch and the Secret Tree. She would've liked for the ceremony to be at a church or even in Boone's fancy office. The tree was in the middle of a field full of cow pies, but compromises had to be made. This one wouldn't be the last.

When she came around the hill, she saw a wagon, Boone's buggy, and a handful of people milling about the tree. While Boone sat in his buggy, poring over a ledger book, a middle-aged man approached her. He brushed his straight blond hair out of his eyes as he neared.

"You must be Miss Kentworth. I hope it's okay that we opened the gate to get the buggies in. I'm Fegus, Mr. Bragg's liveryman, and that there is the pastor." He glanced over his shoulder, as if encouraging Boone to join him. "By the way, you look lovely this morning, Miss Kentworth."

"Just another day," she said. "Not anything that warrants special consideration."

She hadn't meant to shock him, but he shook his head. "Nonsense. It's your wedding day. You look beautiful."

Maisie snorted. "Beautiful? I hardly think so."

"Boone is a smart man," Fegus said. "I'm glad to see he's not marrying any of those silly girls from town. It'd be the ruin of him."

The ruin of Boone? She doubted he'd even notice who he was married to once they got the deal done. Maisie smiled her thanks as another man approached.

The pastor removed his hat and fanned his face. "This heat is insufferable. Can we do this beneath the tree?"

"That was the idea." She looked from one man to the other. She didn't know Boone well, but he was an important part of the ceremony. Why wasn't he coming?

Maisie followed the pastor into the shade of the Secret Tree. Surely Boone would join them directly. What was taking him so long? Second thoughts? Or was he thinking anything at all? Maisie had seen this once before with him. He might need a reminder.

Leaving the curious men behind, she went to Boone's buggy and pulled herself up to his side. Boone's mouth was moving as he recited numbers, but his eyes looked out across the field—not seeing anything, was her guess.

"Boone?" She eased her hand atop his arm.

He raised a finger, a polite request for silence, as he continued his mental recitation. She put her hands in her lap and waited until he reached the end of his calculations. He jotted down a number, then closed his ledger.

"Thank you for allowing me to finish." He smiled sheepishly. "It took me ten minutes to get that figure worked out. I would've hated to have to start all over." Pulling his confidence on like an overcoat, he stretched his legs before him and cleared his throat. "So, we have a job to do. Next we need to . . . we need . . ." Then, taking a quick breath, he asked, "Is everyone here?"

Maisie raised an eyebrow. "The preacher is over yonder."

Boone snapped his ledger closed. "Then why wait?" He helped Maisie down.

The pastor had yet to introduce himself, and Maisie wasn't sure what set of manners applied to events like this, so she followed Boone's lead. He stepped to a spot near the tree trunk, then waited for everyone to arrange themselves around him. Maisie balanced on a root opposite of him, thinking that this would be where the bride stood if they were in a church.

"We don't need a sermon," Boone said. "There's no audience to impress. Just give us the vows to repeat, and then we'll sign the paper."

When Maisie had dreamed about her wedding, she'd imagined a groom who looked at her with longing, love that wouldn't be denied, and a day filled with joy and hope. She'd been singed by love already, and so far her wedding day had been filled with barn chores and potatoes.

"Do you, Boone Bragg, take this woman . . ." The preacher finally looked her in the eyes.

"Maisie Kentworth," she said.

"Maisie Kentworth," he repeated, "to be your . . ."

If Maisie thought the preacher was disregarding her, she couldn't say the same about Boone. His soulful eyes were alive with interest, watching her carefully. When his line came, he held her gaze. Maisie felt all fluttery, and he wasn't even sweet-talking her.

Then, once he had her attention, he went and deliberately put his hand on the trunk of the tree.

"I do," he said.

Despite the chill on her spine, the preacher started saying words toward her, but Maisie couldn't attend. What had Boone meant by that?

"I'm sorry, Preacher, but I'm gonna have to pull the reins on this." She pointed at Boone's hand still on the tree. "What'd you go and do that for?"

His shoulders lifted. "I'm showing you that I mean what I say."

"No, no, no." She grabbed his wrist. Her intent was to pull his hand away, but Boone was being stubborn. "This is the Secret Tree. Any secret can't be shared, or all that bad stuff will happen."

"You said we had to tell the truth." He wasn't budging, no matter how hard she pulled.

"Of course you have to tell the truth, but it's called the Secret Tree, and if you say something with your hand on it, then I can't repeat it to anyone."

The preacher flipped over his book. "This isn't part of the ceremony."

Boone's eyes widened. "You're not supposed to repeat these vows to anyone else. Only me. You're marrying me today, right? Why would you say them again?"

They weren't even finished tying the knot, and he was already being unreasonable. "I'm not going to give anyone else an oath, but these vows can't be secret. If no one knows we're married, what's the point?"

"I was thinking the same," said the preacher.

"Of course we're going to tell people that we're married. Obviously I meant for this to be about honesty," Boone said.

Fegus scratched his head. "You got a lot of trees around here, miss. Why couldn't you enlist some different ones to clear the confusion?"

Digging up potatoes looked like a better activity for her day about now.

"I have a proposal." How quickly Boone forgot the trouble his last proposal was costing them. "Today this will be the Promise Tree. Whatever promises you make with your hand on it are binding forever and forever. Also, they are the truth, but not necessarily secret."

A Promise Tree? Maisie swished her mouth to the side. Finn always changed things to suit his purposes. Why couldn't she do it as well? And when she thought about it, the fact that Boone wanted to show her his intentions was kinda sweet. She released his arm, stepped back to her place, and put her hand on the tree.

"Then it's my turn. Stop your dallying, and let's get this done."

CHAPTER 10

"Ma! Maisie is rolling up in someone's wagon . . . and there's a strange man with her."

Fegus drew in a deep breath at Amos's announcement, which was yelled as he darted inside the house. "That's the brother who whups everyone who harasses his sister?" Fegus craned his neck until it popped. "I should've known Mr. Bragg had his reasons for not bringing you himself."

But the reason Boone had given was that he had a lot of work to do on the mine. Maisie believed him. If he was afraid of her family, he wouldn't have done what he did.

"Pull around back," Maisie said. "That'll make loading my things easier."

The kitchen curtains parted as they drove by, framing her mother's shocked face. She eyeballed Maisie and the wagon even as she waved a hand behind her, trying to silence Amos's chatter. Fegus stopped the horses and pulled the brake, and they both climbed out, Maisie hauling the bushel basket of potatoes down with her.

"Those will be the last potatoes you haul," Fegus said with a laugh. "Your life will be different from here on out."

Feeling defensive, Maisie grunted. "My life isn't bad. It's not potatoes I'm running from."

But her words died as her ma and Amos ran out to the porch.

"Maisie Kentworth, what is going on here?" Her words were directed at Maisie, but she had Fegus pinned in her fiery gaze.

"I got hitched, Ma. I'm a married woman now, and that means Amos and Hank don't have to trouble themselves over protecting my honor. I have a husband to do that for me."

All eyes fixed on Fegus.

"Not me, ma'am. I'm just the freighter." He raised his hands and took a step behind Maisie.

Ma's jaw jutted forward, and her nose flared. She yanked Maisie's hand off thc potato bushel. Maisie had to slam the basket against her hip to keep it from dropping while her Ma bent to study the ring on her left hand.

"Of all the protracted nonsense I've ever heard." She dropped Maisie's hand. "You've gone and tied yourself to a liar."

"He's not a liar," Maisie said.

"If he told you this was a wedding ring, he is. Ain't nobody got a ring that big in these parts, much less Silas Marsh."

When Boone slid the ring on her finger, Maisie hadn't looked at it. Now that she did, her stomach did a little flop.

"It's probably a crystal," she said. "From the mine."

"That's no crystal," Fegus announced. "Mr. Bragg would give you nothing short of a diamond."

"Bragg?" Amos slapped himself on top of the head. "You went and married Mr. Bragg instead of Silas? Woo-ee. My sister done gone and caught herself a rich man."

"We're partners on the Crystal Cave," Maisie said. "Maybe I'm as rich as he is."

Fegus coughed to hide his laugh while Amos just outright snorted.

"There ain't no way, sis, but if thinking so eases your mind . . ."

"I came to get my things," Maisie said. "I'll come back and

visit, but I won't be underfoot anymore. You can be proud of me from now on."

"We are proud of you, Maisie. You shouldn't have . . . What about your pa?" Ma asked. "Does he know? Did Mr. Bragg speak to him before proposing?"

"There wasn't time. I feel poorly about it, but there wasn't time."

"If it's all the same to you, I'd like to get back to town. I need to have the wagon back to the work site," Fegus said.

There was no way Maisie was going to get left behind. Not now. "I'll just be a minute," she said. "Ma, can I borrow your trunk? I'll send it back tomorrow."

"Where is this Mr. Bragg? If you'uns just got married, I'd think he'd want to meet us." Amos kept up with Maisie as she ran up the stairs. Once out of earshot of their mother, he grabbed Maisie by the arm. "What makes you think he's any better than that Marsh character?"

"Because he doesn't . . ." Maisie clamped her mouth shut. She was going to say *because he doesn't love me* but knew that would only sprout more questions. "Because he's an honorable man. I had him swear on the tree, so I know it's true." She walked into her room and opened the low door that led to the attic space. Gripping the handle of the trunk, she heaved backward and pulled it into the room.

"I guarantee you Silas Marsh would've put his hand on the Secret Tree and lied to high heaven without a qualm."

Maisie reached into the top of her chest of drawers and took out an armful of clothing. "Mr. Bragg ain't no Silas Marsh. Once you meet him, you'll know that right off. Besides, we're partners on the cave, and Granny wasn't looking forward to escorting me to town and back for every meeting. This will simplify things."

She could feel Amos's hard stare as she took the last of her hanging clothes out of the wardrobe. That was all she had besides the laundry on the line.

"Maisie, you got to tell me straight. You didn't do this just to keep me out of trouble, did you?" Amos rubbed that long nose of his and tried to hide the worry in his eyes. "If I thought you married yourself to a stranger just so I didn't tangle with Silas . . . well, I wouldn't let it stand. I'd rather go to jail than have you trapped in a lifelong prison of a marriage."

Amos had guessed right, but she could never admit it.

"Mr. Bragg and I hit it off," she said. "It was love at first sight. I just knew I wouldn't be happy until I'd snagged him good." Then, to answer Amos's roll of the eyes, she added, "And he's rich. No more digging potatoes for me."

"Pa is going to . . ." Amos frowned. "I don't rightly know what Pa is going to do, and that's a worrisome thought."

"And all the more reason I need to get to town." She slammed the lid of the trunk closed and lifted one end of it. "I don't suppose I'll need my bed linens and my towel. Surely he'll have an extra set I can use."

Amos lifted the other end of the trunk. "Extra set? You're a married woman, Maisie. Don't you figure Mr. Bragg will be happy to share his bed linens with you?"

When Maisie colored at her error, Amos swore under his breath.

"You're flat out lying to me, Maisie Kentworth. You no more care about Bragg than you care about the well-digger. You did this for me. You tried to save me when I was trying to save you. You've made a horrible mistake."

Maybe it was a mistake, but it was too late to change now.

If Maisie had thought that Boone's office was high-dollar, it was only because she hadn't seen his house. The redbrick structure soared straight up to the sky with a steep gray roof that looked pointy enough to hook a star. The windows covered more space than the brick walls. It looked like she'd given up potato digging for curtain washing.

"It's this way." Fegus grunted as he lifted her trunk up the stone steps and bumped his knee against the door three times by way of knocking. "Don't worry about Mrs. Karol," he said. "She's got an inflated opinion of herself. Boone's mother lets her think she's the boss, but when it comes down to it—" He stopped as the door opened. "Mrs. Karol, Mr. Bragg sent home a surprise."

The lady turned her wide-spaced eyes on Maisie.

"Why are you looking at me like that?" Maisie asked. "This isn't a livestock inspection."

The housekeeper's turned-down mouth dipped even further. "I beg your pardon?"

"Mrs. Karol, this is Maisie Bragg. She married Boone today." Fegus dropped the trunk to punctuate his pronouncement.

"I don't appreciate your joke," she said. "Mr. Bragg won't appreciate it either."

"It's true," Maisie said. "Boone sent me here to get settled in. Now, where do I put this trunk?"

"I haven't heard anything from his parents. Unless they tell me . . ."

"They don't know," said Fegus. "He only told me on our way to the ceremony. About the trunk?"

"It doesn't belong in the house, and it certainly doesn't belong in the entryway." Mrs. Karol produced a hankie from her sleeve and dabbed her forehead. "You've caught me at a disadvantage. I don't know what to do."

"You can take a chair in the parlor," Fegus suggested to Maisie.

"Do you think that's where he'd want me?" asked Maisie.

"He's never wanted ladies anywhere in the house," said the housekeeper.

"But he's never married one before either," said Fegus.

Making a decision, Mrs. Karol stuffed the hankie back into her sleeve. "Fegus, if you say this one needs to stay, then I'll allow it, but if Mr. Bragg disapproves, it's on your shoulders."

"I'm willing to risk it." Fegus tipped his hat to Maisie. "Mrs.

Bragg, I've got to run, but you'll see me around." Then, with a covert look toward Mrs. Karol, he added, "Good luck."

The women waited until he'd gone before starting over.

"The parlor," said Mrs. Karol. "I'm sure it's good enough."

Maisie entered the sunny room and chose the tufted sofa between the elegant armchairs. Across from her was a fireplace set diagonally in the corner of the room, but it was unlit, seeing how it was summer and all the light from the windows made the room toasty. The sofa was more comfortable than the wooden chairs at home, but she wasn't home. Above the fireplace was an aged painting of an intimidating young woman—a woman who would know that Maisie didn't belong here. But it was the deal she'd agreed to. She'd live with the consequences.

There was nothing to do but wait. She studied the portrait of the beautiful young woman over the fireplace. Who was it? Boone's sister? Did he have a sister? Lands sakes alive, she should know that. Maisie heard footsteps as Mrs. Karol came and went, but she avoided the parlor, leaving Maisie entirely to her own devices. There were books aplenty, but Maisie was too jittery to concentrate.

The giant squares of light from the windows had inched across the floor before she was offered some tea and cookies. When the tea came, it was hot and in a tiny cup. Maisie refused to take it from the housekeeper.

"I want a big glass," she said, then, thinking where she was, she added, "Do you have ice? Iced tea. This getting married business has made me thirsty."

Was it wrong that Maisie felt a sense of triumph at the housekeeper's disapproval? But Mrs. Karol expressed her disgust in a turned lip instead of using words that could be quoted against her. The iced tea arrived with a grudge. Maisie took it politely, her mouth watering.

But before she drank it, she asked, "You didn't spit in this, did you?"

Mrs. Karol gaped. "What? How dare—" She worked herself up to her full height by a series of squirms. "I don't spit, miss."

Maisie leaned forward. "Everybody spits. It's the design of God."

"Absolutely not. And I would never spit in your drink. That you would think of such a vile act—"

Convinced that her iced tea was pure, Maisie ignored the rest of the complaint to gulp it dry in one go, but as soon as she did, she regretted it. What was she to do for the rest of the day?

It was well into the afternoon before she opened the window. Another hour found her sitting in the window with her feet dangling outside over a beautiful flower bed. Actually, she wasn't that far up. If she lowered herself down from the windowsill, her feet would nearly reach the ground.

Maisie looked at the door of the parlor. She wasn't locked in. She wasn't a prisoner. But she rebelled against the thought of asking the housekeeper for anything. She'd rather explore on her own.

Maisie rolled over so that her stomach was against the windowsill with her feet hanging down. The drop wouldn't be that far. She gripped the ledge and started her stretch down. If there was more fun to be had in the garden, why was she waiting in the parlor?

CHAPTER 11

If all Maisie wanted out of this marriage was freedom, then Boone was more than happy to oblige. He handed his horse off to Fegus and headed to his house. For long stretches of the day, he'd put the quick ceremony beneath the tree out of his mind. Occasionally, the thought of avoiding a particular woman would resurface, but then, like the glimmer of galena shining through rock, he'd remember that he didn't have to worry about being chased anymore. Once everyone knew he was married, they'd never trouble him again.

He hoped that Maisie felt as relieved as he did. He hoped her day had passed as pleasantly.

As he left the carriage house, he heard a feminine voice in the backyard. Mrs. Karol was never so exuberant. Could it be his wife?

He opened the garden gate to see Maisie standing in the lawn with an open jackknife balanced on her nose. Her eyes darted to him, but she held her head steady with her chin tilted up and her index finger on the point of the blade. Whatever she was doing, it took strong concentration. She lifted her other hand in his direction, bidding him to halt. Boone waited as she flipped her hand downward, sending the knife flying through the air, then sticking neatly in the grass.

"Five points!" Maisie crowed. She bent and retrieved the knife from the ground and wiped the blade on her skirt.

"What's this game?" he asked.

"Mumblety-peg. I'm up to twenty-five this round."

"Don't let me interrupt you." From the jumbled mess on his lawn, it appeared she'd been playing for a while.

"That's okay. Playing this was a last resort. I had nothing else to do."

"Didn't Mrs. Karol show you around?" Seeing the look on her face, Boone's brows drew together. "She left you to your own devices all day?" He shouldn't have trusted Mrs. Karol to smooth things over. He drew a deep breath to summon the maid.

Quick as silver, Maisie covered his mouth with her hand. "Let it go. I don't want to make enemies," she said.

Boone's eyes widened. Her hand was pressed against his mouth, but the rest of her was pressed against him too.

Annoyance at being forced into such close proximity with a lady flared, but just as quickly he remembered there was nothing to fear. There was no one watching, looking for gossip, or trying to manipulate him. Without the complications, this wasn't unpleasant at all.

Taking her wrist, he gently pushed her hand down. "I won't let on that you tattled." His mouth twitched at her obvious relief.

"Sorry. I don't mean to tell you how to deal with your hired help."

"My parents hired her, not me, but she has to treat you with respect." And so did he. He released her hand. "Speaking of parents, how did yours react to our news?"

"My pa wasn't there. I expect we'll hear from him soon. My ma, well, she didn't quite know what to think. And this . . ." Maisie held up her hand to display the sparkling diamond ring. "I tried to tell her it wasn't real."

"It's real. It better be real. I paid the jeweler more than my buggy cost."

"You bought this?" Maisie whistled. "I thought it might be a family heirloom."

"My family hasn't had money long enough to have heirlooms. They think a trip to Fort Lauderdale is as fine as a European tour, and they think Mrs. Karol is sophisticated enough to teach the lot of us some manners."

"And then you ruined all their plans by marrying me. What do your parents think about this?"

Boone would rather not discuss that topic. "If they want a fancy daughter-in-law, they'll have to apply to Grady, my brother. I haven't told them. What's the use? There's no sense in them hurrying home from their trip. It's done. I'm happy." With his chin tucked, he peered at her through his lashes. "Are you happy?"

Maisie crossed her arms. "I am now that I have some company."

Clearly he shouldn't have left her for so long, but he didn't have any idea what to do with her. "I thought you'd be busy today moving in."

"All I have is one trunk."

He winced. "That's all? I don't know what all a lady needs, but I'm certain it's more than that." Then, with a quick shake of his head, he looked away. "Whatever you feel comfortable with."

"I feel comfortable helping you. What can we do tomorrow?"

We? He looked again at the disturbed turf. It stood to reason that if she was restless on a sprawling ranch, she wouldn't be satisfied in his garden. "I've got to find someone who can advise me on the water pumps. That's my task for tomorrow. You're free to do whatever you want."

She ran the flat side of the knife's blade against her thumb. "That's what I wanted, freedom." She turned her back to him and placed the knife on her forehead. "Freedom to spend my day doing this."

Was that sarcasm? But then Boone heard more voices, and they weren't as shy about voicing their discontent.

Maisie recognized the voices at once. Upon reflection, perhaps she would've been wiser to have spent the day smoothing things over with her family instead of waiting around the Bragg home. She'd left things untended that her father was obviously of a mind to tend now.

"This is Bragg's house. I remember when it was being built." That was Uncle Oscar speaking. Maisie crept to the fence to listen without being seen. "Bill, your boy is already in trouble with the law on account of Maisie. If they are truly married like she claims, you haven't been wronged."

"It's not wrong to have my daughter spirited away from under my nose? It's not wrong to take her to wife without so much as a by-your-leave?"

Before she could respond, Boone walked out to meet them.

"Can I help you, gentlemen?" he asked. Although dusty and soiled from his time in the mine, to her family, his suit would mark him among those who spent their time moving figures on the page instead of weight across the scales.

"Bill Kentworth," her father announced, but didn't extend his hand. "Do you know where Maisie Kentworth is?"

"Boone Bragg." If Boone was nervous, he didn't show it. "I married your daughter today."

"So I heard, but you didn't have time to come by and meet me?"

"No, sir. Events unfolded rapidly. I'm going to speak to my housekeeper about scheduling a dinner to meet your family. As soon as she makes arrangements, we'll get a date formalized."

Boone wasn't raised to drop by and say howdy like her family would expect, and Mrs. Karol wouldn't be in any hurry to plan a dinner for Maisie's people. Letting the gate clang shut behind her, Maisie ran forward. Uncle Oscar smiled despite the seriousness of the situation, but her father had a different greeting for her.

"I didn't raise you to turn your back on your family," he said.

"I didn't, Pa. That's not at all what I wanted. I did it to protect our name. To protect Amos and Hank." She might not admit it to Amos, but it was the best excuse she had, and true to boot.

"And this man took advantage of your situation?"

Maisie snorted. She'd spent the day bored to tears with the freedom to do whatever she wanted. Boone hadn't taken advantage of anything.

"We'll get out of your hair, Boone," she said. "Pa and me can finish this discussion alone, and you can get washed up."

"No, I'm his son-in-law," Boone said. "He's right to feel insulted. Besides, I should get used to being inconvenienced by your family."

This made Pa do a double take. "If things had been done differently, we wouldn't have got off on the wrong foot like this."

"I apologize. I make mistakes with etiquette and social niceties, but there's one thing I can promise." Boone's gaze was level. "I don't make mistakes with women or with my character. So if you'll give me grace on communication, I can promise that you won't have cause to be ashamed of me for my behavior."

Maisie's heart fluttered. She was impressed. Not many people spoke with such conviction, especially when staring down her pa and uncle.

Her pa grunted. "Maisie, are you sure you don't want to come back home?"

She looked over her shoulder at the garden. Now that she'd seen her new home, was this really where she wanted to spend the rest of her life? But if she backed out now, it'd mean even more embarrassment on her family.

"This is where I'm staying, Pa. It's for the best."

Pa pulled his bandanna out of his back pocket and wiped his forehead. "If that's how it's going to be, then it's settled." He stuffed the bandanna away, then held his hand out to Boone. "You treat her right, and we'll stand with you. Come calling when you need us."

Boone hastily accepted the handshake. "Thank you, sir. I'm honored by the trust you put in me."

Trust put in Boone to take care of her? Maisie chewed the inside of her cheek. That sounded about right, because her pa didn't trust her past his line of sight. But now she was someone else's problem, so he was satisfied.

Yet there was still a problem, and Uncle Oscar was just the man they should talk to.

With her hands on her hips, she waited for the menfolk to finish establishing their pecking order before interrupting them. "Now that we're all a cozy family, there is a conundrum you might could help us with. Boone wouldn't up and ask you for help just yet, but seeing how I'm part owner in this venture, it's my concern as well."

Boone looked flat out flummoxed as to what she was talking about. Just as well. They wouldn't blame him if her request was out of line.

"This new cave we've got to clear—it's full of water. Boone was going to sell the mine when he hit the waterline because others have more experience with the new pumps, and he didn't want to put out the expense when his funds are limited. But with my discovery, we've got a bigger reason to hold on to the property and get the water out." She turned to Boone. "Is that the gist of it?"

Poor Boone looked as embarrassed as if he'd been caught naked in the middle of Sunday service. "I'm not going to bother your family. I don't expect anything from them. We'll figure it out. I've got some ideas."

"So do I, and my first idea is to ask Uncle Oscar. He's the supervisor of the Fox-Berry Mine. They have pumps, don't they?"

"Actually, we installed the new Cornish pumps last year. At first, we had problems with the exhaust from the generators getting back down the shaft. We had to cut some adits in for ventilation." Normally, Uncle Oscar was the quietest of the Kentworth family, but he possessed the heart of a teacher. "If you're talking about the place on the edge of the ranch, then I don't know if there's enough slope, but there's a way. Do you have a piece of paper?"

"Follow me." Boone had forgotten his embarrassment. He'd also forgotten Maisie and her pa as he led Uncle Oscar inside.

"I guess you'll want to see my new house," Maisie said to Pa. "You won't believe how lucky I am."

He hadn't lost that stern look. "He's the lucky one, Maisie. I understand why you left the ranch. Same reason your brother Finn took out. You want to set your own course, and I can respect that, but you gotta know something. Bragg has done himself well marrying you. Don't let him forget it."

Maisie looked at the massive house standing behind her. She snorted. "I don't think he married me to get ahead in life. If anything, I'm going to hold him back."

"Horsefeathers. The only thing holding you back is that you don't know what you're worth. You're a Kentworth, and that's nothing to sneer at."

Maisie knew when Pa was laying down a lecture like this not to sass him, but she couldn't help speaking plain. "I have an inkling of what he's worth. That's why I say I'm lucky."

"There's more to a person's value than what properties bear their name. If the person behind that name ain't worth shooting, then what's the use? It doesn't matter if you have Kentworth or Bragg as your name, the name Maisie Gail is a name to be proud of, and I expect you to see that everyone understands that."

She nodded. What else could she do? It was nice of him to prop her up like that. If only she believed it as much as he did.

CHAPTER 12

"I wasn't sure how that was going to shake out," Maisie said as she and Boone waved good-bye to her father and uncle. "Goodness, but it feels strange to stay in this big house while my family is leaving me behind."

"It's past time for dinner, and I haven't even shown you around. We'll be quick." Boone closed the front door and motioned her ahead of him down the hall. "You've already seen the parlor. This is the library. Not as big as my office downtown, but it's where I get most of my work done. The morning room is on the east side, where you'd expect it, and the dining room you'll see later. What you're probably most interested in is your personal room, and I have just the one picked out for you."

They went up a staircase with more carved wood than Uncle Calbert's workshop. It was as long as her staircase at home, but then it stopped, did a U-turn, and went up just as far again to make it to the next floor.

"I thought of this last night," Boone said. "You want your freedom, and you won't want to feel in the way of Mother and Father when they return. Also, it might keep us from having to address uncomfortable observations about the nature of our marriage until we get that straightened out."

"I didn't know there was anything to straighten." Things were how they were, and that was how they would be. At least, that was her understanding.

"This room was the happiest place in the house I could think of." He took her down a long hallway lined with doors, little tables that looked sawn in half and pushed against the wall, and fancy electric lamps that looked like giant eggs hanging above her head.

Boone burst through the door at the end of the hallway and strode through the room. Maisie halted just inside, relieved to see a simple white bed with an iron frame and a plain wardrobe and nightstand. After the opulence of everything downstairs, she knew she'd found the perfect space for her.

Boone didn't even pause. He'd already opened a closet door and disappeared inside.

"Aren't you coming?" he called.

Maisie looked longingly at the thick mattress and feather pillows. Where was he going? "Right behind you," she answered, and went to see how he'd disappeared into the magic closet.

It wasn't a closet. It was another set of stairs, narrow and winding. She paused halfway up to look out the small window low on the wall, charmed by the view.

"Where'd you go?" Boone was as excited as a boy.

Maisie ran up the last few steps and landed in a dust-filled room . . . of toys.

Boone stepped back against a chalkboard to clear her view of the room. And what a view. The circular room was almost all windows. Between two of the windows was a boy-sized suit of armor, decked with a stale popcorn chain and pheasant feathers stuck in the visor. A homemade catapult waited on a dusty shelf next to a guitar and a bleached turtle shell.

"You're putting me in the attic?" She looked at the exposed

beams above her head and wondered what kinds of spiders made those webs.

He drew back his head. “It’s not the attic to me. It’s my favorite room in the house—or it was, at least. I haven’t been up here in years, but I thought you would like it. Look at the view.”

Maisie stood next to him in front of the window. It was like they were in a secret passageway, spying on people around town without them knowing. Skipping over the common houses and mortals on the street, she could see downtown Joplin and the upper stories of the Keystone Hotel rising above the rest of the buildings. Beyond that she could see the headframes, elevators, and conveyor belts that carried the ore out of the mines. In the distance were faded hills rising and falling toward the real mountains of the Ozarks.

Boone ran his hand along the telescope that pointed up at the sky. “There’s another room you could use if you want. It was my brother’s before he moved to Indian Territory. But I think our rooms should be close. In fact, no one besides Mrs. Karol even needs to know you’re staying up here.”

What was he going on about? Why would anyone care where she was sleeping? Besides, the little bed in the corner was as big as the one she had at home. It felt good knowing she would have some room to herself instead of being crowded in with his family—wherever they might be.

“This suits me just fine.” She picked up an eraser from the tray of the chalkboard. “Can I clean it up?”

“I’ll have it cleaned while we eat. There’s no wardrobe up here, but I have room in mine.”

They’d made it down the winding stairs before his words landed. “Wait. I’m going to keep my clothes in your wardrobe?” Looking around the tidy bedroom they stood in, she asked, “Why can’t I stay in this room? It has a wardrobe.”

Boone found a razor on the dresser that needed straightening. “This is my room,” he said as he became suddenly involved in the arrangement of some toiletries.

Maisie spun to take in the staircase behind her, then the welcoming iron bedstead before her. "I have to pass through here?"

"You'll be out of the way of the rest of the household."

"You mentioned that." Now it was making sense. "And your parents will assume that we're sharing a room."

"If you'd rather have a different one, I'm happy to oblige you."

Maisie had no answer. After a day alone, she didn't relish sleeping in a far corner of a vacant mansion. On the other hand, having this kind of access to a man who was being far more charming than required carried its own danger.

"I want my own wardrobe upstairs," she said. "Is there a lock on my door?"

His eyebrow quirked. "To lock you in or lock me out?" He laughed at her expression. "I'm not going to harass you. C'mon, I bet dinner is getting cold."

Maisie allowed him to lead her to the dining room, comforted by the thought that she was a light sleeper and the suit of armor had a spear she could have at the ready.

CHAPTER 13

Boone rose before morning light. It had been a messy business, getting Maisie settled in properly. Mrs. Karol's reluctant compliance had shocked him. Her grunts of disapproval when asked to do anything regarding their new tenant had Boone convinced that she was choking on something. Persuading Mrs. Karol to do the work was nearly as difficult as preventing Maisie from doing it herself. He finally decided it wasn't worth his trouble and turned Maisie loose on the bedroom, much to Mrs. Karol's relief.

It had taken a few hours to get the room settled to Maisie's standards. He no longer heard furniture being scraped across the floor above him, so he took that as a good sign. Or maybe she'd work on it again today. As long as she had something to keep her occupied. Or maybe she didn't want to be busy. It was up to her. He wouldn't get in her way.

Pushing thoughts of his new wife behind him, he swung his feet up and propelled himself out of bed. If the figures Oscar Kentworth had given him were correct, they should be able to get an adit cleared by the end of the week. He would order the Cornish pumps this morning, and they could start the tunnel to the cavern from the new entrance today.

Boone turned on the spigot and splashed water on his face. His balbriggan undershirt had gotten hot during the night, but now the room felt brisk to be standing only in his underwear. He pulled on some britches. Today wasn't a day for a suit—not if he was down in the mine, which he hoped to be soon. He lathered up his face and reached for his straight razor.

He heard a door open, but he was picturing what kind of guest center they'd need to construct. A waiting area, certainly, and room for a souvenir shop. Maybe a café? Why not? Then people could get refreshments while they waited for their tour.

"Am I up too early?"

In the mirror, Boone caught the reflection of Maisie standing behind him. What was she doing there? He hadn't planned to encounter her until that evening. Not that he didn't like seeing her. If he had to have a wife, she might as well be pleasant company.

"It'll be light soon," he said.

She lingered in the stairway as if afraid to come in. "I could go downstairs."

"Stay." He scraped the razor up his neck and over his jaw, then rinsed it off beneath the flow of the faucet. "Sorry I'm not ready. If I'd known you'd be up this early, I would've prepared sooner."

"I'm an early riser. Especially when I'm excited for the day."

With another look at her in his mirror, he realized something was amusing her. What was it? Had he done something obtuse?

Then he saw what else was in the mirror—his bare chest. A quick look down revealed that the only clothing on his body was his britches.

"Should I put on a robe?" He turned to address her, but she hurriedly turned her face away.

"It's . . ." She laughed nervously while stealing another peek at him. "It's your room. I'll go."

"You have brothers, right?"

"You're not my brother."

"No, I'm your husband." He persisted until she met his gaze.

He had to know if she was repulsed. Sometimes he offended people without realizing it, and if this was one of those cases, he would have to make amends. But instead of outrage, he watched as she settled into her decision. "It's going to be all right," he said, more to himself than to her.

Her eyes flickered down his form and filled with laughter. "It's going to be all right," she repeated. She straightened the blankets on his bed and perched at the foot of it. "What do you have planned for today?"

He placed his blade against his neck. "I'm making plans for a visitor's center. I'm in search of a builder. I was thinking of hiring Maxfield Scott. He's got an excellent reputation." He scraped the razor over the last glob of shaving soap.

"I know a builder." Maisie crossed her legs and snagged one of his pillows to hug. "She designed and oversaw the Lighthouse Center at the Fox-Berry Mine."

"I know that place at your uncle's mine, but I don't think a lady designed it."

"Yep. My cousin Olive. She studied architecture while confined to the house, tending to Aunt Myra."

"I'm not sure—"

"I'll have her draw up a sketch. If you don't like it, then don't use it. On the other hand, you could refuse to give her a chance despite all the help Uncle Oscar is giving you."

Boone scrubbed his face with a towel. "I didn't realize your uncle's help came with strings attached."

"No strings attached. Just more help offered."

"I'll look at sketches. That's all I can promise." He opened a drawer and pulled out a clean cotton undershirt, then dove headfirst into it before reaching for his shirt. "Where are my suspenders?" he asked. "I thought I took them off my pants last night."

Something slapped against his cheek, and he felt a metallic sting on the back of his head.

"As far as slingshot materials, I've worked with worse," Maisie said. The bed creaked as she settled back onto it.

Boone untangled the suspenders from his neck. "Is your aim that good with everything?"

"Hardly. I've got a good arm for rock-skipping and stone-throwing, but when it comes to rifles, I'm nothing to brag about. Now, give me a shotgun and I can knock a bird out of the sky, but a lady doesn't have to be as accurate with a shotgun."

He pulled on his boots. "I'm eager to test the veracity of your claims." Why did he have to sound so pompous? Because he didn't know how else to talk to women.

"Name the time and place, and we'll do some target practice," she said. "That would be so much better than counting the squares on the parlor rug."

"I have a board meeting today. That comes first. But if I can finish everything before dark, I'll send for you. Be ready." What he expected her to do to be ready, he had no idea, but the thought of her waiting for him at home cheered him considerably.

"A board meeting? Ain't I on the board?"

Boone kept telling himself that his marriage had solved all his problems. He'd forgotten he still had a Kentworth to contend with on the board.

"You could come if you wanted."

"I do. I will." Maisie dropped her chin and paid close attention to a fingernail that needed picking. "I don't have any hats like that other lady, Mrs. Penney. Do you think I have time to buy one this morning?"

Boone didn't notice such things, but he imagined she was right. He opened a case on his bureau and dropped some folded bills on the bed. "Buy whatever you need. When the bank opens, I'll get you some more."

"I'd rather work than shop, but if you have nothing else for me to do before the meeting . . ."

"Adding to your wardrobe seems like a good start."

"First breakfast, then I'll head to town. Maybe Calista will help me pick something suitable." She bounded off the bed and hurried out of the room, wearing the same dress she'd worn the day before.

Down in the breakfast room, Boone had cleaned his plate before he realized that Maisie hadn't said a word the whole meal. Or maybe she had and he'd been too distracted to hear her. He looked across the table, but to his shock, she was gone. When had she left? Where had she gone? Had he gotten too engrossed in his plans again?

He looked through the windows of the breakfast room to make sure she wasn't just outside. He checked behind the potted palm to see if she was tucked away in a cushioned chair next to the tea tray. No, she'd truly left him. One more look out the window, and his day grew darker.

Justina was walking up to the house with that determined going-on-calls walk she had when she was stalking him. Sometimes when she was with her mother, Mrs. Karol could turn her away, but when she was by herself and walking like that, she was as difficult to turn as an underground river.

"Maisie," he hollered as he searched the main part of the house. "Maisie, where did you go?" He had married Maisie for this moment. If Justina didn't know about his wife, what help was she?

He peered through the colored glass pane in the front door and saw Maisie walking away from the house. This was bad. Or was it good? He couldn't tell. He peered around the drapes of the picture window. With her arms swinging and her chin up at a good-natured angle, Maisie was plowing ahead, showing no signs that she feared Justina's approach. Justina's steps slowed. Her flat hat leveled straight as she eyed Maisie, then looked at his front door. Maisie waved as she passed and smiled without guile, unaware of any distress she was causing.

But Justina didn't look stressed. Only angry.

"Is something amiss?"

Boone gritted his teeth. Even worse than getting caught by Justina was getting caught hiding by his housekeeper.

"These drapes." He buried his nose into their velvet folds and took a deep breath. "Do you think they smell musty?"

Mrs. Karol raised an eyebrow. "Your mother sent them out for cleaning before she left. She was satisfied. Why should I do anything further with them?"

The inevitable knock at the door kept him from answering. "It looks like I have a guest." He smoothed his shirt. "If you'll excuse me."

"If you'd like, you should ask Miss Caine's opinion of the drapes. She knows how things should be done."

Of all the miners' widows who needed work in Joplin, why did they have to hire this snooty bore? "Wonderful suggestion. Thank you."

He reached the door and swung it open himself, not waiting for the proper form to be observed.

Justina's eyes widened, and she flashed her teeth. "Boone, I didn't expect you to be home. *Quelle surmise*."

He stepped aside, allowing her to enter. "The sun is barely up, and I just finished breakfast. Where else would I be?"

She giggled. "You're such a busy man. I myself get antsy sitting at home, waiting for the sun to come up. Idleness, it's the curse of our times. So this morning I thought, why let the day get away from me? I might as well get busy doing something productive."

"Which is?" When the door swung closed, it echoed through the house like the detonation of blasting caps.

"'Which is . . . ?' I don't understand the question." She blinked like coal dust had fallen in her eye.

"You set out on a mission to do something productive, but here you are, talking to me. How did you get distracted so early in the day?"

The corners of her mouth tightened. She hadn't expected him to say that. Boone was getting better at recognizing the signs. "Well, you see, I am accomplishing something. I'm speaking to you. I woke up determined to do it today, and now it's happening." She lifted her finger and wagged it in the air. "Check off one accomplishment for me."

He was about to mention that she might put more care into her list making when he remembered that he possessed news she needed to hear. He stepped back as a matter of self-preservation before beginning. "I accomplished something recently as well. I found a wife."

Justina's eyes flashed. Her lips pulled into an uneasy smile. "You did? And you want me to be the first to know?"

The question confused him. Fegus and Mrs. Karol knew. So did Maisie's family and the preacher. In fact, there were a host of people who knew.

"Don't be nervous, Boone. You can ask me. You've already broached the subject, so the difficult part is behind you." Justina bit her lip as she beamed. "I'm going to say yes, Boone. You just have to get the words out."

He stepped back again, bumping his thigh against a marble table. "The words. I need to say the words." Why did she have to look so hopeful? Boone hadn't planned to make any enemies today. "The words are—" He cleared his throat.

"Yes?" She clapped her hands together and bounced on her toes.

"The words are . . ." He gulped and turned his eyes to the sconce on the wall. "Miss Caine, I'm married. I got married to a wife. My wife. I'm really, really married and can't get married to anyone else. Not now."

There. He'd said it. And what did she think? He squinted as he dropped his gaze to her. Justina had turned a sickly green. Tints of the color hovered around her mouth, and blotches of red were on her neck. The color variations were terrifying.

Boone cocked his head. "Are you feeling unwell?"

"Married?" she spat. "You're married?" She gulped a big breath of air, but then spat it back out at him. "How dare you get married! What made you think you could do such a thing?"

"The preacher had no objections—"

"Who? Who is she?" Justina's fists were thrust down by her sides. "Is it Fern Dillard? Her mother said you'd fall for that ruse, but I thought you had more sense."

"Miss Dillard?" Boone winced. Another woman he'd been avoiding. "It isn't Miss Dillard. It's Miss Kentworth. She's a lovely, sensible woman. We'll do very well together." He believed what he said. Doing well together meant no conflict, no fuss, and totally staying out of each other's way. Besides her unexpected appearance in his bedroom that morning, he and Maisie were doing fine.

"I don't know a Miss Kentworth," she said, "and neither do you."

"Ask your father," Boone replied. "He met her earlier this week."

For the first time, Justina looked worried that he might be telling the truth. "My father . . ." Her eyes narrowed. "Was she leaving the house just now as I was coming up the walk?"

"Yes. That's Miss Kentworth. It was Miss Kentworth. Now we're married."

"You can't be serious." Justina covered her forehead with her hand. "Oh, Boone. What have you done?"

She believed him. That was all Boone was trying to accomplish. He didn't need to justify his decision or wait for her blessing. He just needed her to believe.

"If you'll pardon me." He kicked his work boot against the leg of the hall tree. "I have to prepare for my board meeting. I wish you the best, Miss Caine."

He walked out the front door and left her to fume in the entryway.

Despite all the numbers Boone could compile that morning, the conference with his directors would be grueling. Much had happened since they'd first discussed this novel venture. Although he was in contact with each director, he looked forward to presenting their progress as a group. It was a good reminder that he wasn't doing this alone. His father had helped him recruit capable advisers, even if he chose to disregard their advice on occasion.

"Good morning, Boone." Mark Gilbert entered the conference room, the first to arrive.

"Looks like you're doing well." Boone made a show of inspecting his foreman's new suit coat. Maisie wasn't the only one trying to keep up appearances. "I heard you weren't at the cave today."

"Not when I have my new clothes on, nope." Gilbert spun and flared his collar. "I thought it was time to replace that tweed jacket. We're starting a new venture, so we should start it with a new look too." His eyes, always a little too round, sparkled in excitement. His buoyancy carried over even as they discussed the progress made on the preparation for the pumps.

Mr. Yates from the Keystone Hotel arrived next, followed by Mr. Hunt. When Mrs. Penney and Maisie stepped through the door, Boone knew without asking that his secret had been discovered.

"Mr. Bragg, how could you marry this darling girl without telling us?" Mrs. Penney took Maisie by both shoulders and steered her to stand before Boone. Maisie's tidy straw hat looked adorable but was a far cry from the more elaborate structures Mrs. Penney preferred. "I knew from the minute I saw the two of you together that there were sparks. Right here in this boardroom, you couldn't keep your eyes off her."

Boone groaned inwardly. If Mrs. Penney didn't stop, Maisie might suspect that he'd been less than truthful about his reasons for marrying her.

But Mrs. Penney wasn't slowing down. "You have squandered your golden opportunity. Aren't I right, Mr. Yates? Mr. Hunt? Maisie informed me that you have no photographs of the ceremony."

Sorry, Maisie mouthed to him. Keeping her head down, she ducked into her chair.

Boone had to get ahead of this. "I'd like to inform the board that since our last board meeting, I married Maisie Kentworth."

Mr. Yates huffed. "Shouldn't there be some sort of discussion before the president of the board marries a board member?"

"I'll know to ask next time," Boone said.

"And there will be a next time," Mrs. Penney announced, ignoring his sarcasm, "and this time you'll do it right."

"The young lady did mention using the Crystal Cave for special events. Perhaps they should be the first?" Mr. Hunt asked.

"Precisely," said Mrs. Penney. "We'll arrange another ceremony in the cave, because I'm not missing out on the best publicity stunt since Erik the Red named Greenland. And if you think you're going to have the first wedding ceremony in the Crystal Cave without a photographer, then you are out of your minds!"

"The cave isn't ready," said Gilbert. "It's still half full of water."

Boone didn't know much about weddings, but he did know about getting in and out of mines. "We can both get down there, we know that. If we could widen the opening that we used the first time, maybe we can construct a little platform just inside the cave to give us a place to stage the vows. Mrs. Penney could get her pictures, and she'd have something to begin the publicity with."

"I know just the dressmaker to sew your gown, Mrs. Bragg."

"Sew a gown? We need to do this quickly," Maisie said. "I can't go around town planning a wedding when I'm already supposed to be wed."

Mr. Hunt leaned heavily on the table. "I thought this was a meeting about mining. If we need to reschedule—"

"Mr. Hunt is right." Boone was grateful for the crotchety man's complaint. "We have the water pumps ordered, and they are being shipped even now. With the help of Oscar Kentworth from the Fox-Berry—"

"Some relation, I assume?" Mr. Hunt asked Maisie.

"This seamstress has sample gowns available," said Mrs. Penney, "and I think there's one that will work with a few alterations. I'll have her make Mr. Bragg a cravat to match your gown and a veil for you if you don't already have one." She turned to Boone. "How big is the platform?"

"It's not built yet. If we could stop talking about seamstresses, maybe we could get to it."

"Well, it needs a raised portion big enough for the maid of honor and the best man to join you with the preacher. If it isn't raised, then the attendees can't see you."

"Attendees?" Boone shook his head. "We're already married. We aren't inviting guests."

"Then not a big platform, but your parents can't stand on crystals. They need somewhere to watch from."

"My parents are out of town," Boone said, "and the Kentworths are . . . ?" He widened his eyes at Maisie.

"Not inclined to attend," she said.

Mrs. Penney ran a finger over the grosgrain ribbon on her collar. "I see." Maybe she saw a lot, but she wasn't saying what she saw. "So this marriage was opposed?" Her eyes narrowed as she looked at Maisie. "How could your family object to Mr. Bragg?"

"You don't have to answer that," Boone said.

This was why he avoided women. Invite two of them into his office, and they started discussing his suitability as a groom at his own board meeting.

"They don't know him well, and we decided we'd rather not wait around for them to get better acquainted," Maisie said. "Seeing as how we're going to be working together, it made more sense to get this wedding behind us so we won't have to worry about chaperones and propriety."

"I'd assume Mr. Bragg has worked with a whole host of people in his career. He hasn't needed to marry any of them so far," said the reliable Mr. Hunt.

"This is a special situation," Boone replied.

Mrs. Penney's enthusiasm for the project had dimmed. She

smoothed her hair as her eyes darted toward the floor. "Miss Kentworth is so young. I don't want to contribute—"

This discussion was not on the agenda. "We can get some pictures if you'd like," Boone said. "And if you want to bring along a preacher, he'll make the pictures more authentic."

Mrs. Penney looked at Maisie with a slow shake of her head. Boone dropped his eyes to the column of figures on his spreadsheet. Why should Mrs. Penney pity Maisie? He was helping her. For someone whose job involved showing people how wonderful everything was, Mrs. Penney was casting a gloomy cloud on his plans.

"If you're already married, I suppose we might as well make the most of it." Mrs. Penney sighed. "A dress, a cravat, and a preacher. Is there anything else required?"

CHAPTER 14

"You certainly surprised me, Mrs. Bragg." Maisie's cousin Olive flipped through a binder of loose-leaf sketches. "Between you and my sister marrying these wealthy men and Calista's stint with the detectives . . ."

Maisie lowered her boots off the coffee table and leaned forward. "I thought the detective job was a secret."

Olive lifted a sketch and held it to the window to catch the light. "My point is that I shouldn't be surprised by anything anymore, but you've managed to catch me, just the same." She smiled at the sketch. "But to build a visitor's center? Now, that's even more surprising than you becoming a Bragg."

Unflappable Olive was getting her digs in, but at least she was taking Maisie seriously about the new project. After the board meeting, Mrs. Penney had hit Maisie with a thunderburst of odds and ends to prepare for their re-wedding and the publicity surrounding it, but Maisie hadn't lost track of what was most important, and that was getting Olive to build the visitor's center. Without a place for people to buy tickets, all the publicity would be meaningless.

"I made a good match." Maisie propped her feet on the coffee table again and studied her new white boots that were to be part of her wedding ensemble. "When a whopper is nibbling at your bait, you don't piddle around before reeling him in."

"I wouldn't use the phrase 'nibbling at your bait' again, dearest. Not after that mess with Mr. Marsh."

"You know what's really annoying about you?" Maisie asked. "You can't ever let a person forget their mistakes. Why don't you—"

Olive held up a hand. "You're right. I'll stop. I'm just trying to make sense of all this. I remember how you talked when you were in love, and that's not what I'm hearing now. Yet it's a welcome change, so let's move on. What's the budget for the building? How big should it be? What purposes will it serve? I've never seen an office for mine tours before."

Back on safe ground, Maisie and Olive quickly dug into the meat of the project. There were many questions for which Maisie had no answers, but she carefully jotted them down to present to Boone later. More than anything, she was amazed at Olive's knowledge. True, Olive had always enjoyed building elaborate birdhouses that resembled the Murphysburg mansions, but when Maisie had heard that they'd used Olive's plans for the Fox-Berry Mine's community center, she'd thought Olive had merely drawn a picture of a building. She never would've guessed that she had figured the dimensions, estimated the supplies, and had given a price range. While Maisie had been working the farm, Olive had been sitting patiently at her mother's sickbed, studying up on a skill that Maisie would've never credited her.

Maisie had a page full of information and questions when a horrible wet cough sounded from the closed bedroom door. Olive stood.

"Has Aunt Myra woken up?" Maisie stood too. "Does she feel like a visit?" If there was anyone who would understand what Maisie had done, it was her sympathetic aunt.

"The doctor is worried about contagion when she's this bad.

And she frets over people seeing her when she's not at her best. I'll tell her you send your regards." Olive looked up and waited for Maisie to meet her eyes before continuing. "We have to be prepared, Maisie. She can't go on like this for long."

Maisie felt a chill run up her arms. When Aunt Myra was feeling well, there was no one Maisie would rather chew the fat with, but lately her aunt's good days were few and far between. "I wish there was something I could do."

"We all wish we had a cure." Olive had been so happy while they were talking about the new building. Now she looked as old as Granny Laura. "Working on these plans will be a good distraction for me. I can't bear to just sit here and wait."

Wait for what? Maisie was afraid she knew.

"See you later, then," Maisie said. "I'm praying for your ma. And you. And your pa."

"Thanks. Good luck on your mine . . . and your marriage."

Maisie blinked at the ring on her finger. It didn't seem real. In fact, she'd almost forgotten she was married. Somehow she'd already prepared herself for the long walk back to the farm, completely forgetting that she didn't live there anymore.

She let herself out of the house and turned toward town. Downtown Joplin separated the simple house of Oscar and Myra Kentworth and their daughter from the Murphysburg neighborhood where the Braggs resided. Maisie had never aspired to live in such a fine neighborhood. Her oldest brother, Finn, used to say don't ever jump off a hill in the dark, and that was exactly what she'd done. She'd gone and leapt before she knew what she was landing in. She couldn't imagine what the next day or next week would look like, much less the rest of her life. All she knew was that Amos and Hank weren't in danger and that Silas Marsh would have to find another lady to harass.

The skin on Maisie's arms puckered like gooseflesh. Had she conjured him by thinking of him? For here was Silas, headed out of the butcher's shop with a wrapped hunk of pork on his shoulder.

She skidded to a stop, but it was too late. His face broke out into that adorable smile.

"Sweetheart, you found me! Boy, are you a sight for sore eyes. How have you been doing?"

"I didn't come to see you, you swine. I came to see my cousin. It had nothing to do with you." She lifted her hands, keeping them extended between them. "You've got no right to pester me."

Maisie possessed a pair of healthy lungs, but maybe she shouldn't be taxing them so on a city street. She was drawing attention. The man in a tailored suit who'd stepped out of the butcher shop even looked familiar. Had she seen him at Boone's meeting?

"I'm concerned about you," Silas replied, and by George, he looked for all the world like he was. "How've you been feeling? Have they loosened the chains? Are you free to visit yet? I know how much you've been missing the soda fountain. C'mon, let me buy you your favorite drink."

Boone didn't know she liked the soda fountain. He'd never taken her there. He'd never taken her anywhere but a board meeting.

Silas sensed weakness. His voice sweetened even more. "I only want you to be happy, Maisie, and we were happy together. You can't argue against that. Just think of all the fun times we had."

"It wasn't fun when I found out about your illegitimate children." She stomped her foot to clear her head. "That sort of information is something you might want to make known."

"That was in the past." He noticed a girl smiling at him and was temporarily distracted, but he pulled his attention back to Maisie. "That was the past," he repeated. "I'm looking to the future."

"I am too," she said. "I'm planning for the future, and I knew that I wouldn't have a good future with you, so I took care of it. I got married, Silas. I'm a married woman."

He scrunched up his face. "You're talking nonsense, darling."

In Maisie's opinion, the crowd around them needed to move along and mind their own business. "No, I'm not," she said. "I'm married, and that's why I'm here in town. I live here. With my husband. So you can just skedaddle back to your claim and forget about me."

An older woman with sausage links draped over her shoulders began clapping. "Way to tell him, honey. I hope your new man does right by you."

Maisie crossed her arms over her chest as Silas weighed his response.

"Married, you say?" He lowered the hock of meat from his shoulder and switched it to the other side. "But are you happily married? That's the real question."

"I have nothing left to say to you."

She turned to start home, but not before she noticed Silas casting an alluring gaze at the young girl who'd witnessed their exchange. That figured. Silas wouldn't go long without feminine companionship.

The crowd was dispersing, but the man who looked familiar met her eyes, and she was struck by the coldness in them. Where did she know him from?

She shivered as she continued down the street. Marrying Boone was supposed to settle the Silas situation, but had it caused more trouble ahead?

"You're looking at a couple hundred electric lamps to get an area that big illuminated." Charles Belden, Joplin's foremost electrical engineer, tapped his desk in his small warehouse off Virginia Avenue. His electric company was new, and like everything else in Joplin, it was quickly outgrowing its space. "Of course, I can get a better estimate once I see the cave. It's hard to figure an irregularly shaped room, especially one with no natural light."

"Of course." Boone felt a twinge of unease at the scope of what he was proposing. It had cost plenty to get electricity run to his office, and that had involved only a dozen lamps. "Have you handled a project this large before?"

Mr. Belden nodded. "It's not the size but the uniqueness of the situation that will take special consideration." He reached for a large roll of paper. "Have you seen the plans for the Schifferdecker Electric Light Park? There'll be enough wire going around that place to reach to the moon and back." He spread the plans out on the table and pointed out different features to Boone. It was the most ambitious project Boone had ever seen. From roller coasters and skating rinks to swimming pools and a boating lagoon. He couldn't think of any attraction that it lacked.

"Mr. Belden, may I ask what you're doing?" Standing in the open door was a short man in long pants and a round hat. He eyed Boone suspiciously as he crowded into the office. "Aren't those my plans?"

Mr. Belden drew back his shoulders. "I was showing Mr. Bragg an example of my work on a project similar to his, Mr. Peltz. Your Electric Light Park isn't the only amusement center under construction in Joplin."

"Mr. Bragg? I haven't heard of you." Mr. Peltz studied Boone closely. "Don't tell me you're aspiring to make a second electrical park that covers four city blocks."

If it had been in Boone's power to do so, maybe he would have, so strong was his instant dislike for this man. "Not at all," he answered. "I'm hiring Mr. Belden to install lights in a cave I found. You can keep the aboveground entertainment to yourself."

"A cave? For tours?" Peltz hoisted his pants up over his belly.

"Yes, that's the idea."

"Do you think Joplin can support two such attractions? People could spend a week at our Electric Light Park and still not see it all. We have everything you could imagine." He waved his arm over the blueprints on the table.

Boone regretted every wasted moment, and this was adding up to account for several. "You do have everything," he said with a smile. "Everything except for a crystal cave." He picked up his hat. "Thank you, Mr. Belden. We'll be in touch. Mr. Peltz, good day."

And that was the last appointment of a very busy afternoon. Already Boone had met with the surveyor to stake out the boundary of the property that Bragg Mining had leased from Mrs. Laura Kentworth. While stepping it off with him, Boone had even taken time to appreciate the sturdy barbed-wire fence his wife had constructed the day they met.

The water pumps had arrived, and they were moving ahead with the installation. Soon the water would recede and more of the cavern would be revealed. If Boone's guess was correct, the floor would be covered with marvelous crystals as well. The new access hole was well underway, and he'd gotten a contract signed for the delivery of lumber to begin constructing wooden flooring and stairways for visitors. Progress was being made, and what tickled Boone the most was that he had ample work for his men. Even though the mine had gone dry, no one would be without a paycheck. Sure, his borrowed funds were getting low, but the venture would pay out. He was sure of it, or he wouldn't be risking his inheritance on it.

Boone took his horse to the carriage house to pass it into Fegus's hands, but Fegus was nowhere to be found. The wagon was still there, so he hadn't gone to town for supplies. As Boone was tending his horse, he heard the sound of a hammer echoing off the brick house and over the fence of his backyard. Had he forgotten some repair that was underway? Maybe Fegus had told him and he didn't remember. People often swore to conversations that Boone had no memory of, and what could he do besides believe them?

The garden gate was topped with ironwork swirled to look like vines in bloom. This green spot was his mother's favorite place, and despite his best efforts, her absence was visible in the spindly arms of the hydrangea and the wilted petunia blooms. What was new was the woman kneeling on the brick walkway, hammering a block of wood to a narrow plank.

Fegus saw him first. The weathered gent grinned broadly and motioned him forward. "Good evening, Mr. Bragg. We've cooked up a surprise for you."

Maisie lifted her flushed face. Scrambling off her knees with the hammer in hand, she picked up two of the planks.

"Thank you for the use of your tools." She handed the hammer to Fegus, who beamed his scraggly smile.

"I'm not leaving until I see you try those things. Go on." Fegus nodded at the planks.

They were stilts. Boone used to have a set when he was a boy. He'd never wanted to play on stilts since. Not until now. But he didn't want to intrude.

"I'll be in the library," he said. "Enjoy yourself." He had no business loitering with Maisie when it was evident that she could entertain herself. Fegus could help her if she needed.

He'd turned to leave when he heard her squeal. In a flurry of calico and petticoats, Maisie was leaping forward off the blocks of the stilts. Keeping a grip on the boards, she didn't let them drop, but pulled them upright and put them in position for another try.

Boone's breath caught at her expression. Her eyes were focused, her lips tight, but every inch of her face radiated the joy of determination, the thrill of finding a challenge. He recognized that look because he often felt the same way. She'd managed to climb on the blocks and stumble forward and back, searching for her balance. Perhaps he wasn't in such a hurry.

"Here ya go." Reading his mind, Fegus handed Boone a second pair of stilts. "These were our practice run. They ain't as good as the ones Mrs. Bragg is using, but they'll do the job."

Boone balanced the stilts on their ends as Fegus left. He watched Maisie as she swayed and straightened, bent and bowed. She was fire and light bound up in a freckled mess. So far he'd left her to her own devices, just as he'd planned, but would she mind if he intruded on her time?

Maisie laughed. Staggering around with the stilts' ends tucked beneath her arms, she caught him in her laughing gaze. "Are you going to stand there, or are you going to try it?"

Boone felt the warmth of the lingering sun burn through him. "I'm trying it," he said. He hopped up on the stilts but started out too fast. When he dismounted, his left stilt dropped, nearly hitting Maisie, who was already clomping around with speed.

"Watch it!" she hollered.

"Sorry!" He felt the cares of his enterprise lessen with each effort he made on the toys. He'd shouldered so much responsibility since his parents left him to sink or swim alone. So much concern when his best-producing mine hit water. He hadn't realized how badly he needed relief from his burdens.

"When are you going to be ready for the wedding?" Maisie tried to straighten to her full height but lost her balance and put a foot down to catch herself.

"I have the lumber for the platform." His voice jerked with each step. "It'll be done soon."

Every morning, he journeyed into the cave with the anticipation of seeing the beautiful sight. By tomorrow, the water level would start dropping. More of the cave would be visible.

"Boone, what are we going to tell people when they ask about our wedding?"

He stepped off the stilts. Her question confused him enough that he wanted to have both feet on the ground.

"What do you mean? Why would they ask about our wedding? In mining, we never have to explain why we're digging up ore. It's self-evident that it's beneficial."

She cocked an eyebrow. "People will understand how it was beneficial to me, but I don't think anyone will understand what you're getting out of the deal."

He gazed down at her pert, freckled nose and choked on the feeling rising in his chest. This was why he needed to stay busy at work. When he let down his guard, things whirled out of control.

"Be that as it may, it's none of their business. Why would anyone care why or when we planned our wedding?"

"People care," Maisie said. "If you'd listen to women talk, why and when weddings take place is one of their most favorite topics of conversation. Mrs. Penney aims to let everyone know about our wedding in the cave. It'll be conversated over for months, if she has her way."

"It'll all blow over soon enough. Then we can live in peace without people bothering us." Although this evening was turning out to be better than the peace he thought he wanted.

"I bought you something," Maisie said. "You told me to get myself what I needed, and I did, but I wanted to get you a present too." She dropped the stilts and ran to pick up a small wrapped package that was sitting on the kitchen steps. "Open it," she said, her hands clasped beneath her chin.

He had to drag his eyes away from her face to see what he'd unwrapped. "It's shaving soap." He held the round bar up to his nose. "I detect lemon."

"Lemon and sandalwood, the label says. I don't know that I've ever seen a sandalwood tree, but I liked the way it smelled."

"Very nice." Boone drew another deep breath of the scent. It troubled him that she was so excited to give him something when he'd tossed money at her without a second thought.

"Normally I would've done my shopping at Daniel's Drug and Miscellany, but seeing as how I'm banned from there, I had to go to the mercantile by your office."

"That's as good a place as any," he said. "I'll try out the soap tomorrow morning. Now, I've got to sketch some plans . . ."

He read the disappointment in her eyes. Had he not responded with enough enthusiasm to her gift, or was she wanting something else?

"Unless you want to look at the plans with me?" he offered.

Maisie tossed her stilts toward the fence. "That sounds like fun. I really want to see what you have in mind."

Boone led her into the house. He didn't like the conflict warring in his heart. The part of him that was so settled and sure knew this was a mistake. The time Mr. Peltz had wasted would pale in comparison to the task of sketching out the footprint of his cavern operation with Maisie Kentworth. He knew that, so why had he offered?

Because a new part of him thought it was worth the risk. Maybe he'd regret it, or maybe she'd lead him to a new discovery, just like she had in the cave. He owed her a chance.

If Maisie had thought it was dull staying on the farm with all the space, animals, and her family, she hadn't realized what living in town with Mrs. Karol would be like. True, she could leave at will, but she'd learned that an aimless young lady on the streets of Joplin was like to attract attention. It was better to get her business done and skedaddle back home. Problem was, she had run slap out of business. She could only spend so many hours a day shopping.

She followed Boone through the back door of the house, past the kitchen and back staircase to his desk in the library. He dropped his satchel next to his desk and removed his suit coat while Maisie poured him a glass of water.

His brows lifted like he thought it funny that she was serving him, but he drank it anyway.

"Thank you." He reached for a chair and pulled it behind the desk, next to his.

Maisie took the glass away, proud that she'd helped him and resolving to help him more when given the chance. 'Course, if he never came home, how could she be a help?

She had seen the map he pulled in front of them before. Through the straight property lines was an off-kilter oval shaped like a hound dog's ear.

"That's the cave," she said as he centered it on the table.

"That's the cave. This here is where the ground is low, which means the visitors will enter from this side, on your family's land. We'll put the water pumps and the generators on the Kennedy side so they won't be seen or heard from the visitor's center."

"I talked to Olive about the visitor's center." Maisie rocked in her chair. "She had a lot of questions about the size of the building and budget. I didn't know what to tell her."

"If it was mining, I'd have some notion, but this is completely different."

"Have you ever been to a cave tour?"

"I grew up in mines. I've seen plenty of caves."

"I mean as a tourist. Have you paid for a ticket, waited in line, bought a postcard?"

Boone's gaze lifted and rested on the far side of the room in an action that was becoming familiar. His hand found his pencil and, without looking down, he began making a list. Maisie leaned over his arm to read it.

Souvenir shop, ticket counter, waiting area, refreshments and café.

She waited until his pencil slowed before nudging him. "Do you know you're doing that?"

"I know exactly what I'm doing. I'm working." His eyes were focused now as they reviewed his notes.

"But do you have to ignore everyone in the room to do your work?"

"If I want to get my work done, then yes, sometimes."

Maisie leaned back in her chair. If her family shared a trait, it was vigilance. You didn't dare drop your guard, or you were bound to be at the dangerous end of a bull's horn, a boar's tusk, or a cousin's prank. Absolute silence to ponder a problem was a new strategy to her. When the Kentworths had an issue, it was discussed by one and all, and at a healthy volume. But if Boone knew what worked for him, who was she to complain?

"Here's something you might find diverting." Boone flipped over his paper and began sketching on the back of it. "Have you heard anything about the Schifferdecker Electric Light Park that's being constructed?"

"I don't reckon I have."

"I saw the plans for it today," he said. "It's going to be massive. Four city blocks full of every conceivable attraction. These are the gardens when you enter, and at the center of them is going to be a swimming pool. There's to be a tower filled with lights that stands a hundred and twenty-five feet tall at the center, and here will be a German village and biergarten to honor Joplin's founders. There's a stage, concessions, exotic animals, and even a souvenir shop. When you mentioned postcards, I realized we need to have one of those for ourselves."

"Do you think we can compete with something like that? Why would people come to our cavern when they can go to all of that?" Maisie had never doubted the Crystal Cave. Not until now.

"They have several obstacles to overcome that we won't face. First is the expense. They are building all of this from scratch. Tickets will have to be expensive, which means many of our mining families can't afford them, and just imagine the cost of maintaining this place. The grounds have to be mowed, the trash picked up, and the electric bill . . . that expense alone is mind-boggling. They are trying to do too much from the start. I don't think they'll survive.

"Secondly, it's all artificial. The lights, the pool, the German village—none of it is real. It'll be fun, but I don't think it has that sense of awe that comes from our cave. You haven't been back down there, Maisie, but it's amazing. There's nowhere like it. All the electric lights in the world can't compete with what God made and hid beneath our feet."

He was a man she barely knew, and she was getting all soft in the head about him already. Maisie bit the inside of her cheek. It was a good thing she was married and didn't have to worry about that foolishness anymore, for she obviously hadn't learned her lesson.

"I'm sure you're right," she said, "but I'd still like to go to that Electric Light Park, just the same. It seems so romantic."

Romantic was the wrong word to use. Boone shifted his chair and looked at her before bursting into laughter.

"What's wrong?" Maisie asked. "Did I say something funny?"

"You have no idea how relieved I am that I never have to walk through Joplin's Electric Light Park as a single man. Oh, Maisie, it would be a nightmare. This promenade here—a man wouldn't make it ten feet without some lady bursting out of the bushes and into his path."

"I wouldn't be able to see it at all, since I'd still be stuck on the farm. If I did sneak away, I'd have to row a boat to the middle of their lagoon to keep my family from hauling me home." She mimicked rowing for all she was worth. "This marriage is hands down the best deal."

Instead of numbers and plans, Boone was seeing the comedy played out before him. "Without a doubt, some desperate girl will hurl herself into an animal's cage, then insist on being rescued by a disinterested chap, and I don't even want to imagine what traps could be set on the roller coasters."

Maisie stood up and staggered around the room. "I'm so dizzy, I don't think I can stand upright." She purposefully caught her toe behind her heel and tripped forward, spinning just as she fell into Boone's lap.

He caught her with skill and plastered a horrified look on his face. "Excuse me, miss. I'm a married man. You'll have to fall for another gentleman with a ready lap. This one is spoken for."

Maisie batted her eyes. "What a pity. This is my third trip on the Dazy Dazer, and I can go no further." She pressed the back of her hand to her forehead and imitated a faint.

Boone had a nice laugh. He also had nice arms, but the way they made her feel as he pulled her against himself was unwelcome. What was she doing? Hadn't she determined not to be unwise again?

Maisie sat up. She kept on her giddy smile, but there was caution behind it. Boone helped her upright.

Smoothing her skirt and her conscience, she said, "Remember that man I told you about? The one who was pestering me? I ran into him today. He commenced with his usual nonsense, but I cut him off. I told him I was married now. He was surprised, but I don't reckon we'll hear any more from him."

"That's good," Boone said after a long pause. "My troublesome female also made an appearance. She didn't respond well to the news, but it accomplished what we wished."

Was this woman more persistent than Silas? Somehow Maisie couldn't imagine that she wouldn't be. Who would let a gentleman like Boone get away?

CHAPTER 15

The platform was built, the water was down, and so it was time for Maisie's wedding day—her second wedding day—and she still didn't feel like a woman who had a husband.

She'd talked to Boone as he'd gotten dressed that morning—the smell of his new shaving soap would always remind her of those morning visits with Boone before he had the accounts in front of his face and the worries on his back—and he'd promised the platform would be ready for their pictures. It'd been a week since Maisie had gone down in the cave, and she was anxious to see how it had changed, but she was more interested in the newspaper interview they had scheduled afterwards. What would Boone have to say about their joint venture?

Mrs. Penney loaded Maisie's arms full of boxes from the wagon and pointed in the direction of the mine office. Maisie could barely see over the flimsy boxes in her arms, but they weren't the least bit heavy. She walked inside the office and dropped them on the desk.

She wasn't disappointed. How could she be? She had everything a girl could want. Plus, she was married, which meant she would never have to fall in love again. She'd be spared that indignity. At times, she did wish that Boone was more companionable, and at other times, she feared she was becoming too fond of him. But they seemed to have reached a good balance.

Even above the smell of rock was the scent of a room that working men frequented. Maisie tapped a hard-shelled hat with her fingernail. Was this the hat she wore for her unauthorized adventure into the mine? She should either keep it to remember that lucky day or throw it into the burn pile for the trouble it had caused her.

No, not trouble. This was her way out. Boone Bragg wasn't her problem. He was her solution.

"Let's get you ready." Mrs. Penney took the boxes and started pulling pieces of clothing out of them. "I'm afraid this is the only room available for your preparations. I did what I could to clean it out so your dress won't get dirty, but you'll have to be careful. We've got to hurry. When that generator runs out of coal, it's going to go dark down there. We can't take pictures with only these hat lamps."

"How am I ever going to make it down in a cave without getting these duds dirty?" Maisie asked as she removed her outer garments.

"I'm wondering the same. Let me help you with this corset," Mrs. Penney said.

"I don't know about these fancy unmentionables." Maisie sucked her stomach in and pressed against her ribcage. "They're so pretty it's indecent." Lands, did all married women wear such ruffled underthings? Of course not. She did Ma's laundry. She knew better.

Mrs. Penney scooted a stool closer and hopped up onto it, then motioned to Maisie to hand her the gown.

Maisie hadn't had someone help dress her since she was in diapers. When was that? Three years old? Ma believed in letting nature take its course, which explained a lot about Maisie's upbringing. Obviously, even Ma expected nature to stay in line when it came to young men, though.

Maisie handed the gown to Mrs. Penney, who unfurled it from on high, then jutted her chin, showing Maisie where to stand. With her arms over her head, Maisie threaded her hands into the gown. She sighed at her first feel of the softness of the fabric as it slid over her arms.

"Oh, that feels so delicious," she cooed. "What is it?"

"It's silk." Mrs. Penney hopped off the stool and tugged the dress down, working it into place. "Too tight in the shoulders and almost too short. We'll make sure the camera doesn't catch that." She turned Maisie around and buttoned up the back of the gown. "Fits nice everywhere else. Thank goodness for your healthy frame. It could use a little more padding, but your breadth makes up for it."

Maisie didn't have a sister to fret over her figure with. Her cousin Evangelina had opined over Maisie's muscular form, but Maisie hadn't given it much thought. Not until she wore someone else's gown were her shortcomings evident. But Maisie thought she'd never looked lovelier, and she didn't need a mirror to know it.

"Remember, when we are telling the story about this wedding, we don't need to divulge this part. Let people assume you picked out your gown, had it fitted, and spent months planning your special day." Mrs. Penney pointed to the white leather boots that Maisie had brought with her and motioned for Maisie to put them on. "And *this* is your special day. Forget about whatever happened before. By the time the cave is open, no one will remember that your wedding happened with no forethought."

Maisie would never forget.

Bustling her to the stool, Mrs. Penney spread Maisie's white skirt and had her sit. It sure was tough to lace up new boots while Mrs. Penney yanked a brush through her hair, then began back-combing it.

"I didn't know marriage was so hard," Maisie grunted between strokes. She'd never taken a beating this bad without fighting back.

"You're just getting started, sweetie." After a few pins scraped

Maisie's scalp, Mrs. Penney dropped the brush on the table and came to stand in front of her. Her smile was genuine. "My, my. What have I created? You are a vision. Now, let me get the preacher before we run out of time and the photographer doesn't have the light he needs. Don't wander off."

Maisie rose slowly, like she was waking from a long and distorted dream. Her head felt slightly off-balance with all that hair piled on top.

Not knowing what to do with herself, she followed Mrs. Penney outside. When she exited the building, a whistle made her spin to face a row of Boone's miners. One hat was removed, then all of them as they looked at her.

"Go on," Maisie said. "I'm nothing that requires studying."

With a soot-covered face, a grizzled man smiled. "It's your wedding day, dear. You look beautiful."

Maisie snorted. "Beautiful? I hardly think so."

"Mr. Bragg's a smart man," another miner said. "Marry a strong woman, I always say. Someone who can weather life's storms with you. You remind me of my Drusilla."

She was about to give her thanks when a bright flash erupted near her face.

Her hand flew up as a shield. "What in tarnation?"

"Great shot, miss." A man straightened from behind a tripod that had gone unnoticed until then. "The Queen of England has never had such an appreciative audience."

"I don't know that it will work for our advertisements," Mrs. Penney said, having returned with the preacher. "I can't imagine many brides requesting a dozen dirty miners to line their approach to the ceremony."

"They would if the miners were as nice as these fellas," Maisie blurted to the cheers of the group.

The photographer raised an eyebrow. "She's a natural," he said to Mrs. Penney. "You should enlist her to work on some of your other campaigns."

A natural what? Maisie wondered. There was no talent to talking to a group of people—especially guys as good-hearted as these were.

"Let's get through the day first," Mrs. Penney said. "We have work to do. Let's go."

Mrs. Penney led them through the office and into the mine shaft. Obviously safety wasn't an issue, because Maisie wasn't allowed a protective hat on account of it smashing her hair. But once they stepped into the dark cavern, Mrs. Penney was doubtful.

"You think you can find the cave from here?" Her lamp shone in Maisie's eyes because no one cared what Mrs. Penney's hair looked like.

"I found it the first time, didn't I? And I didn't have these lines from the generator showing me the way either." Feeling more comfortable now that she was out of the watchful eyes of the crew, Maisie held up her lantern and forged ahead.

It was surprising that what had seemed like a long expedition was now a quick walk through the tunnels. Boone had been busy. The way was broader now, and she could hear voices ahead, along with the sound of hammers.

"Is Boone already here?" she asked Mrs. Penney.

"He's been here all morning, getting the way cleared and getting the platform set up. Such a thoughtful groom, but it's bad luck for him to see you before the ceremony anyway."

"This isn't a ceremony. It's only some pictures."

"Don't ruin it for me."

Maisie wasn't sure, but it seemed like the crystal cavern was near. Another turn, and she spotted light reflecting off the damp, shiny wall of rock. Instead of a narrow tunnel, the walls disappeared into distant sparkling like a wet sky of brilliant stars.

"We're here," she said.

If Maisie thought a bride was guaranteed a grand entrance, she was mistaken. Mrs. Penney took off, dragging the photographer ahead. There was a delay as they figured out how to get the camera and Mrs. Penney down the ladder, but soon they were stepping over carpenters doing last-minute work on the platform.

"This looks good. Very good, indeed. John, let's get the camera set up just there. Yes. How much of the background can we catch with a shot from here? Where's the pastor? If we have you stand here with the bride and groom on either side of you, that'll cover the state of this platform. And let's not get a picture of their feet. Nothing from the knees down. We want to get the crystals hanging over their heads, anyway."

In all the hubbub, everyone had forgotten about Maisie. She held her hands against her stomach as everyone scurried around, moving lights and peering through lenses while at their feet men were constructing planks over the dark water of the cavern.

"It was nicer when it was just the two of us," Boone said.

With all the racket, Maisie hadn't heard him approach.

Standing behind her, he continued, "Those bright lights blind you to the depths of the cavern. I can't wait to take you exploring, Maisie. It's so massive . . . you wouldn't even believe it. When everyone else is gone—"

"There's the happy couple." Mrs. Penney waved them forward. "We're ready for you, Mrs. Bragg. You stand here on the pastor's right, and Mr. Bragg, you know your place. Oops, don't step backward or you'll fall off the platform. Can't have you soaked. And let's keep your veil back, Mrs. Bragg. No use in covering that beautiful face."

With so many people crowding the platform, every movement was deliberated before executed. Maisie found herself pressed against Boone as the preacher squeezed past them to take his place. They stood still as the last of the tools and wood scraps were gathered from around their feet and tossed onto a raft and out of the way.

"Those wood scraps would make a lot of stilts," Boone said so that only she could hear.

"We already have stilts. Next we'll build a tree house."

“I’m agreeable. I spend too much time underground as it is.”

The damp cave air chilled her through the gauzy dress. She rubbed her arms, but that bumped her against Boone. “Sorry,” she whispered as they adjusted the light poles. All she could see of him was the white spread of his shirt front, but it rose and lowered with a pained sigh.

“How long does it take to take a photograph?” Boone growled.

“We’re ready, we’re ready.” Mrs. Penney balanced on the edge of the platform, trying to get distance between herself and the participants. “Mr. Bragg, if you would step back so we can see the pastor between you. Good. Where are Mrs. Bragg’s flowers? Someone was supposed to carry the flowers. Good. Hold them there. No, Maisie, lower than your waist. We want to see your stunning figure. Now, face the camera.” Then, turning to the photographer, “Can you get them? Do we need more light?”

Maisie found it hard to believe that she’d been digging potatoes just before their first wedding ceremony. The potato patch seemed a world away from this magical place, but it could be directly above it.

The lights flickered as they were readjusted. Maisie could feel Boone looking at her.

“You’re beautiful,” he said. “I wasn’t expecting that.”

But was she, or was he only seeing all the fluff Mrs. Penney had trespassed against her? “Mrs. Penney is paid to make things seem nicer than they are,” Maisie said. “As soon as this is over, I’ll fade back to my unspectacular self.”

“Thank you,” he said. “I’ve suffered enough.”

She cast a quick look, but his face was as bland as his dry remark.

“Look this way, both of you,” Mrs. Penney called. “Hold still.”

Whoosh! A flash blinded Maisie. She closed her eyes, trying to reorient herself. One dizzy misstep and she’d fall into the pond.

Mrs. Penney’s voice was the only constant through the following flashes. "Two more. Tilt your heads up more. Good. Now, face each other. Let's get one of the ceremony."

The pastor opened his Bible as Mrs. Penney knelt to rearrange the train on Maisie's gown. With the lights full on them now, Maisie looked the preacher in the face. He was the same man who'd wed them at the Secret Tree, and he looked just as a preacher should—honest, trustworthy, and friendly. Maybe too perfect.

"Are you a real preacher?" she asked. "Or just a miner Boone thought could play the part?"

"I'm a real preacher. My church is in Carthage."

She twirled her flowers. "Can't ever be too sure about these things."

"I took no chances with that detail the first time," Boone said. "Don't you worry."

"Lady and gentlemen, can we get back to business?" Mrs. Penney called. "We're going to run out of light. We want a picture of you looking at each other as the vows are read. You've been to weddings before. You know what to do."

Maisie looked up at Boone and found the same concerned expression on his face that must surely be on hers. "This will never do," she said. "No one will want to be married here if we make it look so terrible."

The photographer laughed. "I don't take many wedding pictures, but I have to agree."

Boone drew his face out long, then relaxed it. "I have to think about happier thoughts."

"The stilts?" Maisie asked.

"My new shaving soap," he replied.

They must have been doing something right, because Mrs. Penney cooed at them. "That's what we're looking for. Pure adoration. Take another picture. We've got to get this."

Between the blinding flashes, Maisie found herself smiling deeply into Boone's eyes. The whole situation was ridiculous, and she appreciated that Boone shared her opinion.

If she thought the pictures in front of the preacher were odd, the picture of them alone was worse. Mrs. Penney had to take Boone's hands and put them on Maisie's waist. Maisie froze. It would be better to be here with a stranger rather than Boone. She had to face him every morning and night. For his part, Boone stayed as unbending as a statue until they gave up trying to elicit more convincing poses from him.

"That's it," Mrs. Penney said. "Job well done. These pictures will be worth hundreds of tickets sold once we're up and running. Until then, we've got other work to do. Let's get back up top and talk about the float. I'm putting you both in the parade—"

Without warning, the room was pitched into darkness.

Maisie didn't move. No one moved. Silence.

"Jerry, light your head lamp," Boone said.

There was a fumbling, then a weak beam of light from the corner of the platform. "Sorry, boss. Someone topside must have forgotten to put more coal in the generator."

"If it's the same to you'uns, I'd like to get out of here," the photographer said.

Maisie stood still, unable to tell what Boone was doing. Something brushed against her flower arrangement, so she put out a hand and found Boone's searching for hers.

"There you are." He held her fingers in a warm grasp. "I think this is my wife."

More head lamps were getting lit, including Mrs. Penney's, and the men were gathering their equipment. As they moved through their work, the beams of light reflected off the crystal walls, sending sparkles over her beautiful white dress and Boone's dark suit.

"I'm following them up," Mrs. Penney said, "before these little lamps run out and we're stuck."

Maisie shared her concern, but Boone's ease showed that he'd spent hours beneath ground. Darkness was no threat to him.

"You all go on up. I'll stay with my crew and get some work

done down here." Boone took the offered head lamp from one of his men, then turned to Maisie. "Mrs. Penney will get you home."

"I'm not going home. We're supposed to talk to the newspaper after we're finished here." Maisie wrapped the cool silk skirt around her hand to lift the hem off the ground. She couldn't see his face in the shadows, but hers was lit up from his lamp.

"I'll meet you there. It won't take me long to finish up. You'll have Mrs. Penney to show you the way."

"What do I need her for? I found this place without anyone's help, didn't I?" Maisie waited for his answering smile, but he'd already gone to join his crew, regardless of his new suit.

"Not your typical groom," the preacher said as he took Maisie's arm, "but I've never met a bride who wanted to get married in a cave either."

"I hope to meet many, many such brides," she said. "Or else this whole circus was for naught."

CHAPTER 16

Mrs. Penney was wasting no time in getting Maisie in the newspapers. Here she still couldn't find her way to her own parlor on the first try, and she was going to be interviewed on being Mrs. Bragg and all about the cavern. This was a test she hadn't studied up for.

Wearing newer clothes that she'd bought for herself, Maisie still felt like a country bumpkin next to the finely dressed women of Joplin. They probably didn't wear whatever Sears and Roebuck orders had gone unclaimed at the post office like she did. They didn't fit any better than her wedding dress, but she'd bought them herself, and of that she was proud.

Once they reached the newspaper office, Maisie wobbled her foot from side to side as Mrs. Penney spoke to the man at the desk. Soon they were escorted to an office where a black lady sat at a desk with a pencil stuck behind her ear and a pair of narrow spectacles perched on her nose.

"Mrs. Penney! How have you been?" She stood as they entered and shook Mrs. Penney's offered hand.

"Just fine, Estella. Business as usual. How about you? Has Antony convinced you to marry him yet?"

Estella's dark eyes sparkled. "I'm keeping him on the hook, but

I haven't reeled him in yet. We get along just fine, but I'm afraid marriage will tie me down. I love my job. You understand."

Not getting married because it would tie you down? Maisie had gotten married for the freedom. Was there more than women's fashions that she didn't understand?

Mrs. Penney made the introductions. "Maisie, this is Estella Harris. She and I have been collaborating on projects since we started our careers."

"But she'd already raised a family," Estella said. "Me, I jumped in as a pup."

Mrs. Penney laughed. "She would've noticed our age difference without you pointing it out."

"Just in case, Mrs. Penney. Just in case." Estella winked at Maisie. "Now, have a seat, and let's get started. I can't wait to have my byline on this story. I do appreciate you requesting me."

"Who else do I trust with my clients? Especially when I have a story that might need some extra finesse."

Maisie didn't like the silent message that passed between Estella and Mrs. Penney, especially as it was most certainly about her.

Estella picked up a notepad off her tidy desk and plucked the pencil from behind her ear. She leaned back in her chair and crossed her legs. "Tell me about yourself, Mrs. Bragg."

Maisie moistened her lips. Her life was just like every other person's. Nothing special. "My folks are Bill and June Kentworth. They live on the Kentworth ranch with my Granny Laura, and I have some cousins across the river. I don't do anything noteworthy—just feed the chickens, fix the fence, and help with the cattle when called upon."

Miss Harris's smile gleamed. "And discover amazing geological features underground?"

"Oh, that?" Maisie shifted in her chair. Was she allowed to talk about that? She'd thought she would be in trouble if the truth came out, but here Mrs. Penney was encouraging her to tell the newspaper. She might as well. If Mrs. Penney trusted Estella, she did too. "Welp, I was bored out of my noggin and looking for adventure. I'd already got the fence fixed so Mrs. Callahan couldn't get loose. Mrs. Callahan is our cow. She has the best calves, but she's a regular specter when it comes to fences. Nobody was looking for me, so I set out looking for trouble, I reckon. And I found it at Mr. Bragg's mine."

Maisie felt like she should wait until Miss Harris's pencil stopped moving, but Estella urged her on.

"Anyway, those boards over the mine entrance weren't nothing I couldn't get through, and the lock on the chest was pretty flimsy, considering. So I helped myself to a hat, a lantern, and a pickax and went down to explore."

"Maybe we should omit the part about the abandoned mine not being secured well," Mrs. Penney said. "It might look irresponsible on the part of Bragg Mining."

"Consider it done," said Miss Harris. "Please go on, Mrs. Bragg."

"Call me Maisie. I haven't got used to the *Mrs.* yet." Maisie was growing more comfortable, and her storytelling was getting better as she went. "So I took out through the tunnels, and I don't mind telling you that I was a bit worked up. It'd been a bad day, and smashing something to smithereens sounded like a good idea. There ain't many places you can swing a pickax and not get in trouble, but an abandoned mine is the exception. I mean, I'm sure everyone has had days when they'd like to take a pickax to a wall. Am I right?"

"I'm with you, sister," Miss Harris said.

"Yes, ma'am," Maisie replied. "So that's what I did. I took out through that damp cave and swung my pickax at the wall every now and then. It felt good. But one time when I hit the wall, it didn't feel the same or sound the same. It rang hollow, and the ax didn't bounce back with the same strength. I started whaling away at that same spot until it crumbled into a hole big enough that I could poke my head through."

"Amazing," Miss Harris said. "What was your first thought when you saw the cavern?"

"When I first saw the sparkles, I was hoping it was diamonds. If all those crystals would've been diamonds, can you imagine how rich I'd be?" Maisie slapped her knee, then saw her sparkling wedding ring and wondered if she wasn't that rich, anyway.

"Could you see how big the cavern was?"

"No, ma'am, but I heard my echo while I was hooting and hollering. That told me I had to show someone what I'd found. And the someone I happened to run into was Mr. Bragg."

Mrs. Penney looked at her watch. "He should be here. He must be running late."

"Is he usually tardy?" Maisie asked.

"Mr. Bragg does have a propensity toward distraction," Mrs. Penney said. "Let's continue without him."

"Tell me about first meeting your husband," said Miss Harris.

"Mr. Bragg?" asked Maisie.

Estella's eyes narrowed. "Who else would I be talking about?"

"Well, I didn't get a good look at him, seeing as how we were in the dark, and then he wasn't acting fondly toward me, seeing as how I was trespassing on his property, but I finally convinced him to follow me down the mineshaft. From there his manners improved."

"Go on," said Miss Harris.

"I say they improved, but there was an incident when we both tried to get in the cave at the same time. I stepped on his face, and he caught my skirt on fire. That's likely why he never wanted to talk to me again."

Miss Harris's forehead wrinkled. "But somehow that turned to love?"

"Love?" Maisie snorted. This reporter lady had the wrong idea. "I don't know about that."

"Don't be shy, Maisie." Mrs. Penney cocked her head and widened her eyes at Maisie. "Estella wants to know about Mr. Bragg courting you and the romantic wedding you had in the cave. Everyone wants to know that story. Then brides from around the country will want to get married in the Crystal Cave just like you did."

Oh, that was what they wanted. Maisie scratched her nose. It was one thing to take romantic pictures but quite another to make up stories about loving a man she barely knew. A man who might hear and marvel at the lies she was telling.

"We took pictures," Maisie said. "You'll have to see them."

"There's a story behind the pictures," Miss Harris replied. "A wonderful, romantic story. That's what readers want to hear. Now, if my guess is correct, you're a humdinger of a storyteller, aren't you?"

Humdinger didn't sound like a word Miss Harris had ever used in her life, but Maisie appreciated that she was trying to be friendly.

"I can be as windy as a cyclone," Maisie said. "If that's what you want . . ."

"Within reason," Mrs. Penney said. "There'll be scientific interest in the cave, but you are adding the mystique. You're providing us with the romance. Every bride looks at the world through rose-colored glasses. Turn those glasses to your story and tell it to us just like it was a fairy tale."

Maisie wished she didn't know what they were talking about, but she did. When she first met Silas, she thought he could do no wrong. Every interaction delighted her. Every comment was deemed the most clever, the most romantic. Meeting Boone was nothing like meeting Silas. She'd played on stilts with Boone like he was one of her kin. He was nothing like Silas, but she could tell a whopper, and it sounded like telling whoppers was her new job.

"It wasn't love at first sight." Maisie spotted a piece of lint beneath her stubby fingernail and began picking at it. "Down there in the dark, I could hardly see him. He was kinda like that cave. At first I didn't know what I had discovered, but it only took a few seconds of exploring to realize we had found a treasure. That's what meeting Boone was like. We shared that discovery, and it bound us together. The longer we stayed there, exclaiming over the beauty of the crystals, the brilliantosity of the room, the more we saw that there might be something between us, as well. I reckon our fate was sealed from that moment."

"Excellent," Mrs. Penney whispered.

"How did he arrange to see you again?" Miss Harris asked.

"Perhaps I was a bit forward, but I hightailed it to town to meet him instead of waiting for him to come to the ranch."

"And he was surprised?"

"You got that right." Maisie looked at Mrs. Penney for a warning, but the way was clear. "He was in the middle of a board meeting when I showed up."

Mrs. Penney lifted her hand as if she were in the classroom. "Seeing them together, we all knew immediately that matrimony was imminent. You could tell by the change in Mr. Bragg when she walked in the room. His heart was hers."

"And you knew it too?" Miss Harris asked Maisie.

Here she could be honest. "No, ma'am. He surprised the dickens out of me after the meeting when he proposed. I didn't know what hit me. At first I said no, but then after thinking it over, I came to my senses."

"Mm-hmm." Miss Harris was pleased with what she was writing. Mrs. Penney liked her answer too. This story wasn't hard to relate. Maisie felt like she might have a talent for it. "And the wedding?"

"It was really something special. I didn't spend too much time getting it ready, but it was a humdinger of a ceremony." She shot a glance at Mrs. Penney before adding, "In the most beautiful location on earth."

"Poor farm girl meets rich miner in Crystal Cave and weds at once." Miss Harris beamed. "It's a real, local Cinderella story."

"Exactly what I was thinking," said Mrs. Penney with a nod of satisfaction. "I'm sure you can fill in the blanks."

"With a few more details," said Miss Harris. "What about Mr. Bragg made you fall in love with him?"

Maisie closed her eyes and tried to picture the man she'd known for little more than a week. She'd spent more time with the armored knight in her bedroom than with Boone. Creativity was required. "He's got the most beautiful eyes. They are a deep . . ." What color were they? She wasn't sure. ". . . color and so loving. And he's very gentle. Besides setting my skirt on fire, he hasn't bested me at any game yet. Then there's his intellect. He's brilliant. Sometimes he's like a heavy wagon getting stuck in a rut and you have to get your shoulder down against it and rock it so it can go again, but when he's going again, he's the smartest person I've ever met."

"And he's rich?" Miss Harris added.

"I reckon. I didn't know that at first. He told me that it was his mine, but mine owners go bust all the time. I sure wasn't expecting a house like he has. Or even these clothes."

Mrs. Penney patted her hand as Maisie lifted the skirt to show it off. "It'll be an adjustment for Mrs. Bragg, but I think her quaint manners make the story that much richer."

"I quite agree," said Miss Harris. "It's been a pleasure, Maisie. This will be the first part in the series about the cave. Hopefully, I can tour it myself before the next installment."

"Contact me and I'll make the arrangements," said Mrs. Penney. "I'm sorry Mr. Bragg didn't make our appointment. Something urgent must have distracted him."

Maisie got back on her sore feet to leave. She'd done good. Mrs. Penney and Miss Harris were both impressed, but what would Boone think, and why hadn't he been there to help?

Besides the wedding, Boone had had a successful day. The Cornish pumps were operating, and by the time Boone had left, they'd had enough dry room to lay the electrical lines and install some of the lighting on the walls.

Bounding up the stone steps of his home, he swung the door open, then bent to unlace his dirty work boots. He hummed as he ripped the waxed laces through the eyelets, then pulled the high boots off his feet. When he heard someone coming through the entry hall, his heart lifted, but it was just Mrs. Karol, up way past her bedtime.

"Here's a hot towel for you," she said. "I thought you'd want one after working so late."

He eyed her suspiciously. Why was Mrs. Karol being thoughtful? Normally, she'd be in her room by now. "Did you wait up to tell me something?" He scrubbed the hot towel against his face. His good mood was fading at the prospect of enduring one of Mrs. Karol's legendary complaints. "It's late, so if something's amiss, you're going to have to tell me."

"It's Mrs. Bragg. She came home in a frightful mood. She's cross and restless and underfoot. Much to my relief, she finally confined herself to the library. I don't know what she's been doing in there, but I'm afraid to disturb her."

Boone had dealt with problem employees before, but he'd never been married to one. With another look at the grandfather clock tucked beneath the staircase, he thanked Mrs. Karol, then headed toward the library, worried about what he'd find. After all, he'd seen what Maisie could do with a pickax.

The thick carpet silenced his footsteps as he approached the door. Had he been thinking, he wouldn't have walked in unannounced, but when he did, she spun around mid-stride with her eyes flashing and hands outstretched.

"I didn't mean to startle you," he said. "I thought you were expecting me."

She dropped her hands. "I was. Twelve hours ago."

"I'm here now. What do you need?"

"I don't need anything. I did fine without you, or that's what Miss Harris said." Her chin lifted, and with it, a challenge.

"Miss Harris?" The name was familiar, but . . . then Boone

remembered the interview. He'd let Maisie down. "I fully intended to go, but then we got started on the electricity, and people kept coming with more questions, and . . . well, I've been at the mine since you left."

"It's fine. Miss Harris said I was a natural."

He bet she was. He'd noticed from the start how people enjoyed being around Maisie. She attracted attention wherever she went. And she probably got tired of people telling her how marvelous she was.

"I'm sorry about missing the interview. What can I do to make amends?" It wasn't the first time he'd missed an appointment, and it wouldn't be the last. "Maybe it'd be better to talk in the morning. You're probably exhausted."

"No, I'm not," she snapped. "I'm peevish, and there's no way I could sleep right now."

At least she didn't expect him to guess her moods. "What did you do on the ranch when you were out of sorts?"

"You don't have any bulls that need castrating, do you?"

Boone shuddered. "No. What other activities do you suggest?"

Her eyes drifted to the ceiling as she thought. "Saddling a horse, but Joplin's not a safe place to ride this late. Same with taking a stroll. Swimming would be divine, but . . ."

"Swimming?" Boone was often surprised by women, but no one surprised him as much as Maisie. "I'm afraid we're limited to indoor pursuits for the night."

"A good tussle might burn off my frustration." Her arms tightened, and when she leveled her gaze on him, her eyes were calculating. "Whooping up on you might ease my ire. You willing?"

He looked over his shoulder at the library door to buy himself time. Did she understand what she was asking? "Willing to fight you?"

"Not fight—wrassle. No punching, pinching, pulling hair, or biting. Just trying to pin each other down. We used to have matches all the time at the ranch." She came closer, not looking sleepy at all. "I'll try not to hurt you."

Boone set his hands on his hips. "I'm not sure you want to do this. I have a distinct advantage—"

But before he'd finished saying the word, she'd hooked his leg while at the same time shoving her weight against his shoulders. Boone's arms flew up as he crashed to the ground. Before he could gather his wits, Maisie sat on his chest with her hands pressing his shoulders into the carpet.

"That's one point for me." She rolled her eyes in boredom before leaping off him.

Boone got to his feet. Of all the tricks women had pulled to get close to him, no one had ever thought of this before. "That's how you play this game?" He circled her warily on his way to shut the library door. He wasn't sure privacy was a wise decision, but he didn't want a shocked Mrs. Karol looking in.

Maisie stood bent forward, never letting him behind her. "It's how we play it on the ranch. I'm not as strong as my brothers, but I'm hard to pin down. Amos says I'm as squirmy as a worm."

Giving her a chance to thrash him was an appropriate penance, but Boone didn't want to make it too easy for her, lest she not get her deserved satisfaction. A few swipes made it clear that a half-hearted attempt would not catch her. He had to commit if he wanted to be any competition.

Boone faked a lunge to his right, then dove left to catch her, but she spun back too fast for him. He tried to draw back, but his momentum was already working against him. Maisie bounced against him as he stumbled past, and her body weight was the final straw causing him to lose his balance. With her help, he hit the floor again, but this time he caught himself on his hands and knees.

She was on his back, and when he felt her tug against his elbow, he let it give before he even thought about it. That was a mistake. With almost no resistance, she'd managed to roll him onto his back again, and instead of the crystal chandelier over his head, he saw her freckled face framed by loosened hair and illuminated from behind.

The weight of her against his waist was intoxicating.

"That's two." She hopped off him. "You don't have to give in. I'd like a bit of a challenge."

"I'll get better. I'm learning." But what he was learning was that this woman he'd brought into his house wouldn't be satisfied arranging the flowers and overseeing dinner. She needed action and attention, even if it meant waiting up all night for him to come home.

Determined to give her the challenge she wanted, he kept his feet moving. When she darted forward, instead of relying on his strength, he jumped back so she couldn't knock his feet out from under him. The more he thought about it, the more he was convinced he could best her. She was using his weight against him. If he could protect his balance, she would have fewer weapons.

His caution seemed to delight her. Her face lit up, erasing the frustration that had covered it before, as she dodged around, trying to find his weakness.

Boone loved his business. He loved handling the challenges, turning them over and over, looking at them from different angles until he found the best solutions. He loved completely losing himself in his work, but now, being chased around his library, he had an appreciation for how good it felt to have an interest outside of his industry.

And she was definitely interesting.

Maisie had stopped watching his feet. She kept her eyes glued to his as if she could read his intention before he acted. And maybe she could. He darted an arm out, but she'd already juked away before he moved. The next time, he committed to his move. He caught her by the wrist, and then the struggle began in earnest.

He managed to reel her in, get his arms wrapped around her, but she tried him at every turn. She was swimming in his arms—pushing away, throwing herself against him. Just when he started to feel guilty for noticing the lovely feel of her body, he'd get a sharp elbow or knee that kept him focused.

She was as slippery as an eel and as strong as an ox. Boone was stronger, but with her twisting, he didn't know where she was going to attack. Shoving back against his arms made him lurch forward, and then, quick as a wink, she threw herself against his chest and got in a half twist, which left him with a weaker grip. When he went to tighten it, she found her opportunity.

With her leg between his, she hooked his ankle and shoved. Boone didn't let go, but he did crash to the floor, pulling her down on top of him.

He'd like to think it took her longer to pin him this time, but that was probably just his pride at play. The result was the same—Maisie grinning down at him with her weight thrown against his shoulders, only this time her hair was tousled and she was breathing nearly as hard as he was.

"That's three." Instead of immediately rolling away, she took a second to catch her breath.

Why in the world had he waited so long to get married? Boone reached up to push a lock of her hair behind her ear. The innocent grin she gave him told him two things. One, she'd forgiven him for his thoughtlessness and would give him another chance. Two, if he ever met the man who had hurt her, he would throw him into a deserted mineshaft to disappear forever.

He was grinning from ear to ear as Maisie climbed off him. She stood over him with her hands on her hips and her chest heaving as he sat up.

"That's the perfect way to end the evening." He draped his arms over his knees and smiled up at her. "Do you feel vindicated?"

She dusted off her hands. "I feel better about the day, I'll admit, but what are we going to do tomorrow? Can I go to the cave with you?" Her eyes showed an uncertainty that wasn't there before.

Boone had always retreated into his own world, and he'd married Maisie with the understanding that she too wanted to be left alone. He was confused, but the chiming of the clock told him that this day had seen enough. Their questions would wait until tomorrow.

"I'll think of something. C'mon," he said.

He opened the door and escorted her out of the library, turning off the light as they passed. He didn't know what he'd find to entertain Maisie all day, but if he could have this much fun at night, it would be worth his effort.

CHAPTER 17

Boone had said he'd find something for her to do, but when she woke, she found his room empty. When she checked the library, there was no sign of him there either. What was wrong? Hadn't he understood what she wanted? Maisie grumbled to herself as she went to the door. Instead of waiting on him, she would go to the cave. It was half hers, after all.

Maisie took out on foot, rolling her eyes when Mrs. Karol cheered as she left. Why did the housekeeper have to be so tetchy? Maisie wasn't asking for much from Mrs. Karol or Boone. Mrs. Karol just needed to act like a Christian lady. Boone just needed to remember that she existed.

She didn't want any romance. Life was simpler without it. No restless days trying to capture his attention. No sleepless nights trying to decipher his looks. No nothing of anything that meant something to anyone.

But independence had its price.

Maisie kicked a tin can out of the road and into the ditch. Amos would say that she was being an ingrate. She'd gotten what she wanted—to be off the ranch and to be left alone by men. It was a trial to remind herself that it was for the best. Especially when Boone went to playing on stilts with her or wrestling. Hearing him laugh got her heart all fluttery and put her of a mind to see if his heart had any flutter to it, but that was the wrong thing to do. There was no flutter in his chest for her. He was too kind to do that when she'd specifically asked him not to.

Even from the road, Maisie could see progress being made. Already, on the Kentworth side of the property, an uncovered headframe was at work, pulling ore buckets of debris out of the ground, but instead of piles of chat, the bucket held wet scraps of lumber from the construction down below. The passageway from this side must have been cleared if they were hauling from it.

"Mrs. Bragg!" Mr. Hunt waved his hand over his head and left his conversation with Mr. Gilbert to greet her. "I guess you're here about the pumps. It's a sorry business."

Maisie cocked her head. Come to think of it, she didn't hear any steam pumps, just the low motors on the generators. "What's wrong with the pumps? Didn't they get installed?"

"The vacuum piston overheated and warped. It has to be replaced. Now we're waiting for a part to get shipped in. Boone's as mad as a hornet. He has to get all the electrical out before the cave floods again."

The electrical? Last she'd heard, it was just going in. But if the pumps malfunctioned, the same water that had created all those crystals would be seeping through the porous rock and destroying all the work they'd done.

"Is Boone down there?" When Mr. Hunt nodded, she said, "I want to see him."

"Yes, ma'am. It's not safe for you to go down. I'll send word, and he'll be right up."

Or would he? Boone had promised her freedom, not companionship. He was under no obligation to give her more.

"Mr. Bragg, there's someone to see you up top," one of his new miners by the name of Howard Hughes called over the hum of the generator.

"I'm busy," Boone replied. The water might only be knee-high, but it was rising steadily. He squatted in the cold pool to reach the electric light just below the walkway. This line had been cut and the light was dark, otherwise he'd never feel cold again. With the pump down, he was in a race to get everything removed before it was ruined beneath the ever-rising waterline.

"Yes, sir. I'll tell them to come back later." Howard turned and disappeared up the newly cleared passage.

While building the platforms and walkways, Boone's first goal had been to do as little damage to the crystal floor as he could. Scalenohedral crystals was what they called the big pyramid-like structures jutting out of the ground and walls. They were pretty, but sharp and tricky to walk over, especially when they were hidden by a few feet of water. He'd felt a few give way as he found his footing, but it couldn't be helped. When possible, he marked the broken areas so he could step in the same place on his way back.

With a tug, he removed the light from its fixture and set it above him on the walkway. Four down and thirty-two to go. He shivered as he searched for another safe spot to place his foot.

"Why'd God have to make the water so cold down here?" Lewis, one of his favorite foremen, waded toward Boone with a lamp beneath his arm. He held his cold fingers out before him and flexed his fingers.

"It's this water that made this marvel," Boone said. "Thousands of years of flowing through this porous rock left all these minerals behind. Without the water, there'd be no crystals."

"It was a rhetorical question," Lewis said. "I know how crystals are made."

Boone splashed water at him. "Go on and laugh. You're the one who asked."

"I have another question that's not rhetorical. How's your

bride? I heard you were here last night until nearly one in the morning. I hope you haven't abandoned her in that empty house."

Leave it to Lewis to call him to account. Boone had sworn to himself and Maisie that he'd come up with something for her to do, but the early-morning message notifying him that the pumps had broken had changed his plans. Just when he'd made progress, the threat of failure had reappeared.

"I'll make amends tonight," Boone said, "but first we have to salvage all the electrical we can before the water gets too high. After that . . ." Boone had just reached another light when a wall of water splashed against his face.

"We both know this is going to take all day. You aren't going to see her until midnight. . . ." Lewis's voice trailed off, earning him a second look from Boone. "He's back."

Boone followed his gaze to Howard, who had reappeared in the shaft.

"I know you said you were busy," Howard said, "but Mr. Hunt thought I should mention that it's Mrs. Bragg who's hunting for you."

Boone's eyes widened. "My mother is back?"

Lewis snorted. "Your wife, moron. The one you need to spend more time with. You'd better not keep her waiting."

He really didn't have time for a chat. Not now. And even if he'd had the time, he wasn't in the right frame of mind.

Boone splashed across the floor of the cavern, only slowing down when a painful blow to his shin reminded him of the consequences of recklessness. He shouldn't have been surprised to hear that she'd come. He'd assured her that he wouldn't forget her, but he had. Now here she was at his cave . . . her cave.

He came out of the water, stumbling as his feet slipped on the uneven floor. He hauled himself up onto the platform, then hurried up the stairs to meet her.

Maisie's yellow blouse was a beam of sunshine after being in the near-dark below. She turned to him, the wind stretching stray wisps of hair across her face and teasing her cheek.

"I heard that pump turned belly up," she said. "I guess that's why you skedaddled so early this morning?"

"I apologize. Ever since I got the message, I've been in the water, salvaging what I can." He pulled on the legs of his wet trousers to get them loose from his knees. "I can't figure out what would cause the vacuum pump to burn up like that. It doesn't require any coolant."

"Has Uncle Oscar looked at it?"

"I sent for him. He'll come by after work. We've already sent off for the part, but we're going to miss out on days of work while we wait. Not only that, but it's going to destroy what we've done already. I've got to remove all the electrical lines, and I'm not sure how these walkways are going to hold up after being submerged for a few days. My men will be idle until . . ." The thought of idle workers reminded him of their last conversation. "What are you doing here?"

"I had nothing else to do, remember? Besides, I haven't seen it with the lights on."

That's right. She was coming to see the cavern, not him. "The lights are going out. We're pulling wire right now, and the water is rising."

"I was only aiming to help," Maisie said. "I should've thought to wear my old clothes. Then I could get down there and make myself useful."

It was a pity he couldn't allow it, because Boone would enjoy Maisie splashing around in the water and carrying out lines with him. He pictured her sitting on his chest, smiling down at him last night, and he thought of something he could show her.

Taking her hand, he dragged her to a cleared area. "This right here is where we're putting your cousin's visitor's center."

"Has Olive designed some plans?" Maisie crossed her arms. "I thought we were going to talk them over first."

"I wanted to. I want to. We still can. She had them delivered to me, but she's open to adjustments. We'll make some modifications, but overall they are perfect. We'll even use the rock we dug up as our primary building material." Boone pointed at the pile of rock that had come from below.

Hang on, were those chunks of zinc in the pile of discarded rock? He'd depleted the ore in the Curious Bear and hadn't expected anything on this side of the cave, but sure enough, that was what he was seeing. Little good a cache of ore would do on the walkway up to his visitor's center. Mining on this side would wreak havoc with his plans for the cave. If the water level went down on the other side, though, he'd have some breathing room in his finances. A reprieve from the threat of missed payments.

But he could think it through later, while working with the electrical lines. As long as Maisie was here, he should make the most of it.

"The front doors could go here. The waiting area needs to seat a group of twenty or so, which is how many people we'll take down at a time. Of course, the entry to the cave will be this opening here, but we'll clean it up and make it look like a normal room from the outside."

"And on the other side of this door will be a nice, wide staircase?" she asked. "Room for lots of visitors, but what are you going to do if you get one down there that can't make it back up? It was a challenging climb when we went down the first time."

"I hadn't thought of that." What else had he and his board not thought of? He needed to bring Maisie out here more often. "Any ideas?"

"You should have a warning in the visitor center. Show them how many flights of stairs it is and how small of a spot they might be required to squeeze through. Even with that, people are loath to admit they can't do something. Mark my words, someone will get down there and then run out of gumption. We used to have an old cow that would get down in the creek and then couldn't make it back up the bank. We'd hook up a come-along to her and rachet her back out of there. I don't know that it'd be legal to do that to customers, though. She'd bellow her head off while we were about it, so I imagine it rankled her a lot. Visitors probably wouldn't like it."

All this wisdom was dispensed while never slowing or losing her breath as she walked around the area. In fact, the more she talked, the faster she walked.

"Maybe you should keep up your headframe? It'd be easier to haul a person up in that rusty old ore can than to use the stairs, and if someone who isn't fit sees it, they might rethink the risk."

They'd reached his satchel, which sat next to a pile of lumber. Taking out the sketches for the building, Boone stepped off its dimensions, showing Maisie exactly how it would fit around the mouth of the cavern. She nodded in approval and moved around the area like she was already seeing it built.

"There will be some changes needed," he said. "Could Miss Kentworth meet with the board to listen to their concerns and advise us on how to solve them?"

"Olive? She's more the retiring sort. I'll ask her, but I don't know that she'll be up for it, especially with the state her mother is in." Maisie lifted her shoulders and grimaced. "Who is that man? I've seen him before."

Mr. Caine was approaching, wearing a smile as big as the hat he was fanning in front of his face.

Boone's stomach twisted. He hadn't seen Caine since he'd told him the Curious Bear was no longer for sale. He hadn't talked to him since before Justina had found out he was married. But business was business. Caine was professional. Surely he wouldn't hold a grudge, even if his daughter did.

"Mr. Caine, nice of you to come out to visit," Boone said.

"I came to see this magical cave that's got you distracted from pursuing profitable opportunities." Caine looked as if he were thinking of greeting Maisie, then decided against it.

"I think the Crystal Cave will be profitable," Boone said.

"Son, people don't pay to look at rocks. If those rocks build railroads, engines, and automobiles, that's what they pay for. I'm worried that you're wasting your time on this project instead of prospecting for your next big strike."

What he was worried about was that Boone wasn't going to sell him the mine or join in his cooperative. When he'd first made his offer to buy the flooded mine, Boone had been relieved, believing it to be a generous gesture to help him out. The more experienced miner might think he could bring up ore that Boone couldn't get to. But the more Caine complained about the lost opportunity, the more Boone wondered how charitable his offer had been.

"If there are better opportunities, why don't *you* buy those lots instead of recommending that I do so?" Boone wiggled his toes in his water-logged boots.

"For one thing, they are further afield. It would mean greasing the wheels of another municipality. But more importantly, I know what's at stake for you. Not many men are entrusted with a fortune as young as you were. Even fewer can hold on to it, especially in as volatile an industry as mining. Your father would expect me to advise you in his absence. Those pumps might do well at first, but they are difficult to manage. It takes someone with a lot of mechanical knowledge to keep them going. You've been lucky so far—"

"The pump broke," Boone admitted. "It overheated last night."

"The vacuum piston? Yeah, I could've warned you about that. Well, the offer is still on the table. If you throw in the Cornish pumps, I'll keep the bid at the original price, but you'd better hurry. Your crew is too expensive to keep waiting around with no work. Your brother wouldn't make the same mistake."

Boone had tried not to think of his parents and Grady. Stopping production on mining, investing in a tourism site, and, on top of that, getting married. He couldn't predict how his family would respond, and he'd rather not speculate on it.

But there was still another reason that Caine had taken an interest in Boone's business, and that was because of his daughter. Caine had yet to acknowledge Maisie, and that seemed to suit Maisie just fine.

But Boone was a proud man. He wouldn't let Caine snub his wife, even if it was unintentional.

"I apologize for not introducing my wife, Mr. Caine." He nodded in her direction. "This is the former Miss Kentworth. This is her family ranch, and they are leasing Bragg Mining the mineral rights as well as selling us a few acres for our project here."

What was wrong with Maisie? She was as stiff as his starched collar and kept eyeing Mr. Caine like she was afraid he would strike if she looked away.

"My pleasure, Mrs. Bragg," Mr. Caine said in a voice like maple syrup. "You're a Kentworth? That sheds some light on this unusual arrangement, doesn't it?"

Maisie swallowed hard. What was she upset about? Their arrangement *was* unusual. She and Boone both knew it, and Boone wasn't surprised that Mr. Caine recognized the fact.

When Maisie moved, she did it decidedly. Boone wasn't expecting her to wrap her arms around his waist and shelter beneath his arm.

"My husband and I are very happy together," she said. "It would be a mistake to assume otherwise."

Boone *was* happy, but that didn't explain her actions. Why was she acting like this in a field full of his employees?

Maisie grunted a warning at him and squeezed him with a strength that made him wince.

"Yes, we're happy." His brow wrinkled as he looked at her, wondering at her sudden need for reassurance. But the knowing look on Mr. Caine's face showed that Boone was the only one confused.

"I didn't mean to suggest otherwise," Mr. Caine said. "How fortunate to find love right where it's most beneficial, but I'll repeat my concern that this venture isn't going to be beneficial at all. I wish you well, nonetheless. Forgive me if I don't stay. I have other issues to address today."

Maisie didn't move until Mr. Caine had ridden over the rise. Then she released Boone, turned her feet toward town, and left without a word.

How did men ever puzzle out what their wives were thinking? But she was gone, and now Boone was free to look after all the lights that had gone out in his cave.

Mr. Caine did not like her.

Maisie covered the road to town. It had come to her that he was the man who had walked into Boone's office the day Boone first offered her the proposal. He'd also witnessed her and Silas arguing in front of the butcher shop. Were his hackles always raised, or was it only when Maisie came around? She'd had those high-on-their-horse types snub her before when she came to town, but it was usually women, and it wasn't usually so personal. What did this Mr. Caine have against her?

Maisie came over the rise near the Joplin Children's Home and saw Mr. Caine's horse. He'd stopped to exchange pleasantries with Mrs. Bowman, a young caretaker employed by the home. This was Maisie's chance to set him straight.

Maisie sped up her footsteps, barely catching him as he bade Mrs. Bowman farewell.

"Mr. Caine, we need to settle something," Maisie said as she approached his horse.

Mr. Caine's surprise at seeing her was quickly covered by a welcoming smile. "Mrs. Bragg, how may I help you?"

Maisie didn't like standing on the ground, looking up at him, but she wasn't intimidated. "What have I ever done against you?" she asked. "I would consider that maybe you have a feud with my kin, but you didn't even know I was a Kentworth and still you showed your teeth."

His polite smile froze in place. "What have you done against me?" He lifted his eyes to a point on the horizon before deciding on his answer. "I saw you at the Bragg offices and knew you looked familiar, but it wasn't until that day at the butcher shop that I remembered where I'd seen you before. I used to see you about town with a miner who'd had a bit of luck. Marsh was his name, I think. There was one night on a streetcar that I saw the two of you . . ." He raised an eyebrow. "Let's just say I was thankful that my own daughter doesn't carry on like that in public . . . or private."

Maisie tried to swallow, but her throat refused to cooperate. "I thought he was going to marry me," she said at last. "If things had worked out—"

"I'd say they worked out very nicely for you. Boone's parents always feared some woman would catch him unawares. Some woman not afraid to barter her charms. What was it, three months ago, that you were with Marsh, and now you're married to Bragg? You don't even know him." He shook his head. "I applaud your success, but don't expect me to approve. Good day, Miss Kentworth."

He reined his horse toward town, leaving Maisie choking in shame.

CHAPTER 18

Ever since her confrontation with Mr. Caine, Maisie had floundered. She was ashamed of her previous behavior. She'd already tried to make amends to her family for the disgrace she'd brought on them, but she'd thought that once she was married, that reputation would be left behind. With Olive's blueprints ready and the publicity for the cavern beginning, Maisie was excited about the progress they were making, but she had to be careful. She lived in dread that she'd do something unladylike and Boone would decide she was a common trollop. Just like Mr. Caine had.

Better to play it safe, follow the rules, and keep a healthy distance. If only Mrs. Penney wasn't coming to coach them for their public appearances.

Maisie spread muscadine jelly on her toast as she regarded Boone at the other end of the breakfast table. She'd reminded him about Mrs. Penney's visit today. He'd nearly cut himself shaving when she mentioned it, but he'd agreed to stay home until they'd met.

He eyed her over the edge of his cup of coffee. "What shall we do while we wait for Mrs. Penney?" he asked. "Do you need to get any wrestling out of your system?"

It wasn't the first time he'd asked, but ever since Caine's accusations, she couldn't tussle with a clean conscience.

"And get all frazzled before she gets here? No, thank you." Maisie smoothed the braid lying over her left shoulder. "We could do some shooting." That sounded safe enough. "What kind of firearms do you stockpile?"

"I didn't know a stockpile was required. Are we anticipating an invasion?"

Before she could answer, Mrs. Penney arrived.

"Good morning, dear ones!" She outpaced Mrs. Karol, who gave up on announcing her and spun to exit the room. Mrs. Penney positioned herself next to Boone and presented a folder. "Look what I have here. Guess. Well, I'll tell you. They're the pictures from the cavern. Gorgeous, they are!"

She slid Boone's plate of fried potatoes aside and dropped the folder before him. Maisie was out of her seat in a heartbeat and leaning over Boone's shoulder as he pulled a thick, glossy paper out of the folder.

Maisie gasped and wrapped her arms around her waist. Was that really her and Boone? She remembered them posing together in the cave. How could she forget the awkward instructions where they had to all but threaten him with financial ruin to get him to put his hand on her waist? But the picture didn't look awkward. She tilted the image to catch the morning light. Maisie had had two photographs taken in her life, so she wasn't used to seeing herself on paper, but this was beyond belief. She looked like some glamorous lady. As she studied the picture, Maisie pressed her hand to her cheek. Was it really that smooth? And her eyebrows? She ran her finger along her brow.

"It's really you," Boone said. "Don't you remember taking the picture?"

"How could I forget?" She looked at Boone's image. He was handsome, but she couldn't understand how elated he looked. "I just didn't expect it to come out like this."

"We look so happy. Like a real bride and groom." He shook his head. "I didn't expect that either."

"Why not?" Mrs. Penney gloated. "You *are* a real bride and groom, and a more handsome couple has never felt Cupid's arrow. People are going to be enchanted with you. All it's going to take is a little training to stop some of those less-than-ideal statements coming from your mouth."

Maisie chuckled. Boone might be the one who signed Mrs. Penney's paycheck, but she had him dead to rights.

"What am I supposed to do?" Boone asked.

"I'll tell you what you're supposed to do. Give this wife of yours whatever she wants, because she's golden!" Mrs. Penney sashayed to Maisie's side and gave her a dramatic kiss on the forehead. Maisie laughed roughly to hide her wistfulness as she took a seat. She yearned for the people who knew her best, her parents and granny, but Mrs. Penney was becoming a friend.

"Maisie is a natural, Boone. So much character. She had Estella eating out of her hand. If we're not careful, Maisie will be a celebrity."

"I don't know about that. . . ." Maisie shot a glance at Boone to see how he was taking her praise.

"Isn't that what we want?" he said. "The more attention she gets, the more people hear about the cave."

"Estella wants to interview you before she runs the piece, so we have to make sure our story is consistent. We can't have our little country girl telling everyone how the rich prince fell in love with her in the magical cave if the prince isn't willing to put on a show as well."

"It's fine," Maisie said. "He doesn't need to say anything about me."

"I'll just act normal," Boone said.

"No, you won't," said Mrs. Penney. "A man does not act normal when in love." She took a seat and reached for a piece of toast. "It's common knowledge."

Boone's chest puffed out. "Did you see this picture?" He held up the photograph. "I did a good job there, didn't I?"

"And we need more of that." Mrs. Penney gave them each a look-over. "Boone, you can be the reclusive bachelor who evaded all the ladies of town."

"No one will question that," he said.

"Right. And it won't surprise anyone if Maisie does most of the talking for the two of you. Let her take the lead, especially on the romance. If they ask some technical questions about the mining, the novelty of the work you're having to do, then of course you'll speak up, but otherwise, you sit back and let Maisie talk while you gaze at her longingly."

His eyes darted to Maisie, then quickly away. "I'll try."

"Then do it now," Mrs. Penney said. "Come over here, Maisie. He's going to gaze longingly at you." She pulled out a dining room chair beside Boone and motioned Maisie into it. "Now, I'm going to talk to Maisie, and while I'm doing that, you act your part, Boone."

Leaning forward with her elbows on the table, Mrs. Penney waggled her eyebrows. "Tell me about your ranch, Mrs. Bragg. What was life like before you discovered the cave?"

"Just like any other ranch, I reckon. Granny Laura runs several hundred head of cattle, and she and my pa—"

"Look at her, Boone," Mrs. Penney said. "Listen like what she's saying is the most important information in the world."

"I listen with my ears," he said, "not my eyes." But he leaned toward Maisie and widened his eyes.

Maisie drew back her head. "He looks like a hoot owl about to gobble up a mouse. How am I supposed to talk with him looking like that?"

"This is worse than I thought," Mrs. Penney said. "You can't have your face like that."

"How about this?" He blanked his expression until it looked like he might drift off to sleep.

"Try again," Mrs. Penney said. "Now, Maisie, about the ranch . . ."

Maisie swallowed before continuing. "My granny and my pa work the cattle, and then my pa is in charge of the farming. We grow lots of vegetables to feed ourselves. Got walnut and pecan trees too."

"You have walnuts?" Boone perked up. "You think you could get me some? I haven't had walnut ice cream all summer." He looked up at Mrs. Penney's grunt of disapproval. "What? I'm listening to her, aren't I? I heard about the walnuts."

"Then don't listen to her." Mrs. Penney bounded out of her chair and took Boone by the chin. "Turn your head this way and take her hand. Now, instead of listening to her, I want you to think thoughts about how special Maisie is. Think about how gorgeous those brown eyes are. Think about the joy in her smile. Think about a time when you saw her and were just flabbergasted by her beauty."

At first, Boone's eyes cast about as if not knowing where to land, but then something must have occurred to him. He suddenly fixed Maisie in his gaze, and she felt like she was being scorched. Her heart thudded against her ribs. She shouldn't feel this way. The last time she felt this way, it led to disaster.

"Good," said Mrs. Penney. "Whatever you're thinking of, that's the look we're searching for."

"I'm remembering her on the floor in the library the other night," Boone said.

A crash jerked Maisie's attention away from him. It was Mrs. Penney. Stepping backward, she had gotten tangled in the chair and fallen. She was sprawled out on the floor with her feet kicking in the air.

"What in the world?" she huffed. "I thought my chair was beneath me, but when I went to sit in it . . ." She pulled herself up, smoothed her hair, and tugged down her bodice. "Shocking. I was shocked." Her sputtering was more confused as it went on, but then she caught up with herself and collected her thoughts. "Whatever you say to the newspaper, Boone, you can't say that!"

Boone stood and dropped his napkin on the table. "This is getting me nowhere. I have pumps to repair and electric lamps to install. Just tell me where to be and when. I'll keep my mouth shut."

Mrs. Penney covered her mouth and giggled like a schoolgirl right there next to the upturned chair. "I declare, I've never had a subject to work with like the two of you, but I couldn't be happier. This man is besotted with you, girl. I knew it the first time you walked into the boardroom."

Maisie felt the sharp twist of worry before she convinced herself it wasn't true. She'd had a man in love with her, and Boone acted nothing like him.

"Now, what do you say we plan the float for the Founder's Day parade?" Mrs. Penney availed herself of another piece of toast. "I have some spectacular ideas for the Crystal Cave float. It will be—"

"We'll have to plan that later," Boone said. "I need Maisie's help."

Maisie sat taller in her chair. "You need me to fix the pumps and ramps?"

He winced. "That can wait. We need to pick out the hardware and electrical items for the visitor center."

Maisie's brow wrinkled. She knew more about construction than pumps, but it was still next to nothing. But Mrs. Penney was gathering her papers.

"I'll get to work on the float and present my ideas soon. I don't want to get in the way. Enjoy your day together." Mrs. Penney beamed at them, then sashayed out of the room, humming to herself.

"She was never going to let me leave as long as she had you in there," Boone said. "Dragging you along was only a matter of self-preservation."

All that talk about marriage and romance had thrown Boone off track. He had plans for the day, and everyone should know by now that once Boone had a plan, all other matters faded into oblivion. Mrs. Penney and Maisie should be careful. If he ever got it into his mind to woo Maisie, then he wouldn't be able to attend to any other business until he'd succeeded. For now, he'd better think less about Maisie and more about completing the work on the cave.

"So we aren't going to shop for the visitor's center?" Maisie hurried to keep up with him.

"Might as well," he said. "We have Olive's plans completed and a good idea how much to order. I'm glad her estimate is so specific. We don't have a penny to spare."

"I don't mean to pry into your family's goings-on," Maisie said, "but ain't they rich? Why fret over the cost of furnishing the cave when the paneling in your parlor uses five different kinds of rare wood?"

This wife of his was a quick study. Boone hadn't thought about how it would look to her, but he understood her question.

"My parents are wealthy. The house belongs to them. They didn't want me and my brother to struggle like they did starting out, but neither did they want us to be wastrels, so they decided to gift us with our inheritance when we each turned twenty-one. Grady took his to Indian Territory and has had success with his mines there. I had some early success with the Spook Light Mine, but the Curious Bear has been a disappointment. I've borrowed against the Spook Light to fund the building of this cave. If it fails . . ." He shrugged.

"What about all your parents' money? Where is it going?"

"They already have it promised to charity, and I don't blame them. I'm starting out with much more than most people. If I can't make it a success, then I don't deserve an easy life."

Maisie thought this over. "All those women who chased you, did they know about this arrangement?"

"What do you think? Do you think it was my charm that beguiled them, or the thought that I had unlimited funds?" He had to laugh at himself. He'd done everything he could to be disagreeable, and still they were relentless. Boone plucked a bloom off a trumpet vine growing out of the fence. "They never knew, and I wasn't about to babble family business all over town."

"So instead, you married a simple woman from the country who wouldn't expect riches and easy living?" The freckles dusting Maisie's nose were fading the more time she spent away from the ranch. He'd have to remedy that.

"Anyone who thinks you're a simple woman is deceived." He tossed the bloom in the gutter as they reached Fourth Street and turned toward the business district. "I'm finding more and more complications as time goes on."

He met her concerned look with a reassuring grin, then looked down at the gutter. He should have given her the flower instead of throwing it away. Mrs. Penney would be so disappointed.

They reached Mr. Belden's shop. As Boone held open the door, Maisie passed inside and headed toward the basket of lamp bulbs on the counter. When Boone was a boy, no one had electric lamps in their homes or businesses. Now you could find as many shapes and designs of electric fixtures as gas fixtures. It was amazing how quickly the world could change. Electric lights, water pumps, crystal caves, and a wife—who could tell what the future held?

Evidently, the immediate future held another awkward meeting with Mr. Peltz.

Upon seeing Boone enter the shop, Peltz cut off his conversation with Belden. Pinning Boone in his gaze, Peltz squared up as Boone approached.

"Mr. Belden," Mr. Peltz said, "before you sell Mr. Bragg any of your wares, you should consider our agreement. I must have ample supplies to construct our electrical park, or I'll take my business elsewhere."

"There's no need to do that. I'm capable of meeting the needs of both projects," Mr. Belden replied.

"I'd hate to find myself short because you allowed someone else to use them. Mr. Schifferdecker's park will be the biggest order of your lifetime. You wouldn't want to lose it."

"Mr. Belden shouldn't have to choose between us," Boone said. "I'm not looking for a fight with you."

"But that's what you're going to get," said Peltz. "Everyone will have to choose between us. Every weekend they'll have to decide if they want to spend the day enjoying the sights and sounds of the magical Electric Light Park, or if they want to look at a hole in the ground. You'd be better off closing your doors today."

If Peltz thought he was intimidating Boone, he was mistaken. When Boone refused to be cowed, Peltz bustled out of the shop, bumping Boone's shoulder as he passed.

Belden breathed a sigh of relief once he disappeared. "Sorry about that, Mr. Bragg. That Mr. Peltz gets hired on by Schifferdecker, and he thinks he owns the town. Let me assist Mr. Daniel, and then I'll be with you."

Maisie had been tense before, but now she shrank behind him.

"Don't worry about Mr. Peltz, Maisie," said Boone. "He's just afraid we're going to take business from Schifferdecker's Park."

"Maisie Kentworth?" It was Mr. Daniel, the drugstore owner. Boone knew him but didn't understand why he was storming toward them. "Those escapades of you and your kinfolk are the reason I'm here. Your cousin broke my lamp bulbs when you rioted in my shop."

"It wasn't a riot," Maisie said. "Just a misunderstanding."

"Fighting over some man." Mr. Daniel turned to Mr. Belden. "I wouldn't let her within a half mile of a store that contained this much glass. Trouble waiting to happen."

Boone felt obligated to protect his wife's honor. "Maisie is Mrs. Bragg now, and I can assure you that she would never entertain the notion of—"

"Boone Bragg, is that you?" Heidi Kleinkauf darkened the doorway like a cave-in blocking escape. "Is it true? Did you marry Justina Caine?"

"No!" Boone tugged on his collar. "I most certainly did not." He had stepped aside in an attempt to present his wife, but Miss Kleinkauf advanced and slapped him across the cheek. "What was that for?" he asked.

"If you were going to marry anyone besides me, it was supposed to be Justina Caine." Miss Kleinkauf rubbed her red palm against her festooned skirt. "She was the only one I could fathom catching you if I didn't. How dare you lower yourself with some backwards—"

"Ain't nobody going to hit my husband besides me," Maisie bellowed as she snatched at Miss Kleinkauf's hat.

Boone caught Maisie by the shoulders. Had he not spent time wrestling her, he would've been unprepared for the strength of her attack. He pushed her away, pulling Miss Kleinkauf's hat off with her. Maisie threw the hat on the ground and clawed at Boone's arm.

"You call me backwards, but here you come in and slap my husband across the face. He don't owe you nothing," Maisie yelled.

If they were home, Boone would have enjoyed this activity, but not at the risk of marring Miss Kleinkauf's spotless complexion with alley-cat scratches. When Maisie lunged again, he had no choice but to pin her against the counter. One flying elbow, and the basket of lamp bulbs bounced off the counter and disintegrated into shining shards of glass on the floor.

The room went silent.

Mr. Daniel whistled. "I warned you." He walked to the exit, glass crunching beneath his feet.

Miss Kleinkauf's face was streaked with tears. "You deserve what you have coming," she said to Boone. "Years of misery." Keeping her eye on Maisie, she snatched up her hat and retreated to safety outside the shop.

Maisie snorted. "Serves her right."

Boone looked at the broken bulbs on the floor. "I'll pay for those," he told Mr. Belden. "My apologies."

Mr. Belden rubbed his forehead. "If your Crystal Cave is as entertaining as that, you'll sell plenty of tickets."

"Maisie?" More crunching glass as another couple entered the small shop.

Boone didn't want to look. So far, everyone who had entered had brought trouble. But this time, it was Maisie's parents.

Her pa removed his hat and stepped forward, his face pale and his brow lowered. "Your housekeeper told us we could find you here."

"What's wrong?" Maisie asked.

Her ma's tear-stained eyes only sought her daughter's. Maisie's chin trembled. Boone looked at her pa, and he had the same stricken look.

"It's your aunt Myra," he said. "She's gone."

CHAPTER 19

Boone draped black crepe on his wagon as he waited for Maisie to come outside. For the first time since his marriage, he wished his parents were home. Seeing Maisie's tears made him feel helpless. It was special, the way her family gathered together and supported each other, their sorrow made more poignant by fond memories and shared stories, but he was an outsider. Graham Buchanan and Matthew Cook, the other two men who had married into the family, weren't excluded. They joined in, comforting their wives, helping with arrangements, offering the right platitudes, and maybe the family would have welcomed the same from Boone, but he didn't feel like he'd earned the right. His marriage didn't feel authentic.

Boone had done what he could. He sent some of his men to help on the ranch while the family grieved. He offered to help Oscar's boss, Mr. Blount, while Oscar was absent from the Fox-Berry Mine. Practical help, but it didn't touch the pain Maisie felt.

Maisie's black gown looked like a dismal blot against the cheery flowers along the drive. With the help of her family, she'd prepared for the day. Calista had taken her female cousins to shop for appropriate mourning clothing—the older generation having already suffered enough losses to have a suit in their closets. While in town,

Maisie had gone with her mother and Granny Laura to tend Uncle Oscar's home and be with Olive and Willow, Olive's sister. At least they had each other. A few days of Maisie's absence had affected Boone in ways he didn't fully understand.

He helped her into the buggy, proud of her poise as she sat straight-backed on the seat. He'd missed her. He was tired of only hearing his own voice in his head. He needed more Maisie. But now wasn't the time. No rowdy physical contests in the evening. No boring her with progress reports and business decisions he was contemplating. It was killing him, but he'd give her space. He'd stay away if that was what she needed.

He wouldn't claim a spot in her heart he hadn't earned.

It was the best funeral Maisie had ever attended. Reverend Dixon at the Tabernacle Church had let Matthew use the building on account of the size of the crowd. If Matthew's preaching for the funeral was any indication, he'd be in high demand ere long. He told family stories about Aunt Myra and her younger days, when she was strong and active. Told about how she and Aunt Polly had hit it off when Myra was being courted by Uncle Oscar. About what a good mother she had been to Willow and Olive. How the character of the daughters was testament to the goodness of the mother.

No matter how obedient and good Maisie tried to be, she'd never be as nice as Aunt Myra had been, and Aunt Myra had died anyway. Aunt Myra's kindness didn't keep death at bay. What would people say about Maisie when she passed? Would she have any children to mourn her? Was she apt to do any charitable deeds that others might recollect at her funeral?

Why couldn't Maisie be a gentle woman like Aunt Myra? She wished she had someone to hold her hand and tell her it would be fine. Boone was sitting right next to her, but he might as well have been down in the cave for all the company he'd been.

She was feeling low-down and sorry for herself until Matthew turned it around and started talking about heaven. He reminded them that Aunt Myra wasn't gone forever but had gone to a new home. No matter how nice Aunt Myra had been, she couldn't earn her place in heaven. That place was bought by the sacrifice of Jesus, and faith in Him was what gave Aunt Myra the right to call it home.

Maisie breathed easier. She knew that her hope lay in Christ's righteousness, but the words of the Scripture had never felt as important as they did now. No matter how badly she'd bungled her life, her salvation wasn't dependent on her efforts. Aunt Myra believed too, and she was finally healed. She could finally laugh and run and not get winded or break out in that horrible cough.

Maisie's eyes smarted with tears. What she'd do to hear that cough again. And then there was Olive to think of. Olive had spent most of her life taking care of her mother. They'd been impossible to separate. How Olive would miss her!

Matthew finished up his remarks, and the crowd started passing by the coffin to pay their last respects. From the church, they'd go out to the ranch and bury Aunt Myra in the family cemetery, then everyone would gather at Granny's for a meal provided by their neighbors.

After the last people filed out, the family was left for their final minutes. Uncle Richard and Aunt Polly had Evangelina and Calista gathered together with their brother, Corban. Uncle Calbert, aged for his young family, had gathered his children to approach the coffin together. Uncle Oscar was supported by Willow and Olive as they helped him out of his seat. Her own pa was heading toward her, trying to gather his chicks for the final visitation.

"I don't want to intrude," Boone whispered, his eyes on her father. "I'll wait for you outside."

Had she not been in a church and at a funeral, Maisie would've cried her protest. Why was he leaving her? Didn't he know that she wanted him with her? Her parents were a comfort, but they weren't the ones who should've been with her.

Seeing poor, distraught Uncle Oscar was the last straw. Maisie needed air. She needed Boone and his calming influence. Dabbing her eyes with her black-edged handkerchief, she took out the same door she'd seen Boone use. Outside, people were clumped into sad groups, old friends reunited and connections to the Kentworth family being compared. Here, among the respectful talk, were also words about the price of jack, the completion of Mr. Blount's house, and the plans for the parade. Proof that life did go on for the rest of the world, even if Aunt Myra wouldn't be in it.

But Maisie wasn't ready to think about tomorrow. She wanted to pour out her grief, and it wouldn't be right to do it on Willow or Olive. They had their own burdens. That was why she needed Boone. She needed someone she wouldn't burden more. Someone who was strong enough to handle her grief.

Maisie pushed through the crowd, ignoring the pitying looks. Where had he gone? She wandered to the grounds where the horses and buggies had been left . . . and saw him.

Not Boone. It was Silas, and he was headed her way. Maisie pressed her hand against her forehead. Silas was not who she was searching for, but he'd been searching for her.

He approached, as confident as a rooster in his own coop. "When I heard about your aunt Myra, I had to come." His face carried all the appropriate trappings of grief and concern. "I know how you respected her. How are you doing, Maisie?"

He said her name with the tenderness she'd been seeking ever since the awful pronouncement.

"You shouldn't be here," Maisie protested. "If Hank or Amos sees you—"

"I don't care. I couldn't live with myself if I didn't at least try to check on you, Maisie-girl. I wanted to remind you that your aunt loved you. You were special to her. Just like you're special to me." He took a step closer.

Maisie put up her hand. "Stop right there. Don't come any closer." She needed Boone, and Silas was no substitute.

"A funeral isn't the place for wooing," Silas said. "I know better than that."

"Plus, I'm married," Maisie said.

"That puts a damper on it, but don't you worry. I'm watching out for you. As long as I'm around, you don't need to worry. That's what I told that Mr. Caine too. If you need any help from me, he just has to let me know."

Caine? The mention of his name, on today of all days, angered Maisie.

Silas, who knew her as well as anyone, realized his mistake. "My only reason for being here today was to talk to you. I was worried that you might get forgotten in all the hubbub. I didn't want you to be sad without anyone noticing."

But Silas had noticed. What was she to do with that? He was showing her the compassion and sympathy that her husband had failed to show.

Did Silas recognize the gratitude in her tears? He must have because he seemed satisfied. He tipped his hat, then, with a ghost of a smile, turned and left before anyone spotted him.

Maisie's tears ran anew. Silas was a sorry character. He didn't deserve her regard. But it broke her heart that the one who did wasn't there when she needed him.

CHAPTER 20

The carpenter sanded the benches as Boone watched the road. In the week since the funeral, Boone had repaired the water damage to the walkways and the stage, replacing the warped boards and reinstalling the electrical lines. Finally, he was making progress on the cave again. He drew a deep breath filled with the scent of fresh lumber and the gritty smell of the drainage coming out of the pumps. If everything went well from here, they would be ready to open on schedule.

While the electrical man was rehanging the lamps, Boone was focused on the construction of the visitor center. He hoped Maisie approved of what he had done with Olive's designs. He had some questions about her sketches, but with the recent loss of her mother, he didn't want to bother Miss Kentworth. If he was giving Maisie her space, how much more would he give her cousin?

But today Maisie would see it. He'd put off the invitation as long as he could, just to give her time. Today he'd finally mentioned the possibility of her coming to see the center and the cave, and she'd jumped at the chance, to his relief. Perhaps mourning was over. Perhaps they could recover the ground they'd lost between them.

Here she came, walking the dirt road toward him.

"I left the buggy for you," he said. "You didn't have to walk."

"I needed to hit the trail," Maisie said. "Nothing like seeing this to make you want to take a long walk out of town." She held out a folded newspaper.

Local Bachelor Finds Treasure and Love Beneath the Surface, read the headline. Boone felt his stomach flip. He'd done just as Mrs. Penney had instructed for their interview with Miss Harris. He'd felt like a fool, gazing at Maisie while the reporter asked them questions, especially since they hadn't as much as shared a laugh since the death of her aunt, but he'd followed instructions.

On the front page of *The Joplin Globe* was the picture of him and Maisie, looking as romantic as any bride and groom could. He shook his head. "It makes me question every photograph I've ever seen. It looks so real." He flattened the page but couldn't focus on the words. Not when he could feel Maisie's stare.

"What do you think of the interview?" she asked. "Miss Harris must have done some digging on you. There's a lot I didn't know. Like the fact that you own the Byers Building too. I didn't know that. I got my first professional haircut in that beauty parlor."

"Father thought it was important to diversify."

"My lands, Boone. To read this, every single woman in Joplin was covering themselves in flypaper hoping to catch you."

"I thought I mentioned that in my proposal." He tugged on his collar. "What's this? It quotes you as saying, *'Boone has the most beautiful eyes. They are a deep color and so full of love. He's also brilliant. Whenever I'm stuck, Boone knows just what to do to get me going again. He's the smartest person I've ever met.'* Did you really say that?" He watched for her response, hoping that she'd meant a portion of it.

She didn't meet his eyes. "I did just like Mrs. Penney said. And did you read the part about how you did all the shopping for the wedding? You shopped for my wedding dress and put the whole ceremony together. Somehow Estella made that sound romantic. I was afraid it would sound like I didn't care about my own wedding."

"It sounds very romantic," Boone said, "because this is a fairy tale. It's not true. I don't know how we're supposed to act when the whole town is reading this." How was he supposed to act, period? It was dawning on Boone that he was failing as a friend, not to mention failing as a husband.

Maisie took the paper from him and folded it up. "According to Mrs. Penney, this is ad copy. It's going to be quoted in the ads we run across the tri-state area. All we need is for them to enjoy the story and come see where it happened. It shouldn't be too taxing on you."

He'd looked forward to showing her the visitor center and the cave, and he'd already gotten crossways with her. "I'm sorry, Maisie. It was brave of you to come out this soon after your loss. I didn't mean to be curt."

"Brave of me? I've been itching to get out of the house. How can I heal if all I do is sit around and stew?" She leveled her shoulders like she was preparing to tear into a wall of granite. "Now, show me this building that you and Olive built."

Olive was the absent architect. Maisie's brother Amos had taken care of all the correspondence between them, passing messages back and forth during her time of mourning, and Boone had learned to appreciate raucous Amos. Observing the stubbornness and character behind her brother's pranks, Boone better understood Maisie. Despite her easygoing attitude, there was an unyielding toughness that you didn't want to run afoul of.

Her eyes never left the new building as they approached. Made of limestone, calcite, and other minerals that had been excavated there on site, the building blended well with the surroundings, modestly refusing to compete with the gorgeous countryside.

"I love how you left the rocks at the top uneven," she said. "It makes it look like a castle."

"Olive added that detail in a later draft."

"The doors are so narrow and tall. Was that the plan all along?"

"They aren't narrow. It's just the height that throws the perspective off."

She seemed pleased as she ran her hand along the line of mortar that curved between the oddly shaped stones. “I’m glad you decided to build with these rocks. It wouldn’t seem right to have a smooth, perfect facade out here. Rough can be beautiful.”

Boone looked at the faded calico she wore. He’d noticed that she had taken to wearing her farm clothes after the funeral, but she was beautiful indeed. “The rough exterior was Amos’s idea.”

“He and my whole family are planning to come for the grand opening. I told them that I expect them to buy their own tickets. No freeloaders on Bragg’s dime.”

“Your family can come for free, Maisie. I can’t wait to show them what was here beneath their farm.”

“Don’t you be doing them any favors,” she said. “You bought a few acres and are leasing the rights for the rest. It’s yours now. Be firm, or next thing you know, Evangelina, Corban, and Hank will expect you to put them up in town and feed them buttered rolls every day.”

“Thanks for the warning. Now, I didn’t let them move the furniture inside until you were here to show them where it should go. If I remember rightly, you had strong opinions on the subject.” If Boone remembered rightly, Maisie had strong opinions on every subject.

He didn’t have to say more. The Maisie who had first crashed his board meeting was back, directing his men on where to put the benches in the waiting room, where she wanted the ticket desk, and speculating on whether there’d be room for tables so people could enjoy their refreshments as they waited for their tour. He only had to stop her three times from lifting the heavy benches herself and remind her that if she’d just point, the men would move them for her.

“Will this wall be enclosed, or are you leaving it open?” she asked.

“For now, it’s open so we can get the construction equipment down below. Once we’re finished, we’ll close it up.”

"Or you could leave it open and build an arbor here. Put some tables out, and in nice weather, people can eat outside."

"I like that idea." He could picture the day when the building would be filled with people and he and Maisie would come to visit. They'd stand here and listen to the awestruck tourists when they came back up. They'd see faces lit up with the wonder and majesty of God's creation. They'd get to share it with the world . . . and each other.

"And this area? What are we going to sell here?"

We. The word meant so much coming from her. "We'll have postcards, pictures, jewelry . . ."

"Jewelry?" Maisie touched her neck. "What kind of jewelry?"

She didn't have a necklace, did she? Boone would remedy that. "I've hired a jeweler to make items from the crystals." When her face hardened, he hurried to assure her, "Just from the crystals that were broken in the construction. We aren't damaging any purposely."

"Well, that's a dandy idea," she said at last. She toed the staircase that led into the ground. "And this is the entrance?"

As if in response, Gilbert came out of the tunnel. "The lights are all set, boss. We're just coming up for dinner."

Perfect. Boone wanted to show her, and it would be better without the crew down there.

"We'll go down as soon as the stairs are clear," Boone said to Maisie. He watched with pride as the men filed up out of the inconspicuous hole in the ground and greeted his wife. Instead of hanging back, she shook their hands and thanked them for their work. Boone saw appreciation in their eyes that was sometimes missing when they spoke to him. He paid them a wage. It was what they expected and what they needed, but evidently they craved something more—a kind word and appreciation from the owner of the mine. He'd do well to remember that. Maybe even Maisie would like a kind word from him.

The line of men ended with the stragglers huffing and puffing as they hauled themselves up the last flight of stairs.

Boone motioned to Maisie. "Shall we?"

She clapped her hands together. "Do we need lanterns and hats?"

"Not anymore, but I'll bring one just in case."

It was strange to be in a cozy little building and step through a narrow passageway, knowing it would lead to a huge expanse. Boone started down the staircase, trying to imagine what it would be like to take this journey for the first time. Where his imagination ran thin, Maisie was there to supply the details.

"Those lights are hot. I can feel them warming my head when I pass under them. How long is this staircase? It feels like we're going all the way to China. Why is there a divider on the staircase? Why make it smaller? Look at the water dripping down the wall. Is it clean enough to drink? Can I taste it?"

Her voice cheered him. "The lights are close in this part, but we need a lot of light so people don't trip on the stairs. The divider is so groups coming up and groups going down don't get in each other's way. The water is clean, but let's not lick the rocks." He'd remember this day all his life.

Her chatter continued as they descended, commenting on every twist and turn of the shaft and every inch of workmanship on the stairway. Boone was torn between wishing the stairway would continue forever and anxiousness to show her the cave immediately.

The steps widened, and the angle flattened. He paused, blocking the opening to the cavern. "Close your eyes," he said.

Maisie searched his face before her eyes slid closed. He took her hand, surprised when she gripped his with a sure grasp.

"Step down," he said. "And another one. Now forward."

Their footsteps on the wooden platform echoed faintly from across the expansive room. He positioned her in the center of the dock on the subterranean lake. At first, he moved to stand behind her, but on second thought, he decided he wanted to see her face.

Boone took one last look at the sparkling fairyland before them, then said, "When you're ready."

Her eyes opened, and her face immediately went blank. Her smile disappeared and her forehead creased. Her eyes darted from spot to spot as if searching for something that was missing. She looked above her, then at the water, smooth as glass and reflecting the colored lights and crystals like a mirror. She pulled on his arm. Boone frowned. Did she want to leave already?

Then, without warning, she sat on the floor and lifted her face to the sparkling ceiling above them.

Boone was flummoxed. What was wrong with her? The tears in her eyes troubled him, but instead of leaving as he had at the funeral, he squatted next to her, offering his company.

Maisie sniffed loudly, the only sound in the expanse. "I'm sorry. I didn't mean to get overcome."

Kicking his feet out in front of him, Boone sat. "If you can tell me what's wrong, we can fix it. Is it the lights? Or the platform? What is it that you don't like?"

"Don't you dare change a thing." She wiped her eyes with a strong swipe of the back of her hand. "It's so beautiful, it's overwhelming. I'm crying for the grandeur of it. It's like my heart just got bigger than it ever was before, and I can't hold it all in."

Wasn't that something? Boone relaxed and waited, letting her have her moment of wonder. It was bigger than their relationship, bigger than the both of them.

"It makes me ponder how many surprises God has for us," Maisie said. "How many treasures waiting just around the corner that we never see coming. That building above, it's wonderful, but it's small and humble. Then there's this little hole in the ground that we go through. It looks like a dead end, so dark and confining. From looking at the structure above, you would never guess what wonders are down here. What a glorious world exists below the surface."

Boone was grateful that she had the words he lacked. A rich treasure hidden beneath a rough surface. He was growing fonder of that type of treasure day by day.

Sitting next to her, he took her hand and cradled it in both of his. How had it happened that he'd found someone who appreciated this wonder as much as he did? She looked at their joined hands, and then her eyes rose to meet his. Boone hoped she knew how much he was growing to value her.

She squeezed his hand, then went back to admiring the cave. "I know one thing," she said. "You're going to have to put fainting couches down here, because you're going to have people get plumb overcome."

"Do you want to look around?" he asked.

"Is there more?"

He stood and helped her up. "Let's explore."

The day they found this place, they had both stood on the brink of a flooded mine with no room and no solid footing. It had been dark and disorienting. The day of their wedding photographs, they could see better, but the small platform they'd stood on was crawling with workers and photographers who made them act in the most unnatural ways.

Today, the cavern was fully lit, the water pumped down to a beautiful lake surrounded by crystal, and the two of them were alone.

"Look how much bigger the platform is now. This is where the tour group will gather for a speech from the guide. They'll learn about the minerals in here, how this was formed, the dimensions of it, and about its discovery."

"Will the guides mention me?" she asked.

"They'd better." He pulled her to a walkway that curved around the edge of the cavern. "After that, they'll walk along here until they reach this stopping point. From here you can see the highest point of the cavern, and over on that far side is the hole we first came through."

Maisie gasped. "Way up there? That's terrifying. What if we had taken one more step? We would've fallen to our deaths."

"It was full of water, remember? We would've gotten scratched up from the fall, but as long as you could swim . . ."

"I can swim," she retorted.

"Either way, I'm glad we didn't fall. From this vantage point, we move the tourists to the main area."

Still holding her hand, he led her farther, but she stopped in her tracks.

"Look, Boone. The light is shining through the water. I can see crystals there too."

"The whole place is lined with them."

"Are there fish?"

"No. There isn't a river coming through. The water seeped through the rocks. That's why the minerals came through to make the crystals. No fish, though."

Maisie kept looking into the cloudy water. "That's a pity. I'd really like to see a catfish swim through that light. Or a rainbow trout. Wouldn't that be pretty?" She watched for a second more before smiling up at him and taking his arm again.

"Here's our ballroom." This floored area was only as big as the dining room of his house, but it was plenty big enough for dancers. Brass chains were draped between posts to form a railing so dancers wouldn't get carried away and fall off. The same barriers also protected the crystal walls from tourists who might want to climb off the platform and break off a souvenir.

Maisie walked out to the middle of the floor, then tilted her head back to look above at the lights shining down. "I've heard of a crystal chandelier before, but this takes the cake." She turned deliberately, taking in every detail. "This is the spot we're hoping to lease for weddings?"

"We took our pictures here." He looked for the open shaft behind him to get his bearings, then stepped to his left. "I stood right here."

"And I was here." Maisie took her place before him, but the grandeur of the twinkling lights among the crystals kept her face turned toward the lake. "It was dark that day. If these lights had been on, I would've had a hard time paying any attention to you or that photographer."

And yet here the lights were on, and Boone couldn't take his eyes off her. "But you weren't dressed so fine on our real wedding day," he said. "You were dressed just like you are now."

Her face dropped. "I came ready to work," she said. "I didn't want to get my new duds dirty."

"I like the way you look today," he said. "I do."

His chest got warm when he remembered that day. He'd barely known her. Hadn't spent any time with her to speak of. Hadn't heard her laugh. When the preacher had told him to kiss the bride, he'd done the minimum to fulfill that obligation. It had been odd to kiss someone he didn't know.

Now that he knew her, it was growing more difficult to stay aloof. He would obey the rules of their agreement, but his actions weren't showing what his heart felt.

Her eyes were moist again as they roved the spires that emerged from every angle. Her mouth was soft, lips parted. His hands clenched as he thought of the feel of her when they played her games—her strong body with its surprisingly soft places, her skin smooth despite the sun-kissed cheeks.

"When I married you, you were a stranger." Boone hadn't foreseen the feelings he was trying to express, and he wished he wasn't doing such a poor job of it. "You're not a stranger anymore, Maisie. You're someone I care for very much."

"Thank you," she said. "You're trying to care, but you don't always know how to show it. Hearing you say it helps."

"Do you want me to show it?" he asked. "I thought we'd agreed—"

Her eyes flashed. "Showing that you care means sticking around when times are tough. Not leaving a person when they need you. It has nothing to do with kissing and pawing at a person. There's some who do that without any love in them at all."

Love—it was a word he didn't dare utter. Not yet. "That's not who I am, Maisie. You know that." He had left her at the funeral because he hadn't known what she wanted. Now he knew. "I can do better."

He smiled to diffuse the tension, but as he began a lecture on the different types of crystals in the cavern, he realized that even after a week of barely speaking, she was giving them another chance.

CHAPTER 21

It was their first social occasion, and Boone would give two inches off his index finger to avoid it. He'd had to leave the cave early that afternoon to wash up and don his evening suit. As he slid his arms into the vest, he felt akin to a prisoner getting metal bars closed in his face. The only grace was that his sentence would be a matter of hours, not years.

Maisie's room above his was silent. She'd slammed drawers up there for half an hour or so before thundering down the spiral staircase, running through his room holding her dressing gown closed, and disappearing down the hallway. Boone still couldn't get over the image of her stockinged legs flashing as she ran through.

And that was the biggest reason he resented this event. Instead of sipping tea with businessmen who refused to discuss business over dinner, he could be working, or even better, learning what would convince Maisie that he cared.

No one had ever made him laugh like Maisie. He hadn't had many schoolyard friends. He and his older brother weren't close. Maisie was the nearest thing he had to a companion, and he was jealous of her time. He'd been irate at Mrs. Penney for accepting the invitation on their behalf and had ordered her to cancel the invitation until he saw the look on Maisie's face.

"Don't you want to go to a party?" she'd asked.

He'd felt his face growing warm. "You said you wanted to arm wrestle tonight. We already have plans." They hadn't wrestled since the funeral, and he was eager for another carefree evening.

Her shoulders had drooped as she swirled her knife through the jam on her toast. "If you want to go to the party, we could arm wrestle afterward. I bought a new dress all by myself, and I'm going to wear a corset beneath."

And that was how Boone found himself buttoning on a new paper collar while Maisie ran the length of the house to get Mrs. Karol to help with her stays. Mrs. Karol showed up to grumble about Maisie's need for a hairdresser and to do whatever else it was that Maisie required while Boone ordered the buggy made ready.

Even with his preparation, they were still late. If the corset made Maisie's waist any smaller, it wasn't noticeable beneath the loose-fitted gown she'd chosen. Boone was at a loss. She looked pretty, ethereal in the floaty lace, but she might as well have been as large as Mrs. Penney from the way the fabric draped. Maisie was proud of the fact that she'd chosen the dress herself. He just hoped no one noticed how ill-suited it was for her.

Boone hopped out of the buggy once they reached Mr. Landauer's house. He had started toward the double doors before remembering that it was his responsibility to escort his wife. But he was too late. Maisie had hopped down from the buggy without help and lifted her skirts to catch up with him.

"I'm sorry," he said. The indoor lights streamed through the glass panes of the door and blended with the light from the setting sun. "I should've helped you."

She waved him away. "Granny Laura doesn't need help getting out of a buggy. Why would I?" Then, instead of waiting for him, she strode up to the front door and pulled on the handle.

Boone rushed to stop her. "You can't let yourself in."

"Why not? They know we're coming." She yanked against the handle again, but Boone held it closed. "We're already late, Boone. No reason to have them get up from the table."

This party was a bad idea. He should have waited until he could prepare her better. "Listen, Maisie. I'm not the most astute person, but I've been in this situation before. You have to follow my lead. I don't know what the rules are for parties in your neighborhood—"

"Rules?" Maisie laughed. "We don't have rules for our shindigs."

"There are rules," Boone insisted. "Maybe the rules are that you don't wink at someone's girl, or everyone brings their own fried chicken, but there are rules. Think about it. And these rules are different."

Maisie's eyes got big. "Was I supposed to bring chicken? You didn't tell me."

"Not to these parties, but you aren't supposed to walk into the house on your own either." He held out his arm. "And you should be escorted by your husband, seeing as how you have one."

She twisted the finger of her glove before taking his offered arm. "I want to do good," she said.

His confidence was rising. She'd listened to him and trusted him. Maybe this would be a good party after all.

The guests had already taken their places at the table when he and Maisie left their gloves and hats with the servant. Even if they hadn't been late, they probably still would have had the room's attention at the first introduction of his new wife. Every head turned their way as they stood in the doorway. Soup spoons and glasses were lowered in expectation. The host, Mr. Landauer, stood, followed by all the gentlemen.

"There you are, Boone. We've been anxious for your arrival." Mr. Landauer didn't seem offended in the least. "Would you please do us the honor of introducing your guest?"

"Certainly. This is Maisie Kentworth Bragg." What else did one say at such a time? Boone added, "My wife."

The table erupted in exclamations of cheer and congratulations, although some of the looks were more speculative than celebratory. Such a brouhaha. The wedding ceremony itself hadn't been as big of a production. Boone stole a glance at Maisie, surprised to see her beaming smile undiminished by all the attention. She really was beautiful, despite the yards of excess fabric draping her figure. No one would ever guess that he'd married her for the sake of convenience.

He allowed the guests to exclaim over her for what seemed an eternity, then steered her to their seats. This was one meal he'd get to enjoy without the danger of feminine wiles.

"I read your story in the evening paper, Mrs. Bragg." Boone chilled at the voice. Why did Justina Caine have to be the first to address Maisie? "Quite a whirlwind romance, I understand."

Boone's spoon clattered into his soup, splashing the tablecloth. He dabbed at it with his napkin. "The newspaper isn't always accurate," he said. "The interview was primarily about the cavern and its discovery."

"The discovery of your love." Mr. Hunt raised his glass with a grin.

"I didn't get to read it," said Allison, Justina's friend. "What did it say?"

"Why don't we let Boone tell us," said Justina. "I'd like to hear from the lucky groom."

Boone gaped. Why hadn't he gone back and read that article more closely? Maisie had shown it to him, but reading it had made him so uncomfortable that he hadn't finished.

"Well, I'd gone to retrieve some gear at the mine when I noticed that the barrier on the shaft had been forced open. I was concerned there might be a child inside, so before I nailed the boards back in place, I decided to walk through it."

"Wait a minute," Mr. Wolstead said. "You mean you weren't going to go inside until you found that the opening had been disturbed?"

"That's right. I'd planned to sell the mine and had already cleared the inside, but seeing the entrance pried open made the tour a necessity."

"Lucky for you there was a trespasser, or the new owner would have found that cave," said Mr. Clarke, who owned the smelter.

Justina's mouth tightened, and her eyes darted to Allison.

"I might have toured it again just to make sure, but I didn't get far before running into Miss Kentworth. Although I tried to eject her from the cave immediately, she insisted that I follow her."

"And what did you think of her?" asked Mrs. Landauer. "A beautiful maiden appearing out of the dark deep of a cave."

"She wasn't beautiful," Boone said. Because of the gasps around the table, he expanded on his answer. "She was covered in mud and black dust. Besides, her lantern was shining in my eyes, so I didn't get a good look at her until we came outside. Even then, I didn't think—" Maisie's knee knocked into his. He stopped to lift the tablecloth to see what was the matter. That only made Maisie hit him with twice the strength. "What?" he asked.

Maisie addressed the table. "My lands, I don't know why I bothered to get all decked out for you'uns tonight when my husband is bound and determined to recollect how dirty I was that day."

The snickers chilled his blood. The older women were smiling pityingly at her. The men seemed enchanted, but the ladies of his set were merciless.

Mrs. Picher, seated next to Maisie, laughed. "Despite Boone's claims, he obviously recognized your beauty soon enough, since he married you immediately after."

"Exactly how long after meeting was the ceremony?" Justina dabbed her napkin to the corner of her smug lips. "Two days, maybe three?"

Boone felt like he'd just experienced a cave-in. He'd thought he was on solid footing talking about the cave, but now they wanted to hear something else. "I don't remember. It was all a blur."

"Those pictures in the paper were so romantic," Justina continued.

"No one plans a wedding that fast. Surely you'd known each other before then."

"No, I had never met her before in my life. We just threw together that ceremony in a matter of days." He was telling the truth, so why did Maisie groan?

"Where did you get your wedding gown, Maisie? You couldn't have had it sewn so quickly. Was it an heirloom?" Why couldn't Justina just let it go? Boone hadn't thought such details would be important. He didn't know where he got any of his clothes. They just appeared in his wardrobe.

"As a matter of fact"—Maisie kept her voice even, but there was steel beneath it—"it was given to me by a friend. I didn't have it made."

"What a friend you must have," said Justina. "That dress looks like one Madame Duvalier has had on display since last season. I'm surprised a lady would choose a dress that everyone in town has walked by for the better part of a year."

Maisie's chin went up. "My dress isn't important. What is important is the man I married, so you can stop with your little jabs. Everyone here knows you're just jealous he didn't marry you."

Boone's mouth dropped open along with everyone else's at the table. Justina's eyes burned with murderous fire. Maisie didn't understand how the game was played. Justina could make catty remarks endlessly and still be considered acceptable, but Maisie's blunt statement would never be forgotten. Or forgiven.

"That's enough of that," Mr. Caine erupted. "Boone, it's one thing for you to marry poorly, but you must not allow your choice to corrupt our society."

"Don't look to him for help." Maisie ripped a dinner roll in two and stuffed a piece in her mouth. "I'm just repeating what Boone told me. Everyone knows it's true. Isn't that right, Boone?"

Boone had been raised to follow these rules. Even though he did it poorly, he tried, but he had no idea how to recover from such a breach. The only thing he knew to do was to drop his head and choke down another bite of a dinner that had suddenly gone tasteless.

The ride home was silent. The dinner had been a disaster, but Maisie didn't understand why everyone seemed to blame her. Justina had started the row. She'd had her claws out from the get-go. What was Maisie supposed to do? Ignore the slights? Pretend she didn't understand the insults? And when she'd enlisted Boone's help, he'd left her to fight alone.

"We should've talked about that story before we went," she mumbled into the dark night and away from her husband. "Then maybe you would've answered better."

"My father always said to tell the truth, and then you don't have to remember which lies you told."

Maisie's fist clenched as she turned to face Boone. "You told me to obey Mrs. Penney and do the promotional work for the cavern. In case you forgot, that includes painting a picture of our whirlwind romance and our deep love for each other. It's going to be hard to portray that when you look like a gigged fish every time someone asks you about your beautiful wife."

He jangled the reins over the back of the horse. "I wasn't prepared. If you'd told me everything you said that first time Miss Harris interviewed you—"

"Now it makes sense, the way Mr. Caine looks down on me. You should've told me that was his daughter picking me apart. The one who wanted to marry you. It's all starting to add up." They'd pulled up in front of the redbrick house. The downstairs windows were ablaze with light, but her bedroom in the turret on the third floor was dark.

"I told you about the ladies lying in wait for me. Miss Caine was one of the most determined. She even brought her father into her plans."

"Let me get this straight. You married me to convince her and others that you are no longer looking for love, yet when they ask if you think I'm beautiful, you can't say a simple *yes*?"

"Sometimes you tell me to keep my distance, other times you want me to tell everyone how besotted I am."

"If someone makes a complimentary statement about your wife, just agree with them, Boone. How complicated is it?"

"Sorry, I didn't know which act I was supposed to perform tonight." He waited, and when she didn't move, he rattled the reins. "I'm going to put the horses up. Fegus is already asleep."

Maisie climbed down unaided. The buggy rolled around the corner to the carriage house as she went inside.

She'd made a horrible mess of the dinner and wished she could right the situation, but she didn't know what to do. All she knew was that Boone had every right to be embarrassed of her, even if he hadn't helped matters one bit.

She'd made it to Boone's room before she remembered that she couldn't undress unassisted. Why did women put themselves in such helpless situations? At Maisie's knock, Mrs. Karol cracked her door downstairs with her hair tied up in rags and a cigar in her hand. With a roll of her eyes, she carefully balanced the cigar on the edge of a tea saucer, then followed Maisie to the unused bedroom where she'd gotten dressed for the evening.

As Mrs. Karol's cold fingers worked their way down the buttons on Maisie's back, Maisie pondered the unfairness of the world. Why were cultured women allowed to be cruel and heartless, and common people were supposed to ignore their slights? Smile and pretend that everything was fine? Boone might not be able to fake a romance, but Maisie couldn't ignore a slight.

With the buttons unfastened, Maisie stepped out of the gown and reached for the silk dressing gown that she'd worn earlier that evening.

"I suppose you want your hair down," Mrs. Karol said as she hung the beaded gown on a hanger.

It'd be nice, but Maisie needed to get back in her room before Boone returned. She didn't want to face him again. Not tonight.

"I can do it myself, but please loosen my stays. I can't never sleep all tied up like this."

After Mrs. Karol had loosened the ties, Maisie took a deep and grateful breath. Her chest was bound lightly, so at least she could bend a little. She tied the belt of the robe as she stepped out of her heeled slippers.

"Leave them here with that dress," Maisie said. "I won't wear them without it."

Ma had always got after her in the winter for walking about the house in her sock feet on account of the rough boards snagging them, but this house had rugs, and her silk stockings felt good against her skin. She hurried up the grand staircase and slipped through Boone's door, only to see him hanging up his suit coat.

"Sorry," she said. "I thought you were with the horses."

"This is your place. You're not a visitor," he reminded her as he went back to hanging up the coat. "Fegus was awake after all." He began unbuttoning his shirt.

Maisie turned toward the stairs.

"Wait, you promised me . . ."

She paused with one foot on the first step. What else did he want from her? Hadn't she been through enough? "What do you want?"

"Arm wrestling?" He removed his shirt and tossed it into the bottom of the wardrobe. His short-sleeved cotton undershirt stretched over his chest in ways that the coat didn't. Too bad those women hadn't asked Maisie what she'd thought upon first seeing Boone. She could've burned their ears with her thoughts.

But he didn't have the same thoughts toward her.

She pushed up the loose sleeve of her robe. What had she expected? She'd told him she didn't want to be his wife but then had her feelings hurt when he treated her with indifference. Clearly, he regretted marrying her. How could he not, when every person in the room that night knew she didn't belong?

Maisie knelt by the corner of his bed and anchored her elbow in the mattress. He took the opposite corner and grabbed her hand, but the mattress sagged beneath the force.

"The floor," she said, and crawled to the rug at the foot of the bed. Lying on her stomach, she stretched her robe beneath her to stay covered. Boone flopped down opposite her, propping himself up on his elbows. Maisie did the same, her wide sleeves falling to expose both arms. She kept her eyes averted, not wanting to communicate anything further to him. Not wanting to see more disappointment in his eyes.

She wadded the sleeve beneath her elbow to keep it from rubbing raw, then took his offered arm. Boone had to scoot back to adjust for the size difference in their reach, but then all was settled.

Maisie had been the champion arm wrestler of the family when they were young, but as the boys matured, she'd lost more matches than won. Still, she put up a good fight and could sometimes win through pure perseverance, especially when she was riled. If the fight in the dog was the most important, Maisie would beat a dog twice her size tonight.

She gave a twitch to test him, but Boone didn't tense. Maisie braved a look at him. Boone stared at her over the tops of their joined hands. He'd insisted that they do this, but gone was any sign of competition. Not a trace of jovial, good-natured fun either. Just determination.

Another of his inscrutable ways that made her feel adrift. She'd had enough of it. At the dinner, he'd pulled the rug out from under her, but this was familiar ground. She knew how to play here. Maisie tightened her grip, leaned her shoulder into it, and pushed against his arm. There was always that first engagement when her arm tightened and she thought she was pulling hard, but then in a few seconds more muscles engaged and it seemed her strength had doubled. This time, her strength was there, but Boone wasn't moving.

Maisie looked up, and he hadn't changed a thing. He was still watching her as if he didn't know there was a contest on. She growled and increased her efforts. Sweat was dampening her forehead. How dare he not even try? Her anger was being met by something unmovable, and it made her furious. She felt tears starting, and his expression finally changed.

He let his arm drop an inch, but then the uncertainty cleared from his eyes. "No. I'm not going to let you win just because you're angry," he said. "Sometimes you don't win, Maisie. It's alright to lose."

But it wasn't alright. She'd given up on a future with anyone but him. She'd given up on anyone telling her that she was beautiful and speaking words of love. She'd given that all up for an easy escape, and she hadn't thought about how it would cost her. She hadn't thought about the disparity between her world and the world of the people at that dinner. She hadn't considered how they would look down on her. She'd lost so much. She didn't want to lose anything more.

She kept pushing, straining, but nothing was changing. Her elbow stung as the skin rubbed raw against the carpet and the sleeve of her robe. Her neck ached as she threw her shoulder against his hand, little caring that she was breaking the rules. When that didn't work, she got to her knees and pushed with her whole body against Boone's arm. He moved his bracing arm to balance better, but he didn't waver.

This was no longer a fight against him. It was a fight against all the confusion and disappointments of the last few weeks. How dare Silas profess his love to her when he should've been looking after the children he'd sired? How dare he embarrass her publicly? And how about her brother? If Amos had minded his own business, Maisie wouldn't have felt like she needed to save him. Look where his concern had landed her. Married to a man who couldn't even admit to his friends that she was pretty.

Maisie growled as the tears sped down her face. She flipped around to her left side and, instead of pushing, began pulling against Boone's arm. She slipped on the silk gown beneath her and fell to her back, her hand still in his—his hand still upright and unmoved by all her efforts.

The tears ran down the sides of her face and into her hair as she lay flat on her back. Boone loosened his grip, but he didn't relinquish his hold on her hand. Maisie wasn't a baby. She didn't cry at nothing. When trouble came, she faced it squarely and fought. And that was what she was trying to do, but she didn't know how to win this fight, and now she was making a fool of herself, bawling on Boone's bedroom floor like an overwrought, hysterical female.

The thought made her cry even more.

"Shush." Boone came into view, his face upside down. He lowered her hand to the floor, then brushed the tears from her face. He rocked her head to the side and pulled out the combs that held her hair. With gentle movements, he unwound the thick strands that Mrs. Karol had bound up, stretching her hair out on the carpet behind her and combing his fingers through it.

Maisie closed her eyes. Her chest rose in gulped breaths and lowered in ragged sobs, but slowly her cries ceased. The tightness of her throat eased, and frustration gave way to resignation.

Boone's caresses soothed her exhausted spirit. He wasn't a bad person. Many people lived with worse. Besides, Maisie had set the rules for their relationship. She had no one to blame but herself.

She took a deep breath to cleanse all the wounds and slow her pounding heart before she spoke. Keeping her eyes closed, she said, "I feel like a fool. I'm sorry."

"It's fine." He brushed his fingers over her forehead as if to erase the creases of worry there.

Maisie opened her eyes, but she couldn't see his face. She rolled to her stomach and found herself closer than she'd bargained for. "It's not fine," she said. They were both on their stomachs, elbows to elbows. The stubble on his cheek caught the light from the sole lantern in the room. The color of his lips looked deeper in the shadows. "I had no call to carry on like that." She pushed her hair behind her ear so she could see him better. "You must think I'm off my rocker."

The way he kept searching her face was intoxicating. "I might not always understand you, but that doesn't mean I don't care." His eyes narrowed in orneriness as he said, "Actually, right now the only thing I care about is that I finally beat you at a contest."

Maisie laughed and punched him in the shoulder. "You beat me? Is that all you can think about?"

"That and how your robe is falling open. Maybe I shouldn't mention it, but I'm credibly distracted."

"Yikes!" she yelped. Overt immodesty would not help the situation. Tucking the edges of the robe together, Maisie dared a look up again. He was the same obtuse man who had left her to the wolves at dinner, yet somehow, with his simple inappropriate observation, he'd made her feel more beautiful than any woman at the party that night.

Boone got to his feet, then offered her his hand. "Tomorrow we'll read that newspaper article, and you can tell me how you want me to answer any further questions about our romance. I won't go to the cave until we get that straight."

What could he say about their romance? Maisie wasn't sure where they stood minute to minute. She let him help her to her feet. "And I want to talk to you about the Founder's Day float Mrs. Penney has planned. It'll be a great advertisement just in time for our opening."

"I'm looking forward to it." With a squeeze of her hand, he let her go and turned toward his bed.

Maisie had started to her staircase when he spoke.

"Maisie." His hands were clasped before him, and he was twisting on his fingers. "You should know that I'm happier right now than I've ever been. Maybe it doesn't matter, but you deserve to hear it."

It did matter, and it made all the difference. Maisie took a step forward, yearning to give him a hug. Just to hold him and show him her appreciation. She could imagine how his firm chest would feel, how his arms would slide around her thin silk robe, and how gently his hands would comb through her hair again.

Or maybe if she did that, he'd hear rumors of her someday, and he'd think back to her forward behavior, and he'd know the rumors were true. He'd be embarrassed to have married a woman like her.

She came no closer.

"Thank you, Boone. I think we're going to be good friends," she said, then turned and climbed the stairs to her bedroom.

CHAPTER 22

If only they'd had more time to work on the float. For the last week, Maisie had kept busy getting the visitor center ready as well as preparing for the parade. Stains from the black paint she'd used on the side of the wagon still graced her fingernails, but the lettering reading *Bragg's Crystal Cave and Auditorium* was clear. Yesterday, she'd enlisted Amos to add chicken wire to the wagon so they could recreate the bumpy walls of the cave, and she'd dredged up Christmas tree tinsel from the Bragg attic in order to make the black drapes sparkle.

She hoped Boone would find everything satisfactory. He'd had little time at home. One problem after another was popping up at the cave. The pumps had failed again. Thankfully, Boone had thought to order extra parts ahead of time, so the repairs had been made before the water rose. A load of lumber for an outbuilding had been stolen despite Gilbert setting guards at night, and Boone had found the bank unwilling to loan him any more money to replace it. It was only upon speaking to the loan manager that Boone had realized rumors were circulating about the cave. That it was a carnival trick, not what it was billed to be. That there was nothing down there besides an everyday cave dusted with rock salt to trick the gullible.

Maisie reached for a hammer hidden in the wagon bed and popped in a loose nail to keep the drape from sagging. Boone had a lot on his mind, and the closer they got to the opening of the cave, the more pressure he was under.

A band was lining up behind their float. At least there'd be music to entertain her and Boone as they rode through town. Maisie watched the bandleader get the men into line amid the random honks and squawks of them tuning up. Completely unaware of their formation, Boone walked through their ranks to reach the float.

At least she wasn't the only thing he didn't notice.

"Sorry I'm late," Boone said. "There was another theft last night."

Maisie felt the hair on the back of her neck rise. "I thought Gilbert was standing guard."

"He was out front of the visitor center with the building supplies, but the thieves came through the old mine entrance into the cave. They took all the electric lamps they could get unhooked."

"Oh, Boone!" Maisie's jaw clenched. "Who would need that many lamps?"

"There's only one outfit I can think of." Boone's face was grim. "One that will use thousands of lights and doesn't want us as competition."

Boone had already mentioned he suspected that Mr. Peltz from the Electrical Light Park was behind the rumors that had reached the bank. "Surely Peltz wouldn't stoop to thievery."

"Your cousin Calista got me a detective to keep tabs on Peltz and his crew. We'll catch them. You wait and see."

Calista had hired someone else? Maisie would bet her last firecracker that Calista was doing the job herself, but she wouldn't rat on her cousin.

"Without any help from the bank, will you be able to replace the lamps?" Without the lamps, there was nothing to see below ground.

"It'll mean putting a mortgage against the Byers Building. That'll put me up to my neck in debt. If we don't start a profit soon, something will be on the auction block."

Maisie shuddered. She'd been around ranching long enough to have seen such events, and she couldn't stand the thought of Boone facing that humiliation.

"We're going to keep that from happening today," she said. "We'll be all smiles and happiness. Show them that we're excited about what's down there. That's the best thing we can do for now."

"Why do people want to see us?"

"Because they've heard our story. They feel like they know us, and while they are waving at us, they'll decide to follow this float right to the end of town and buy themselves a ticket for next week."

"And that's why you're the best decision I've ever made." Boone nudged her with his elbow.

"Don't forget to do more of that." She felt selfish asking for more praise, but in this case it had a purpose. "Everyone's going to be looking for signs of our passionate romance." Especially after the disastrous dinner. If Boone had faced any criticism for it, he'd hidden it from her. Maisie wouldn't hear what was said. No one was speaking to her.

"That band sounds like a gaggle of geese flying in." Boone tugged on his tie to loosen his collar. "We'll hope everyone is looking at them, not us."

"Getting people to look at us is the whole point. We did this to get attention, not to hide."

Maisie lifted her hands to straighten his tie, but then thought better of it. She wouldn't straighten his tie, although she had to admire how nice he looked. Maybe once they had this awkward exposure behind them, the relationship would mend. It would help if the cave wasn't consuming so much of his time.

She'd been distracted too. Maisie had been so busy looking

after the details of the float that she'd forgotten to plan her own appearance. Mrs. Penney was always thinking ahead, but unfortunately Mrs. Penney's idea of a farmer's costume was a garishly colored calico that was so ugly it'd sour the cows' milk. If the colors weren't bad enough, there were mismatched patches sewn randomly about in a theatrical attempt to make her look poverty-stricken. Mrs. Penney claimed it necessary, since their story of a country girl capturing the rich man in the mine was the foundation for their publicity, but next to handsome Boone, Maisie felt like an already-plucked hen.

The whistle on the ten o'clock train sounded. It was time to mount up and ride. Maisie lifted her skirt and took that first big step up to the back of the wagon. She picked her way through the fabric-draped chicken wire to reach their stand. It had been tricky designing this float. Recreating the wonder of the cavern was impossible. She knew she couldn't come close, but she had to represent it to catch people's imagination and get them to come and see.

The love story that had purportedly begun there was stirring up a lot of talk. It was selling newspapers around the country, but would it sell tickets to the cave? Starting today, they'd find out. She only hoped there was a cave ready for them to visit by next week.

She pressed against the chicken wire, making room for Boone. The parade was lined up in an alley. Everyone was hurrying to get to their places. The ladies' riding club came before their float. Mr. Blount questioned a young woman dressed like a western rider, made a mark on his clipboard, then approached the side of their wagon.

"Bragg's Crystal Cave," he read from the panel on the side of the wagon. "Since this is your first entry in the Founder's Day parade, I'll show you the ropes. Follow the lovely riders in front of you. At least you're on a wagon so you don't have to worry about dodging their droppings. That'll be the band's problem. Once we reach Fourth, that's where most of the observers are. If you throw candy, you'll need to do it from both sides."

"Candy?" Boone frowned at Mr. Blount. "I didn't bring candy."

"Then just smile and wave. That's all people will expect." He looked at his clipboard, then did a second take at Maisie. "So you're the country bride, huh?" He looked again at Boone, his smile widening. "A diamond in the rough. But us miners know to watch for such treasures down there."

Boone scratched his ear. "She's the best treasure I ever found in a mine." That was the line Mrs. Penney had prepared for him, but it fell flat when it was basically what Mr. Blount had just said on his own.

"Alright, then. Don't forget the grandstand. It's at the corner. When you get there, you'll stop, and they'll announce the name of your business and say a few words. Most of the audience will be right there, so that's your moment. Don't miss it."

"Fegus?" Boone called to their driver.

"I heard, boss. I'll stop right on time."

Mr. Blount was satisfied. "Good luck, then!" He moseyed past them to the band.

When the horse brigade in front of them moved, Fegus picked up the reins of their four-horse team, and they rolled forward. Until they turned the corner and reached the main thoroughfare, there really was nothing to do besides watch alley cats scatter and friends of the other participants move out of the way.

A group of schoolchildren waved grubby hands at them. Maisie was surprised at their enthusiasm, but when Boone held up his empty hands and shrugged, they turned their attention to the band. The crowds got thicker in front of the business district. Eyes flickered over the sparkling black of their float. Mouths moved as they read the banners on the sides. Girls dipped their heads together as they evaluated Maisie and Boone. Had they read the news article? Did they think them in love, or were they making plans to visit the cave? Maisie held her head high and even remembered to give Boone a sweet look every now and then.

Riding in a parade turned out to be more work than she'd

bargained for. Smiling all the time, disappointing kids looking for candy, trying to keep her balance while being on display in front of the whole town—it required skill.

The wagon wheel dropped into a pothole. Maisie swayed. Boone steadied her with a hand at her back.

"How are you doing?" he asked. "Do you need some water?" He lifted a canteen dusted black with ore.

"I'm glad you thought of that." She smiled even though her cheeks were sore. "I wasn't prepared. It's as exhausting as a dinner party."

"I'd bring a canteen to dinner parties if they let me."

When exactly was she supposed to take a swig? It didn't seem fitting to do it while on a stage before a hundred people.

"Go on," Boone said. "The grandstand is ahead. Do it before we get there."

He kept his hand on her back as she took a satisfying draw. When she handed him the canteen, she let herself lean against his chest. His eyes met hers. He looked unsure but willing. Hoping, maybe? Maisie didn't know what to hope for. They'd gone from strangers to a close friendship to the verge of romance, and now . . . what? Impersonal, polite, and wary. His fingers brushed against hers as he took the canteen. She felt his hand tighten on her back, holding her. He wasn't acting. Maisie had seen him try to fake affection and knew he wasn't behaving this way for the benefit of the crowd.

Best not to push their luck. She stood erect as he dropped the canteen at their feet. The tall buildings of downtown rose on every side of them. The midmorning sun fell right between them and dried up what little breeze trickled through. No longer were there country folk and schoolkids on the street. Men in fine linen suits and ladies with the wide-brimmed hats occupied the prime spots by the grandstand. Their mouths didn't move while they read the banners, but their eyes showed interest just the same.

Maisie had never had an audience this big before. Had it been a barn dance, she would've cut a jig to raise the roof, but Mrs. Penney had taught her to behave differently. Maisie's strong hands gripped the stand in front of her. She knew the part she was supposed to play as the marketer of the cave. She knew the story to tell to excite the reporters, but she didn't know how to act it out with Boone.

The wagon stopped as a lady's voice introduced the horseback riding club in front of them. Maisie waited as they rode through a series of maneuvers to showcase their skill.

She was such a dolt. Here they were, stopped in front of the most crowded area, and she was staring off into the great yonder when she was supposed to be waving and carrying on. Maisie plastered a smile on her face and lifted her hand. The mine owners and society leaders didn't respond with the same delight as the miners and children at the beginning.

"If I had candy, I wouldn't give it to them," Maisie gritted through her smile.

The riders finished their drill and rode ahead, moving the Bragg's Crystal Cave float into the limelight. Fegus rolled them in front of a stage constructed on the side of the street. The way had narrowed here because of all the people crowding around. Maisie reckoned those people sitting on the stage above them were important folks for some reason or another. She only hoped they wanted to rent the cave for their meetings.

"And now we have a new entry, Bragg's Crystal Cave." The voice sounded like a high-pitched screech coming through the megaphone.

Maisie tilted her head back to see who was speaking, but the sun glinted at the brim of her hat.

"We've all heard the fairy-tale story about Mr. Bragg discovering his bride along with the cavern. I'm sure all the bachelors in Joplin will go there with the same expectations."

"It's Justina," Boone growled. "Who gave her the megaphone?"

Justina? Maisie looked again and caught Miss Caine's gaze bearing down on them.

"So instead of worrying about their dusty mine, let's celebrate this newlywed couple. Aren't they lovely?"

Maisie felt her anger rising along with the cheers from the crowd. Forget the cave? That was the only reason they were doing this.

But Justina wasn't finished. She waited for a lull in the cheers before delivering the fatal blow. "Since you robbed all your friends and family of the joy of attending your wedding, why don't you give us a little reenactment? Go on, Mr. Bragg. Kiss your bride. We'd like to see that."

Justina's father criticized Maisie for being wanton, and Justina pushed her to be publicly demonstrative. Well, Justina was barking up the wrong tree. Maisie was made of stern stuff. She could take a dare with the toughest of them.

"Let's get this over with." Maisie tilted her chin up at Boone as her eyes narrowed with her smile. "She's not going to win."

"Kiss the bride, kiss the bride!" the crowd chanted.

"Get it over with?" Boone lifted an eyebrow. "I'd rather kiss you without Justina's irritating voice ringing in my ears."

"We're trying to sell tickets, remember?" This was what he wanted, wasn't it? Then why couldn't he brush his lips against hers? She grasped his lapel as she rose on her tiptoes, and the crowd's cheers grew louder. "Just another inch, dear . . ." If he'd just bend down a smidgen, they could give the crowd what they were after.

But Boone wasn't looking at her. Maisie followed his gaze and spotted a middle-aged couple pushing their way through the crowd.

"Boone Bragg, what is this?" The man held a traveling case and the woman a hatbox and a parasol. Both stood agape, as if unable to understand what they were witnessing.

Boone blinked as his face went pale. "I'm sorry, Maisie." He removed her hand. "I should've warned you."

Maisie's stomach dropped as he moved to the edge of the float. "Where are you going?"

The wagon rocked as he hopped off it to join the couple in the crowd.

"He's leaving you, Maisie."

Of all the voices in the crowd, Maisie knew this one, and it made her courage drop like a hot potato.

Silas Marsh swaggered closer to the wagon, an uncorked whiskey bottle in one hand, the other hand pressed against his chest. "Maisie, he doesn't love you, and you don't love him. Not like you love me."

The crowd had gone silent, everyone straining to hear his words. Maisie looked around, but Boone was leaving, not concerned that she was alone on the float. Alone to deal with Silas herself.

"It's time to stop this farce," he slurred. "Everyone knows you two aren't suited. You belong to me, Maisie-girl. You'll always belong to me."

Mrs. Landauer pressed the tips of her fingers to her mouth and shook her head in pity. Mr. Hunt crossed his arms and scowled, his disapproval evident. With a smirk, Justina was whispering to Allison behind her hand. Even the band members had paused to listen.

"C'mon down here, Maisie. Leave these heels to clean up their own messes." Even sloppy drunk, Silas was a handsome devil. "You're just after his money. You don't love him," he said, "and you know what you're missing by not being with me."

The blood rushing through her ears drowned out all the noise except Silas's cruel words. How dare he talk to her like that? How dare Boone walk off and leave her? Picking up the canteen, Maisie leapt off the wagon. She cleared the draped fabric and landed on her feet. She might be dressed like a clown, but she was still as strong and healthy as a colt.

The crowd parted, leaving Silas standing there with a stupid grin on his face. That grin didn't budge until Maisie swung the canteen by its strap and smacked it against Silas's head.

"Oww . . ." His reaction was delayed, but his complaints were hearty. "What'd you do that—"

"I don't love you. I can't stand the sight of you. Don't you ever come near me again."

Whirling the canteen like it was David's slingshot, Maisie pelted him again. The leather strap came loose just as she swung, and the canteen flew wide, hitting one of her horses in the hind end. The horse startled and pulled the team forward. Maisie spun around. The float she'd planned, worked on, decorated . . . it was leaving her.

She jogged a couple of steps before coming to a stop. What was she going to do? Ride it alone? Smile and wave at people after this? Maisie pushed her patched sleeve up to her elbow. She couldn't ride it now. Not with the laughter and the pity.

Not when Boone had left her too.

"Get out of my way." Maisie pushed through the paradegoers and ducked through the first doors available. It was a saloon, empty except for the bartender, who was polishing a glass. She stomped her foot in frustration. Of all the places to end up, she found herself in the only place that would make her granny even madder.

Ignoring the bartender's questioning gaze, she covered her face. She'd shamed her family. Granny Laura would be horrified. But for all the embarrassment Silas had caused, Boone had hurt her more.

The only reason she'd married Boone had been to save her family from shame, but she'd made a bigger spectacle of herself than she ever would've managed from the ranch.

"Maisie! There you are!" Her cousin Calista ran across the room and wrapped her arms around Maisie. Humming noises of comfort, Calista rocked her and stroked her hair as she collected herself.

Maisie couldn't cry. She was too shattered. Dressed in a clownish costume, pretending to be poor when her family had never lacked, pretending to be professional when she had never worked away from the farm before, pretending to be loved when she was only humored. There was nothing about her life that was real.

But having Calista there proved that there *was* something real: her family.

"Why did he have to act that way? It was so humiliating."

"Matthew is dealing with Silas. He'll be behind bars until he sobers up."

"I'm talking about Boone. I understand Silas. He's a rascal. But Boone? Why did he leave me?"

Calista sighed heavily. "You're coming home with me. We'll figure this out."

Maisie lifted her head. "Here I dragged you, a pastor's wife, into a saloon. I can't do anything right today."

"Don't you worry." Calista winked at her. "I may have seen the inside of a saloon before."

She tipped her hat to the bartender and escorted Maisie outside, sheltering her from the scoffing stares of the crowd that had found something more interesting to watch than the parade.

CHAPTER 23

"When I left home, you had zinc and lead mines. I return to find that you've got a carnival sideshow going on underground." Wallace Bragg fanned himself with his bowler hat as they walked through the Murphysburg neighborhood to their home. The neighbor's cat slunk around a fence post, watching them pass. "We had to cut our vacation short because of it."

"What about the girl?" Boone's mother asked. "When were you going to tell us about the girl?" Boone should slow down for her, but his legs were taking off like he had no control over them.

"Are all of the mines closed down? Have you disappointed your smelters and told them that you'll no longer be their supplier?" his father asked.

So far, Boone had heard dozens of questions but hadn't been allowed to answer one. It was about time.

"No, sir. The Spook Light is still producing. The Curious Bear had gone dry and hit water. I was preparing to sell it to Mr. Caine to raise capital for another venture, but that's when I discovered the cave."

"What about the girl?" his mother persisted. "The newspaper showed pictures of your wedding. Please tell me that was a stunt."

The neighbor's gardener had started on a new flowerbed and left gravel and loose dirt scattered over the sidewalk. Boone and his father turned to give Mrs. Bragg their hands to help her through the obstacle, then set their course straight ahead as usual.

"What percentage of employment do you have?" his father asked. "Are you keeping everyone in wages?"

"Yes, sir. Once the mine played out, I set them to building ramps and stairways to the cave. They also constructed a visitor center."

"Who is she? All the paper said was that she was local, but the only Kentworths I know of are from the rancher family," his mother said.

"What are the men going to do now?" his father asked. "You don't need forty men to take tickets and do tours. How can this attraction support that many?"

It was a problem that had troubled Boone as well, but he was hopeful. "Running into water in the Curious Bear was why we'd stopped. If I can keep the Cornish pumps working, it'll be clear for more exploration."

They'd reached the house. His mother let her shoulders sag. "I've been away for a long time. Let's go inside and discuss this."

"I can't stay," Boone said. "I have to find Maisie."

"That girl?" Once his mother got on a subject, she was relentless. "Do you think she wants to be found? From the way it looked, there was another man demanding her attention."

Boone picked up his parents' luggage and strode into the house. He'd been so shocked to see his parents, so disoriented by Maisie and the crowd, that he'd fled without checking on her. Was she still in the wagon? And what was this about another man? It had seemed there was something she was doing, someone she was talking to, but he couldn't remember. All he'd known was that Maisie was asking him to kiss her, but his parents had shown up, and he remembered that he'd forgotten to tell them he was married.

Not forgotten. Not really. More like he'd postponed sharing that information because he'd been afraid they would rush home and raise a ruckus. He'd forgotten about the newspaper interviews that had been published all over the region.

Boone dropped the luggage at the foot of the staircase. With Fegus hauling the empty float through the parade, Boone would have to saddle his own horse. He had to find Maisie. He hoped she had gone out to the cave to do ticket sales. That was the point of participating in this spectacle.

"Ahem." His mother stood in the doorway. "About this girl."

"Now's not the time."

"Was that story in the paper—that picture—a ploy?"

"No." Boone stared at the finial on the banister. "We're married."

He didn't have to see her expression to know how terrible it was. "Oh, Boone, what have you done? I've spent the last two years running off ladies so you wouldn't ruin . . . I was afraid that if I left, one of those girls might sink her claws into you. I thought I warned you about the Caine girl, but I never dreamed you'd marry a stranger before we had a chance to intervene. This is a disaster."

"I agree." It was a disaster. How would Maisie feel when she realized that his parents didn't approve of her? "But it's too late. We have to make the best of it, Mother. You can't mistreat her. If you'll excuse me, I have work to do today. That's what Father would expect." He picked up his satchel and kissed his mother on the cheek as he headed out the door.

Boone got on his horse and headed toward town. The parade must have finished, because people were streaming down the sidewalks, men and women walking arm in arm, kids dodging and darting through the crowd as they discussed the races that were to take place at the park. Remembering the parade route, Boone headed to where his wagon and Fegus should have stopped. The closer he got to town, the less likely the people were to look him in the eye.

If he'd been thinking, he would've kissed Maisie. Of course he would have. He'd just gotten distracted thinking about how this wasn't how he wanted to kiss her. How many better opportunities there were. Then, next thing he knew, he saw his parents. By the time he'd come to his senses, they were filling his ears with their rebukes and Maisie was gone. He needed to find Maisie and make amends.

He met Fegus coming toward him. The team's heads were hanging as they pulled the wagon, its shredded black cloth waving in the wind. Fegus pulled the reins as Boone stopped next to him.

"This is a wreck. What happened?"

Fegus turned in his seat to look behind him. "When Mrs. Bragg jumped ship, she pulled the fabric loose. The farther I went, the more dragged behind and got caught up in the wheels."

The float was tattered and a horrible reflection on his new business, but Boone had bigger concerns.

"Where did she go?" He looked up and down the street for the figure he had grown to appreciate.

"She got in a tussle with some fellow. I didn't see it all, but your canteen saw some action. After that, she ran off into the crowd. No telling where she disappeared to."

Tall buildings stood shoulder-to-shoulder on both sides of the road. Buildings and businesses lined every side street and alley. She could be anywhere. Boone's horse twitched, its skin rippling beneath his saddle. So much rode on the success of his cave. He had bet everything—his workers' jobs, his other investments, and his future—on it being a success. Despite that, he'd forget it all to find Maisie.

When he thought about it, the places she was most likely to run to were the cave or her family farm. Boone patted his horse. He didn't like leaving town without knowing for sure, but he wasn't helping anything standing here in the middle of the street.

Sending Fegus home, Boone headed out toward the cave.

The shops of Joplin were taking advantage of the crowds on the street by hawking their goods from crates and barrels pulled out to the sidewalks. Miners strolled along, ripping bites out of greasy turkey legs and washing them down with bottles of beer. Little girls dressed in white ruffles and black boots chased their brothers down alleys. It seemed that every home in town had emptied out onto the street, and as Boone reached the outskirts of town, the crowd barely thinned.

Where were all these people going? They didn't all live in the country. Wagons and horses trotted along, and people talked excitedly. Boone got so caught up in scanning the crowd, looking for Maisie, that he didn't realize they were all heading to the same place until he arrived at the visitor center in front of the cave property.

After the talk with his parents, Boone was ready to throw in the towel. He'd almost let their skepticism convince him that this had been a bad idea. But it hadn't been. If a float of cheap black material and a painted sign impressed people enough to come, just wait until they saw the real cave.

He had to dismount and maneuver his way between horses to find a place at the hitching post. The door to the office was open, and people were crowded in the doorway, going neither out nor in.

"Excuse me," he said to a silver-haired couple leaning against the doorframe. "Can I pass through?"

Boone looked over his shoulder at all the excited faces. With this many tickets sold, he might have enough to pay for the stolen lighting.

"He's the owner," a kid said. "He was on the float with that lady."

"Where's your wife?" a woman in a nurse's uniform asked. "Your story in the paper was adorable. I'm hoping maybe I'll meet someone during my tour of the cave." She cast her eyes at the lanky man next to her.

"Yeah, where is your wife?" the portly man in front of her turned to ask. "I saw her come flying off that wagon and lay into that fella after you left. I wasn't close enough to hear what he said, but I'm sure he had it coming."

"Excuse me. I need to get inside." Boone removed his hat and turned sideways to squeeze through the line of people.

"No cutting in line," a man behind the desk charged. It was Amos. "Oh, sorry, Boone. I didn't see who it was. C'mon in."

"What are you doing here?" Boone asked.

"We came to buy our tickets, but when I saw how shorthanded you were, I pitched in to help." Amos craned his neck. "Where's Maisie?"

Boone didn't think it prudent to go into details. "We got separated at the parade. I was hoping to find her here."

"I can't believe she's not. She was all fired up about selling tickets."

"She's not at the ranch either?"

"Why would she be there when this is going on?"

Boone had no answer. All he knew was that he wanted Maisie with him. The cave didn't mean anything without her.

If Maisie had thought that Calista's house would be a quiet refuge where she could lick her wounds, she was wrong. Calista and Matthew had more people coming and going than the train depot. A poor miner's wife stopped by to ask if they had any spare groceries on hand. Calista loaded her down with a bag of potatoes before sending her on her way. A miner nearly fell through the front door, barely keeping his bottle of whiskey upright, and hollered for Matthew to save him from the demons hounding him. Matthew took away his bottle and told him he was free, then apologized to the ladies and escorted the miner to the guest bedroom to sober up.

"I'm sorry for the interruptions." Calista added more water to the teapot before joining Maisie at the kitchen table. "Now, I don't want you to be worried. I'm sure Boone had a good reason not to tell his parents about you."

"The reason is that he knew they'd hate me." Maisie picked at the doily under the table's centerpiece.

"No one hates you, sweetie. They just don't know you."

"The fact that I married their son without their knowledge isn't going to incline them in my favor."

Calista sipped her tea as she thought this over. "But once they see how happy you make him, they'll learn to love you."

Did she make Boone happy? For a while, she and Boone seemed to be going the right way. They spent time together, and she thought they both enjoyed that time. But lately he'd changed his mind about her. Lately he had regrets. She could read the signs. She might have done well enough for a partner in a business venture, but she'd never make him a suitable bride. Not with the way she constantly embarrassed him in public. He'd realized it before his parents ever showed up.

There was a timid knock on the door. A tear-streaked and rouge-painted face appeared at the screen.

"Mrs. Cook," the lady whispered as she pulled up the neck of her tattered gown. "I gotta get out of town. The madame has sent me to that brute for the last time. I won't take another beating." Then she spotted Maisie. "I'm sorry. I'll come back when you're not busy."

"Come inside, hurry." Calista set down her teacup and glided to the door. "Don't mind my cousin. Did anyone see you coming here?"

Maisie went to the stove and poured herself some tea so the woman and Calista could have some privacy. Here Maisie was, feeling sorry for herself, but she didn't have it that bad. She should be ashamed, taking Calista's time when other people needed her. Boone was nice to her. He'd never hurt her. She'd never go hungry or want with him. She had a lot to be thankful for.

She looked at the poor woman trying to escape her misery and felt ashamed. She didn't know what she could do to make amends to Boone's family, but she was no coward.

Matthew cleared his throat before easing into the kitchen. "Can I come in?" he asked cautiously.

Calista looked at the woman she was interviewing before waving her husband forward.

"Maisie." Matthew had the kindest face Maisie had ever seen. "There's someone at the door for you. The front door," he clarified.

Calista rose. "You can stay here," she said. "If you need some time to figure things out . . ."

"You gave me all I needed," Maisie said. She hugged her cousin tight. "Thank you for being you and doing what you do. That's more than enough." If only she could be more like Calista. As Maisie passed, she even threw her arm around Matthew's shoulders. "I don't know the next time I'm going to get a hug, so I might as well collect some of them now."

"You let me know if you're in trouble. You know we'll be there for you." Matthew had the same heart as Calista but more muscle behind his offer.

"You and the rest of the Kentworth clan," Maisie said. "It's prayer I need. Just remember me in that."

Maisie's feet dragged her through the parlor, but the peace and love she had with her cousin bolstered her resolve to face what was ahead. She'd made a decision on her own. She couldn't blame anyone else for it. It was up to her to deal with the consequences.

Boone stood by his horse at the edge of the porch. Without a word, Maisie walked past him to the street. She heard the jangling of the bridle and knew he was following.

"I owe you an apology," he said. The gravel scattered before him as he took long steps to catch up with her. "I don't know why I didn't do what I was supposed to do."

"Kiss me?" Maisie had wondered what offense he thought the most grievous. If that was where he wanted to start . . .

"Even worse, I left you at the parade. Those were my parents, and I wasn't expecting them home for another month. It was our article in the paper that did it. Someone mailed them a copy—someone who couldn't mind their own business."

"You getting married *is* your parents' business," Maisie said. "They shouldn't have heard it from a newspaper."

Boone shoved a hand into his pocket. "They mentioned that, and they're right. I should've written them, but they hadn't been in touch, and I had a lot to tend to. There was no reason to involve them."

"Or you didn't want to tell them because they would've told you not to do it, and you didn't want the confrontation," she said.

"Is that why you didn't tell your family until we'd already made it legal?" His raised eyebrow was all the censure she needed.

Maisie hung her head. "We both acted irresponsibly. Our parents deserved to have their say. They care about us."

"They would've convinced us to wait and make sure we weren't making a mistake." Boone focused on a streetlight on the corner ahead.

Had it been a mistake? Did he think it was? Maisie didn't like second-guessing her decisions. It was better to figure out what to do next instead of crying over what had already been done.

She drew a firm breath to steady her voice before continuing. "What do I need to know about your parents? Are they going to let me back in the house?"

"Yes!" Boone's eyes flashed. "You're a Bragg. You belong there."

That was something to build on, Maisie figured. "Are they terribly angry with me?"

"They'll blame me. Believe me, they know how stubborn I can be."

"But it's their house. If they don't want me there . . ." She paused, giving Boone a chance to reassure her. To tell her they would learn to love her and everything would work out in the end.

Instead, he said, "That man at the parade. That was your old beau?"

Her stomach flopped. "That was him."

"From what I heard, he seemed confident that you would be

happier with him." Boone's jaw twitched. Avoiding her gaze, he turned to check on his horse as it followed them.

Maisie looked up at the evening sky. What would Calista advise her to say? She wouldn't be happier with Silas, but was Boone trying to find an excuse to let her go?

"I don't want him," she said. "I'm ashamed that I ever associated with him. I left him when I saw what manner of man he was, and I don't regret that decision."

Had she laid on the *that* too heavily? Because Boone winced.

"You might not be happy with him," Boone said, "but I don't know if I can make you happy either."

The lights of the Bragg home flickered through the trees. Maisie knew the courage it took to leap over a gully. She knew the courage it took to dive into a lake. But courage was also needed when you found yourself in a fight with a runaway calf and you had to decide whether to let it go or to keep ahold of the rope, knowing that you were going to get some bruises and scrapes in the fight. Courage was for hanging in there, even knowing how tough it might get.

"It's not your job to make me happy," she said. "No man can keep a woman happy unless she has set her mind to it. I've just got to decide that I'm grateful for what I have and make the most of it. Happy or not, I can do my duty. That's the surest road to happiness that I know."

Brave words as they reached the house, but now she had to find the strength to live them.

CHAPTER 24

Before the sun had cleared the rooftops visible from Maisie's third-story window, she was up and dressed. Today she was going to meet Boone's parents, and she was ready to face them.

Last night, Boone had brought her through the servants' entrance and up the kitchen staircase to avoid running into his parents before she was ready. Maisie didn't think she'd be any more ready the next morning, but he'd mentioned that she looked a mess, and when she thought about the scuffle she'd had with Silas along with the long day on the float in the sun and wind, she realized that waiting until she could wash her hair and put on clean clothes was wise.

But it meant a sleepless night of pacing, wishing the first meeting was already behind her.

When she heard Boone moving around in the bedroom below, she went down her stairs and pressed her ear to the door for a sign that he was ready for her. This morning it was the sound of his boots dropping to the floor that told her it was safe to tap on the door.

"Come in," he said.

The faint pink tint in his eyes spoke of a wasted night for him as well. She wished she could smooth his tousled hair. This whole ordeal would be so much easier if she knew she was fighting for the two of them. As it was, it felt like Boone and she were fighting to maintain the status quo when neither of them cottoned to it.

He lifted his chin to the side and stretched his neck out to her. "Go on, take a whiff. I think you like the smell as much as I do." He kept her in his gaze, hopeful as she approached.

Maisie dropped her hand onto his shoulder as she leaned in and filled her lungs with the scent of lemon and sandalwood. "Smelling sweet," she said. "Too fancy for working in a mine." This was what she'd never had with Silas. The slowly growing together. The friendship, the uncertainty, the little steps that might someday mean more than instant attraction.

"Today we need to test the safety of the stairways and finish the café area," Boone said. "You can come if you want, but you'll probably get dirty."

"I'm not going to sit around here. I've had enough of that." He was engrossed with his shoestring, so Maisie added, "I could bring Olive to the visitor center. She needs to get out of her house."

"Good idea. I'll have Fegus drive you to pick her up, if you'd like."

"I can walk." She moved to the door, but Boone stopped her.

"Wait. I should go down with you. If you'll give me a minute . . ." He was really flummoxed by that shoestring, but Maisie was ready to face her dragons.

"I'll see you at breakfast," she said.

"If you'll wait—"

Maisie wouldn't hide behind Boone. She needed to stand on her own feet.

The breakfast room was a beautiful rectangular space that ran the length of the house and seemed to be made entirely of glass. Because of the sunlight, potted plants of every size and shape crowded the edges of the room, their greenery framing the view of the lawn. Even the breakfast cart was covered in small pots of herbs that reminded Maisie of her mother's kitchen garden back home.

"Mrs. Bragg," Mrs. Karol said with a smirk, "Mrs. Bragg would like to see you in the parlor."

Since her first day, Maisie had barely made it back to the parlor. She and Boone spent their time in the library or in the yard, making up some contest between them. When she saw a tall, handsome woman pounding on a pillow, she looked about to make sure she'd taken the right turn, but then she recollected the portrait above the fireplace and reasoned it out.

"Maisie?" Mrs. Bragg pounded on the pillow one last time, then tossed it onto the sofa. Her mouth twisted to the side as she took in Maisie, from her head to her toe twisting in the deep rug. "Have a seat, dear."

"I'm faster on my feet," Maisie said with a quick glance at the door.

If Maisie's answer surprised Mrs. Bragg, she hid it well. "I think I'll sit, if you don't mind." She eased her way onto the sofa and fluffed the pillow one last time. "You can imagine our surprise when we were mailed a newspaper that told us our son had wed." No beating around the bush for Mrs. Bragg. Maisie understood who her son took after.

"Yes, ma'am. I can imagine. Then again, you must know Boone. He's not one to blather on about things."

"I do know Boone, thank you." His mother's tone was hard to read. "And while he isn't the most communicative, he's never failed to involve us in a matter of this importance."

Like what? Maisie wanted to ask. What else had ever happened in his life that was this important? And what did they expect when they'd been gone for weeks? Her own folks had to be home by dark every night if they wanted to get up for milking the next day. She couldn't imagine parents who left for months. But Granny Laura had taught her that not all her thoughts were worthy of breath, so she held her peace.

Mrs. Bragg clapped her hands over her knees. "You seem like a nice young lady."

"Yes, ma'am."

"I said you *seem like*. I haven't had time to make that determination yet. If you are eventually going to decide that being married to our son isn't agreeable, it will take years for the scandal to fade. For this reason, I think we should avoid that scenario by biting the bullet and making the removal as quick as possible."

"I don't understand." Maisie crossed her arms. "If divorcing him is disgraceful, why would you tell me to do it?"

"I'd rather give him a chance to put this unfortunate incident behind him while he's still young, instead of letting the idea become well entrenched around town before you make your exit. If it's inevitable, let's get it behind us."

Maisie's neck burned. "It's not inevitable," she said through clenched teeth. "You should give your son more credit. He didn't marry a gal who would bring disgrace on his family." Perhaps her own family, but she'd learned a thing or two since then.

"I would hope not, but Boone has had girls after him since he started shaving. Most of them are pushed by their parents because they want their daughters to have this house, this life, and to move in the highest society."

"You can keep that society," Maisie exclaimed. "Bottle them up and put them on the back shelf of the root cellar. The house is nice, but I've got more room to roam at home. Your yard is puny compared to our ranch. My family isn't penniless."

"Why, then? Don't tell me you fell in love with him immediately. I'm not buying that."

"I'll stay married to him because I promised to," Maisie said, "not because of how I felt when I said the words. Feelings have nothing to do with it."

"You'll stay out of a sense of duty?" Mrs. Bragg twisted the tassel on the corner of the pillow between her fingers and pegged

Maisie with her skeptical gaze. "Even though your heart isn't engaged?"

With a clearing of his throat, Boone stepped into the room. "She isn't in love with me," he said. "You wanted her to admit it, and she did. Does that answer satisfy you?"

Mrs. Bragg had the grace to look embarrassed. "You shouldn't lurk in hallways. I'm trying to ascertain what's to be done here."

Had Maisie walked in to hear Boone saying that he didn't love her, she would be devastated, but he didn't seem to be affected.

"There's nothing for you to do," he said. "She's my wife, and that doesn't require any further action."

"I appreciate your goodwill, but look at her, Boone. You're doing your family a disservice if you think she can represent us dressed as she is. And there will be consequences for her, as well. She won't be accepted or happy until she better understands the life you've thrust upon her."

"She understands the business that we've partnered in. There's work to be done today. You must be tired from your traveling—"

"Nonsense. I never shirk my duty, and if you are insisting on keeping her, we must help her acclimate to life as a Bragg. The first thing she should realize is that Bragg women don't work in mines."

Maisie wondered if Bragg women had adequate hearing, because they were carrying on like she wasn't in the room.

"It's a cave, Mother," Boone said. "Hundreds if not thousands of women are going to go into this cave. Maisie has been a godsend when it comes to marketing the business."

"Word is spreading," Mrs. Bragg said. "We heard about the Crystal Cave all the way in Florida. And then, when we arrived home, we found a girl dressed in a hideous costume atop a wagon with our name on it. Everyone in town saw her. And half the town saw her get into a brawl with a strange man."

"I've laid off brawling," Maisie said. "From now on I'll only fight with Boone."

Mrs. Bragg blinked.

Boone dropped his hand on Maisie's shoulder. "If you want to grab some breakfast, I'll get the horses saddled."

"I'm in earnest, Boone," his mother said. "You've neglected her development. If you insist on keeping her, you must minimize the damage. Let me take her for a fitting before you parade her inadequate wardrobe through town again. Who is your dressmaker?" she asked Maisie.

"My ma, when she has time. Otherwise we order from the Montgomery Ward catalog."

Mrs. Bragg flung both hands in the air. "Do you see how badly I'm needed?"

"It's up to you," Boone said to Maisie. "You can come with me to the cave or go with Mother to the dressmaker. Whatever you feel is best."

Maisie bit her lip. She'd rather go with Boone. One hundred times over would she rather go with Boone than spend the day with his prickly mother, hearing more about how her wardrobe was inadequate, her family was inadequate, her manners were inadequate. But she needed to make another friend in this household, and that wouldn't happen if she rejected Mrs. Bragg's offer. Besides, she'd embarrassed Boone horribly at the party, and she never wanted to do that again. His mother was right. She had a lot of work to do that didn't involve the cave.

"I'll go with your mother." Maisie pulled her mouth into what she hoped looked like a smile. "I need her help to get all gussied up."

"If that's what you want."

What she wanted was to help Boone. If making his family happy put his mind at ease, then that was what she'd do.

Despite him asking, Boone's father had no interest in coming to see the cave that morning.

"Son, I've been in more caves than a bat. I just got back in town. I've got to see how my investments are doing."

Boone lifted his satchel to the desk in his father's office downtown. "I've kept accounts on everything of yours while you were gone. You should find it in good order. I was able to negotiate a better rate at the smelters for the Spook Light Mine, so I included your mines in that as well. Last month the output of the Rosemary was down ten percent, but they've hit another good patch and are hauling ore out on schedule now. You shouldn't have lost anything."

"You're a good mine operator, son. Why would you throw that away?"

Boone's eyes were drawn past Maxfield Scott's architectural wonders lining the street to the morning light cascading through the leaves.

"You taught me and Grady that we're supposed to be good stewards of our gifts—whether talent, intelligence, or wealth. God entrusted us with those gifts for His glory and the benefit of our fellow man."

"And that's why it's a shame for you to let this distract from your mining. That's where your talent lies."

"There's no lack of men in Joplin who can do the mining. God gave that gift liberally, but He gave me something unique. He gave me—Maisie and me—a piece of His creation that is unlike anything in the known world. When you see it, you can't help but think of the One who created it. No man has ever designed its equal—no matter how many electric lamps they steal."

His father's head jerked at the accusation. "Someone's stealing from you?"

"Yes. I can't prove who, but that Electric Light Park going in sure doesn't like that we're taking attention away from them."

"I read an article about the construction. You're going to be up against a behemoth. There's no way you can compete with them."

That was why Boone hadn't told his parents anything. If they had stayed gone for two more weeks, he would've had figures on paper to prove his success.

"At least I'll know in good conscience that I did what I could." If God had wanted to hide the cavern until Caine discovered it, He could have.

"I've been gone too long," his father said. "The mine managers need to see that I'm back at the helm. Are you coming with me?"

Boone picked up his hat. "We've sold a lot of tickets for the upcoming weekend. Everything has to be ready. I'm sorry."

The heaviness of his parents' disappointment stayed with him all the way to the work site. He arrived to see a wagon unloading crates of mugs for the café. Boone grabbed a crate to carry inside and saw Mark Gilbert coming up out of the shaft.

"How's it look down there?" Boone asked.

Gilbert held the door to the shaft open behind him as the rest of the construction crew came up. "It's hard going. We had to reset all the lamps, and we're nearly finished with the handrails. We'll be set if the pumps hold out."

"They'll hold out," Boone said. "The repairs have held, and I know what to do next time." And with his newfound experience, he would never have to shut down a mine because of water again. If he was still solvent after this venture, anyway.

"I heard your folks are back in town. What do they think of your new project?" Gilbert asked.

"I'd rather have been able to tell them about it myself instead of them forming their opinions while at a resort in Florida."

"Not happy, are they?"

"Mining is all my father knows. He doesn't see any profit in this, but we'll show him. We'll get this open soon enough, and it'll start earning its keep."

"Or Peltz is right. It'll fail, you'll lose this investment, and you'll have to sell to Caine, regardless of all your work."

Boone wanted his workers to be passionate about their jobs, but sometimes they took on so much ownership that they forgot who was boss.

Boone paused just long enough for Gilbert to feel the stare and drop his head.

"I'm going below," Boone said. "Help move these crates inside."

He walked through the entryway and down the steps, pausing for his eyes to adjust to the electric lighting above his head. He wasn't deep enough for the normal scents of a mine to catch him, but this one would always smell different. Instead of gunpowder and floating dust, the air smelled like paint and varnish. The handrail was smooth as he descended, and the stairs were even.

The tight path the customers would come through gave no hint of the glory beyond it. Boone wouldn't be surprised if many people became anxious and reversed course before reaching their destination. Hopefully they'd buy some postcards in the gift shop on their way home.

He'd gone down five or maybe six flights of stairs when he heard someone approaching from the bottom. Boone waited on a landing, because from the racket they were making, it sounded like they were loaded down like a pack mule.

His light caught the miner's surprised face when he turned the corner and looked up at Boone. It was young Howard Hughes.

Noting the bucket of paint and the paintbrushes stuck beneath his arm, Boone said, "They left you to tidy up, did they?"

"Forgot all about me," Howard said, "but if we leave this varnish open, it's going to dry out."

"Then you better get on up there." Boone moved to the side of the platform to give him room to pass.

"Hey, boss, I've got a question for you, if you don't mind." Howard's dark-rimmed eyes darted about as if someone might be in the shadows listening. "I noticed something strange going on in this tunnel."

As if his parents weren't bad enough, even the youngest miner was questioning Boone. "What's the matter?" he asked.

"The foreman said we needed to paint the sides of this entrance in places, so they're easier to see and people won't bump their heads. I think that's a fine idea, but some of the places he has marked for me to paint aren't in the way at all." He looked again over his shoulder. "I swear, the foreman only seems interested in covering up the ore spots. Wherever that shiny silver galena shows through, sure as shooting, that's where he'd have me slap a coat of paint. It's like he's just covering all evidence that this is an ore-rich mine. Now, if he's doing it on your orders, I'll shut my trap and move on . . ."

Boone nodded. "Drop your things and show me."

"Right by your head is one spot." Howard pointed to the squared-off side of the tunnel.

Boone reached up, caught the lamp, and turned it to the side. The beams created sharp shadows that weren't consistent with a smooth rock wall. He ran his hand over them. Through the paint, he could feel the squared corners that were particular to the ore.

"I knew there was ore here. We processed what we found when we cleared the shaft, but I didn't expect this much. We shouldn't paint over it. It'd make an interesting item for the tour guides to show the tourists."

"You don't have any desire to mine it?"

Boone shook his head. "Not if it means disturbing the cave. This is too close to it to be dynamiting."

"What if we could drill instead of dynamite?" Howard beamed as his words came quicker and quicker. "What if there was a drill of two, maybe three cones rotating against each other? It'd practically eat the rock away. It'd revolutionize mining." Even in the dark, Boone could see his enthusiasm for the idea.

"Wouldn't that be something?" Boone said. "I'll tell you what, you invent a drill like that, and I predict you'll become a very wealthy man. In the meantime, we're stuck with pickaxes and dynamite."

"I think about it all the time," said Howard as he hurried on up the stairs with the varnish cans.

Boone took one last look at the ore. A lot of good stuff in a bad place. If the Curious Bear had blossoms this abundant, he'd still be mining it. He could only pray that there'd be some beneath the waterline in the mine. Otherwise, the Crystal Cave carried his whole future on its shoulders.

Mrs. Bragg the elder was a force of nature, flying through town like a cyclone. She greeted people as she hurried by and let the responsibility for their surprise at her sudden reappearance in town fall on Maisie, who didn't know what to say beyond, "Her showing up was as unexpected as finding a snake in the hen's nest." Which, now that Maisie ruminated on it, was probably not a flattering thing to say about her mother-in-law.

Turning abruptly at a double door, Mrs. Bragg nearly took Maisie off her feet.

"I'm taking you to my dressmaker." Mrs. Bragg tugged on Maisie's waistband to straighten it. "*My dressmaker*. If you say something outrageous to her or behave in an untamed manner, I will be humiliated."

"Why?" Maisie asked. "She works for you, don't she?"

"Madame Duvalier accepted me as a client. I don't have the time and you don't have the education to understand how significant that is. I would rather have to find a new husband than a new dressmaker." Her eyes narrowed. "Forget I said that about my husband. I'm not looking to replace Mr. Bragg, you understand."

"You were talking big potatoes," Maisie said. "I follow you."

"Be on your best behavior." Then she reconsidered. "Remember that I'm trying to help you and do better than your usual best."

Mrs. Bragg's warning had no effect on Maisie beyond making her wonder what her mother-in-law thought might happen. Goodness, but people spent a lot of time worrying about matters that would never come to a head.

Maisie stepped through the brass door. The round sofa inside looked like a tight, prissy pincushion with no more softness than an overdone biscuit. On the table next to it, a marble pyramid paperweight held down a local newspaper. The chandelier would've impressed her at one time, but ever since she'd seen what God had made down in the belly of the earth, she couldn't be awed by an electric contraption of broken glass wired together.

Maisie stood before a full-length mirror as Mrs. Bragg consulted with a young lady toting a stack of fabric bolts. Maisie didn't spend much time brooding over her reflection, but since she'd stopped with her outside chores, she noticed her skin had grown creamier and smoother. Her figure still had the good proportions that were considered lucky as far as fashion was concerned.

The girl with the fabric glided past a brass birdcage and through a curtained doorway.

"Ellie is asking Madame Duvalier if she'll accept you as a client." Mrs. Bragg plucked at the lace on her wrist. "I even offered to give up my fall appointment if it would make room for you."

"There was no call for—" But at the pained expression on Mrs. Bragg's face, Maisie amended. "Thank you. You're awful generous."

When a woman parted the curtains and made her entrance, there was no doubt that she was Madame. Her peacock-blue turban was held in place with a glittering pin shaped like a monkey with ruby-red eyes. Instead of a fitted working dress, she was wrapped in a robe that was soft and flowing. If it hadn't been for the richness of the fabric and her flowered boots, it would have looked like she was still in the process of getting dressed herself.

Madame Duvalier's eyes lit on Boone's mother. "Ah, Mrs. Bragg. What a pleasure to have you home. If I weren't in such straits today, I would be able to see your new daughter-in-law, but as you understand . . ."

Those were the longest eyelashes Maisie had ever seen. Were they real? How could they not be? How would you get fake eyelashes? People wouldn't glue stuff to their faces, would they? Maisie reached up and tugged at her own eyelashes. Could you glue so many lashes to your eyes that it made them too heavy to blink? What a mess that would be. Just thinking about heavy eyelashes made her drowsy. She felt a yawn building in her chest and locked her jaw to keep from erupting right there in front of the priceless madame.

"But, Mrs. Bragg, is this the young lady in question?"

Madame Duvalier grabbed Maisie's forearm in cold, unyielding hands and turned her around. She pinched the skin at Maisie's waist, sniffing in surprise when she didn't get what she expected. Maisie felt her hackles rise. She wasn't used to being manhandled without defending herself.

"She is not my typical client, but she has potential," Madame said.

"You could do wonders with her," Mrs. Bragg cooed.

"And everyone has already seen her like this? They would know of my success?"

"It would be a credit to your skills."

Madame Duvalier turned Maisie away from her and ran her hands from the base of Maisie's neck out to her shoulders. "Broad," she said, "but a good anchor to hang marvelousance. I will accept her." Then, turning to Maisie, she said, "Remove your clothes."

Maisie put her hands on her hips. "I beg your pardon?"

"She can't measure you wearing this lumpy ensemble," Mrs. Bragg said. "You can keep your underclothes on."

"I never," Maisie grumbled as she unbuttoned her blouse. These fancy people liked to put on airs and act like they were so proper, then they behaved in the most indecent ways. It didn't seem right, getting undressed in a room bigger than their parlor back home. Especially as Madame Duvalier's assistant was coming and going at will.

Maisie didn't feel very proud standing in her homemade drawers.

Madame flicked her finger at Maisie's feet. "Shoes off."

Maisie hiked her foot up on the back of a chair and ripped the laces through the eyelets. Drat. Why hadn't she checked to make sure her socks didn't have holes in them?

Her mother-in-law sighed. "A full set of undergarments too, please. And stockings."

"She will need shoes for every outfit I design her. Those are unacceptable."

Maisie pulled the drawstring of her drawers tighter. "These shoes are comfortable. They have a lot of wear left in them."

Mrs. Bragg and Madame exchanged a look that let Maisie know sharing her opinion wasn't necessary.

"I can measure." Madame snapped her fingers, and her assistant placed a measuring tape in her hands.

Maisie stood stock-still while the woman pressed the strip of paper against her and around her.

"Is that twine in your drawers?" Mrs. Bragg whispered.

Maisie looked down at the drawstring just below her bellybutton. "Yes, ma'am. My drawstring snapped, and I found this in the carriage house. I didn't want to ask Boone for a drawstring for my drawers." Yet somehow she felt that talking to Boone about it would've been less embarrassing than this ordeal.

"Knock, knock?"

In the mirror Maisie was facing, she saw the curtain sway, and then a woman entered. The skin on Maisie's arms pimpled up before she even remembered the woman's name. Justina Caine.

Justina's face hardened as it lit on Maisie but then split into a smile as she saw Mrs. Bragg.

"Mrs. Bragg!" She ran across the room and threw herself into Mrs. Bragg's arms. "I heard that you and Mr. Bragg had returned to town. I'm so relieved! Things weren't the same without you."

Maisie tensed. Justina had humiliated her in front of all of Joplin, and Maisie had no doubt that Justina had done it deliberately. Now she'd shown up to make Maisie even more miserable. And all Maisie could do was stand here in her feed-sack underclothes.

"Be still," Madame Duvalier whispered.

"Indeed, they are not," Mrs. Bragg allowed. "Is your mother with you?"

Maisie had thought Mrs. Bragg treated *her* like a louse found after Saturday baths, but she was even colder to Miss Caine. And Miss Caine didn't seem to notice.

"No, I brought the buggy and Gus to haul my purchases. Madame Duvalier has a trunk of my new duds, and I can't wait to see them. I have a brunch today, and I know the morning dress she designed will do just perfectly."

"Another brunch? How charming." Mrs. Bragg smoothed her eyebrow.

Madame removed the pencil from her mouth to answer. "Your trunk is by the door, Miss Caine."

"Aw, thank you," Justina simpered, but she showed no signs of departure. Instead she turned her attention to Maisie. "My, my, Maisie Kentworth. Flour sack unmentionables? I'm shocked." She turned to make sure Mrs. Bragg was listening. "Everyone said that your family were well-respected ranchers. I didn't imagine they needed to make clothes out of twine and feed sacks."

"No use in wasting money," Maisie said. "The cows don't care what we wear." It was bad enough that Maisie had to stand in her underwear while Justina circled her like a wolf, but that her underwear should have been so inadequate was doubly shameful.

"You'll look lovely when I'm finished with you." Even Madame Duvalier was feeling bad for Maisie.

But Justina had turned her attention back to Mrs. Bragg. "I'm sure Boone told you about how he and Maisie met. That mine on the Kennedys' place—the one my father had a contract to buy—it was all locked up, but Miss Kentworth decided to illegally trespass on it. How was it that she got into that mine?" Justina tapped her chin. "Broke into it with a pickax? Just think, if Maisie hadn't been so handy with a pickax, Boone would be a free man right now."

Maisie's fists clenched. She was being insulted, and the truth put no shine on her, but she remembered her lesson from the dinner. She couldn't lash out. No matter how cold Justina was, she couldn't get hot.

"Your brunch must start soon," said Madame Duvalier to Justina. "We won't waste any more of your time. My girl will help you carry the trunk out."

Justina dusted her fingers. "The two of us can't lift a trunk that size. Gus will come inside and get it, but of course, he'll have to wait until Maisie has some decent clothes to wear."

"No need to wait," Madame Duvalier said. She gently rested her hand on Maisie's bare arm. "Mrs. Bragg, if you'll step behind the curtain, Miss Caine's man can come inside, and she can be on her way."

Looking at the floor, Maisie saw her bare toe sticking through the hole in her sock. She wasn't one to run and hide. To her way of thinking, Justina was showing herself to be uglier than Maisie's home-sewn underthings. She wouldn't make the same mistake twice, but she could deal with the problem in her own way.

Maisie strode to the trunk. Squatting, she got a good grip on both handles and neatly snapped the trunk up to her chest.

Refusing to look at Justina, she turned to Madame Duvalier. "Where do you want this?"

Madame's eyes held a sparkle of respect that hadn't been there before. "Put it in the entryway. Then we'll be undisturbed by Miss Caine and her driver."

Maisie might be wearing her tatty underwear, but she was still as strong as Samson. The awed silence in the room felt good as she strode through with the trunk held securely against that old twine drawstring. A matron sank back in her cushioned chair as Maisie burst through the door into the entryway. Maisie met her astonishment with a level gaze and lowered the trunk to the ground.

"Is it locked?" she heard Justina ask Madame inside the fitting room. "I don't want her going through my things."

Maisie's eye fell on the padlock of the trunk and the shining brass key that was still in the keyhole. Picking up the marble paperweight from the table, she hammered it down against the key, snapping it off flush. The waiting woman covered her mouth as Maisie swooped down and picked up the broken end of the key.

Holding the bent and broken piece of brass before her, Maisie entered the fitting room and dropped it into Justina's hand.

"Your trunk is locked," she said. "No one will be stealing your things from it." She expected her mother-in-law to be aghast, but instead there was an ornery smile on her lips.

Justina seethed as she turned the broken key over in her hand. "I need that dress immediately! What am I supposed to do? Call a locksmith?"

Maisie marched her holey socks across the thick rug to where her clothes lay in a pile. She snatched her blouse off the ground and had one arm in it before answering.

"Or you could learn to use a pickax. I've found it to be a valuable skill."

CHAPTER 25

"Mr. Bragg, we have a problem." Mrs. Penney wiped at the sweat dripping down the side of her face as she stepped into the visitor center.

It must have been a big problem to bring her all the way to the cave on foot. Boone thought she'd take a moment to appreciate the nearly completed visitor center, but to his surprise, she didn't seem the least interested.

"You hired me to stir up publicity for this venture. We all agreed that, in addition to talking about the geological wonders and discoveries, part of the marketing campaign was a story of true love discovered in the cavern."

"We agreed." It hadn't been his idea, but he'd agreed.

"Then why are you and your wife trying to destroy the image that we've constructed?"

"I don't understand," Boone said. "We're doing everything you told us to do."

"Did I tell you to abandon her in the middle of a parade? Did I tell her to have a row with a former beau in front of the grandstand?" Mrs. Penney pulled a folded newspaper from beneath her arm. "You'll want to see this."

No, Boone was fairly certain he didn't. "Enlighten me."

She quoted without reading, "'Cave Operator's Story Doesn't Hold Water.'"

"If only it were the cave that didn't hold water."

"All you had to do was ride through town and look happy together. I didn't think that was too much to ask." Mrs. Penney dropped the newspaper in a chair and retrieved her handkerchief to mop her sweaty brow. "It hurts our credibility. It hurts our narrative. And it's going to hurt sales."

"Come here," Boone said. He looked over his shoulder to make sure Mrs. Penney was following him to the office. Once there, he pulled out an account book and pointed to a number written on a light blue line. "These were our ticket sales after the parade."

She looked, rubbed her eyes, and looked again. "People bought that many tickets?" She stiffened her spine. "This was before the newspaper came out, but it's a good show of intent. Once the cave is open, word of mouth will do its part, but until then, you two need to hold steady to the plan."

Protect his wife, protect his business. With every day, Boone was finding that Maisie meant more to him. She hadn't deserved to be shamed in front of the crowd. She hadn't deserved to have to explain herself to his parents. He should've prepared them. He should've made it easier on her.

He should've kissed her when he had the chance. In fact, he'd kiss every one of those freckles if she'd let him.

After Mrs. Penney left, Boone waited anxiously for the hands of his watch to move to the correct placement, and then he packed up his gear to go home.

What had Maisie gotten into while he was gone? Had his mother succeeded in running her off? Overall, he was glad they were home. He'd missed his father's steady partnership and his mother fussing over him. The fussing had been taken over by Maisie, so maybe he hadn't missed it as much, but he wanted to get everyone to the place where they could appreciate each other.

But to do that, he had to show his parents that Maisie would be good for him. That she wasn't a poor interloper whom he'd had pity on and unwisely brought into the family. He had to convince his parents that Maisie Kentworth was good enough for the Braggs.

Now that his mother was home, walking straight from the mines into the parlor was not allowed. Maybe Maisie would be in her room. After leaving his horse with Fegus, Boone entered a side door and was skirting through the kitchen when he heard feminine voices in the parlor. Trying to be discreet, he eased past the doorway. His mother had her back to him, entertaining her guest with an animated account of some disaster. The lady on the couch was a beauty, but Boone knew a trap when he saw it. Had his mother invited another prospect to the house in the hopes of convincing him to abandon Maisie? His blood boiled at the thought.

He'd escape before he caused a nasty scene. But before he could, his mother turned.

"Boone? You can't mean that you have no comment."

He had a lot of comments, but none that were fitting for a mother's ears. Where was Maisie? He looked up, on the off chance that she had climbed the bookcases, but she was not there.

His mother crossed the room to sit on the sofa next to her visitor, and Boone realized he was about to get reprimanded for not introducing himself. But another look told him that he had made a mistake.

Maisie was holding a teacup, hiding her smile behind it, but her eyes were tilted with merriment. How had Boone not recognized her? Maybe it was the giant platter hat balanced atop her pillow of hair. Maybe it was the pearl earrings as big as grapes. Maybe it was how she was seated at the edge of the sofa with her feet crossed daintily beneath her. All of those things made her look like someone other than Maisie.

His mother beamed at him as she reached up to twist one of

Maisie's escaped curls around her finger. "Doesn't she look superb?" Then, to Maisie, she said, "He didn't even recognize you."

Maisie lowered her teacup. "What do you think, Boone? Didn't your ma do me up good?"

"Let me see," he said. Surely when she got up, he'd see she was the same girl.

True to form, Maisie stood, stretched her arms wide, and spun on her toes. She acted like Maisie, but she looked like the women his mother had rightly warned him about.

Mrs. Bragg the elder patted the sofa. "You've learned a lot today, dear, but never, ever get up and twirl for a man, no matter how he seems to appreciate it."

"No twirling? Yes, ma'am. Boone, watch this. I used to walk like this. . . ." Moving so that her back was against the wall, Maisie took out across the room, swinging her arms and thunking her heels into the floor in an exaggeration of her normal gait. "Your ma said I walk like a hawker on the sidewalk trying to lure people inside a new saloon. But she taught me how to walk like a lady. Instead, I'm supposed to walk like this. . . ." Running to return to her starting place, Maisie pressed her back against the wall, lifted her chin, and let her smile fade away. With bored indifference painted on her face, she eased forward one foot, then the other, slowly but perfectly gliding across the floor.

"Isn't she amazing?" his mother cooed. "She's a talented mimic. It doesn't take her any time to get the imitation down."

Every detail, even to the arrogant tilt of her nose. She didn't look like the Maisie he knew. She didn't look like a woman he'd want to know either.

"You should've gone with us today, Boone," his mother said. "You've really done a disservice to this young lady. This poor child has been thrown to the wolves, and you haven't helped her."

Boone wanted to defend himself, but his fearsome mother had called it true. "What wolves did she encounter today?"

"The leader of the pack—Justina Caine."

Maisie snorted. "Justina Caine has no more manners than a pig with a slop bucket."

Boone looked at his mother in alarm.

"Maisie is fine," Mother said, "but Justina will be stewing for a while. Maisie put her in her place quicker than we ever could. I'm telling you, boy, this girl is a treasure, but she's going to need help."

Boone was flabbergasted. He hadn't expected his mother to come around so quickly. What was she up to?

"What kind of help?" he asked.

"The kind I can provide. You see, society loves an ingenue, assuming they are presentable enough for them to relate to. I'm taking Maisie under my wing and am going to prepare her for her place in society. All you have to do is stay out of the way."

For the first time in this conversation, he saw the shadow of misgivings flit across Maisie's face. Could that mean she'd rather stay with him?

"The cave is almost ready," Boone said to Maisie. "I even hired a few of your cousins to work in the café."

"You don't have a dress for the grand opening, do you?" His mother tilted her head the way she always did when picturing a solution. "Whatever we do, it should have some sparkles on it. Something to reflect the beauty of the cavern. I wonder if Madame Duvalier has time to sew some Austrian crystals onto the velvet trim we ordered today. That would be perfect."

"You have to see the cave before it opens, Mother." Boone sat. "You should be one of the first."

"I suppose there are a lot of steps," she continued, not seeming to have heard him. "Maisie's dress shouldn't be too slim at the ankles, and no train at all, then. We'll have to rethink our decision. Can't have you tripping and falling down the stairs. This is my first shot at having a daughter of my own. I can't fail this early."

"I can wear whatever," Maisie said. "People aren't going to be looking at me. They'll be there for the crystals."

"Nonsense. I've spent twenty-four years picking out Boone's

clothes, and he isn't nearly as interesting to dress as you are. I'm not missing out on the fun."

"We could go tomorrow," Boone said. "No one will be there, so it doesn't matter what you wear."

"We'll come when we're ready, Boone." Mother stopped gazing at Maisie long enough to pat his hand. "You don't want us at your great and glorious cave if we're only going to be an embarrassment."

"What are you talking about? How could Maisie embarrass me in front of my men? They're already besotted." And so was he, but evidently his opinion didn't matter.

Boone waited, hoping to catch Maisie's eye and drag her away from his mother, but he never got the chance. Leaning forward with her beautiful lip between her teeth, Maisie was intently noting every word out of his mother's mouth like an earnest student.

Boone was only in the way.

It had been two days, and Maisie had barely seen hide nor hair of Boone. She'd agonized over the rough start she'd had with Mrs. Bragg. She'd thought she would never have her mother-in-law's approval, but now she realized that she could have it if she was willing to work every minute of the day to keep it. Mrs. Bragg seemed delighted with her and more than capable of turning her into exactly the kind of wife that Boone needed, but the more Maisie worked to please Boone, the less she got to be with him.

Maisie bent over the marble-topped end table and gathered a Napoleon clock along with a bronze figurine of a nearly naked woman and carried them to the dining room table.

Mrs. Bragg entered the dining room backward, dragging a rocking chair behind her. "We've nearly got the area clear. I'm not going to rest easy until that rug gets beat out. I don't know what Boone was doing while I was gone, but it looks like he's dumped buckets of dirt in the parlor."

Now that she knew Mrs. Bragg, it was easy to see the resemblance between the haughty young bride in the portrait over the fireplace and the determined matron hefting ponderous cabinetry to and fro. Maisie helped her carry out the end table while Mrs. Karol took the cushions off the sofa.

"I've beat out rugs before," Maisie said, "but this rug is big enough to cover the whole ground floor of my house. How in the blazes are we going to carry this thing outside?"

"Not by ourselves, I assure you, but it won't be easy. Once Mr. Bragg and Boone see me starting on my spring cleaning, they find urgent business that needs doing away from the house. We'll have to enlist Fegus."

Was that why Maisie hadn't seen Boone? He came home every night, but he was either already asleep when she tiptoed past his bed, or she heard him rummaging around late at night after she'd retired. Their timing was all wrong, but everything else seemed right. Boone and his father left for work at their mines every morning, while Mrs. Bragg kept Maisie busy, which helped push the loneliness away. Maybe this was what Boone had imagined from the beginning.

Taking little steps so she didn't run over Mrs. Bragg, Maisie carried the round table into the dining room so they could roll up the rug. The three ladies lined up on the far side of it and began folding it over.

"Maisie?" Boone walked across the rug, oblivious to their task.

Maisie straightened and brushed her hair out of her face. Was she smiling too big? Mrs. Bragg was teaching her that enthusiasm could be off-putting, but she was so glad to see Boone that she didn't care.

"Do you need me?" she asked.

Her smile was reflected in his eyes. "The final board meeting before the opening is about to commence. They'll want to hear from you."

Maisie beamed. Despite the sweat on her brow and the grit on her hands, she looked the part of a lady. She wiped her hands on her chintz skirt. "I want to hear from them. I have some ideas for our opening—"

"Wait." Mrs. Bragg jammed her foot behind the rolled rug to keep it from unwinding. "Boone, is it appropriate for a lady of Maisie's station to be involved in this venture?"

"Mrs. Penney is on the board."

"Of Maisie's station, I said."

Boone's smile faded. "Maisie knows I don't mean any disrespect."

"But others might not understand. This young lady has to overcome a multitude of disadvantages. Let's not give her the added stigma of being a woman in mining."

"I was in ranching," Maisie said. "I don't think mining is a step down from that."

"But it is a step down from socialite, and that's what you're going to become. I already have plans for you to accompany me to Fort Lauderdale in a few months. The ladies who winter there will find you delightful."

More time away from Boone? Maisie smiled bravely. Learning the right way to behave was the best way to help him. Once she got her lessons down, it would correct this awkwardness between them.

"Because beating rugs is more exalted than a board meeting?" Boone asked. "I have something in the carriage house that might help you with your chores." His eyes telegraphed a heartfelt message to Maisie before turning away. "Follow me."

CHAPTER 26

Boone hurried out of the parlor, a tight, choking feeling working up his chest. He wasn't all that astute when it came to women, but he was learning to read Maisie, and something was wrong. He should've known she'd be uncomfortable under his mother's tutelage. He should've guessed that she'd feel constrained with the new wardrobe, new manners, and new rules. So why was she doing it? Did she really prefer this life to the freedom they'd had before his parents returned?

Boone had never wanted a woman interfering with his life, but once he'd made room for Maisie, his day felt empty without her. He could finally understand how she felt when he worked long hours—watching the clock, anticipating meetings, and the disappointment when the meeting never materialized.

Maisie had ducked her head and fallen into step behind Boone before his mother could object. She didn't speak a word as they wound their way to the kitchen door and then through the garden.

Now, in the privacy of the carriage house, Boone felt the words grow thick. There were questions you might not want to know the answers to, but they needed to be asked just the same.

Boone lifted some planks away from the wall to help his search for the pulling cart. "What are your true feelings?" he asked.

He heard her feet scuff against the hard-packed floor. "About what?"

"About what my mother is expecting of you." He tossed the planks aside and reached for more.

"I've got as many thoughts about that as Blue has fleas."

"I can understand why you'd like it," he said as he piled the scraps of lumber out of his way. "Most girls enjoy getting dressed up and fawned over."

"Cricket's wings," Maisie exclaimed. "I don't give a hoot about looking like everyone else. You're the reason I'm doing this. I embarrassed you at the Landauers' dinner. I don't want to do that again."

Boone turned to look at her. "You're doing this for me?"

"For you. For us. I've got to figure out how to smooth things over. I don't want to be a liability as a partner."

The cart was visible now. Grabbing it by the corner, he rolled it out from against the wall, even as his thoughts tumbled along.

"Boone? Maisie? Are you coming back?" His mother stood in the garden, shading her eyes as she tried to spot them in the carriage house.

"I have a board meeting. I can't stay," he said to Maisie. He pulled the cart outdoors. Glancing at his mother, he added under his breath, "Tonight, I want another contest. I don't care what it is, but I miss our bouts." He missed everything about her, including her propensity to astonish him with her sweetness when he'd done nothing to deserve it.

"You think your luck has changed?" Maisie crossed her arms.

Boone grinned as he held the door open for her to pass. Win or lose, if he was keeping Maisie company, he was the luckiest man in Joplin.

Maisie had worked harder cleaning the parlor than she'd ever worked with a hoe and shovel. Once back in her room and out of her new clothes, she stood at the basin and ran the washcloth down her neck.

These city women were a sight to behold. All proper and dainty, but they decorated their houses in heavy furniture, carpets, and drapes that would take a pulling team of Clydesdales to move. She thought back to the simple furniture at her Granny Laura's house—the maple breakfast table, the ladderback chairs, and the braided rugs. Besides the piano and the pie keep, there wasn't anything that couldn't be moved by one person. Simplicity had its benefits.

Picking up the plush towel, Maisie dried her neck, then reached up to unpin her hair. She rolled her head from side to side, knowing that she'd feel the soreness the next day, but preferring sore muscles to idle ones. Her brush, the same wooden-handled one from home, caught the tangles as she held the locks high to reach the ends. She was focused on a particular snare when she heard footsteps on her stairs.

Boone had promised her a visit tonight. She hadn't forgotten. All day she'd fretted over what could happen, what she wanted to happen, what she dreaded happening. The uncertainty made her skittish.

"Knock, knock," he said. "Can I come in?"

All day she'd waited in an uncomfortable but beautiful dress, and here he would see her at her worst, in an old nightgown. "Come in," she said.

The door was ajar. Boone paused when he saw her, his foot on the last step. Maisie had watched him get dressed in the mornings, but he'd never seen her so unpresentable. Whatever he was thinking, he hid it well.

"The board meeting is over." He stepped inside and, without commenting on her unusual appearance, headed toward the suit of armor. She was in her nightclothes, and he was still dressed for the office. His suit coat was gone, but his dark vest and tie remained.

"How did it go?" she asked.

"There's cause for concern, no doubt about it, but the early ticket sales are outstanding. We're getting letters from all over the country wanting to know about our cave. Most of the newspaper articles are positive, and there's no evidence that Peltz has caused any more trouble." He lifted the visor on the knight. "It looks like our work might pay off."

"Let's pray it's so." Maisie reached for her robe, but Boone snagged it off the hook first.

"I always wondered if this knight got tired of being the same, day after day." He draped the robe over the knight's shoulders. "He can't change. He can't bend, or learn, or adapt."

Maisie's nose tickled at the dust he sent aloft. She rubbed her nose with the back of her hand as she found the belt to the robe and tied it around the knight's waist, careful to thread it around the spear balanced against the floor. Maisie didn't have to look up to know that Boone was watching her. He was standing so close that she could feel the heat of him through the capped sleeve of her nightgown.

"This knight must have been bored when you moved downstairs. I bet he missed not seeing you every day," Maisie said.

"I miss him too."

She was one-hundred-percent sure that Boone wasn't talking about that armored man.

"But you're here now, and you promised me a game." Maisie looked around the room, trying to keep the conversation light. There was no space for wrestling. No room to throw things either. There was a chessboard on the shelf, but she'd never had the patience for that game, preferring to throw the pieces at her brothers instead of learning the moves. Neither the ball, the knight's spear, nor the kite were of any help.

Her eyes lit on an oblong rock. "This isn't from the cavern, is it?" She held it between her finger and thumb.

Boone shook his head. "I've had that for years. It's quartz. Just something I thought was pretty and brought home."

"We could play thimble, thimble," Maisie said. "Since you don't sew, we'll use this crystal."

"I was hoping for something with more exertion."

"I've moved every piece of furniture on the ground floor of this mansion." Maisie rocked on her bare feet. "If you wanted exertion, you could've helped. Now, step outside."

Boone ducked his shoulders as he passed through the door, and Maisie shut it behind him. The piece of quartz was nearly the size of her pinkie finger. She'd have no trouble hiding it, and her gaze fell first on the knight wearing her robe. She gritted her teeth as she opened his visor, wincing at the slightest squeak, and settled the crystal inside. Once she had the visor closed, she stepped to the other side of the room and called for Boone.

Boone entered and, without giving her a second look, began searching the shelves. "I don't want you to feel obligated to do everything Mother suggests," he said. "Especially on my account."

"I'm a practical person," Maisie said. "Colder. You're getting colder. If it helps us, then it makes sense."

"There are things that lead to success in society or business that aren't helpful for a marriage." He wandered toward the windows and looked behind the curtains.

"Even a marriage like ours?" Maisie regretted her words as soon as they left her mouth. Why did she have to go and kick the hornet's nest? Why couldn't she leave things be? "Warmer," she said as he started toward her.

"Do you remember our contract, Maisie?" Boone wasn't looking for the crystal. He was looking at her. "We agreed there'd be no romance until the Crystal Cave is successfully launched."

"No discussion of romance," she corrected. "You wrote it yourself. Colder."

Boone's eyes fell on the suit of armor. "Ticket sales exceeded my expectations."

"We haven't had our first visitor. Warmer."

"Everything looks promising."

"Warmer. That's what I'm hoping."

"Are you?" He stopped with his hand resting on the visor. "Are you hoping it's a success?"

For financial reasons, of course, but that wasn't the heart of the question. Did she want romance with Boone? Could she give him her affection and love? She wiped her hands against the worn cotton of her nightgown.

Seeing that no reply was coming, Boone opened the visor and produced the crystal as if he'd known it was there all along. "My turn," he said.

Maisie felt no relief as she stepped out of the room. The games they played, the roles they pretended—there was a safety to knowing that at any time she could step away without risking her heart. If Boone disappointed her as Silas had, she could claim that she wasn't hurt. It had all been a ruse. That was where she was, but was that where she wanted to stay? If she was honest with herself, it wasn't.

She entered at his bidding and moved without thought.

"Warmer, colder, colder, warmer." She let his voice direct her toward the telescope. When she honed in on it, he stepped out of the way.

"I've been thinking about our future," he said. "A lot depends on how the mines and the cave do. Maybe a few years from now we'll have started construction on our own home. We'll have our own group of friends. Our own lives, separate from my parents. Colder. You're getting colder."

He'd directed her straight to the window, then switched his call. When she turned toward the shelves, he indicated that she was on the right path again.

"What if the mines fail? What if you had to take a job in town and you lived in a modest house like Uncle Oscar's?" she asked. "Would you be devastated?"

"The failure would crush me, but if that was where God wanted me, I'd learn to be content. As long as I have work that I feel is important. As long as I have . . ." His eyes followed her as she ran her hand along the shelving over her head. "Warmer. Warmer." He stepped out of the way so she could explore, and immediately changed his advice. "Colder. Now you're moving away."

Maisie turned to survey the room. He'd told her she was getting closer by the window, then by the shelves. Now she was cold again, and the only thing that had changed was his location. "I don't think you're playing fair," she said.

He shrugged. "I don't remember any rules discussed." As Maisie came to stand in front of him, he asked, "What if I had only modest means? Would you feel cheated by our deal? Warmer. You are definitely getting warmer."

Maisie took his hand and pried it open. It was empty. She took his other hand, but there was nothing in it.

"You're getting so warm," he said as she stood holding both of his hands.

And she was. She took one look at the knight and, remembering the visor, asked, "Boone Bragg, you did not put that rock in your mouth, did you?" Maisie took him by the chin. "I am not digging through your mouth to find it."

"Colder."

Her hand fell to his collar.

"Really warm. You haven't answered my question. What if our future doesn't look like this? Would you be satisfied without the money and the society and the jewels?"

Maisie was on a mission. He had to have that narrow piece of rock somewhere in his collar. Being so close to him was flustering. Being so close to winning was flustering. With shaking hands, she unknotted his tie and yanked it through the collar. Standing on her tiptoes, she ran her finger beneath his collar, all the way around, but all she could feel was the tickling of his breath on her neck. She bent his lapels, but there was no stone beneath them. She ran her hands over the breadth of his shoulders but didn't feel anything that wasn't Boone himself.

"You didn't answer my question," he said.

"You stopped playing the game," she replied.

"Hot. So hot you're melting."

With her heart pounding, Maisie started at his collar bone and ran her hands slowly down his chest. His heart was pounding too, strong beneath her palm. She went lower, and then she felt it. A bump like a pencil inside some hidden pocket. She swallowed hard as she slid her hand inside his vest. She felt the seam of a pocket, but then his hand clamped down on hers, pinning it against him.

"Take away the expectations of my family," he said. "Take away the comforts that wealth can provide. Take away whatever happens for good or ill with our investments. Could you be satisfied with me?" His hand held hers firm even though his breathing was bumpy. "Only me?"

Maisie closed her eyes. She'd thought she would have to protect herself against an overly amorous husband, and instead she'd found herself with a generous, caring companion. A companion who had done his best to preserve her independence and had left her incredibly lonely. She dropped her forehead against Boone's chest. Despite his mother's best intentions, Mrs. Bragg was no substitute for Boone. No one was.

"Maisie, you must know that I'm devoted to you." His hands traveled up her back to cradle her head. "I've given you everything I thought you needed or wanted, but now I'm going to ask for something in return. I want to know what you think. Do you think you could ever love me?"

"Losing the money doesn't scare me," Maisie said. "I'm not afeared of hard work or modest means. You can take society and jewels and toss them in a sinkhole, for all I care. The only thing that frightens me now is losing you."

Suddenly, it wasn't just her tattered nightgown that made her feel exposed. She'd gone and said words that she'd promised herself she'd never say again.

Boone's chest lowered with a long exhale, and he wrapped his arms around her. Maisie felt the comfort of his body against hers and the safety of his arms. They stood there with only the knight as a witness, until Boone planted a kiss on her head, then pulled away.

"You won't lose me," he said as he dropped the crystal into her hand. "We might lose everything else, but you were never in danger of losing me." His eyes were so full, so earnest.

Could it be true? Boone didn't think her inferior or shameful. For whatever reason, he thought she belonged to him, and with him.

With a promise to see her in the morning, Boone backed out of the room, watching her with fondness until the closing door interrupted his view.

Maisie wiggled her fingers, unsure that she was still in the same body. She switched off the light and felt her way through the dark to her little bed, feeling more at home than she ever had at the ranch.

CHAPTER 27

No matter what words were said the night before, Maisie and Boone were destined to spend the day together. They were going with Mrs. Penney to meet some journalists before the cave opened on Friday. Mrs. Penney had invited journalists from afar to come for an interview, an early tour, and pictures. If they managed to squash some of the rumors from that one catty newspaper article, all the better.

Maisie tossed a baseball into the air and caught it as she dallied between two outfits. The horrible farm outfit that Mrs. Penney had scrounged up was folded atop Boone's chessboard, neat and cleanly pressed. The other dress hung on a padded hanger from the dressmaker. The morning light caught the sheen of the fabric and made it glow like it was warmed from the inside.

She was warmed from the inside too, especially when she thought about Boone's visit the night before. Clearly, Boone was probing into areas that they'd set aside before. While Maisie wasn't satisfied with where things were, she wasn't sure where she wanted them to go, but it bore looking into.

"Boone?" she called down the staircase. "Can you help me for a second?"

She heard a dresser drawer rasp closed and then Boone jogging up the staircase. Maisie knew she was taking another step away from safety, but after Boone's declaration last night, it wasn't as harrowing. He hadn't laughed at her nightgown. Surely she could trust him with this situation as well.

Boone didn't come inside until he'd done a complete inspection of her in her dressing duds. She was wearing her corset and liked the way it cinched in her waist and pushed up her bosom. Upon first wearing it, it had made her feel self-conscious, like she was a peacock strutting around so everyone would notice what was being emphasized. Once she realized that everyone from Mrs. Penney to her mother-in-law wore the same apparatus, she didn't feel as guilty. In fact, the apparatus had been most helpful in getting Boone to notice her, just like he was doing right now.

"I don't know what to wear," she said. "This ensemble that your ma got me is beautiful, and I'm leaning toward it if I'm going to be in front of a gaggle of newspaper people, but Mrs. Penney sets a lot of store by that tale we tell. She expects me to be the country bumpkin, so she might rather I be dressed in the outfit she got me. What do you think?"

Maisie stepped back so he would stop gazing at her and direct his attention to the clothes displayed before him. There was a lot riding on his answer. Boone swore that he didn't need her gussied up, but ever since she took to dressing fine, he'd started paying court.

He went from one dress to the other while Maisie held her breath, unsure of what she wanted to hear. She'd melt if he told her that he liked her no matter what kind of bizarre costume she wore. On the other hand, if he said he wanted her to wear the new outfit, she'd feel proud. That would show that he appreciated the hard work she was doing to fit in with his friends. Which would he choose?

"We've got to tell them our story, right? The poor farmer's

daughter wandering into the rich man's lair and trapping him with her beauty?"

Maisie nodded. "That's the plan."

"On one hand, if you're all dressed up fancy, the story won't be as dramatic. You'll look just like every other rich woman."

"True."

"On the other hand, if you wear this monstrosity, you won't have any reason to dress like *that* underneath." He lifted an eyebrow. "I'm very much an enthusiast of whatever *that* is." He pointed at the lacy shaper and the things it was shaping, but his eyes never left hers.

Maisie felt light and giddy. "I'll wear whatever you think best."

"I'm happy with you no matter what you are or are not wearing," he said. "And I'm sorry if I didn't make that clear earlier."

"Mr. Bragg." Mrs. Karol's voice sounded from Boone's room below. "Mrs. Penney has arrived. She's waiting for you and Maisie."

"I have to get ready." Maisie stepped carefully around Boone, not sure what would happen if they touched each other but knowing that whatever it was, it'd take more time than she had allotted.

"I think farm clothes would be best for today," Boone said. "But not those. That's not what Maisie Kentworth wore."

"You're right." Maisie went to the window and opened it. "I'll wear what I wore to my first board meeting. Not this." She lifted the costume and tossed it out the window to fall three stories to the front yard. "But they don't need to know what I'm wearing beneath."

"I won't forget," he said and left, which relieved and disappointed her.

By the time she went downstairs, Mrs. Penney was pacing before Boone, coaching him on his lines and wondering aloud what was keeping Maisie.

"I'm ready," she said, and when Mrs. Penney's face fell at her clothing, which was neither impressive nor ridiculous, Maisie hurried to add, "When I lived on the ranch, this is what I wore to town, so it's authentic."

"Too late to change now." Mrs. Penney smoothed her unruly eyebrow. "The buggy is waiting."

Maisie sat between Boone and Mrs. Penney. At first she held herself away so that she didn't crowd Boone by bouncing against him, but he didn't seem to be bothered by the contact. It felt good to be back in the sunshine, behind a trotting horse, wearing comfortable shoes—herself, not the horse—and it felt good to be safe and secure next to her husband.

Boone smiled down at her, and Maisie leaned into him even more.

They turned early, before reaching the Kentworth road, on a new road that led to the visitor center. Maisie would never stop being amazed at the fact that this building was conceived in Olive's head, drawn on paper, and now stood here in solid rock. She reckoned it was like how she and her ma planted seeds in the spring and had an inkling of what the garden would look like by summer. Only this was a skill she had never acquired, and she couldn't imagine where shy, retiring Olive got the idea to take up such an interesting hobby.

Buggies were lined up at the north entrance of the visitor's center, and horses stood at the hitching post. A group of men and a few women waited beneath a shade tree, every eye turning toward them as they rolled up.

"We're late," Mrs. Penney said, nearly jumping out of the buggy before it stopped rolling.

"Sorry I took so long to get dressed," Maisie said.

"I'm not sorry," Boone replied. He climbed down, then reached for her. Taking her by the waist, he pulled her against him. "Not sorry at all."

Maisie didn't see Mrs. Penney coming until she appeared at Boone's side. "You're doing marvelously, Boone," she said, "but save it for the interviews. No one can appreciate your act from over there. Now, come on. They're waiting."

To Maisie's surprise, Boone took charge of the group immediately, introducing himself, welcoming the journalists, and leading them inside the cool, thick walls of the visitor center. Maisie's cousin Hilda Kentworth came out of the kitchen with a tray of glasses of sweet tea to serve as everyone found their seats in the waiting area.

"What are you doing here?" Maisie asked.

"Hannah and I got hired on. We're working in the café."

Which made perfect sense. Her cousins from across the river lived closer than workers in the city. They wouldn't have a chance for work if it weren't for the cave. Maisie began to understand some of Boone's concern for his employees and the importance of keeping them in jobs.

"Thank you for coming out to our Crystal Cave," Boone announced. "I know some of you traveled for a couple of days to get here, and we appreciate it. This geode was formed when water permeated the walls of the cave. . . ."

Maisie stood off to the side with Hilda and watched the crowd. Confusion started sprouting on their faces like dandelions in spring. Heads were turning, looking around the room.

"I don't see anything that spectacular," a man wearing a bowler hat whispered to a woman with a pad of paper on her lap.

"I can't believe I came all this way to see a rock building," she agreed. "We have prettier buildings in Lincoln."

Maisie twisted her mouth to the side. They didn't think this building was the cave, did they? No one had even noticed the door to the shaft. They had no idea what they were waiting for, but Maisie didn't want their first impression to be bad. The smarty-pants types who wanted a full discussion about how calcite crystals were formed would be happy to stick around and hear from Boone. The rest of them were looking for a story and to see the site.

"Wish me luck," Maisie whispered to Hilda, then made her way to the front. Boone followed her approach with his gaze. He seemed relieved when she reached him and he could wrap up his explanation.

"I'm sure many of you will have questions after the tour. My wife and I will be available, but now it's her turn to say something." He stepped away from the center of the room so Maisie could saunter up, but she caught him by the arm to keep him from disappearing.

"How are you'uns doing?" Maisie dug her heel into the floor and swayed. "I'm the one who discovered this place, but I can tell from the looks on your faces that you aren't too impressed. That's alright. Don't judge the steak by the way the steer smelled, we say. This building is not what you came to see. What you're here for is behind that closed door, and we'll go there in the shake of a honeybee's tail."

Her audience settled in with her pronouncement, alert but more content. Maisie dusted off her hands. She might be throwing in a few more colorful phrases than she would normally use, but it was part of the role she was called to play.

"Now, you might not be able to tell, but I'm a farm girl." Chuckles floated up from the group. "In fact, this bit of land that you're standing on right now used to be part of my family ranch, but I happened to wander off our property and down into an abandoned shaft belonging to Mr. Bragg." She went on to describe her journey through the deserted shaft and her amazement at finding the cavern. She kept it short and peppy, knowing that the better she did at stirring up their curiosity, the more anxious they would be for her to finish her talk. Before she lost them, she reached her favorite part of the story.

"My mind was about to bust with what I'd seen. I had to get out of that mine and tell someone, and who should I run into, but the very man who'd least appreciate finding a woman trespassing on his property."

This was Boone's cue, and he didn't disappoint. "I'd spent considerable time keeping interlopers off our property, so I was prepared to escort Miss Kentworth out of my mine, but when I saw her, I wasn't prepared for her beauty."

Maisie felt his eyes on her, burning more intensely than ever. She kept her head modestly ducked while he continued.

"I'm sure you gentlemen can imagine my surprise to round the corner of a mine and find this lovely lady coming up out of the depths. I was so stunned I could hardly understand what she was telling me." Boone gently took her hand. "Thank goodness I followed her to where she'd pickaxed a hole in the wall of rock. What she showed me changed everything." He lifted her hand and pressed it to his lips, which had never been a part of the routine. "If my lovely wife will accompany me, we'll show you what we found."

Maisie held his gaze, oblivious to the people gathering around.

"This is our moment," he said. "I'm proud to share it with you."

Despite her clothes and her manners, they were partners, and they were partners in much more than a business venture.

"Let's show the world," she said.

Boone rolled open the door.

The excitement of the journalists was building as Boone and Maisie led them down the staircase. He got goosebumps with the dropping temperatures. The moment of truth was before them. Would everyone else share his wonder at the discovery? He carried a kerosene lamp—a safety feature in case the electricity went down—while Maisie led the way down the staircase, as natural and welcoming as if she'd been inviting someone into the kitchen for a cup of coffee. A female reporter who had introduced herself as Mrs. Betsy Puckett from Pine Gap was asking the usual questions about how long they'd been married and whether he'd proposed in the cavern or not. Maisie tried to answer over her shoulder while Boone held on to her arm so she wouldn't lose her footing.

"Still newlyweds," Maisie was saying. "And it's been a whirlwind, with everything that was needed to get this place open."

"But even with all the busyness, I'm finding myself more in love with my wife with every day that passes." Boone had done the impossible. He'd shocked Maisie into silence.

She wasn't the only one. Even though the voices echoed in the tight quarters, it was getting quieter as they continued. People usually became quieter as they went down into the earth. Whether it was nervousness or the feeling that they were approaching holy ground, a sense of awe always seemed to settle over people as they left the surface behind. Boone tried to see the tunnel as though it were his first time too. The damp rock, the buzzing lights over them, the jagged walls . . . with patches covered in paint. That still troubled him, but he had more on his mind today.

There was one last flight of stairs before the cave was revealed, but Boone and Maisie were the only ones who knew they'd arrived. He squeezed her arm. In return, she stepped sideways, purposefully bumping against him.

"I'm happy for you," she whispered.

"I'm happy for us." He slid his arm around her waist, torn between the desire to be alone with her and the desire to show the world what they'd found. When they stepped off the last stair and followed the wooden walkway to the cavern entrance, Boone stopped. The sight before him would always fill him with awe. The scope, the size of the room, and every inch of it covered in dazzling gems. The different colored lights along the walls picked up varying hues in the crystals and reflected off the water like a garden filled with blooms. To think that this other-worldly treasure had been hidden under the Kentworths' cow pasture for centuries.

How long had he stood here? Long enough for the people behind him to grow impatient.

"I can't see anything."

"We must be getting close."

Maisie took the lantern from Boone's hand and set it against the wall. "Let's step aside and let them in."

Without waiting for an invitation, the crowd pushed past him and Maisie, but the first ones to reach the viewing area did exactly as he had. They stopped in their tracks and stared, their mouths agape. Those behind them pushed through, nearly toppling some in the front into the water that pooled at the bottom of the cavern.

"There's room for everyone," Boone said as he directed those stuck on the stairs to come to the far edges of the platform so they could see too.

The moment of awe stretched, but it didn't last forever. These were people who lived to spread the word, and as soon as they recovered their senses, they realized they had a story to tell.

Flashes of light from the photographers illuminated dark corners that the permanent lights didn't reach. With one such flash, the small original entrance shone out of the shadows. The ladder that had been built to it as an emergency exit was nowhere as grand as the walkway for the visitors, but it always drew Boone's interest, regardless.

He walked the boardwalk around the perimeter as the journalists explored. Now came the questions he was most suited to answer. Now came the appreciation for the innovations it had taken to light up a dark masterpiece. Notepads were out and held to the lights as the men and women scratched down every word out of his mouth. His facts and knowledge about the minerals had turned more interesting now that they could see what he was talking about.

Before long, some of their guests bounded away, jogging up the stairs as soon as they had their story, hoping to beat the competition to the telephone lines at the Joplin hotels. Others lingered, many besotted with Maisie, hovering around her and hoping to get another colorful quote from her to share in their articles.

True, had she not wandered through the mine that day, he wouldn't have found this cave, but even beyond her discovery, she had changed his life for the better. If tomorrow the place was sabotaged and the cave refilled with water, he'd still look forward to working with her on some new project. He'd still want her at his side as he went about town. He'd still rather go to uncomfortable parties with her than stay home without her.

Her eyes darted to him, standing alone on the dance floor. A flash of uncertainty crossed her brow, but he nodded encouragement to her. Without another hesitation, she plowed on with her riveting tale of their climbing through the hole and nearly falling off the ledge. She even mentioned that he'd set her skirt aflame.

If Boone had only known then what he knew now. He hadn't been looking for a wife, but he'd found just what he needed to get along in the world.

"Thank you for coming," Boone said as he invaded Maisie's circle of admirers. "You are welcome back on Friday for the grand opening. If you'll follow our guide, Amos is here to help you back up the stairs."

"I don't want to leave." An old-timer was looking out across the cave instead of taking notes. His pad of paper swung crumpled in his hand. "I might never get a chance to see this again in my life. It's just a wonder what God has done, isn't it?"

Boone's eyes drifted to where Maisie was posing for a picture with a journalist and his wife. "His works are beyond explanation. Stay as long as you like. We're in no hurry."

The old man reached in his coat pocket for a handkerchief and laughed at his foolishness. "That's the problem, I *am* in a hurry. I've got to get this story on the wire before midnight tonight. They'll want it to run in tomorrow's paper. No one will believe it." With a sniffle, he reached for Boone's hand. "Thank you, young man, for saving this. We can find our lead and zinc somewhere else, but this is unique."

Boone's spirit settled. There were times you prayed for God's guidance, prayed for His wisdom, and then you had to act without knowing for sure that you were doing the right thing. But a moment like this—when someone spoke words that you knew were planted in their heart from the Father—was the approval he'd sought.

With final farewells, the reporters left in a contented silence, probably each mulling over the exact wording for their articles. Maisie started to follow, but Boone had other ideas.

"We're not going up with them? Is there more work to be done down here?" Maisie pushed her sleeve up her arm like she was about to grab a pickax and take to work.

"There's more to life than work." Boone couldn't believe he'd just said that, much less that he actually believed it.

He led her toward the stairs and across the platform, now much bigger than it had been on their wedding day. Much had changed since then, including him.

Maisie watched as the last of the stragglers headed up the stairs. "Everyone's going up. We don't want to get left behind." She reached for the railing.

"Don't go," Boone said. His dark form was outlined by a light behind him. "Stay with me."

"What if they forget we're down here? What if they shut the lights down?"

"We have a lantern." Boone sat on the bottom step of the staircase, turning so he could view the cave. "How did I do with my presentation? Am I improving?"

"You're no Maisie Kentworth Bragg, but you were pretty convincing." Her cotton skirt was easy to gather as she seated herself next to him on the step. "So smart and knowledgeable. And then the way you went on about me. If I wasn't careful, I'd find myself falling for you."

"I'm your husband. Why would you be careful?" He'd angled himself toward her with his back to the balustrade.

Her throat tightened. "I was reckless before. I gave my heart to someone who wasn't worthy of it. I'm wiser now. You don't have to worry about me being foolish again."

"Loving isn't foolish." He moved the lantern from the wall,

adjusting it so they were both in its warm glow. "Only in loving the wrong things is a person foolish. When I think of the things I love about you—your strength, your goodness, your selflessness—I don't feel foolish at all."

Maisie didn't realize she was holding her breath until he placed his arm around her waist. Lifting her slightly, he pulled her closer until she was nestled against him. This wasn't foolishness. Foolishness would be rejecting the husband who meant so much to her.

"Boone." She rested her hand tentatively on his leg. "I know how I feel, but the contract says . . ."

"Contracts are very important," he said. "It's also very important that you know that I love you. I want you to be perfectly clear on that point. On the other hand, you were adamant we shouldn't *discuss* romance until the cavern is successful. You were very specific on that point."

"Yes." Her hands felt jittery. "Does that mean . . . ?"

"That means we'd better stop talking. With you, here in our cave, I can think of better ways to convince you." With the lightest of touches, Boone drew her closer. He slanted his head just so, and Maisie found herself sighing into him, finally joining what had always belonged together.

He kissed her, was kissing her, and she was kissing him back with a response that felt as spontaneous and natural as breathing. But the breathing part was getting out of hand. Never had anything so slow and gentle made her blood roar like Shoal Creek over the falls. Her heart was pounding like the hooves of cattle in a stampede, but she wasn't running anywhere. And her skin was burning like a tin roof at noon. In fact, combined with the scent of his lemon soap was the smell of smoke.

Maisie opened her eyes. Her heart leapt at the sight of her handsome husband so incredibly close to her. Maybe it was the sparks they were putting off, but the cavern seemed to be getting lighter. Her legs were getting hotter too, until suddenly they actually burned.

Maisie straightened her arms, pushing Boone away. Then she saw what she feared.

Her skirt was on fire.

Her hem had brushed the open lantern, and once again, Maisie's wardrobe was burning in the cave.

She bent to slap at the flame, but Boone was quicker. Diving, he wrapped his arms around her knees, pulling her off the stairs and suffocating the flames against his chest.

With the smoldering fabric under control, Maisie lay on her back and laughed. Boone rifled through her skirt, looking for hot spots until he was satisfied that she was no longer in danger, then shifted to lie beside her, propping himself up on his elbow. Reaching over her, he pushed against her shoulder.

"You're pinned. I win," he said.

"Cheater." But Maisie didn't hop up to defend her record. Instead, she lay still, looking up into his eyes. How could this unusual arrangement have resulted in so much happiness?

"A cheater at wrassling, but faithful in every other way." Boone ran his finger over her cheek before helping her to her feet and up the stairs to take more questions about their miraculous discovery . . . and the Crystal Cave.

CHAPTER 28

"Your grandparents are eager to meet your wife," Mrs. Bragg said to Boone over the cantaloupe Thursday morning. "And if you're traveling to Cape Girardeau, you might as well swing by Willow Springs and see the Rippees. Aunt Bobbie has always been so good to you."

Maisie kept her head down and tried to catch the slimy fruit with her fork. It sure did like to squirm away from her on the slick china plate. Although she didn't know the people her mother-in-law was talking about, and there would have been no way for her to have informed them of Boone's marriage, she still felt like the offense was on her shoulders. After all, if it weren't for her, Boone wouldn't have messed this up.

"The cave opens tomorrow," Boone protested. "You know we can't leave town now. Maybe this fall when it cools off, but not before then."

Traveling alone with Boone and having him all to herself? Maisie sipped her milk, surprised she wasn't jumping up and grabbing her bags immediately.

"What do you think, Maisie?" Mrs. Bragg asked. "Wouldn't you be ready for a change of scenery by this fall? At least you might be able to prevent Boone from locking you in a mine every day."

"Speaking of the Curious Bear." Boone turned to his father. "Now that construction is finished on the cave and the water is down, the men on that team can go back and explore what we passed on before."

"I agree. As long as the pumps are trustworthy." Mr. Bragg wiped his mouth with a fine white napkin. "I wouldn't invest more, though. If it went barren so quickly on top, there might not be any ore below." He turned to his wife. "What do you have planned today?"

Mrs. Bragg rocked in her seat with a closed-mouth grin. "A bit of a surprise, actually. In all of Boone's rush to be wed, he forgot to commission a portrait of his bride. I'm taking Maisie to visit Mr. Rose this morning."

"We got our picture taken in the cave at our wedding," Maisie said. "It was in the newspaper."

"Not a photograph—a portrait. Mr. Rose is a painter. When Wallace and I married, we couldn't afford a painting, but we had one commissioned from my wedding picture a few years later. You should have one hanging in the parlor too."

There wasn't a room in the house that Maisie less wanted to be hung in. Besides, sitting still while her picture was being painted didn't sound entertaining. The only photographs taken of her family were blurred because she, Amos, and Finn couldn't stay still long enough. She shot a look of despair at Boone, but he only shrugged.

"And don't forget the dinner party at the Caines' tonight." Mrs. Bragg pinned her cantaloupe as firmly as she pinned Boone in her gaze.

"What?" Boone and Maisie said in unison.

"If it were a small gathering, I would've refused, but they invited everyone in town," Mrs. Bragg said. "I know Maisie is having a squabble with Justina, but I hope she can move past it. There's a lot Maisie needs to learn if she's going to fit in. Besides, Darin has always been a good friend to your father."

"If you hadn't found that crystal cave, he was willing to keep you from sinking," his father said. "You shouldn't sneeze on a friendship like that."

How Boone kept his calm demeanor in the face of such horrendous news, Maisie could not understand. She felt her hands going numb and her stomach turning. They should be preparing for the opening of the cave, not wasting time with a lady who wouldn't loan Maisie a used corncob to save her life.

Mr. and Mrs. Bragg continued their chatting, but Boone wasn't attending. He had that same faraway look that he got when he was in his office unraveling a problem. Feeling alone, Maisie was about to excuse herself when Boone suddenly addressed his parents.

"We need to have a talk about good friends and fitting in." Boone set down his silverware and wiped his mouth with his napkin before continuing. "I've been thinking, and I've come to a conclusion. Every conversation seems to be focused on how Maisie needs to change and what she needs to do to please our friends. Have you ever considered that there are things we could change?"

What was he saying? "Boone . . ." Maisie put her hand on his arm, but he shrugged it off.

"Mother, you have no use for Justina. You think her a horrible person. So why are you holding her up as an example to Maisie? And, Father, you know of the Kentworths. Why haven't you reached out to Maisie's parents or her uncle Oscar? You say we are the ones with the social skills, but I don't know of any invitations that have been sent to her people."

Boone knew how to control a boardroom, but Maisie had never seen him use those skills at the breakfast table.

Mrs. Bragg surrendered her fork. "We've only been home—"

"Long enough to meet the dressmaker. Long enough to commission a portrait. Long enough to accept an invitation that you know will be difficult for us. All this before you've even met her family." Now Boone took Maisie's hand, covering it with his own on the table. "At first, I was afraid to interact with Maisie. I knew there'd be some conflict, some misunderstandings, so I left her to her own devices. It didn't take me long to realize what I was missing. Maybe you should take some time to get to know her before you change her into something less appealing."

Maisie held her breath. What had prompted this defense? Where had these notions come from?

"Your point is well taken," his father said. "I've been remiss. We'd be glad to entertain the Kentworths soon. On the other hand, your mother is just trying to help. Surely you appreciate the progress that's been made since she's taken Maisie under her wing."

"Why do you'uns talk around me like I'm not here?" Maisie asked. "I am grateful for the help of Mrs. Bragg. She showed me how the ladies in town do things, and for that I'm beholden. Now that I know, maybe it's up to me to decide if I want to do it like they do or not." She shot a nervous look at Boone. There was nothing but pride and love in his eyes, but this dreaded lump in her throat was going to make the rest of breakfast impossible to enjoy. "That is, if Boone agrees."

"I think you have our son quite under your spell." Mrs. Bragg pushed her chair back from the table. "That's how it should be, I suppose, but please give thought to the dinner tonight. Just make an appearance. We want to smooth any ruffled feathers over Boone's refusal to sell them the mine . . . and his refusal to marry their daughter."

Mr. Bragg stood, gulped down the last of his coffee, and handed the cup to Mrs. Karol. "I'm headed off to the mine," he said. He rested his hand on Mrs. Bragg's waist and planted a friendly kiss on her lips before gathering his things.

Boone stood and pulled Maisie to her feet. "I'm headed off to my mine too." He put a hand on Maisie's waist. "Are you going to wish me a good day?"

"In front of your mother?" Maisie whispered.

Mrs. Bragg's eyes sparkled fondly at her son, the same son who was tormenting Maisie. "Find me in my room when you're ready, Maisie, and we'll pick out an ensemble for your sitting."

"See you outside." Mr. Bragg disappeared through the front door, leaving the two of them alone in the breakfast room.

"What kind of good-bye do you think you're getting?" Maisie asked.

"When a man leaves his wife of the morning, a kiss is customary. Didn't your parents kiss?"

Ranch life didn't mean a parting every morning, but yes, if her father went to town or was going to be out for the day, he usually did grab her mother for a quick kiss . . . or sometimes a not-so-quick kiss.

"That's different. They're . . ."

"Married?" Boone smiled, but his eyes gentled. "We're not foolish or reckless, Maisie. We're married. A kiss in the breakfast room isn't going to distress you, is it?"

Somehow she couldn't imagine that her parents kissing in the kitchen was the same thing as when Boone kissed her. It was the difference between moonlight and moonshine. But he had a point.

"I reckon it's okay," she said, "as long as I don't lose control."

"Please, wife. Please tell me what might happen if you lose control. Just imagine me trying to focus on business with that possibility in my head." He pecked her on the cheek, and although the kiss was chaste, the message in his eyes was not.

Maisie pressed her hand against her face. "Cricket's wings," she whispered. "I'm turning beet red. I'll ruin my portrait."

Boone only laughed and headed toward the door. "I don't think it'll be as bad as you think, but try to enjoy yourself regardless."

Maisie watched him depart, then ran up the stairs to find Mrs. Bragg.

Once they settled on an outfit, time passed like a whirlwind. Mrs. Bragg, Mrs. Karol, and Maisie were a flurry of cloth, lotions, and combs until she passed inspection. The next thing she knew, she was sitting on a leather stool in the painter's studio, being reminded for the hundredth time to sit up straight.

Maisie tucked in her lower back and lifted her chest. "If I'd known this was going to take so long, I would've picked a more comfortable chair." She looked at the portraits Mr. Rose had hanging around the messy workspace. "I don't see any pictures of girls resting in haystacks. Seems like you might want some variety instead of everyone doing the same pose."

"Shh, Maisie," Mrs. Bragg said. "We are not commissioning a picture of you in a haystack. That is not the tone we are trying to set. Now, can you stay still while I make some calls? There are many ruffled feathers I need to smooth on account of my son getting married without inviting our friends to the ceremony." She stood and shook out her skirt. "If you'll behave yourself . . ."

"I've got nothing else to do," Maisie grumbled as her mother-in-law left.

It turned out that she would've been happy to sit if it meant she could have avoided the next interview.

Forgetting about Mr. Rose and her posture, Maisie was daydreaming about Boone when she heard the door behind her open.

"I'm looking for Maisie Kentwor—Bragg."

Maisie recognized the voice. It was her cousin Calista.

Without shifting her position, Maisie lifted her hand over her head. "Over here, Calista. Mr. Rose is painting me, so I'm not supposed to move."

"She's over here," Calista said.

Calista stepped into view, dressed to the nines as usual. Maisie was fixing to ask Calista how she endured dressing so fine every day when she saw who Calista had pulled along in her wake.

It was the man from the Electrical Light Park, Mr. Peltz.

The normally confident Mr. Peltz looked like he'd been dragged behind a wagon through a field of cactus. A tuft of grass rode in his crushed hat band. A button had gone missing from his shirt, and the knee was ripped on his trousers.

Maisie narrowed her eyes at Calista. "What did you do to him?"

"You'll thank me. Take a break from your portrait and hear what he has to say."

"Don't you dare move," Mr. Rose warned. "You're arranged perfectly."

"Just tell me, Calista." Maisie had been so worried about keeping Amos and Hank out of trouble that she'd forgotten to account for her former Pinkerton operative cousin.

"This *lady*"—Mr. Peltz obviously felt that Calista little deserved the title—"has been following me relentlessly. Last night, I had one of my men follow her back to her house. When he didn't return this morning, I went looking for him."

"You went looking for trouble," Calista amended. "You don't send a man to lurk around my house."

And what happened after that, Maisie could imagine.

"This fella better not show up in my painting," Maisie ordered the painter. "Maybe you should take a break while I settle this."

Mr. Rose nodded, but his brush kept moving. "Just a few more strokes. Your face is so animated. I think I've got the perfect expression—"

"For crying aloud." Maisie turned on Calista. "What good does getting all gussied up do me if my portrait is going to look like I'm fixing to light into someone?"

"Then we won't take any more of your time than necessary." The look Calista gave Peltz carried enough of a threat to make him wince. "Tell her what you came to say."

Mr. Peltz scuffed a shoe on the floor. "I'm not involved in whatever is being perpetrated against you and your cave, but I might know something."

Maisie met Calista's furious gaze before returning to him. "Go on."

"I was at Black Jack's when I overheard a conversation between two men. Their identities were a mystery to me, but their conversation was very interesting." Peltz paused like he expected to be begged to continue. All he got was an elbow from Calista. "The younger man was fairly inebriated, but he was taking in every word the older man was saying. The older told the younger that you'd been forced into a marriage arrangement by your family. That your husband didn't love you, and that you wanted someone to rescue you. That if he didn't intervene, you would be a prisoner locked behind bars of misery and in a dungeon of regret."

"That's not true!" Maisie lunged to the edge of her stool. "It's a bald-faced lie."

"Perhaps, but it was what this young man wanted to hear. Especially the part about you being a wealthy woman now. How you would own half of Boone Bragg's estate once the divorce was final. He commenced to planning how he'd prove to you that you had to leave Mr. Bragg. How to present his suit. He had more plans than my architect. And the older man told him the perfect time and place to implement the plan—the Founder's Day parade."

"Silas!" Maisie kicked the footstool away. "He humiliated me on purpose?"

"We know what kind of character Silas is," Calista said, "but he wouldn't steal your electric lamps. He hasn't got the gumption. If it's not Mr. Peltz, who is it?"

"I didn't recognize the older man," Mr. Peltz said. "I only came to town to supervise this project. I had no intention of getting wrapped up with feuding families and women who kidnap—"

Calista cast a warning glance at the painter. "I don't like discussing my methods in front of civilians."

"Never mind me," said Mr. Rose. "I just paint the pictures."

"Thank you for your help, Mr. Peltz. If that's all you can tell us, you're free to go." Calista cracked her knuckles through her dainty white gloves.

"You don't have to tell me twice." Peltz hurried to the exit. "I wish this Silas and his friend the best of luck."

"We have to get Silas," Maisie said as soon as the door closed. "See who put him up to this and what else they have planned."

"Get Boone to go to Silas's claim," said Calista. "He'll get the story out of him."

Maisie bit her lip. Silas would be tickled pink at the chance to tell Boone how Maisie was planning to leave him. Silas would do anything to drive her and Boone apart. She couldn't let him talk to Boone.

"We'll have to go on our own," she told Calista. "Boone can't know. Not until we learn more. As soon as I'm free, I'll send word."

Maisie bade her cousin thank-you and good-bye, and by the time her mother-in-law had returned, she'd managed to paint on a smile as skillfully as any Mr. Rose had ever painted.

With the cave opening tomorrow, Boone's tour guides needed practice. He'd enlisted a few of his miners who had shown promise, but after a couple of runs, he'd realized they were more interested in talking about the minerals and the excavation that had taken place. Even Boone got bored listening to them drone on in a monotone about the process of draining the water. When Amos Kentworth volunteered, Boone decided to give him a chance. After all, his sister had turned into quite the spokeswoman without any training. A few families from Boone's church had jumped at the chance to serve as the canaries for Amos to practice on.

That was what Amos should've been doing, but when Boone entered the visitor center, he found his brother-in-law eating a warm cookie with his feet propped up in a café chair.

Boone looked at the visitors sitting in the holding area, then took another look at Amos. Amos grinned broadly and lifted a finger in place of a wave.

"How's it going, boss man?"

"Not well, I presume. Are the guests waiting while you finish your cookie?"

Amos jerked his head toward the café, where the two ladies were cooking up snacks for the opening. "Seeing as how you got

Hilda and Hannah to work, it didn't seem fitting to leave their brother out in the cold. So I gave my job to him. Hank is down there leading the first tour."

"How can he be doing tours?" Boone asked. "He's never been down there. He doesn't know what to say."

"You don't know Hank. He's got a skill for chin-wagging. I can't guarantee what he says will be true, but it'll be entertaining. Besides, he's giving me ten percent of his pay for finding him this job. Who else could I trick into doing that?"

The door to the cave opened, and a stranger with a lamp hat came out, followed by a string of customers.

"Looky here." He held the door open while they exited. "We're back topside. I hope y'all enjoyed your visit to the magical Crystal Cave. Be sure and tell your friends to come take a gander tomorrow. It's like nothing they've ever seen before."

"That's your cousin?" Boone asked. "Why'd he bother wearing a lamp hat if he wasn't going to light it?"

"Hank," said Amos, "come here and meet Maisie's husband."

Hank's long face barely moved, but he stretched out his hand to grab Boone's and shake it vigorously. "Nice to meet you, Mr. Bragg. That's one humdinger of a cave you've got there. I've never seen anything like it."

A gregarious lady Boone recognized as his church organist had trouble catching her breath from the climb up the stairs. She grabbed Hank by the arm. "I want to thank you for the amazing tour," she said. "I bet you never get tired of going down there."

"I'll tell you what." Hank leaned closer. "That was my first time to see it too. Ain't it a beaut? But I've got another group awaiting. Better go." He patted her hand as he disentangled himself and announced to the people in line that the next tour was forming.

As they progressed to the door, those exiting were profuse in their praise.

"You'll love it."

"Amazing."

"I'm coming back tomorrow with my parents."

This was what Boone had sacrificed for—so that God's workmanship would be shared with everyone who wanted to see it.

After listening to a few more comments, Boone realized he'd have to talk to Hank about the tales he was sharing of the ancient Indian tribe that lived down there and the artifacts that had been discovered. From the comments of the people exiting, that seemed to be their favorite part of the tour, but it was wholly untrue.

Boone turned to look for Hank but found him in a tight gathering of his sisters and cousin. Just as Boone drew near, he heard news from Hannah—or was it Hilda?—that made his stomach drop.

"Amos, I have a message for you and Hank from Calista. Maisie needs to see that Silas Marsh tonight, and she thinks she'll need your help."

Boone couldn't believe what he was hearing. There was only one Maisie, and if he remembered correctly, Silas Marsh was the one person she swore she never wanted to see again.

"What's this?" Boone read guilt on every face that turned to him. Then Amos's expression settled into stubborn lines.

"Hilda's just passing on some family business." Amos met his stare dead even. "Nothing that concerns you."

"I am family, and I heard my wife's name. I'm concerned."

"We got it handled." Hank stood tall, his chest stretching and straining his buttons.

Boone turned to Hannah. "Where's Calista?"

But Hannah was just as obstinate as the rest of them. "I reckon if she wanted to talk to you, she would've come inside. You really shouldn't be eavesdropping, Mr. Bragg. You'll only catch ill tidings."

Ill tidings. That was exactly what he feared.

CHAPTER 29

Boone's empty stomach reminded him that he'd skipped lunch in favor of getting home early. The cave's opening was important. He would have been tempted to say it was the most important thing, but it wasn't. Something more urgent had arisen, and Boone had to address it.

"Oh good, you're home early." His mother stood at the top of the staircase with her hair pinned in curlers. "I haven't seen Maisie for a while. You might want to check on her. She'll need some encouragement for tonight."

Had Maisie left already? Boone did a quick jog through the family rooms downstairs before taking the steps two at a time to the second floor. He hurried through his room and ran up the winding steps to her bedroom in the tower, the small jewelry box in his vest pocket bouncing against his chest. Forgetting anything but finding Maisie, he burst through the door.

Lying flat on her bed, she didn't even flinch.

Boone paused, catching his breath and taking stock. Maisie had an arm thrown over her eyes as if the light were offensive. She wasn't wearing whatever new gown she'd donned for her portrait.

Instead, she was wearing her everyday work clothes—clothes she'd worn before she'd met him.

"Boone?" Her voice quavered higher than its natural tenor. "I'm glad you're here. I need to tell you that I'm beset with ailments. It'd be better if I didn't go to the party tonight."

She had to have heard him running up the stairs. Instead of reacting when he'd busted in, she'd remained perfectly still. It was an act, all of it.

He came to stand by the edge of her bed. "I'm sorry to hear that. If something hurts my wife, it hurts me too. What can I do to help you?"

"You're so kind, but I think I'd be better off resting. Go on without me. I don't want to stand in your way." Interesting how she kept her face covered as she delivered her lines.

"Go to Justina Caine's house without my wife?" Boone gave a dry laugh. "I don't think so. Let's see what we can do to improve your condition." He slowly lifted her arm off her face.

"No, really, I'm not well." She stopped when the light of day touched her face. Instead of watery eyes and a red nose, her gaze was sharp and direct. She knew she'd been caught, but she wasn't giving up the fight. "You understand, don't you? You know why I'm not going?"

"I can think of a couple of reasons. Maybe you don't want to go to a dinner party, or maybe you have a secret meeting that you don't want your husband to find out about."

The bed squeaked as Maisie bolted upright. "Don't say that. It sounds so . . . dirty. It's not what you think."

"Please explain." Part of him, the self-centered part that had always said women weren't worth the trouble, wanted to turn a blind eye. Let her do what she planned and suffer the consequences. But his nobler nature told him that his hurt pride had no place here. This was a battle worth fighting.

"I need to see Calista." Maisie pulled her knees up and sat cross-legged. "What's wrong with that?"

"Calista seemed to think you needed the help of Amos and Hank."

"She told them?" Maisie slapped her forehead. "They're the last people who need to be involved."

"Involved in what?" When she failed to answer, Boone asked, "Then why not appeal to me? I'm at your disposal." He couldn't think of a valid reason for her to meet with a former beau, but he was willing to listen—if only she'd say something. Her silence did nothing to ease his concern. He moved toward the knight. "Since you aren't ill and you don't have any excuse to offer me, I'm afraid I'm going to have to insist that you go to the dinner."

"I can't." She pushed her sleeve up her arm. "I'm telling you that I can't. Bad things could happen."

Boone hadn't expected her to be so adamant, but he was a stubborn man.

"I can't think of anything worse than you leaving me." He looked the knight up and down. Once he'd thought this soldier the biggest, strongest-looking man around. Now he looked down on the diminutive figure. "I hate to do this, but I'll remind you of our contract. You agreed to three social events per quarter. You signed the paper with witnesses, and I'm holding you to it."

When she didn't respond, the most awful thought assaulted Boone. He'd made an amateur negotiation mistake. When someone was threatening to leave a business partnership, you didn't produce the contract to force them to comply unless you were eager for their departure. That was exactly what he'd done. But he had no choice. He had to bluff his way through.

"I brought you something." He reached into his pocket. This wasn't how he'd imagined giving her the gift, but it might be the perfect time. He handed her the velvet-covered box.

Maisie took it and lifted the lid. Her quick breath of surprise made his heart skip. She lifted the necklace's pendant, rolling it between her fingers against the light. "Is it from our cave?"

"Yes. A calcite crystal, perfectly shaped and clear, just for you."

"Can you help me put it on?"

Just when Boone thought he could breathe again, she knocked the wind out of him. He took the necklace from her, then stood behind her and draped it around her neck.

"Do you need any more help?" He fastened the clasp and tried to imitate the playful banter they so often enjoyed. "I'm pretty good at wrestling now. I think I could get you wrestled into a dress."

"For the record, you are holding me to my contract and forcing me to go tonight?" She held the necklace against her chest and watched for his answer.

"If that's the way you want to look at it, then yes. You must go." No use in sugarcoating it. If she was speaking plainly, then so would he.

"Then you give me no choice." Maisie rose off the bed. "I'll go with you, but I need to send a note to Calista."

"Of course."

He couldn't believe her cousin—the wife of a pastor—would be involved in anything immoral, but Maisie's failure to explain left him no answers. More time with her meant more opportunity to win her heart. He only wished his efforts could take place somewhere more conducive to romancing his wife than the house of Justina Caine.

Had Daniel felt this anxious as they were marching him to the lions' den? God had strengthened him, and he would sustain Maisie, but she hated the thought that someone was trying to hurt Boone and she couldn't do anything to stop them.

"Hold your head up high," Mrs. Bragg said as they reached the porch. "There will be many fine people here tonight. Don't let a few rotten apples spoil it for you."

Justina was the least of Maisie's worries, but if there were rotten apples, Justina was the worm that was ruining them.

The door opened, and the ladies stepped inside first.

Boone reached for Maisie's wrap. His hands rested on her shoulders as he spoke into her ear. "Thank you for coming. I hope you'll let me convince you that you made the right choice."

"I didn't have a choice." Maisie shrugged out of her shawl and straightened her lemon-yellow gown. Boone didn't know the plans that were being made against him, and because of his actions, he wouldn't know until it was too late. At least she'd sent her cousins after Silas. She'd pray they could accomplish what she couldn't.

As they meandered among the different groups, Mrs. Bragg kept to Maisie's side. Under the protective wing of her mother-in-law, not to mention the sharp talons, Maisie's welcome was much warmer than last time. Justina kept a wary eye on her, always managing to keep to the opposite side of the room as the Braggs made their way through, collecting pleasantries just like gathering eggs from the chicken roosts.

"I'm sure you're already acquainted with my daughter-in-law," Mrs. Bragg said to Mrs. Geddes, "but I can't help but introduce her myself. If you could see how happy she and Boone are together . . ."

Justina and a tall, awkward girl were conspiring together by the punch bowl. Without a doubt, they were hearing every word Mrs. Bragg was saying and laughing at Maisie's expense. She clenched her fists. Mrs. Bragg was right. There were fine people here. She could ignore Justina for the sake of a pleasant evening for the rest of them.

But what she couldn't ignore was her brother scaling the brick wall of the Caines' garden.

Amos had one leg thrown over the wall and was pulling himself up. When he finally sat astraddle it, he spotted Maisie through the double French doors and waved broadly. Maisie shook her head. What was he doing? He had no business here. A quick look around the room showed that no one else had seen him. He dropped into the garden, then bent over and crept behind the pergola, disappearing from view. He was supposed to be with Calista. Why couldn't he do what was expected?

Oh no. Maisie stumbled back a step. Now Calista was propping herself up on her elbows atop the brick wall. Although dressed as fine as any woman in the parlor, she was hiking her expensive leather boot over the edge of the wall.

Trying to hide behind a potted plant that was much too small, Amos waved again. He motioned to Maisie, urging her to come to him. Maisie lowered her eyebrows and glowered.

"Evidently your daughter-in-law disagrees," said Mrs. Caine, a larger but more diluted pain than her daughter. "If not Tchaikovsky, who is your favorite composer?"

"What?" Maisie was impervious to the conversation going on around her. Calista was inside the enclosed yard. While it wouldn't be the first time a family reunion involved trespassing, it was the first time it had inconvenienced Maisie. "My favorite composer? I'm sure whoever you just said is dandy."

If anyone looked that way, they couldn't fail to see Amos. Calista must have realized it as well. She scurried to him and tugged on his shoulder. He pushed her away, and she kicked the back of his knee, knocking him flat and out of view.

"Forgive me for boring you." Mrs. Caine sniffed. "I didn't mean to monopolize your time when there are so many others wanting to take you into confidence."

Mrs. Bragg moved only slightly but managed to bump Maisie in the arm with force. "Maisie has had a trying day, sitting for Mr. Rose. She means no offense."

"No offense," Maisie obediently repeated as she watched for Hank to appear next. Or Olive. Or maybe they sent to Kansas City for Corban and Evangelina. Why not enlist everyone to embarrass her?

"You haven't seen the improvements we've made to the garden," Mrs. Caine was saying to Mrs. Bragg. "We hired that landscaper from Carthage, and while his work was adequate, there were some adjustments. The space was crying out for a pergola."

They moved toward the French doors.

Maisie considered falling into a faint but was afraid her errant family might rush inside to her aid. Instead, she blurted, "What about your plumbing in the washroom?"

Mrs. Caine turned in shock. "Excuse me?"

Mrs. Bragg shot a wide-eyed warning at Maisie. "Do you know where the necessary is?" she asked in lowered tones. "If you need it . . ."

"Yes, I know. I availed myself of it earlier." Not true, but Maisie was desperate. "It's a humdinger of a nice place, but indoor plumbing can be tricky. If you drop something down it, like one of those spicy meat rolls—I wasn't partial to those—it doesn't just sit and stew like an outhouse. Instead, it's like to clog. And then when you pull that chain up above your head, the water rises and rises in that bowl." She was talking faster and faster, and no one was looking out the doors where Calista and Amos were frantically trying to get her attention. "That's all fine and dandy unless it's clogged, like I aforementioned, because then that water has nowhere to go. Nowhere unless you have a cellar beneath the main floor." She stomped her boot and listened to the echo beneath the wood floor. "Oh no. You'uns do have a cellar. Then I'm awfully sorry about your room. I was of a mind to come back and mop up that dirty water after the party—"

"Darin!" Mrs. Caine lifted her skirt and rushed from the room, and Mrs. Bragg followed.

Not wanting to miss the drama, the other ladies followed, letting their disapproval show as they passed. Maisie tried to look contrite as she hurried to the French doors and slipped outside.

Stepping out of view of the windows, she was quickly joined by Amos and Calista. "What are you doing?" She pushed up her lace-lined sleeves, ready to whup them both.

"We got Marsh, and he's spilled the beans. They're going to

destroy the cave tonight to stop you from opening." Amos couldn't help but be excited, even if he knew it was serious.

"Who are they? Peltz?"

"Marsh said he wouldn't tell anyone but you," Calista said. "Hank's got him tied up on the other side of the wall."

"You brought him here?" Maisie looked over her shoulder at the house full of Joplin's finest. "He can't be here."

"Neither can you," said Calista. "We have work to do."

And that work involved getting the truth out of Silas Marsh.

CHAPTER 30

It took a jump off a planter to pull herself atop the brick wall. Maisie could've done it easier had she not been wearing one of the ensembles Mrs. Bragg had designed for her. When she felt the satin snag on the brick, she realized she wouldn't be going back to the party, which was for the best. Especially when everyone learned that she'd storied about the washroom being flooded.

She found herself behind the Caines' landscaped yard in the service drive, which was lined with the buggies of the guests. Amos dragged her to the empty lot on the next street, and that was where they found Silas.

"Maisie-girl." Although roughed up, Silas retained a spark of his charm. He removed his hat, and dried grass fluttered free. "I done you wrong. I'm full out ashamed of how I conducted myself at the Founder's Day parade. I was heavily influenced by someone who wished you ill." He stood a little straighter. "I've never wished you harm. I would've taken good care of you. You wouldn't have lacked anything." He looked around at the high-dollar neighborhood. "I reckon you've done well for yourself without me, but I wanted to apologize for my behavior, nonetheless."

"Who?" Maisie stepped closer. "Who told you to do that?"

"I hate to say, but you know I'm always looking out for you."

"Stop with the hogwash," said Amos. "Get to the point, you no-account, fragrant man-swine." Amos's vocabulary in the language of insults was quite extensive.

Silas straightened with wounded dignity. "Sorry if my habit of charming ladies is a difficult one to set aside. I'll help you, Maisie, and I expect nothing in return. It'll be beneficial for me to do something for someone with no gain to myself."

"If you expect nothing in return, then how is it beneficial?" Calista asked.

"Don't be so literal," Silas responded.

Maisie grabbed Silas by the arm. "Spit it out, already!"

"Maisie?" Boone stepped out of the shadows.

Mr. Schifferdecker had stopped mid-sentence at the clamor from the other room. Something had the ladies all atwitter, and Boone was willing to bet Maisie was involved. Ignoring the women streaming past him, he headed toward the parlor with its many windows. It was empty, but a flash of lemon yellow caught his attention before it tumbled off the garden wall.

He felt the weight of disappointment settle on his chest. Boone had thought they could work through their differences—that they could make a future together—but despite his best efforts, Maisie was determined to leave him.

He turned, preparing to rejoin the party, but nothing about doing so appealed to him. Was he really going to give up on her? Was he really going to let her throw away all their possibilities?

Boone headed toward the French doors. The garden gate was locked, so he climbed the wall, just as he'd seen her do. From there it was an easy task to follow the voices. There was Maisie, holding the arm of another man, but from the way she was slinging him about, Boone realized she had other things in mind besides romance.

"Maisie?" He stepped closer. "What are you doing out here? What are all of you doing?" Several limbs of the Kentworth family tree were represented, along with a stranger who he could only suppose was the infamous Marsh.

"We've got ourselves an instigator here." Amos stepped forward with his chest puffed out. "A conspirator, a curly wolf, and he wouldn't spill the whole story without what we brought Maisie to bear witness."

"I'm here now, and he best start talking," Maisie said.

"I had the best intentions," Marsh started. "I heard that you were in trouble, and I wanted to help."

"Forget about that." Maisie clapped her hands together. "We need to know what is planned for the cave and who is behind it."

"The cave?" Boone's eyes widened. "What does this have to do with my cave?"

Amos twisted Silas's arm behind his back. "Time's getting away from us. Talk fast."

"There's a plan to close down your mine site," Marsh squeaked. "They don't want the cave to open, so they're going to tear it up tonight while everyone is at the party."

Boone's stomach lurched. "Who is they?"

"Mr. Caine. He's the one who put me up to harassing Maisie. He wants that mine, and the crystal cave is all that's kept you from selling it."

"Caine?" Boone looked toward the house. "He's here. I saw him not a minute ago."

"I'm just telling you what I overheard."

"What we had to chase you down and force you to report," Calista said. "That makes you a conspirator."

"It doesn't matter," Maisie said. "We have to get there and see what's happening."

"Yes, you should." Then, with a look at Amos, Silas added, "Before Sheriff Bigelow finds out that you're harassing me again."

"We can't let him go." Calista turned to face Boone and Maisie. "Not until we get to the bottom of this. What if he warns Caine that we're coming? We're practically in his backyard."

"This is Mr. Caine's house?" Silas Marsh's throat jogged. "I'm not staying here. If he catches me conversing with you all . . . He's a dangerous man."

Caine, dangerous? Petty and prideful, yes, but dangerous? Did anyone trust this Silas Marsh character? What if he was working for Peltz? What if he was just making up lies to cause more problems?

But at this point, Boone's only option was to see if there was any truth to his story.

"Then c'mon," Boone said. "Let's get to the cave."

Between the Braggs' buggy and Calista's wagon, they managed to make good time to the cave. Maisie sat on the edge of her seat the whole way there, her teeth clenched.

Finding the cave had changed the course of her life. What would losing it do? She and Boone could go flat broke. That didn't scare her. What did scare her was how discouraged Boone would be. He'd stuck his neck out for this unusual project. He'd stood firm when everyone questioned his judgment. If it failed, what would that do to his confidence?

"Darin Caine was still at his house. I saw him in the window when we drove out." Boone turned the team as they rode up to the visitor center. "I don't see how he can be behind this. What are the chances that Marsh isn't telling the truth?"

Maisie had no love for the Caine family, but she had to admit that Silas was prone to tergiversating. "I don't see any harm in taking a look. Besides, missing that party . . ."

Boone hopped off the buggy and reached for her. Once he had

his hands on her waist, he lifted her down and held her before him. "Why didn't you tell me you had to meet with Marsh? Why hide it?"

Looking into his eyes and seeing his pain made her regret it sorely. "I didn't want you to meet him and remember how foolish I used to be, but I couldn't turn a blind eye to the threat to the cave."

Calista's wagon pulled up next to them. Boone released Maisie. "You made the right decision, telling me. I just wish you'd made it sooner."

Maisie nodded as they hurried to the visitor center. From the outside, it looked undisturbed. Boone pulled a ring of keys out of his pocket and opened the door. A flick of a switch, and the lights sputtered to life.

"Where's Gilbert?" Amos asked. "Wasn't he supposed to be standing guard?"

"He was," Boone said. "Maybe we should send the ladies home. If something happened to Gilbert . . ."

"Don't you dare." Maisie opened the door to the staircase that led down to the cavern and pulled the lever for the lights. "Calista and I can hold our own. Now, let's see what's down there."

Not waiting for permission, she took off down the stairs. Nothing seemed amiss. Everything had been locked up neat and tidy, ready for the grand opening. Maybe Silas was windy.

They reached the cave to find it pristine. The unruffled water on the lake sparkled with the lights shining from every angle and the crystals reflecting from above. Boone held his safety lantern up high—a habit that he hadn't ceased even after the electric lamps had been installed.

"Cricket's wings," Calista said, borrowing Maisie's favorite exclamation. She and Silas both stood stunned at the entrance, while Amos, Maisie, and Boone did a quick sweep of the cavern.

"I don't see anything amiss." Amos dropped to his knees and looked under the walkway. "Nothing beneath here or the stage."

"Let me see." Maisie took the lantern from Boone and shined its light beneath the staircase.

"I swear they said they were going to put this cave out of commission." Still awed by the room, Silas kept his head tilted back. "I can't believe someone would want to shut this down."

"The pumps." Boone looked at Maisie. "Remember when we were wondering if someone had sabotaged the pumps? Let's go."

Amos and Hank sprinted to the staircase with Boone right behind them. Calista had reached the doorway before she stopped and waved Silas forward. "I'm not turning my back on you. Get up those stairs." When Silas swaggered past, Calista gave him a wide berth, then followed determinedly.

No one seemed to realize that Maisie was left behind.

Would Calista think to shut down the lights in the cave once she reached the top? Quite possibly, and Maisie had more work to do. She checked the fuel in her lantern, then walked another round of the cave. She believed Silas. He didn't want to get involved, but neither did he want to be responsible for this malicious action. If there was danger at the pumps, Boone would find it. Maisie wanted to look elsewhere.

And where she was looking was the ladder reaching up to the second entrance. The visitor center had been locked, but could someone have gotten in through the mine shaft?

Maisie hooked her arm through the wire handle of the lantern and grabbed the first rung of the ladder. The crystals had their own hard, distinct smell. Sharp, like clean dirt. As she climbed up the ladder, they glittered before her. She closed her eyes as she climbed past an electric lamp fixed into the wall. Its heat warmed her skin all the way through her elaborate gown.

When she reached the top, she set the lantern on the ground, then pulled herself over the ledge through the glittering rim of the cavern and into the darkness of the mine. Standing, she twisted her dress around and dusted off her hands as she got her bearings. Her foot hit the lamp resting on the ground. With a swoop, she rescued it from being tipped over. The last thing she needed was to catch her skirt on fire again.

She steadied the lantern, but there was something piled up near it. Her blood ran icy cold as she made out the shape.

Correction, the last thing she needed was for her lamp to turn over amid a pile of dynamite.

CHAPTER 31

Maybe they were mistaken. Maybe Boone had been the victim of theft and vandalism but with no thought to put him out of business. Or what if this Silas Marsh was concocting a conspiracy out of thin air just to put Boone on edge? If so, he must be tickled over his success, because Boone was running around in the dark, chasing ghosts.

He followed the shadows around the clearing, working closer to the sound of the water pumps whooshing like a giant's heartbeat. When he reached the stream of water that gushed out of the mine and down the hill, he followed it with Amos, Hank, and the rest of them trailing behind. So far, there'd been nothing amiss.

Amos knelt next to the steam engine. "I'll go around this way, and you go that way. If someone's meddling, they'll run into one of us."

"Sounds good." Maisie's family was good in a pinch. Another benefit Boone should've mentioned to his parents.

Amos disappeared into the darkness, his footsteps drowned out by the noise of the pumps. Boone hurried around the other way, waving the others back as he kept his eyes peeled for any movement. As he rounded the pumps, Amos was the only soul he met.

"No one here," Boone said. "Do you think this Marsh fellow was telling the truth?"

"I wouldn't vouch for him. But just in case, I'll stand guard tonight. Ain't nobody touching these pumps as long as I'm here."

Boone slapped him on the back. "You're as good as gold. Thanks. I'm going to check out the headframe and mining offices. I'll take Hank and leave Silas and the ladies with you."

Amos whistled, and Hank approached. "What's the plan?" he asked.

"You're coming with me," Boone said.

"I'm staying with Calista and Silas," Amos told Hank.

Hank nodded. "Lead on."

More and more it was looking like this whole drill had been a false alarm, but there was still time for mischief. Still time to think through the strange events that had taken him from a dinner with his peers to skulking about with his wife's former beau.

Boone reached the works of the Curious Bear Mine. Everything looked quiet and undisturbed . . . everything except the office door.

Hank spotted the open door at the same time Boone did. "You reckon Maisie's in there?"

"Maisie's not in there," said Boone. "Maisie is with Calista."

"No, she's not. I haven't seen her since we left the cave. Either she stayed behind, or she circled around in front of us. My money's on her coming out here. It's not like Maisie to sit around and miss out on the fun."

Boone focused on the office door with new urgency. Had Maisie gone ahead before them? She thought she was indestructible, but Boone feared otherwise.

He burst through the open doorway of the office and ran straight to the open mine shaft. He saw light ahead and raced forward, stumbling through the shadows with Hank at his heels. When he got a clear view, what he saw struck him dumb.

A man was wiring a firing line to what was as familiar as a pickax to Boone's mining experience—a blasting machine.

Boone froze. The man was adjusting the firing line to the terminals. One shove on the plunger, and the electricity generated would race down the firing line and ignite the blasting caps deep in the cave. Where was Maisie? Boone couldn't startle the saboteur without knowing she was safe.

But the moment the man put his hand to the plunger, it didn't matter. Boone and Hank were both airborne, flying at him.

The whirling sound told Boone the plunger had been initiated. The man bent as he forced it down. Boone crashed into his back, sending him sprawling. The blasting machine toppled over, but the firing line stretched down into the darkness of the mine, carrying the electric charge to the blasting caps and igniting whatever dynamite it was attached to.

A distant roar reached Boone's ears. He was too late.

He flipped the man over, and to his wonderment saw Mr. Gilbert.

"Gilbert?" So it wasn't Caine or Peltz who was out to get him? But Boone didn't have time to puzzle it out.

He grabbed the lantern and ran down the mine shaft, leaving Hank behind to hogtie his foreman. Was Maisie down below? How close to the dynamite was she? The charge must have been far away because the ground had barely moved beneath his feet. The blast he'd heard was faint, and as of yet, no cloud of rock dust rolled up from below. Loose rocks scattered as Boone ran through the shafts, following the firing line to its destination. With each turn, he braced himself for what he might see. His pulse rocketed as he saw the first signs of debris in the air. The explosion had ignited.

Boone was almost to the wall that opened onto the Crystal Cave, and still he didn't see piles of rubble. One more turn, and he dug in his heels and skidded to a stop.

Dynamite—a pile of it, enough to collapse the delicate ceiling of the crystal geode and mar it permanently. Boone's heart hammered in his chest. It was untouched. Had the first charge failed to detonate it? What if Hank lost the scuffle with Gilbert? What if the plunger was activated a second time?

"I done pulled the blasting caps," a voice said.

Boone turned to see a light glowing at the next bend. It was Maisie coming back up, covered in soot, walking over the firing line that had been diverted away from the dynamite.

"No sooner had I pulled them out of the dynamite and tossed them down this shaft than they exploded. If I'd been a second slower, I would've lost some fingers," she said.

"You don't toss blasting caps." Boone caught her by the hand to reassure himself she was whole. "I don't want you anywhere near blasting caps."

"How was I supposed to know? I'm a farmer, not a miner." Maisie rested one foot on a stick of dynamite and rolled it along the bumpy ground.

Boone pulled her away from the explosives before she could cause more mischief. "You did the right thing. If you hadn't gotten the blasting caps away from the dynamite . . ."

The dreadful memory of Gilbert detonating the charge was too recent. He'd been too near to losing her.

Boone's words were failing him, so he made use of his lips in a different manner. Framing her face with his hands, he bent and tasted the sweetness of her mouth.

She hummed a note of contentment as he drew her closer. One of her hands held onto her lantern, but the other hand slid around his neck in a beguiling fashion.

"I declare, we're putting off enough sparks to blow this place to smithereens." Maisie smiled up at him.

"Unless you've got something better to do . . ."

"Welp, now that you mention it." She stepped away with an apologetic half smile. "I took off down this shaft to get the blasting caps away from the dynamite, and I saw something interesting. Whoever is behind this was busier than we thought. Come this way."

He knew this cut. It had looked promising when they first started this direction, but it had dried up completely. A dud tunnel. He followed her down the narrow path until something besides Maisie caught his eye. Her light reflected back from the shiny surface of the wall.

"I don't know much about mining, but doesn't this favor those blocks of ore you have in your office?" she asked.

"How is this here? I thought we'd gotten out everything we could reach," Boone said.

"Could it be exposed because the water has been pumped down?"

"If the water had been this high, we wouldn't have been able to cut the tunnel." He took her lantern and shone the light around. "Let's keep going. If we're where I think we are, this direction was abandoned because it was barren. Nothing in this direction at all. Nothing in most directions, and then we hit water. That's why I gave up on it." He walked until he came to a crossroads. "This was another dead end. Let's see what we find here."

True, there was a criminal above that he needed to deal with, but he trusted that Hank wouldn't be bested. Besides, once Boone was enthralled with a question, he couldn't think of anything until he knew the answer.

The lantern light was swallowed as they entered a different tunnel. After years in mines, Boone could sense when he was reaching the end of a tunnel. Maybe it was the way sound echoed back, or the feel of the air moving. After a few more jagged steps, they hit the end. This one stopped in a pile of debris.

"Hold this."

Boone gave Maisie the lantern, grabbed a splintered wooden beam with both hands, and lunged backward with it. Dust kicked up as he tossed more of the rocks and trash behind them. Maisie covered her nose to cork a sneeze. His men had used this as a trash heap once they'd decided it wasn't worth looking at any longer. He pushed debris behind him, working his way to the wall. As the pile of debris disappeared, the wall could be seen.

Holding the lantern close, Boone sat back on his heels. "Ore. It's ore, not twenty feet from where we were already mining. No one could miss it." Such a decision couldn't be an accident. This was done purposefully. Someone wanted to hide the bounty of this mine from him, and the only person who was in that position was Gilbert.

"I've seen enough," he said. "Let's go topside."

"So that's a lot of ore?" Maisie asked as they covered the open area of a well-mined room.

"Enough to build a house like we're living in and to pay off our loans against the Spook Light Mine and the Byers Building."

She whistled. "Then that means we won't be moving to the poorhouse yet?"

"Not unless you want to."

Boone's mind whirled. Gilbert was behind this, but Gilbert didn't want to buy his mine. It was Caine who stood to profit. But how could he be accused? He was at his party with people who would swear he had nothing to do with Boone's misfortune.

So, to the party Boone was headed.

"It was Gilbert?" Maisie trotted along next to Boone. Finally, after days of dress fittings and housekeeping, she was getting some excitement. "I thought Caine was behind this. What's Gilbert have agin the cave?"

Boone's face was grim. "Let's ask him, shall we?"

She heard voices as they exited the mouth of the mine and stepped into the mining office. Bound by ropes and sporting a dirty sock in his mouth was Gilbert. Amos, Hank, and Calista were involved in a heated argument while Silas was trying to avoid notice behind the desk.

Amos spoke first. "I got tired of hearing him blather, so I put Hank's sock in his mouth. Calista disapproves."

"Next time wear socks," said Hank. "Then you could use your own."

"I can't question him with Hank's sock in his mouth." Calista's dark hair was curling in the night air. "We're wasting time."

Boone knelt and, after some hesitation, grabbed ahold of the unraveling sock and tossed it aside. "Trying to blow up a mine is a serious offense. Considering my wife was down there, it could be considered attempted murder. Are you taking full responsibility?"

"You pay me to detonate charges down there. Maybe I was exploring for ore." Gilbert was rolling on his side, trying to sit up.

"At midnight? No one is going to believe that. And from the looks of the dead-headed shafts, you were turning the crews every time they found ore. I can only think of one reason you'd do that," Boone said.

Silas spoke up from the dark corner. "Because Mr. Caine and Gilbert were in cahoots. They wanted to devalue the mine so Caine could get it for cheap. I guarantee you Caine promised Gilbert a slice of the pie." He smiled at Maisie in particular. "That's how I figure it."

Maisie felt like she'd swallowed cold chicken gristle. "Keep your opinions to yourself."

Boone's smile made her feel warm and toasty. "He's right, Maisie. Then Caine planned a big party tonight so everyone in town would swear he was nowhere near the mine. He thought he covered his tracks. Without Silas telling us what he'd heard, the cave would be demolished, and Caine would've gotten off scot-free."

"He didn't tell it of his own volition," Amos said. "Me and Hank did some urging."

"Regardless, I think a visit to the Caines' residence is in order. Amos, will you find the sheriff and bring him along?" Boone took Gilbert by his bound arm and lifted him to his feet. "You need to come, as well. I only hope we haven't missed the party."

"How about me?" Silas asked. "By my reckoning, I've done all that's required."

Calista looked at Boone. "As long as he'll tell his story to the law, there's no reason to keep him around."

"I agree," Maisie said. "Let him skedaddle back to where he came from."

"Thank you, Mr. Marsh." Boone extended his hand. "While I don't relish the idea of our paths crossing in the future, I've appreciated your help."

"They better not cross," Amos said. "Especially if Maisie's anywhere near."

Maisie slapped her brother on the back of the head. "Cricket's wings! Can you just let it be? Let's get going."

Silas took out, and then everyone jumped into the buggy and wagon for the second time that night, with the exception of Gilbert, who on account of his recalcitrance had to be hoisted. Amos jumped out when they reached town to hunt down the sheriff, and the rest of them headed toward the rich section of Murphysburg.

Maisie couldn't help the glee bubbling up inside of her. Boone had wasted his time trying to appease Mr. Caine and his family. Now that he saw them for who they were, he could waste his time appeasing her. Only it wouldn't be a waste of his time. Maisie would do everything she could to appreciate him.

"I'm afraid my dress isn't as tidy as it should be," she said as they pulled up behind Caine's house. "Your mother is going to have a conniption."

Boone's eyes narrowed, and his mouth turned up at the corner. "I don't care. Do you?"

"Just tell me what I'm supposed to do," she said. "I can get savagerous when called for."

But Boone didn't want her to turn loose on the Caines. Not yet.

After working out the details with Calista and Hank, he and Maisie used a side door to enter without being spied. As they expected, the dinner was over, but the socializing had recommenced. Various clusters had claimed the different furniture groupings scattered across the main floor of the house. Boone secured Maisie's hand in his arm and traveled through, ignoring the questioning looks, until he discovered Mr. Caine holding court near the piano with a brandy snifter in one hand and a cigar in the other.

"Joplin zinc is essential to the world," he was saying. "Any other use for the ground beneath our feet should be outlawed. It's a waste of resources. We as mine owners have a duty to cooperate for the good of all."

Boone's father looked uneasy as Boone and Maisie neared. Either his dinner or the conversation was souring his stomach.

Caine continued, "If a few large holders control the minerals, we can cut the waste. We can control the price that the smelters charge and the transportation of our zinc and lead. And with the politicians' help, we can create regulations that will discourage any newcomers from trying to enter the ring. Consolidation would benefit us all."

"If you put us all together, who would make the decisions, then? You?" Mr. Bragg asked. "What about competition? What about the freedom to determine our own destiny?"

"Speaking of destiny . . ." Boone stepped forward. "We just returned from the Curious Bear Mine, where I found a load of dynamite wired to create a cave-in. Do you know anything about that, Caine?"

"What? I've been here all evening. Anyone can vouch to that." Caine set his snifter on the edge of the piano. "Besides, you've hardly been gone any time at all. You haven't been to your mine. Not this evening."

Maisie knew how to read faces better than Boone did. Did he see the skepticism in the room? But even she couldn't tell if the doubt was aimed at Caine's protestations of innocence or Boone's accusations. Somehow, the rest of the house had been alerted to the drama, and people were gathering from the other rooms. A veritable directory of Joplin society crowded around the confrontation in progress.

"I have, and what I found there was criminal." Boone addressed the mine owners around them. "Mr. Caine has been preaching consolidation to us for a year now. You need to know that he is willing to back up his theories with sabotage if you refuse to comply."

"After the friendship I've shown you and your family . . ." Caine let his shoulders slump, as if the disappointment was too much to bear. "I'm afraid I have to ask you to leave."

Maisie looked toward the front door. Where was Amos? Was he having trouble finding the sheriff? Now would be a good time for him to appear.

Instead, Justina Caine waltzed in with her mother and Mrs. Bragg.

Recognizing that Maisie and Boone were the center of attention, Justina zeroed in on them. "You've returned? How quaint. But keeping out of the mud was too much to ask of you for even one evening, wasn't it, Maisie?" She smirked at her beanpole friend as she sashayed around Maisie. "Look at your slippers. Disgraceful. Why, it looks like you've been traipsing through a mine shaft."

The room went deathly silent. Mr. Picher and Mr. Kleinkauf moved slightly away from Caine.

"It doesn't matter where you were, that doesn't mean I was involved," said Caine.

Justina raised her chin and looked at Maisie through narrowed eyes. "I shouldn't pity you after your bizarre episode and claims about our water closet, but it is a horrible tragedy. Still, we had nothing to do with the cave-in at your Crystal Cave. It's just lucky it wasn't full of visitors when it happened."

Maisie's fists clenched. Her sight narrowed until Justina was all she saw. "Was there a cave-in at the Crystal Cave?" she asked. "What would you know about that? Nobody here mentioned it."

Justina cast a quick look at her father, who was as pale as a corpse. The puzzlement on the faces around them was turning to anger.

Mr. Bragg looked at his wife. "Did you hear anything about a cave-in?"

Mrs. Bragg drew herself to her full height. "No, I was in the other room with Justina. No one in there mentioned any tragedy at Boone's property. I'd like to know where Miss Caine got her information."

The pounding at the door could only be the cavalry. Not waiting to be invited inside, Calista glided into the room, looking for all the world like she belonged there in her silk and feathers. Amos and Hank, on the other hand, didn't even notice the mud they were tracking across the roses on the rug.

"Who are you?" demanded Mrs. Caine. "This is a private party."

"Where's the jug band and the dance caller?" Hank asked. "It don't look like much of a party to me."

"We are here as witnesses." Calista's Kansas City enunciation gave her an air of culture. No one would ever suspect her rougher side. "We have some testimony to give and collect."

"I'm not answering to you," said Caine. "If you don't leave, I'm going to call the sheriff."

"I'm already here." Sheriff Bigelow stepped into the room. "Darin Caine, if I were you, I'd send my guests home. Boone Bragg caught your conspirator red-handed, and he's confessed to everything. You need to get your affairs in order and come with me."

Mrs. Caine's hand went to her throat. "What's this about, Darin?"

"Ask Justina," Maisie said. "She knows."

"Dragging your daughter into this?" Sheriff Bigelow's frown deepened. "Forget your affairs. We're going now. C'mon."

Mr. Bragg stepped in front of Caine. "I trusted you to watch over my son in my absence. This is how you treated me?"

Caine stepped around him without an answer. Couples recoupled as wives went to their husbands. Mrs. Caine's dearest friends began to gather with her.

"This time it wasn't us getting arrested." Amos slapped Hank on the back.

Mrs. Bragg took Maisie's hand. "You've withstood a lot, dear.

We don't need to stay any longer." Then she turned to Calista, Amos, and Hank. "I'd be honored if you'd introduce me to your family. I've been wanting to make their acquaintance."

Warm contentment washed over Maisie as she introduced her kinfolk to her new family—contentment and the worry that Amos and Hank would do something to embarrass her. Mr. Bragg shook hands with everyone while thanking them for their role in saving his son's venture and invited them all over for coffee immediately.

It was a loud and boisterous drive through the neighborhood, with spirits high. If Mrs. Bragg was shocked by the Kentworth exuberance, she hid it well. Maisie stayed behind with Boone after he unloaded their passengers and drove the buggy back to the carriage house.

"Something occurred to me," Maisie said. "Since Gilbert was hiding the ore from you in the mine, you never were losing money. You wouldn't have had any reason for closing the mine down or putting it up for sale." She brushed the debris off her skirt before stepping inside the house.

Boone looked her over from head to toe. His mouth twitched like something funny had occurred to him. "If I hadn't closed down the mine, then I never would've met you." He didn't look so tired anymore. "You're a better discovery than all the giant geodes in the world."

Maisie didn't know what to do with her hands. She swung them at her sides. "Ain't that a pretty thing to say? You know you don't have to blather on like that, though. I'm staying married to you, no matter who tries to run me off."

His eyes widened. "Now that you mention it, there is something I need to do." He grabbed Maisie by the hand and dragged her through the house until he found the raucous gathering.

"Excuse me, everyone. Amos, Hank, Calista, Mother, Father." Boone waited until he could be heard. "I want to thank you for what you've done to help me tonight, but there's one other matter I need to address." He took Maisie by the hands and pulled her in front of him, just like they'd posed for those wedding pictures down in the cave. "You've completely changed my life, Maisie, and it needed to be changed. Thank you for sticking by me, even when it was rough."

"Cricket's wings," Maisie said. "If there was anything rough, it was me and how I carried on. It's a wonder you didn't send me away the first time I whooped you at wrassling." This evoked exclamations from her kin about her skills at wrassling, but Maisie silenced them. "Even so, this man has been patient and long-suffering. Even when he had cause to doubt me, he never gave up. For that, I'm grateful."

Boone's eyes shone. "And I'm grateful I have a chance to correct one grievous error. Do you all remember the Founder's Day parade?"

Maisie bit her lip. Why would he mention the lowest point of her life? This was supposed to be a happy time.

But Amos caught his meaning immediately. Reviving the chant the crowd had cheered, he began, "Kiss the bride! Kiss the bride!" Hank and Calista joined the cheer.

Boone pulled Maisie close and wrapped his arms around her. Without so much as a by-your-leave, he bent her over his arm and planted a burning-hot kiss on her mouth, right there in front of all her kin.

With him kissing the daylights out of her, it didn't take Maisie long to forget about those kin. It wasn't until she heard them hooting and hollering that Boone let her stand upright again.

Hank and Amos were clapping and cheering while Calista whistled. Mr. and Mrs. Bragg smiled, but knowing the hour, Maisie forgave them for their lack of enthusiasm. Boone's more than made up for it.

"I'm glad you didn't do that at the parade," Maisie said. "I would've fallen off that float, sure as shootin'."

Amid the laughs and congratulations of their family, they headed to the kitchen for coffee.

"I hope you weren't too worried about me," Maisie said. "I was trying to help without getting you involved."

Boone covered her hand with his own. "I was worried, but not for the reason you think. It's because I heard you were sneaking out with Silas tonight. Wait—" He lifted his hand, stopping her protest. "What matters is that, when I thought it over, I realized you didn't know how much I wanted you to stay with me. I worried I hadn't convinced you that you were valued . . . that you were loved."

Having seen Silas again, Maisie realized she hadn't been irreversibly damaged. Whatever she'd felt for him was gone. It was hard to believe he was even the same species as Boone.

Maisie laid her head against Boone's shoulder. "Even then, I wouldn't have betrayed you."

Boone squeezed her hand. "And I'm going to do my best never to give you cause to consider it."

"After the grand opening?" she asked.

"Nope. Starting right now."

CHAPTER 32

Maisie hadn't let Boone out of her sight all day—or all night. But now that it was morning, he was busy answering questions about the crystalline formations, while she checked on the supply of refreshments the café had remaining.

"I didn't expect all these people," Hannah said. "Hilda ran up to Aunt Laura's to look at borrowing some coffee. We're slap out."

"I can't believe the crowd," Maisie said. "All of Joplin is here."

"And I talked to people from Knoxville. Your story ran in newspapers all the way in Tennessee." Hannah wiped the sweat from her brow, exposing the widow's peak that all the Kentworths shared. "They said when they were done with the tour, they would buy a postcard and see about you signing it. They called you the Cinderella of the Crystal Cave."

Maisie patted the complicated knot of braids that Mrs. Karol had put her hair in for the occasion. "Let them think I was just a poor country girl if they want. City folks think anybody who works with their hands is poor." Unsophisticated, unfashionable, and uncouth maybe, but rich in the things that mattered to her—land, cattle, and most of all, family and love. "I don't want to disabuse them of that opinion."

From the looks of the three scientists from Jeff City, Boone's answers were fascinating. Tapping their chins thoughtfully and looking studious, they clustered together, mulling over the implications of what they had viewed and discussing plans to investigate further.

Boone extended his arm toward Maisie. She caught him by the fingers, enjoying the connection even as he was facing guests and carrying on the conversation with the scientists.

She was so happy for him, for both of them. Boone's biggest concern had been the employment of his men, his biggest thrill bringing the beauty of the cave to the notice of the world. With the reopening of the Curious Bear and the success of the Crystal Cave, God in His goodness was allowing him to do both.

So much goodness.

Voices, animated and breathless, floated up through the door leading to the cave. Maisie fiddled with the crystal pendant hanging from her neck as she drew closer to her husband. With a short jerk of her chin, she messaged to Boone that it was time to cut it short. He nodded his understanding and made his excuses to the scientists, then followed her to the doorway to greet the returning tour group.

Hand in hand, they smiled and chatted with the people coming up the stairway. At some time during the receiving line, Boone's hand slipped around Maisie's waist. She had never felt more loved or protected.

Finally, the visitors they were particularly waiting for stepped up into the room.

"That was marvelous!" Mrs. Bragg threw her arms around Maisie's neck and kissed her on the cheek. "I am speechless, dear. I can't wait for everyone I know to see it."

"I'm proud of you, son." Mr. Bragg reached for Boone's hand and pumped it soundly. "I've spent my life in mines, and I've never seen anything like that. Whatever it cost to bring that about, it was worth it."

"Just think of the events we can have down there," Mrs. Bragg said. "Weddings, club meetings, dances—it's cool during the summer and warm during the winter. You'll have no lack of people wanting to reserve it." She turned with shining eyes to Boone. "Is your calendar full yet? Can we throw a ball here? I want to be the first."

"You and Maisie," he said. "It'll be her reintroduction to society."

Reintroduction as his real wife. They'd gone through the motions before, and the weakness of their relationship had been noted. This time, they didn't have to fake or pretend anything. Maisie knew the truth, and if it wasn't evident to everyone else, she couldn't care less. As long as she and Boone were on solid footing, they could handle the rest of the world together.

Throughout the day, they worked side by side. Maisie's pride in her husband grew with each interaction she witnessed, until it was time to close the doors and turn away visitors until Saturday, when they would begin again.

After refusing a ride with his parents, Boone insisted that he and Maisie take the long way home, cutting through the Kentworth fields instead of going straight to the road. It wasn't until she saw the Secret Tree that she realized he had a plan. She hummed to herself as they stepped high through the prairie hay and over the cow pies.

"I thought you'd be in a hurry to get home," she said. "It's been a long day."

"I want it to last as long as it can." It was dark under the leaves of the Secret Tree, but Maisie gladly followed him into the shadows. "I have a secret." He placed his hand on the tree. "I think I loved you from the beginning."

She laughed. "You say that now, but I don't think so."

"I did. I loved you enough to give you time, I loved you enough to give you room, and I loved you so much that I almost lost you." He paused to pick at the bark of the tree. "Now that I think about it, I didn't love you then like I do now. I had to change before I could love you this much, but it was still love. Only perhaps it was love of a more controlled nature."

Maisie fell against him, hooking one arm over his shoulder. "Your love doesn't have to be of a controlled nature anymore. In fact, I'd rather it not be."

"My wild, untamed wife."

She could barely see his face in the darkness, but she could hear the sincerity, the warmth in his voice. She could sense the glow of a dream realized radiating off him, and she could feel his love when he took her in his arms and granted her every kiss they'd missed out on while entertaining their guests.

It had been a perfect day, and they would get to do it all again and again, with acquaintances and strangers, with family and friends. Their story would continue with the cave that sparkled like a thousand galaxies gathered and hidden until it was time for all to see.

A Note from the Author

Dear Reader,

Thank you for picking up *Proposing Mischief*. I hope you enjoyed the story. I certainly enjoyed sharing some Joplin (my birthplace!) history with you, even if it was wrapped in fiction.

You probably want to know about a possible crystal cave, but first let's recognize the people who made this story possible.

I want to thank the generous Joplinites who helped me with my research and local connections. Thanks to Brad Belk, who fulfills the role of Community Historian and who supplied any information I requested. Also, I and all lovers of historic beauty owe a debt of gratitude to the members of the Historic Murphysburg Preservation. They have saved countless unique structures in Joplin as well as the stories of those who lived in them. In particular, I should mention Paula Callihan and Mary Anne Phillips, who welcomed me into one of their beautiful homes and who continue to send me tidbits for inspiration. All historical inaccuracies should be excused as poetic license and charged against me alone.

When naming my characters, I often used the family names of Joplin's early citizens, although it's only to honor them, not to suggest they were involved in any of my fictional shenanigans.

One name that people outside of Joplin will recognize is that of Howard Hughes, Sr. He did indeed work as a miner in Joplin, and one has to wonder if his experience there contributed to his invention of the drill that made him a very wealthy man.

Schifferdecker's Electric Park was just as spectacular as described, although it was built a little later than this story and opened in 1909. When the amusement park aspects closed in 1913, Charles Schifferdecker donated some of the land back to the city, and it remains a park today. The manager of the Electric Park, M. B. Peltz, probably wasn't so nasty to the owners of the Crystal Cave, but he was responsible for the baby raffle that occurs in Book One of the Joplin Chronicles. If in Joplin, be sure to drive by Schifferdecker's beautiful home in Murphysburg, and watch for more about the Electric Park in Book Three.

Now, what you've been waiting for—the cave. I am happy to announce that there is a crystal-lined geode cave beneath Joplin, Missouri. The real Crystal Cave was discovered by miners in 1893 and is located eighty feet beneath current-day Fourth Street and Gray Street. Measuring two hundred and fifty feet long and completely lined with calcite crystals of various colors, it is a treasure like no other.

Like our fictional cave, the discovery was made possible by the pumps of adjacent mines that had lowered the water level in the area. The cave was opened to the public on July 4, 1908, and was a popular tourist site for several decades.

When the price of zinc fell during the Great Depression, many Joplin mines closed and their water pumps went idle. Not realizing that the water table was rising, the cave's owners left the cave on a Friday evening in 1930, and when they returned the following Monday, they found the stairway flooded.

No one has been in the cave since.

Occasionally, interest is raised in reopening the cave, but to do so would require a fortune in dewatering equipment. Since mining isn't as profitable in the area these days, it's questionable if it will ever happen. In 1998, a hole was drilled and a small camera sent down. The murky pictures showed that the cave remains untouched, although unreachable. It's horribly dissatisfying to think of this lying hidden beneath the city, and there are many who would like to see it reopened. Perhaps this story will reinvigorate interest in the project.

If this short report brings about more questions than answers, please contact or visit the Tri-State Mineral Museum in Joplin. They are the real experts.

Thanks again for reading my books! Be sure to drop me a line at www.reginajennings.com or on Facebook, or sign up for my newsletter. I love hearing from you.

Sincerely,

Regina

Regina Jennings is a graduate of Oklahoma Baptist University with a degree in English and a minor in history. She's the winner of the National Readers' Choice Award and a finalist for the Christy Award, the Golden Quill Award, and the Oklahoma Book of the Year Award. Regina has worked at the *Mustang News* and at First Baptist Church of Mustang, along with time at the Oklahoma National Stockyards and various livestock shows. She lives outside of Oklahoma City with her husband and four children and can be found online at www.reginajennings.com.

Sign Up for Regina's Newsletter

Keep up to date with Regina's news on book releases and events by signing up for her email list at www.reginajennings.com.

More from Regina Jennings

Assigned to find the kidnapped daughter of a mob boss, Pinkerton operative Calista York is sent to a rowdy mining town in Missouri. But she faces the obstacle of missionary Matthew Cook. He's as determined to stop a local baby raffle as he is the reckless Miss York, whose bad judgment consistently seems to be putting her in harm's way.

Courting Misfortune
The Joplin Chronicles #1

You May Also Like . . .

Caroline Adams returns to Indian Territory craving adventure after tiring of society life. When she comes across swaggering outlaw Frisco Smith, his plan to obtain property in the Unassigned Lands sparks her own dreams for the future. When the land rush begins, they find themselves battling over a claim—and both dig in their heels.

The Major's Daughter by Regina Jennings
The Fort Reno Series #3
reginajennings.com

Confirmed bachelor Lieutenant Jack Hennessey is stunned to run into Hattie Walker, the girl who shattered his heart…and she's just as surprised to find her rescuer is the neighbor she once knew. But his attempts to save her from a dangerous situation go awry, and the two end up in a mess that puts her dreams in peril—and tests his resolve to remain single.

The Lieutenant's Bargain by Regina Jennings
The Fort Reno Series #2
reginajennings.com

When her father's greedy corruption goes too far, heiress Emma Grace McMurray sneaks away to be a Harvey Girl at the El Tovar Grand Canyon Hotel, planning to stay hidden forever. There she uncovers mysteries, secrets, and a love beyond anything she could imagine—leaving her to question all she thought to be true.

A Deep Divide by Kimberley Woodhouse
Secrets of the Canyon #1
kimberleywoodhouse.com

More from Bethany House

Assigned by the Pinkertons to spy on a suspicious ranch owner, Molly Garner hires on as his housekeeper, closely followed by Wyatt Hunt, who refuses to let her risk it alone. But when danger arises, Wyatt must band together with his problematic brothers to face all the troubles of life and love that suddenly surround them.

Love on the Range by Mary Connealy
BROTHERS IN ARMS #3
maryconnealy.com

Spiced with Witemeyer's signature blend of humor, thrilling frontier action, and sweet romance, this charming holiday novella collection includes three novellas, "An Archer Family Christmas," "Gift of the Heart," and a brand-new story, "A Texas Christmas Carol," along with a Christmas devotion, holiday recipes, and fun facts about 1890s Christmas celebrations.

Under the Texas Mistletoe by Karen Witemeyer
karenwitemeyer.com

Traveling the Santa Fe Trail on a botanical exploration, Linnea Newberry longs to be taken seriously by the other members of the expedition. When she is rescued from an accident by Flynn McQuaid, her grandfather hires him to act as Linnea's bodyguard, and Flynn soon finds himself in the greatest danger of all—falling for a woman he's determined not to love.

The Heart of a Cowboy by Jody Hedlund
COLORADO COWBOYS #2
jodyhedlund.com

BETHANYHOUSE